THE KENNEDY CONSPIRACY

MICHAEL WHITE

arrow books

Published by Arrow 2012

2 4 6 8 10 9 7 5 3

First published in Great Britain in 2012 by
Arrow
Random House, 20 Vauxhall Bridge Road,
London SW1V 2SA

www.randomhouse.co.uk

Addresses for companies within The Random House Group Limited
can be found at: www.randomhouse.co.uk

The Random House Group Limited Reg. No. 954009

A CIP catalogue record for this book
is available from the British Library

ISBN 9780099569275

The Random House Group Limited supports The Forest Stewardship
Council (FSC®), the leading international forest certification organisation.
Our books carrying the FSC label are printed on FSC® certified paper.
FSC is the only forest certification scheme endorsed by the leading
environmental organisations, including Greenpeace.
Our paper procurement policy can be found at
www.randomhouse.co.uk/environment

FSC

MIX
Paper from
responsible sources
FSC® C016897

Typeset in Times New Roman by
Palimpsest Book Production Limited,
Falkirk, Stirlingshire

Printed and bound by CPI Group (UK) Ltd, Croydon, CR0 4YY

Always for you . . . Lisa, India, George,
Noah and Finn.

"He saw all these forms and faces in a thousand relationships become newly born. Each one was mortal, a passionate, painful example of all that is transitory. Yet none of them died, they only changed, were always reborn, continually had a new face: only time stood between one face and another."

Herman Hesse, *Siddhartha*

PART 1

You never know who you are going to meet.

Prologue

It comes in alternating snatches of super-reality and vagueness, just as most recurring dreams do. Sharp edges jump out, light splits as if through a prism. And, beneath that, an uncomfortable, unsettling feeling, a disjointedness, a nagging anxiety, as though you know things aren't quite right but you can't put a finger on the root of the problem.

There is a line of cars, big chunky old-fashioned automobiles with huge Cold War tail fins and brash headlights. There are two cars in front of us. They look alike, one dark blue, the other black. I'm in the offside rear seat of a Chevrolet with the roof down. I can feel the leather with my fingertips. A slight breeze rustles my hair. On the wind, I smell pizza. The car has a large red sweeping dashboard and one of those huge 1960s steering wheels, white plastic with an inner chrome rim that doubles as a horn. I'm aware of someone sitting beside me, a man. I look down at myself and see that I'm wearing a somber black suit, narrow lapels, middle button done up, white shirt, green tie. I notice my hands, long slender fingers, in my lap. At my feet is a worn brown leather briefcase.

I turn to the person beside me but he has vanished. In his place on the seat lies a newborn baby. She starts to cry and rolls around on the leather as the car accelerates, then slows. We're only just crawling along now. I can see the speedometer reading under ten miles per hour. The driver is wearing a dark suit, spectacles. His hair is graying, greased back.

There is a line of people by the side of the road. They are clutching flags and waving. As we pass, a well-upholstered woman in a tight flowery dress peers into the car, realises that I'm no one famous and pulls back, disappointed. The celebs are in the lead cars. I'm not sure how I know that, but I do.

I look round across the vehicle's sprawling trunk and count five more cars in a curve that sweeps from a yard behind me, left, between two brown brick buildings. Twisting back, I notice the outriders, half a dozen police bikes, big Harleys, cops wearing aviator sunglasses. Then I notice the bright sunlight, the clear blue sky.

The cars keep going, around a corner, a left, then a right. I glimpse street signs but can't make them out. There is a stretch of lawn to our left. Someone is standing there playing a double bass, but the music cannot be heard as the man sways gently, his eyes closed, his fingers caressing the neck of the instrument.

I whirl back to the seat and the baby has gone. There is a pile of newspapers in her place. Then a second bundle of newspapers lands on the back seat, quickly followed by a third. It starts to rain paper, single pages, and whole supplements, reams and reams of paper cascading from the perfect blue sky. I can see more, high up in the air, thousands of growing dots, millions of specks all falling toward us, and I know we'll be crushed under their weight.

I start to panic, pushing away the great pile of paper that has accumulated on the back seat of the car. I try to pull sheets of newsprint away from the face of the driver so that he can see where he's going. Then I slip back again and push myself over the trunk, attempting to retrieve something, but it's just more paper.

I hear a gunshot far off ahead of the car. It's followed by at least two more bangs. And then it's over. I awake.

Chapter 1

Mark Bretton opened his eyes to a view of the white ceiling of his apartment. His head was splitting and he groaned as he shifted across the bed toward the alarm clock and saw that it was 7.01 a.m.; groaned again as he remembered it was Monday morning. Then the memories of his latest dream came back to him. The same weird dreams . . . again.

The phone rang. "Mark."

"Yeah." It was Saul at the paper.

"Just checking you remembered the 7.45 with the boss."

Mark swore silently and scrunched up his face. "Course I did," he lied. "Your shout with the coffees," he added as nonchalantly as he could. He put down the phone and jumped out of bed.

The apartment was on East 10th Street, a tiny one-bed affair four floors above a second-hand record store that had only just started selling CDs as the world had moved on to iTunes. The two rooms and a kitchenette were scruffy and bohemian: "lived-in", as Mark preferred to call the place. This morning it was more than lived-in. Clothes lay strewn across the back of the overstuffed, seriously distressed chesterfield, beer cans covered the coffee table. Mark's vintage Gibson 335 ES guitar in its hard case lay against the wall close to the bolted and locked front door. The guitar was his most precious possession and even after getting in at two a.m., and much the worse for wear after a gig at Mackey's Blues Club, he had cleaned the sweat from the instrument's neck and laid the case carefully against the wall. Cat, the cat, lay in the narrow doorway to the kitchenette, rolling onto her back as Mark stumbled in to put on the kettle. He could only drink tea first thing, a hangover from the days when he thought of himself as entirely British. In the twelve years since he had moved to New York he had lost most of his old habits and picked up many new ones, some good, some decidedly bad, but drinking tea as one of the first acts of the day would, he knew, remain with him until the day he died.

As the water heated up, Mark leaned forward with his arms outstretched, gripping the rim of the kitchen counter, and stared at the wall above the slowly evolving steam. A corkboard hung there. It was covered with reminders, unpaid bills, notes, lists and two photographs pinned with colored tacks from Walmart. On the left was the smiling face of Jill, his ex-wife. They had been apart for more than four years now. He had only seen her twice during that time. The first encounter had been two years after their separation when Jill had come over to tell him that she had met someone she had fallen in love with and that she wanted a divorce. The second time was when he had stood across the street from the registry office on the day when she had remarried. He watched her leave the building in Union City. She had not noticed him. It provided an odd form of closure.

The picture on the right showed an ageless, almost hermaphroditic character. He was bald, his face gaunt. His large brown eyes spoke of youth, but his skin was creased around the eyes and at the corners of his lips. He was wearing a bright red woolly sweater, the sleeves hanging over his long bony fingers. Recently, Mark had been looking at this picture more and more; this picture of Patrick, his oldest friend, the one constant in his life now that Jill had gone. If Mark had believed in the concept, he would have called Patrick his soul brother. He was the one person in the world he could feel free with, could say anything to. They had been closer than most brothers and he missed him, but an ocean stretched between them and he hadn't been in the same room as his friend for far too long. And now Patrick was ill again.

The sunlight, some ninety minutes after dawn had filtered through the buildings, banded the street with strips of dazzling orange and deep shade. But it was already hot and sticky, another steamy August day in Manhattan. Mark dashed across the street and dove into the subway. The ride uptown passed in a semi-conscious reverie. He had gone through a phase of reading novels on the subway, but that had been during a brief period when he'd been trying to clean up his act. He would get to bed at a reasonable time, rise refreshed, drink orange juice as well as his tea and sometimes even go for a run, ending up at his local, Life Café. But that kick had lasted no more than two weeks, ruined when his band had been offered three nights a week at Mackey's. The band, The Gondoliers, meant a lot to him. They were three friends, him, James Trent (bass) and Hugh North (drums), who shared a love of the blues. He would never be as good a player as he would wish to be, and sometimes he felt like an imposter, but playing in the band acted as a nice foil to his day job, the one he had somehow managed to hold down for almost a decade—Features Writer for the *New York Courier*.

Saul Maddox handed Mark a coffee outside the door to the editor's office, triple-shot latte, which he knew would be the first of many that day. "You look like shit," Maddox remarked as he rapped on the door.

"Oh, stop the flattery," Mark quipped and led the way in.

Two other Features Writers were there already, Juney Shriever and Alex Coltrain. They started to get up as Mark and Saul Maddox came in.

"Right. Gotta make this quick," the editor, Sam Helmer, a two-hundred-and-fifty-pound ponytailed Texan, said. He was a man loved and hated in about equal measure in the industry and had been at the helm of the *Courier* for over eight years. In spite of the air conditioning he was sweating profusely, his white shirt stained under the arms and in two lines down his front. "Juney," he said. "You deal with the lead on the Assistant DA in Queens. Sounds juicy. Saul, take the Kremlin story. Needs more meat than your outline suggests, though." Then he turned to Mark. "Got this in last night, Mark. Some psychologist, set up her own research programme here in Manhattan." He glanced at a sheet of paper before handing it over to Mark via Alex. "Professor Abigail Marchant, researching into reincarnation."

Mark looked up from a notebook he had open on his knee, his pencil poised in mid-air. "Oh, for fuck's sake!"

Helmer raised an eyebrow. "You no like?"

"No, Sam, I don't. You had me on some kook only last month, the guy who claimed he could talk to the dead. You know how I feel about that sort of shit." He glanced over to Alex Coltrain. "It's more Alex's bag, isn't it?"

Coltrain shook his head. "Er . . . no, Mark. You're giving me the train crash inquiry, aren't you Sam?" He glanced at the editor.

Helmer nodded. "Mark, listen. She sounds pretty competent."

Mark Bretton eyed his boss skeptically. "Yeah, right. A shrink studying reincarnation. Don't tell me . . . her secretary's a fairy."

"He might well be," Helmer retorted. "Adds color to the story if he is—find out!"

"Sam!"

"Okay, people," the editor said, ignoring Mark's protestations. "I want copy from you, you and you by four," he said nodding in turn to Alex, Saul and Juney. Turning to Mark, he added. "You have until six o'clock. It'll be for the weekend supplement. Right, go." He stood up, his gut wobbling as he pulled on his jacket.

Mark hung back as the other three journalists trooped out. "Sam," he said, "why'd you do that?"

"Do what, Mark?" He saw the anger in Mark's eyes.

"You know I hate all this woo-woo crap."

"Precisely."

Mark stared at his boss, frowning. "So you want an aggressive piece?"

11

"I want an *intelligent* piece, Mark. And I believe that skepticism is the best direction to come from if you want intelligent. At least when it comes to this kinda stuff."

Mark gave him a cynical look.

"Listen, I think this Professor Marchant is an interesting woman. I don't think she's a crackpot. And our readers are hungry for unusual new ideas. This is certainly, well . . . different. Plus it's about people. I want a balanced piece. Hear the woman out. Do some serious digging, okay?"

"You think you can get round me like that?" Mark retorted.

"Don't need to, Mark. I'm the editor. If I want you to interview a psychic researcher, I expect you to do it." Then Sam smiled. "Nothing woo-woo about that, buddy."

Chapter 2

Professor Marchant's office was on West 47th Street close to the corner of 3rd Avenue, a fair distance from the paper's office on 55th. Mark felt like a walk, but after three blocks away from the air conditioning he was beginning to regret it. The whole of Manhattan seemed to shimmer in the summer heat. Some of the visual effect was caused by oil smears on the tarmac and the steam rising from manholes, but there was a very real humidity in the air. He had experienced this almost every summer of the twelve he had spent in the city, but he could never get used to it. It felt as though he had an extra layer between his skin and his clothes, a slippery film that itched.

Out on Sixth Avenue the traffic stood bumper to bumper, a sea of yellow cabs, horns blaring pointlessly. Messengers on bikes dodged between the crawling cars. They must be melting, Mark thought as a Lycra-clad beanpole on a super-lightweight racer shot through a gap between two stationary cabs and almost hit him as he stepped off the curb. "Hey! Moron!" the cyclist hollered and Mark gave him the finger.

The air grated the back of his throat. It was always the same, fumes kept at street level by the fetid Manhattan air. And the catalytic converters made it worse, adding a top note of ammonia. He kept to the shade as best he could, loosened his tie and undid the top button of his shirt. Slinging his damp jacket first over one shoulder, then the other, he finally rested it in the crook of his arm.

His cellphone rang, a blues-guitar riff he had recorded himself and downloaded onto the machine. But it took four rings before Mark heard it above the noise of the traffic. By the time he pushed the "accept" button the caller had rung off. The screen told him that the number was blocked. He cursed and edged into the doorway of the first shop he could, just to get out of the noise and the heat.

He waited for the phone to ring again. It had been a blocked number, so it could have been about his credit card, or some insurance jerk trying to sell him half-assed protection. But it could also have been Patrick; international calls always came up as "blocked". Mark leaned against the wall of the store just inside the doorway and brought the plastic of the phone to his forehead. It felt unnaturally warm.

"Can I help you, sir?"

Mark opened his eyes and saw the Indian shop assistant. Behind him stood an array of glass cabinets filled with electronic goods, watches and models of the Statue of Liberty.

Mark apologized and turned back to the sidewalk, feeling suddenly depressed. He hadn't thought about Patrick since leaving the apartment, and the realization shocked him. Was he already burying his friend? Moving on? How ridiculous. He pushed the thought aside and tried to focus on what he was doing. By the time he reached his destination he had prepared his attitude and his questions for the kooky professor. He was a pro, he told himself. He would do the interview, write the damn piece, duty done.

Professor Marchant's rooms were on the twenty-fourth floor of a nondescript building on the south side of the street. Mark checked his watch as he entered the relative cool of the lobby. It was ten-thirty and he felt he could really do with a drink. He paused for a minute to find the bathroom, failed and asked the doorman who pointed to a narrow corridor just beyond the elevators. At the sink he threw cold water over his face, toweled it off, straightened his tie and pulled on his jacket. The sleeves stuck to his arms, scrunching the fabric, making it bunch at the elbows. He removed it again and cradled it in his right arm. Peering into the mirror, he surveyed his face. It was long and narrow. He had good cheekbones that would usually have made him look a little younger than his thirty-five years. But the benefits from the cheekbones were canceled out by the bags under his eyes, the pallor of his skin and the lines in the skin at his temples. He had striking green eyes and a good haircut. He was sometimes able to convince himself he was aging in an interesting way, that he was clearly a man of substance. But he couldn't manage it this morning. He just felt jaded and actually not very interesting at all.

A slightly overweight young woman with brown hair tied back in an old-fashioned bun met Mark as the elevator opened onto a brightly lit reception area on the twenty-fourth floor. She smiled as he stepped towards her. "Mr. Bretton? I'm Julia Dreen, Professor Marchant's PA. Follow me, please."

Julia led the way along a wide corridor. Mark read the signs on the doors: Matilda Inc., The Brass Screw Company, Lamington's Optical Equipment. The last door on the right carried a brass plaque that read: A. H. Marchant. M.D., Ph.D. The professor's PA took them through an outer office dominated by a wide oak desk. A large window opened onto the sides of two other buildings looming skywards: their concrete lay in shimmering shadow one side, striped massicot on the other.

Julia stopped at a door to the left of her desk and knocked gently. A moment later, a tall athletic woman appeared in the doorway, her hand extended. She was smiling warmly. The PA took Mark's jacket, holding it gingerly by a single finger at the collar.

"Mr. Bretton, welcome," Professor Marchant said. She had a refined voice that fitted precisely what he had learned about her from the preliminary research he had done after this morning's meeting. Professor Marchant was an Ivy Leaguer, old Bostonian money. One of the articles about her had been from the Association of Psychologists website describing the work that had first gained her recognition—a study of post-traumatic stress disorder in troops returning from Afghanistan. Another had been a piece in *Paranormal Investigations*—what passed for a serious publication in the field of occult subjects. The third had been a mention in *Reader's Digest* which had highlighted Professor Marchant's recent clashes with the scientific establishment over her radical new studies into what the magazine referred to as "parapsychology".

And, indeed, she had clashed, very badly—so badly that she had been suspended from the APA, the American Psychological Association, and publicly denounced in the *Journal of American Psychology*.

"Please, come in," she said. "May I offer you coffee? I'm afraid I only have half an hour. Something unexpected has come up and I have to be somewhere by midday."

"Coffee would be great—thanks." Mark looked around the room as Professor Marchant popped out to instruct her PA. The room was large, with cream walls and a high ceiling; the block was old, a deco tower. A large modern desk stood one side of the room, a four-seater sofa the other. A forty-two-inch flat-screen TV dominated the adjacent wall. When Abigail Marchant returned she nodded toward the sofa.

"You're disappointed by how ordinary it is, Mr. Bretton."

"I guess I am."

"Were you expecting some box of tricks with flashing lights and a slightly demented lab assistant?"

Mark grinned. "Reckon I must have been."

"Sorry to be so prosaic. So, I imagine you've done some background research. You probably hold quite definite opinions on my work."

The coffee arrived and Julia Dreen placed the cups on a table in front of the sofa, closing the office door behind her. Abigail Marchant lifted her coffee and took a sip.

"Yes, I have," Mark replied. "You're obviously at odds with the scientific establishment over what you're doing."

Professor Marchant raised an eyebrow. "It is always difficult to divert the course of a driverless juggernaut as it speeds along the freeway, Mr. Bretton."

He studied her face. It was angular: a fine, shapely nose, large brown eyes. He knew she was thirty-four, but she looked a few years younger. Her skin was pale with barely a visible blemish and she wore very little make-up, just a smear of lipstick. Wavy blond hair fell to her shoulders. She was a striking woman, Mark decided. "And that's how you view orthodox science, is it?" he replied. "A driverless juggernaut?"

"I never used to. I was a good girl, did all the right things, believed all the respected and respectable ideas. But when a new concept hits you between the eyes and it doesn't fit the accepted pattern it would be a dereliction of duty simply to turn away from it."

Mark looked puzzled. "I'm sorry, professor, I'm not really sure what you mean."

"You have a scientific training, don't you?"

Mark looked surprised.

"When I knew you were coming to interview me I Googled you—the *Courier*'s website. The only journalist there with a science degree." Marchant took a sip of coffee.

Mark raised his hands. "I own up—physics, Oriel, Oxford. But it was a long, long time ago."

"Well, then, you shouldn't find the reaction of the science community toward my work that strange."

"Well, no, I don't. Science and the occult—strange bedfellows."

She looked away across the room for a moment, staring at the far wall above her desk. There were two rows of framed certificates and diplomas there. "They are today," she said. "But it wasn't always the case. Isaac Newton was an occultist. Einstein often considered things in a bipartisan light."

"Yes, but correct me if I'm wrong . . . they certainly didn't publicize the fact, did they? We've all seen modern careers crumble at the very mention of the paranormal. It's a path followed by only the very bravest scientist."

"Or the terminally stupid?" Marchant asked.

"You said it."

There was an uncomfortable silence for a moment. "Okay, look, maybe we ought to go back a few steps," Mark said. "I've read that until eighteen months ago you were something of a poster girl for your profession. Your work on PTSD was lauded. Then, somewhere along the line, you stirred up a hornets' nest by advocating research into reincarnation. You were booted out of the APA."

She lifted a hand. "I was suspended, Mr. Bretton. There's a difference."

Mark conceded the point with a nod. "Was the tragedy surrounding Senator Roger Gates's granddaughter Peggy the final straw?"

Abigail Marchant didn't answer immediately. She just looked down at her lap and the cup. "You've obviously read the report. I was exonerated. And, more importantly to me, I remain close to Senator Gates, whom I consider a great friend."

"But the APA made the case that your research into reincarnation was, to quote, 'a contributing factor in Peggy Gates's mental decay'," Mark replied.

"They did say that. It's their prerogative. But they happen to be wrong."

"Okay, but how come you're still conducting research?" He waved a hand to indicate the well-appointed room.

"Let's just say I have some contacts who believe in what I'm doing and have the resources to support my work. But look . . ." She stood up. "You're here to talk about my latest work, isn't that right?"

Mark nodded.

"Okay, then. Well, first let's just correct a few things, shall we? First, I call the phenomenon I'm studying 'rebirth', not reincarnation. Second, you seem to have the idea that I came suddenly to this work. But I did not. I was not converted from being a skeptic in some whacko road-to-Damascus moment. I'd been studying what might be called parapsychology for a long time. I'm not taken with much of it. I see nothing in most of the ideas of the occultists. I don't believe in alien abduction, spooks and ghosts or telepathy, or precognition, or any of that stuff, but I do believe that rebirth is a genuine phenomenon. There, I've written your headline."

Mark gave her a rueful smile. "I'm afraid I'm a horrible skeptic, Professor Marchant. You'll have to do a lot better than that."

"Wouldn't have expected anything else." Abigail Marchant bent down, plucked a remote from the coffee table and pointed it at the plasma TV. "I've got something to show you."

Chapter 3

The screen lit up to show a young boy sitting in a small room. He looked scared, his eyes wide. He was seated in a hard plastic chair and was facing the camera. A voice-over, female and British-accented, said: "This six-year-old Greek boy is Andreas Mossikious, and he claims that he has lived before. From the age of two he has been telling his mother about his 'other parents' who lived in a big city. What he calls the City of Angels in a country called America."

From out-of-shot an interviewer asked the boy a question in Greek and the voice-over translated. "What do you remember, Andreas?"

"We lived in a big house. My name was Sam. I had two sisters, Suzy and Fiona. Both of them were older than me."

"What happened to you?"

"I died when I fell into a river and drowned. I was nine when I died."

The image changed to footage of Andreas in his tiny house in Greece, playing with a skinny kitten. The voice-over continued: "At first, Andreas's mother Delia thought it was all nonsense, just the fantasies of a toddler. But the odd thing was that Andreas was consistent. He simply built on his tale, embroidering it, filling in the details as he went along. By the age of four, he was describing the inside of his house in Los Angeles, recalling the color of his 'other' mother's hair, the shape and shade of her eyes, the way she had looked down upon his dead wet body as they had dragged him from the river. Andreas's mother was understandably disturbed by this. She told her brother Petros."

A big man with heavy eyelids and ebony eyes and wearing a leather jerkin over a rough white shirt appeared. His mustache twitched almost comically as he spoke. A male translator took up the voice-over. "I was skeptical, of course," he said. "I talked to Andreas for a long time. I tried to catch him out, just to prove he was making it up. But I couldn't. I know it sounds crazy, but I believe my nephew is telling the truth."

The female voice returned over stills of a growing Andreas. "Another two years passed and Andreas continued to talk about his 'other' family. He told his mother and uncle about his 'other' father, John. John had been killed by a car, knocked down outside the house in LA. He hadn't looked right then left, Andreas had explained. Then, just after his sixth birthday, the boy began to suffer anxiety attacks. He would weep, stay up half the night in tears, shaking, saying he missed his 'other' family and he had to see them, that they would be very worried about him."

Abigail Marchant glanced at Mark. He ran his hand over his forehead and was frowning. He caught the professor's eye. She could tell he was finding it a struggle just to keep watching the clip.

The scene changed again to show a film crew arriving

at Andreas's home in Greece and being introduced to the boy. Then came footage of Andreas, his mother Delia and uncle Petros boarding a plane, flying to America and looking bewildered as they were driven along Santa Monica Boulevard, rain pelting against the sweeping wipers.

The car pulled up at a run-down house in Jefferson Park. Andreas seemed to be at home there immediately. "It's different to how I remember it," he said in Greek to the camera. The male voice-over translated: "The old phone box on the corner is gone and the cars looked different when I lived here. There used to be a store over there." Andreas pointed to a parking lot.

The dilapidated house resembled what Andreas had described as the home of his "other" family. It was small and ramshackle but at least twice the size of the boy's tiny home in Greece. It had been left to decay: the windows and front door were now boarded up, graffiti had been splashed across the walls.

The camera held the boy's expression. He looked stricken for a few seconds and his eyes began to water. The same interviewer, still off-camera, suggested that they should go inside. It was almost as though the bubble had burst and some strange confused realization had hit the kid. Suddenly, the contradiction of it all, the impossibility of what was happening had been made clear, even to a six-year-old.

"This was my room," he said slowly to the camera. Then, walking along a corridor, he pointed to another tiny room. "This was where Suzy and Fiona slept." He paced over to the window and pointed out to the street.

"That's where my papa died," he added, thoughtfully. "Right there. He was hit by a blue car. There was red all around his head."

The scene changed abruptly to show the producer interviewing a local couple, a very old black man and his wife who had lived across the street for fifty-four years.

"We remember the family," the old man said. "The Trebaums. Germans or Swiss, I think. Mother, father, two girls and a boy. A sweet kid, the boy, Sammy. It sure was tragic, what happened to 'em. It musta been '65 when the father died."

"Was '66," the old man's wife interrupted.

"You sure?"

"Damn sure."

"Okay, '66," the old man said. "John Trebaum, hit by a car right there." He pointed a gnarled finger toward the living-room window. "Right outside his house. Then, not two years later, the boy, young Sam, he goes and drowns in the waterway, over there." He pointed toward the back of the house.

"They moved away after that, poor souls," the old woman added. "The ma took the girls, Suzy and Fiona, I think they were called. No idea where they went to. I just pray they found some peace."

Professor Marchant flicked off the DVD and gave Mark a questioning look.

"I'm here to interview you," he said. "Tell me what you think."

"I find it impossible to explain, other than that rebirth is a reality."

"Hardly scientific, Professor Marchant. It struck me as being pure hokum."

"Oh, don't get me wrong. I've applied Occam's razor—that's why I came to my conclusion."

"You honestly think it is the simplest answer?" Mark scanned her face. "The kid could be making it up."

"Bit of a coincidence that he was right about the details."

Mark breathed in, brought his fingers to his lips and shook his head slightly. "He must have known about the family, saw it on the Internet. Maybe the mother made it up and fed him the story."

"Naturally, I considered those possibilities and others," the psychologist replied. "There's one major problem. The Mossikious family in the film live in the tiny village of Kossis on the relatively remote Aegean island of Naxos. No phones, let alone Internet. More importantly, until the journalists arrived and took them to LA, Andreas, his mother and his uncle had never left the village."

Mark looked stunned for a second. "Okay, so someone went to the village years ago and told the story to the kid."

"Possible, I suppose, but unlikely. Both Delia and Petros have sworn on the Bible—and they are extremely religious people—that, as far as they know, no one from outside spoke to the boy."

"They could be lying."

"They could be. But this story is far from being the only one on record." Abigail Marchant stood up and walked over to her desk, picked up a collection of folders and brought them back to the sofa. "These," she said, handing them to Mark, "are the tip of the iceberg."

He glanced at the front cover of the uppermost folder. It said: *UK*.

"Fourteen cases in Britain," the doctor continued. "I have over two hundred from around the world on file."

Mark stared at her, a little taken aback. "Okay." Then he lifted his wrist to glance at his watch.

"I'm so sorry about the rush," the professor said.

"No problem . . . Can I take a look at these?" He lifted the folders a couple of inches.

"Sure. Everything is anonymous or pseudonymous, no real names . . . and they're copies, of course."

"Can we meet up again? I can't say I'm any more convinced, but I am interested. I hope that doesn't sound too patronizing."

"Only a little." Professor Marchant smiled. "How about the same time tomorrow? Say, eleven?"

"Sounds good. I'll have my work cut out for me." Mark eyed the files.

"And remember, Mr. Bretton . . . Occam's razor is sharp. But there's only so much it can cut through."

Chapter 4

As Mark descended in the elevator he put a call through to the office and left a message with Helmer's secretary, Maddie, saying he needed more time on the story and that he was going home to write it. He felt more comfortable in his own place and it bought him time to think without people asking him questions or the phone going off all the time. He had a backup piece, he told her, a feature about suspected malpractice at the New York Zoological Gardens.

It was stifling in the apartment, but it was quiet, private. He cleared a space among the beer cans and takeout containers covering the kitchen table and put down the armful of folders that Professor Marchant had given him. Then he strode over to the window, switched the air-conditioning unit to max and stood in front of the grille, luxuriating in the cooling draft. Back in the tiny kitchen he found a beer in the fridge and settled down to work through the case histories.

They were organized geographically, by country. In this set of records there were fifty-four cases spread over eight nations. He opened the top folder marked *UK*. Five children, all aged between three and seven at the time of their interviews. No discernible pattern among them apart from the fact that they all claimed they had "other" families", "other selves". It was a small sample but there was no statistical skew based on socio-economic classification, parts of the country in which the kids lived, or family circumstances.

Mark read through the first case. It described a deaf boy called Norman M, from Leicester. As soon as he could talk, which, because of his disability, was late, he told his mother Carla about his older brother, Aban. Norman was an only child, so his mother was confused. Gradually, the boy expanded on his story. He talked of bombs dropping, gunfire. His "other mother and father" had died along with Aban when a bomb landed on their house. Over a period of several months, Norman described his other life in Lebanon. He talked of the war there, about his "other" friends and family, and finally how he had himself died when he was crushed under the tracks of an advancing tank.

Mark closed the file and looked around the room. The place was a shambles, but he couldn't care less. His mind was racing. "There has to be a scientific explanation," he declared to the room. Then he opened another file and started to read. When he next looked up he was surprised to see the digital clock on the kitchen counter telling him it was 4.09. He had gone through the entire set of cases, all two hundred and eleven pages.

He pushed back the chair and paced over to the window with its view down onto East 10th Street that was filled with people wearing as little as possible in the cloying heat. He could see steam rising from a manhole towards the western end of the street where it crossed Avenue C.

An oily haze shimmered over the rooftops. It rippled like some weird time-travel portal from a science fiction movie. An urban mirage, he thought. How romantic. A pigeon swooped down from a water tower and Mark half expected it to vaporize as it hit the shimmer, but it just landed on the roof and started pecking at scraps.

The phone rang and he walked over to it. "Hello."

"Mr. Bretton?"

He recognized the voice immediately. "Professor Marchant."

"I'm sorry to call you at home. I tried the office but they said . . ."

"That's fine. What's up?"

"I feel bad about our interview—cutting it short. I know we're due to meet again tomorrow morning but I was wondering." She paused as though trying to make up her mind what to say. "Would you like to meet for an early dinner? To carry on the interview?" she added hurriedly.

"That would be great."

"Good. There's a nice Italian place near my office. Do you like Italian?"

"I like Italian wine."

She laughed. "Good. Well, how about five o'clock? The restaurant is called Falluchio's, on West 47th."

Mark shook his head as he lowered the phone. "Well, what d'ya know?"

Mark arrived ten minutes early and ordered a large glass of Frascati to help him loosen up. He couldn't put a finger on the reason for it, but he felt expectant, even a little anxious. He found himself surprised. He had grown cynical over recent years. He still got a thrill from his job, still loved the chase of investigative journalism and the buzz of creating something and seeing it in print the next day, but in most aspects of his life he had become jaded. He knew why, of course. It wasn't just his age. He used to agonize over that, and still, in some mental recess, he was aware of the fact that he would be thirty-six in a few weeks and that he was now precisely the same age as Mozart had been when the composer had died; that he was three years older than Christ when he'd been crucified. There were still moments when he felt he had wasted his life, that he could have done so much more. He had so many regrets. At the top of this odious list was the break-up with his ex-wife, Jill—and, of course, the loss of Imogen, the daughter they had had for so short a time.

He had very successfully blanked out much of the pain of the past, but he could not perform the trick all the time. The past crept in, an insidious virus. And, once inside, it reproduced with frightening energy. He and Jill had been happy for a few years. He'd been doing well at the *Courier*, making Senior Features Writer by his thirtieth birthday. Jill was enjoying life as a marketing exec. When she fell pregnant, they were both ready. And everything seemed to be going smoothly, until the birth itself. The baby had become entangled in the umbilical cord. The attending doctor was inexperienced and out of his depth. Imogen had been born severely brain damaged and had died after two soul-searching, gut-wrenchingly anguished nights.

Mark never really understood why Jill had blamed herself for what had happened, and he understood even less when blaming herself was no longer enough and she turned her fury upon him. It shattered their former intimacy, driving a wedge through their feelings for each other.

Naturally, they had tried therapy. Mark had struggled with every fiber of his being to rescue their marriage. But he was also trying to work his way through his own grief and bitterness. It could never have worked. And so, in the space of two months, he had lost his daughter and his wife. His life was in pieces. All he could do was work, drink, play the guitar, and try to suppress the pain until it no longer mattered. But he had not yet reached that happy state.

He saw Abigail Marchant before she saw him. There was something about this woman, he told himself. He had talked to her for no more than twenty minutes a few hours earlier, but he could not deny an instant interest in her. It wasn't simply her looks, he reasoned. Neither was it her obvious intelligence, nor her individuality. It was something indefinable, something he would have to work to unearth.

She saw him and smiled, negotiated a path between a clutch of tables and sat down opposite. "Well, you said you liked Italian wine," she remarked and eyed his glass. The waiter approached. "I'll have what my friend is drinking," she said. "Very chilled." Then she faced Mark. "At least it's cool in here." She ran a hand across her forehead theatrically. "It feels like the end of the world out there . . . So, you read the cases?"

"I did."

"No more convinced?"

The wine arrived and Professor Marchant took a sip. "To skepticism," she said with a grin and raised her glass. Mark clinked his against it and then looked at her seriously.

"I'll admit, some of them present a good case. But I face a basic dilemma here. Either I believe that these stories are true, that people are reborn, or I don't. If I go for the first option I have to junk all my training and three hundred years of scientific progress. You can't have both, and there are no half measures."

Professor Marchant held his gaze for a second and then nodded slowly. "When I started to get into this study I faced exactly the same conundrum. I'm a scientist, too. I set out on the accepted path of logical reasoning, mathematical science, but I came to the conclusion that the two are in fact mutually compatible."

Mark gave her a doubting look.

"Hear me out. There is actually nothing about rebirth that contradicts the accepted laws of science. Nothing at all. Researchers have many different theories to try to explain it. Most are ridiculous, but my conclusion is that there must be an interaction between solid matter—our bodies, in other words—and some as-yet-undiscovered energy, what religious people call the 'soul'. This inter-action must operate on a subatomic level, perhaps involving a quantum manipulation of our DNA."

"That's not a very convincing argument," Mark responded, draining his glass and raising it. Catching the eye of the waiter, he glanced at Abigail, who shook her head, and he indicated that he wanted just one refill. "It's unreasonable to argue that things that are possible in the microcosm, the quantum world of neutrinos, bosons and mesons, can be bolted onto the macrocosmic world of people and planets. It just doesn't work like that."

"Yes, it does, Mark."

He raised an eyebrow.

"How do you think a CD player works? It contains a laser that reads the encoded information on a disk by firing a stream of light at it. The laws of quantum mechanics control the behavior of that light. We extrapolate from the microcosm to the macrocosm all the time."

"All right, putting aside the details of how it could happen: Why *should* it happen? What's the point?"

Abigail let out a heavy sigh. "I have absolutely no idea. But aren't you evading the point? The matter of 'why' is a philosophical, perhaps even a religious issue. Maybe we can answer that one day, but right now we're just scratching the surface. The very idea is ridiculed—unfairly, I believe. I know it isn't impossible and that it does not contradict physical laws. I don't have a clue why it should happen, but I'm convinced that rebirth is a real phenomenon."

"And you're basing this—let's face it—pretty bloody radical idea on a collection of reports taken by others totaling perhaps . . . what? A mere few hundred cases around the world?"

"If that were all I had I could understand your doubts. So perhaps I've been expecting too much of you."

"What do you mean?"

"I've been conducting experiments for two years. I

33

have a huge file detailing every aspect of those experiments; first-hand interaction with hundreds of subjects. To me, the evidence is irrefutable."

"Oh, please don't tell me," Mark exclaimed a little more aggressively than he'd intended. "Regressive hypnosis?"

"Yes."

"But that has been discredited over and over again."

"Yes, and rightly so. Those experiments were sloppy. The researchers who conducted the tests practiced very poor science."

"So, tell me, Abigail. How many of your subjects were Marie Antoinette or Adolf Hitler in a previous life?"

Mark's drink arrived and neither of them spoke for a moment. Then Mark leaned forward. "I'm sorry. I didn't mean to be rude."

Abigail shook her head. "I'm used to it. There's a great deal of skepticism and cynicism about this and a lot of it is perfectly justified. My predecessors have done me no favors."

"So what is it that you are doing differently?"

"Well, for a start, I would like to think that I'm more thorough and more honest."

"I wouldn't doubt that."

"I have a filtering system that helps. Initially, I had five and half thousand applicants for my trials—all from one ad in the *New York Times*!"

Mark couldn't help laughing. "Desperation!"

Abigail looked at him, a serious expression on her face. "Perhaps. Anyway, I vetted them and took on four hundred cases. I don't have the resources to do more. I regress the candidates, record on video film everything they say and then I have a team of researchers—graduate assistants from Columbia, actually—who sift through every scrap of information divulged by the subject before trying to corroborate it with historical facts."

"Okay. So what have you found so far?"

"I've been working on this project for nearly three years, the last two dedicated to the trials. I'm still not ready to publish, but I have found a significant level of cross-correlation between the stories told under regressive hypnosis and various historical facts. In many cases it would have been extremely difficult for anyone intent on fraud to discover those facts before undergoing regression. More importantly, perhaps, I have, on a few occasions, found cross-correlation between subjects who did not know each other and who, as far as we can tell, have never met—in this lifetime. Now, if you are willing to believe that those people are telling the truth when they say that they did not get together before the trials to concoct a story, any twinning of past-life experience, where they met or knew each other in a previous existence, is immensely important and dramatically increases the chance that rebirth is a genuine natural phenomenon."

"I'm sorry, Abigail, but I'm still not convinced. It's not rigorous science. It's based on trust. It's not empirical. And if you want the scientific world to accept something so radical, then the experimental findings need to be ultra-convincing, absolutely watertight. Surely you can see that?"

"Yes, of course I can," Abigail responded, an edge of irritation in her voice. "I still wasn't convinced myself. But then I made a rather important discovery.

"Some eighteen months into the study I was interviewing a man I can only refer to as Subject 343. He
is a middle-aged New Yorker, a rather ordinary man
who works in the mail room of a large publishing house.
He underwent regressive hypnosis and returned to what he
claimed was a previous life in which he worked at
the docks. In his regression, he returned to 1926. His
name in that incarnation was Alfred Kingston. When
he emerged from the hypnosis, he described something
I had never heard before from any of my first three
hundred and forty-two subjects. He claimed that he
could "inhabit" his old self. He could feel the emotions
of that person, he had access to their memories. To a
very limited degree, he had *become* them."

"And the others? What did they claim they experienced?"

"Nothing like that. And take a look at the literature,
the accounts of the others who have studied rebirth. They
may have been unscientific, but they documented thousands of individual cases. I'd never heard of such an
intense experience. Mostly the images that people recall
are vague, cloudy. No one has ever said they could inhabit
their former selves."

"So could this man, Subject 343, control the actions
of Alfred Kingston?"

"No, but he claimed he could influence him vaguely."

"How could you possibly know that?"

"This was the experience that convinced me, Mark.
Subject 343 described battering a young woman to death,
a prostitute who had tried to steal from him. His recounting
of the experience is all on film. The subject became very

upset as he reported intimate details of what he was doing. I almost called a halt to the whole thing. I was worried that the guy would have a heart attack in my office. But then it got weirder because Subject 343 tried to stop Kingston, the killer in 1926. He described a witness catching him in the act, a man who saw him stand over the woman just before he delivered the fatal blow. Kingston was caught by the police a few hours later and hanged for the murder the following week."

"It could all have been a story," Mark commented.

"Of course it could. But then one of my researchers unearthed a police report on the killing. It had never been made public. The witness described how the murderer, Alfred Kingston, had stood over the woman and had seemed to be fighting a demon. It seemed like there was some strange struggle going on in the man's mind, as though he were two people, one of whom wanted to kill while the other was trying to stop him."

Mark took a long drink. "It's an interesting story. But . . ."

"What are you afraid of, Mark?"

He looked startled for a second. "Pardon me?" Then he laughed. "Almost had me there."

"No, I'm serious," Abigail retorted. "What are you afraid of that stops you entertaining the idea that rebirth is a reality?"

"You're being ridiculous. Just because I put up arguments . . ."

"No, no. You're right," she said, surprising him again. "Of course, you're entitled to believe what you want to believe."

"Yes," Mark replied uncertainly.

"So you wouldn't object to being hypnotized yourself?"

"Oh! Now hang on!"

Abigail tilted her head to one side. "I don't quite understand, Mark. If you don't believe there is anything in my theories then what's the harm in playing along?"

"It's not that."

"Then what is it?" Abigail had her elbows on the table, her fingers interlocked. She rested her chin on her hands and stared him out.

"Okay. I'll think about it."

"That's called ducking out, Mark!"

He sighed. "All right, let's organize a date . . . I'm game."

"How game?"

He shrugged. "I'll do it. When?"

"Now."

Mark laughed. Abigail stared into his eyes.

"You're joking, right?"

"Am I laughing?"

They walked the two blocks to Abigail's office, hardly exchanging a word. Mark still felt a little shell-shocked.

Abigail flicked on the lights in her room.

"All right," Mark said. "So how exactly does this work?"

"It's actually really straightforward. Hypnosis is nothing more than a technique for channeling specific pathways in the brain—breaking down defences, if you like."

"Yeah," Mark retorted. "I've seen Jerry Springer."

"I do things differently."

"Oh?"

"You know I don't have much respect for those who have worked in this field before me, Mark. One of the things I've always objected to is the level of suggestion by the therapist."

"But I thought that was the essence of it? I've always put the whole thing down to ideas being planted in people's heads. Their own imagination fills in the gaps."

"I take your point. But I won't do that. I'll get you under and then it's entirely up to you what you say. I won't suggest anything to you. I'll be here all the time." Abigail walked over to a cluster of electrical equipment close to her desk—a tape recorder and a control panel for a camera. "Everything you say will be recorded and filmed," she said as she fine-tuned the equipment. "Unless you object."

Mark lowered himself onto a couch. "So you'll be taping it?"

"Yes . . . I want you to talk to me. Keep talking. Describe everything you see, everything you hear, taste, touch, smell. Relate everything as it happens."

"If anything does happen."

"Yeah, sure . . . if anything does happen. I'll be here and I'll hear everything you say. The recording is simply a backup so we can listen again."

"So I just lie here and tell you everything I experience *as I experience it* . . . first-person . . . real-time?"

"Exactly."

"Fine . . . I guess. You got the fob watch?"

Abigail laughed and walked back across the room to where Mark lay. "You comfortable?"

"I suppose so."

"It's perfectly normal to feel nerves."

"I'm not nervous. I'm just, well . . . skeptical, and I'm worried I'll ruin the experiment for you."

"Oh, we do have a high opinion of ourselves, don't we? Now, relax. Try to clear your mind of any worries. Put them out of your head."

"That's not easy."

"No, it isn't," Abigail agreed. "Okay, imagine a box," she went on, speaking slowly. "Open it. It's a big, empty box. Peer inside. Check that it's empty. Now put your thoughts in the box, one at a time. Take the thing that's bothering you most. Dispose of that one first. Is that in the box?"

"Yes."

"Good. Now, the next one. Add it to the box and keep the first one inside. Can you do that?"

"Yes."

"Do you feel the weight lifting from you?"

"A little."

"Keep going. Gradually, you'll feel more and more relaxed. Your head is feeling lighter. You're starting to float . . ."

Chapter 5

I'm running, terrified, my heart racing. Something is gnawing at me, trying to squeeze into my mind, but I can't allow it there, because then whoever is chasing me will know beyond any doubt that I know the terrible secret.

I survey an over-lit reception area and flash my ID at security. Howard, the duty officer, knows me. I reach the closed elevator doors and notice, out of the corner of my eye, that Howard has picked up the phone. He glances over at me and I know that he's been told something I didn't want him to hear. I see Howard lower his hand to his gun and I rush away from the elevators and bolt for the staircase ten yards ahead along a corridor. He shouts: "Mr. Ashcombe. Stop, Mr. Ashcombe."

I ignore the man and reach the first step. My heart is thumping harder now. I'm not as fit as I once was. Ruth has been feeding me too well. Too many TV dinners. I feel sad. I'll never survive this, a voice yells inside my head. I'll never see Ruth again. And then a wave of anger. Damn them. Damn this. I'm not a fighting man. I'm no hero. I'm a White House Press Liaison, for Christ's sake.

And then something else. A horrible memory. Today has been the most extraordinary day of my life. It feels as though I've lived a year during it. And as the dread thought starts to edge in, I force it back. No. I can't contemplate it.

I'm halfway up the stairs and I hear the front door of the building open. Then comes the slap of leather soles on the marble floor. Then voices. I recognize Agent John Maclaren's baritone. It's like sandpaper. The Secret Service guy sounds a little out of breath. Perhaps you won't get me, you bastard, I think. I run faster, my own breath coming now in gasps. I feel my chest hurting, stabbing pains like knives cutting through my lungs.

I reach the top of the first flight of stairs, grasp the metal rail and yank myself round, keeping tight to the wall, faster that way. And then up the next flight, ignoring the pain, driven on by raw fear. As I reach the second-floor landing I hear a wonderful sound. The ting of an elevator door opening. The sound comes from overhead, and I know that the elevator is coming down from the third floor. I dive for the call button, stumble and fall forward, just managing to stab the plastic disk. The elevator stops, the doors open. I ram my finger against the "door close" button, hearing the rush of feet on the stairs growing louder, closer. I glimpse a black jacket, and then the doors shut. I let out a deep sigh and lean forward, head against the wall.

A loud bang reverberates around the inside of the elevator. One of the Secret Service agents has fired his weapon at the elevator door. I can barely believe this display of violence. Then I realize I still have my finger pressed on the "door close" button and haven't touched the other controls to tell the elevator where to go. I leap forward as another bullet to the doors makes the enclosed space shudder. I hit the button marked "Level 6".

I take long, deep breaths. I have to control my heart rate or I'll go into cardiac arrest, I think. And the weird thoughts start to cascade into my mind again. I lean back against the metal wall, straining for some clarity. I catch sight of myself in the mirror to the left. Rivulets of sweat run down my lean ashen cheeks. I look like a wet cadaver. My black hair is disheveled, my suit sweat-soaked, white shirt filthy, tie askew. I check my watch. It's almost nine.

The elevator stops abruptly. I hit the "door open" button and run out onto the landing. This too is over-lit with fluorescent strips running along the empty corridor. I count a dozen doors, six-a-side interspersed with panels of opaque glass. A brown carpet runs along the center of the corridor. There's no one around. I head straight for my office, third door along on the right. A small sign reads: "David Ashcombe, Press Liaison." I unlock the door and dive inside.

The room is small. On the desk sits a telephone. I switch off the light. The view of the room collapses into darkness. I walk back carefully to the desk and reach for the phone.

It feels like an eternity as I wait for someone to pick up. Three rings, four, five. I begin to despair. I tap my fingers on the desk, strain to hear anyone approaching. The Secret Service guys will be here any second. I feel the panic growing. Ruth picks up.

"Ashcombe resid—"

"Ruth."

"Dave, darling."

"Ruth, baby. Listen. I gotta be quick."

"Why?"

"Ruth, get out of the house. Go to your Aunt Joan's in Missouri . . . tonight . . . Right now."

"Aunt Joan?"

"I can't explain. Just, please, do what I say."

"But Dave . . ."

"No buts, Ruth. I'll make my way to your aunt's—meet you there just as soon as I can."

"I don't understand."

I take a deep breath and close my eyes for a fraction of a second, feeling the cold Bakelite of the receiver against my cheek. "Look, Ruth. This is life or death."

"Is it to do with . . . ?"

"Of course. Now. Please."

She starts to sob.

"Please, honey . . ."

"Dave, I have to tell you something."

I'm only half-listening. I hear a sound . . . scraping. Then the whine of a creaky hinge as a door is opened along the corridor.

"Ruth, I have to go. I love you."

In the blackness I tiptoe over to the door, straining again to hear. I think I discern voices, but I can't make out anything. I open the door a crack and peer along the corridor. A man, Maclaren's sidekick, steps through a doorway into the office two along from mine. Agent Maclaren is already inside. I can hear him rifling through the desk. I slip out into the corridor. I don't dare look behind me as I fight back the dreadful thoughts, the panic, the terror. Any second I expect a raised voice to yell out my name, followed by a shot and the sharp sting of a bullet.

I reach the end of the corridor and the emergency exit. I push on the bar and risk checking over my shoulder. A man emerges from the office, sees me, raises his gun and I fall forward onto the bar across the door.

"Stop, Mr. Ashcombe. Stop."

A second later I'm picking myself up from the cold concrete and a bullet smashes against the wall, sending chunks of brickwork over my head. A sharp fragment hits me in the neck and I feel a stab of pain, pull myself to my feet and rush for the stairs, grabbing for the metal rail.

I stumble down the stairs, panting. And I'm talking to myself, panicking. "Oh fuck! Oh fuck!" I keep repeating it aloud. I hit the wall and bounce back. The door to the emergency exit slams open above me and the two men crash into the stairwell. I duck away from the opening in the center of the staircase, keeping to the outside wall. I see a flash of black cloth.

"Stop," Maclaren yells. "David—we will fire again if you do not stop . . . now."

I ignore him. I know I'm dead meat if I stop. My only chance is to run. But I don't really know what I'm doing or where I'm going. They have such an advantage. There are two of them, they are armed pros. I'm a glorified office grunt, a pen-pusher, as my cousin Tom calls me. And the dread thoughts try to intrude again, but I don't dwell on them, don't allow them in.

I reach the second floor of the stairwell. The floor is wet. I rush round the concrete curve, keeping to the outside wall. A bullet smashes into the wall behind me and I feel my stomach flip. The sound of the shot is horrendously loud, a boom from the gun and a crack from the shattered brickwork.

I twist round and see Maclaren's gun pointed straight at me. I see it jerk upward slightly, a burst of light from the tip of the barrel. I'm thrown backwards as the bullet slams into my head. I hear a crack of bone, the thud of the bullet rocketing through my brain, the squelch of organic matter as a chunk of it splatters against the bricks.

The two men run toward me, guns still raised. The right side of my vision has clouded over, a dark veil of blood slithers over my eyeball and I can see nothing on that side. Maclaren crouches down, peering into my face, and I feel a loosening in my bowels. I start to gurgle, feel warm blood on my neck. It flows down under the open collar. I feel drunk, stoned. Nothing works anymore. The view through my left eye fades to nothing.

Chapter 6

"Oh, fuck!" Mark screamed as he jerked upright.

Abigail stood up and took a step towards him, placing a hand on his arm. He shook it away and pulled himself off the couch.

"Sorry," he said, putting a hand to his forehead. His face was covered with sweat.

Abigail said nothing, just stared at him.

"It's all right. Sit back down. Talk to me about it."

Mark took a deep breath, studied his hands and peered around the room as though it were an alien place, his lips trembling.

"Er . . . no . . . thanks. I, er . . . don't think so," he managed to say and snatched up his jacket from where he had put it earlier over the foot of the couch.

"Mark. Talk to me."

He frowned, shaking his head slowly. Then, without another word, he strode to the door and walked out into the waiting area. It was dark and still, a hazy light sifting through the fibers of the drawn curtains. From outside came the sound of car horns and the growl of traffic, a sound that never dissipated completely in this city of eight million voices.

A storm had broken while Mark had been in Professor

Marchant's rooms. He could hear the rain hammering against the front door of the building as he approached it, passing the night porter at his desk. Through the glass door he could see people hurrying past on the sidewalk, umbrellas aloft. Cars splashed by, sending plumes of water high into the air. Horns blared, voices shouted. It all seemed so very real, but at the same time Mark felt an inalienable dislocation, as though he had woken from a dream only to find himself in another one. He paced toward the door and exited onto the busy street.

The rain was almost monsoonal, falling in great sheets, the drops bouncing on the road and the sidewalks and ricocheting at crazy angles. The drains were overflowing and water ran across the sidewalks. He looked up, shielding his eyes, and saw Abigail's building towering over him, the deluge cascading down the darkened concrete. There was no wind, not even a slight breeze. This, he thought, was Nature showing another of its many facets, totally indifferent, it seemed, to the comings and goings of men, sending them scurrying like ants before a garden hose.

He headed off west, not really knowing why. It felt as though he was passing through an unreal world, that everyone was staring at him like some fairground attraction, an alien intruder, Klaatu just set down in Central Park.

In moments he was soaked through. The rain, still warm against his skin, ran down his cheeks, slithered under his shirt collar, and along the length of his spine. He noticed his clothes had changed color: his sand-colored suede boots were now a buffalo brown. He hailed a cab. It pulled up, showering him with more water, but he thought nothing of it. In fact, he welcomed the shock of it, like a pinch convincing him that he was not dreaming. He slipped into the cab, leaving a trail of wet on the seat's velour, and directed the driver downtown. He watched as the city's neon lights flashed past, and contemplated the familiar confusion; the glistening sidewalk, sodden pedestrians like statues in a waterfall: 7-Eleven and Sbarro, Jim's Convenience and Imran's Market, Nail, and Ross Precious Metal Emporium. Mingling with News Talk Radio 702 came the incoherent comments from the cab-company switchboard.

On East 10th Street the same rain was falling, the same crowds milling and running, staring and gazing, the same cars plowing through the flood water. Mark dived through the doorway of his building. The record store was still open. He could smell hot dogs and spilled beer. He flicked on the hall light and took a deep breath, letting the water pool at his feet. Then he climbed the stairs two at a time, panting as he reached the third floor and slowing for the final turn and the eighteen steps to his landing.

Inside his apartment Mark ran for the bathroom, pulling off his clothes as he went and leaving a ragged wet trail along the corridor. Drying his hair and his body, he found a robe and pulled it on, gave his hair a final rub, dumped the towel on the bathroom floor and walked through to the lounge.

He saw the light on the answer machine flashing in the splintered gray light. It could wait. He fixed himself a massive bourbon, added two chunks of ice from the box, took a swig that half-emptied the tumbler and felt the liquid run down his throat like a lover's caress. Flicking on a lamp beside the worn-out chesterfield, he leaned over and depressed the button on the answer machine.

He expected a message from Abigail. But it was not her. "Mark," the voice said. "This is Janet."

Mark sat bolt upright. Pat's wife. Oh God!

"I'm sorry to call so late, but it's about Pat."

He waited for the words to tumble from the speaker. The words of death he had dreaded. But they did not come.

"He's taken a very bad turn, Mark. He's asked for you."

Mark snatched up the receiver and punched in Pat's number in the UK. He checked his watch. He knew that it would be the middle of the night across the Atlantic but this was urgent.

Janet picked up. "Hello?" She sounded wide awake.

"Sorry to call so late, Jan."

"I'm not sleeping much at the moment."

There was an uncomfortable silence, then a quiet sob. "Jan?"

"You need to come over. Now. He's not going to last long, Mark."

"I will. Of course. I'll leave tonight. First flight I can get."

"It would mean so much to him."

Chapter 7

Mark had not been back to England for five years. It was drizzling; reassuring for August, he thought. The plane nudged into Gate 21, Heathrow Terminal 3 at 7.53 a.m. There was a predawn orange smear over the cubes of concrete and iron. He had managed to get a seat on the red-eye from JFK, then grabbed an hour of sleep, but, sandwiched as he had been between a young mother traveling with an irritable two-year-old and a snoring Indian woman with personal-hygiene issues, it had felt like ten minutes.

Switching on his phone, Mark checked his messages. The first was a text from his boss, wishing him well but insisting that he spend no more than two days out of the office. The second was a voicemail from his assistant saying she had found the pieces from his backup collection to use while he was away, and the third was from the dry-cleaner telling him his shirts were ready for collection. He hitched his carry-on bag a little higher on his shoulder and followed the signs for Customs. Using the British passport that he studiously renewed and with only one small bag for luggage he was soon through the main doors and out among the stream of travelers, taxis bumper to bumper, and breathing in the crisp chill air of a Heathrow morning.

The hire car was small and underpowered, but it was cosy and warm and one of the radio presets was already tuned to Radio 4. Pulling onto the M4, Mark kept to the inside lane until his brain adjusted back to the habit of driving on the left. It was a Thursday morning and by the time he reached the junction with the M25 the motorway was gridlocked. The dashboard clock told him it was 8.59. The news was filled with disasters, death and pain, but he found every morsel fascinating. When he had first moved to New York he had gone through a phase of listening to the BBC World Service but Jill had weaned him off it, telling him that he had to adapt. He regretted listening to her. He made a mental note to go back to listening to the World Service on the Internet just as soon as he got home. But was New York really home? Of course it was. He had spent an unbroken dozen years in the city. He had a green card, he had an American ex-wife, a job, a band, an apartment of his own, potted plants, friends. What did he have left in England? A few distant relatives—both his parents had died before he'd left for the States—some old acquaintances, and one very special, very dear friend, Patrick Clifton. Perhaps that relationship was all that linked him to his old life, along with a few fading memories of youthful days spent punting, or sitting in the pub while the snow tapped on the window. And, further back, Saturday afternoons with his dad, watching West Ham play at Upton Park.

The M40 was clear and he began to feel a little more relaxed. Ever since leaving Abigail Marchant's rooms he had made a desperate effort to force away the memory of the experiment in which he had agreed to take part.

Every time it nudged at his mind he shoved it aside. But for one simple reason even that was difficult. It only exaggerated the memory because that was exactly what he had been doing in the regression—shoving something aside, something dreadful, something he could not contemplate.

Pat's wife Janet had sounded all in on the phone. These past few months must have been so terribly hard for her. While they'd been on holiday, skiing in Austria, they had learned that the cancer had returned. Then it began to spread. In June, Pat had been given weeks to live. He had been holding on, fighting, living for every second. He needed to survive, Janet wanted him to survive, but for her and the six-year-old twins, Alice and Peter, life had become a slow descent into Hell. Janet had told Mark in an email that she felt so utterly useless, watching the person she loved so much shrink and dwindle in front of her eyes. In the months since Austria, she had run the gamut of emotions: guilt, anger, shame, regret, dread and fear. Hovering over it all, there was a horrible sense of loss, for she was losing Pat, even while he was still there.

Mark tried to snap out of this dark train of thought. Switching stations to Radio 3 as he drove through the Chilterns, something singularly appropriate came on, a Vaughan Williams symphony. He wasn't sure which one it was but it provided a perfect accompaniment to the view as he swept into an Oxfordshire displaying its best August colors, the sky now a heartbreaking blue. And he could not help remembering the first time he had traveled this road. He had been on a bus from Victoria, en route to his interview at Oriel College. He'd been feeling strangely calm, riding a wave of self-confidence. He had just read *Jonathan Livingston Seagull*, and he'd felt untouchable.

He had also been buoyed up by the fact that his parents, whom he loved dearly, were so proud that he had come this far: to be granted an interview at Oxford. They were an old-fashioned, lower-middle-class family who lived in a three-bedroom house in Croydon. Dad worked at the High Street branch of Lloyds Bank. After thirty years devoted to the black horse, the bank's symbol, he had risen to the dizzy heights of assistant branch manager. He hadn't gone to university. He had attended night school after leaving Kennington Secondary Modern school with five O levels. To Mark's father, his son, their only child, was the great hope for the future.

That day in Oxford everything had gone smoothly for Mark. Before he left he was more or less told he had a place, a fact that he knew would raise his parents' spirits beyond the stratosphere, and he had met a young man named Patrick Clifton, who was also to be accepted and would end up on the same college staircase as him and become the best friend he ever had.

Aged eighteen, Patrick Clifton had been a wildly exotic-looking creature, and when Mark first laid eyes on him as Pat slithered through the doors leading from the corridor into the waiting area outside the professor's office he had felt instantly intimidated—and slightly repelled. Patrick was almost entirely bald and eyebrow-less, and his skin was as pale as paper. He was wearing a suit that had obviously been forced upon him by his parents, but between home and Oxford he had customised it. Dispensing with his tie, he had replaced it with a bolo lace clasped with a silver skull, and he had turned the lapels of his jacket inward to create the effect of a slim, elegantly curving collar.

"Oh good Lord, how tedious," he exclaimed in a perfect imitation of Sebastian Flyte as he eyed the line of interviewees sitting nervously, their hands in their laps. Then, to Mark's horror, he had seated himself next to him on the end chair of the row. Turning to face Mark, Pat had grinned, and then, in a perfectly normal Home Counties voice, said: "*Ulysses* or *Finnegan's Wake*?"

"Sorry?" Mark had replied.

"Which one curdles your milk? Bet that will be the first question. It won't be a physics question for sure— they want well-rounded intellects at Oxford."

"Oh, right."

"I'd prefer Higgins vs. Sheldon myself. But you can't have everything."

Mark had never met anyone like Patrick. They didn't speak again for nine months, by which time they had both been accepted into Oriel. Mark saw him ascending Staircase VI. Pat had been wearing dark eyeshadow and a turquoise green ankle-length linen coat. Beside him walked a girl whom all the "lads" had dubbed "the most gorgeous fresher ever"—Amilia—who was five-eleven, blonde-bobbed and Sophia Loren-lipped. She was gazing at Patrick's face with the sort of longing that Mark could only fantasise about, and he had decided there and then that this strange character, Patrick Clive Staples Clifton (his parents were C. S. Lewis fanatics), was somebody he should know.

It turned out that, two years earlier, Patrick had been diagnosed with leukemia. He had been a promising violinist, fast-tracked for a place at the Royal Academy of Music. But all that had gone and he had turned to Plan B: to read physics at Oxford. Patrick wanted to live big. More than anything, he wanted to live so big that he could defeat death. He embraced each new morning as though it might be his last because, quite simply, it could have proven to be just that. He was in remission, but no one could tell if or when the dreaded dark cells would begin to conspire.

Mark and Patrick became inseparable friends. Mark, the more conservative, more conventional one, was caught up in his new friend's spellbinding world. Later in life, Mark often wondered why it was that Patrick had befriended him. After all, Pat was a star. He could have been friends with anybody, but he had chosen Mark, had created an umbilical link between them. Mark never knew why. He had theories, but the truth was that he did not want to probe too deeply in case he came up with a reason so prosaic as to ruin his cherished memories.

Patrick really had adopted the role of a late-twentieth-century Sebastian Flyte. Because he had already come so close to death, he worshiped life and adopted the same sense of *Carpe Diem* as had his fictional counterpart. And, because of this, he had brought Mark out of himself, heightened his senses, subconsciously molded him to be a better man than he might otherwise have become.

They played music together in transient, long-forgotten bands at clubs with names like Back To Nature and The Jungle. Mark played his old Gibson—an eighteenth-birthday present from his parents—while Patrick, who had switched from violin to guitar, strummed a cheap Strat copy.

Patrick was a master of spontaneity and the glamorous gesture, and many of Mark's fondest memories of Oxford were thanks to him. His favorite moment occurred in their second year when Patrick decided to host a breakfast party in a field somewhere outside the city. Mark had set off in the dark with two friends, Jeff and Grant, in Jeff's clapped-out blue minivan.

They arrived just before sunrise, the three of them spilling out of the van to find Patrick setting up tables and preparing the champagne. Together, they toasted the sun rising to cast its eternal light on a new day.

A year later, the night before their Finals, Mark was awoken at two a.m by the sound of stones being thrown at the window of his bedsit off Iffley Road. Patrick was in a panic and Mark had to calm him down with tea and reassurances. It was the first time that Mark had been in the dominant position in the relationship, the first time Patrick had truly needed him. It felt good in spite of the fact that Mark was as nervous as his friend.

Mark pulled into the driveway of a modest house in Summertown. The curtains were closed. Rain spattered on the windshield. He took three deep breaths, then stepped from the hire car, a bouquet from the local florist in one hand, a copy of Sidney Sheldon's *The Naked Face* under his arm.

Janet came to the door. Mark hadn't seen her in two years. She looked thin, exhausted, pretty much as he had expected. He kissed her on the cheek. "He's very excited about seeing you, Mark," Janet said. "Although he's trying his best to pretend he isn't." He handed her the flowers. She smiled and turned to the kitchen to find a vase.

The kids were at a friend's and the place was unnervingly quiet. It was a rather shabby house, but Mark had a great affection for it. The decor was what many would call quirky. Nothing matched. The house had been decorated in a mixture of styles from Georgian to Philippe Starck and the walls looked as though a box of paintings marked "odds and ends" had exploded and the images had landed intact but had been scattered randomly around the walls.

Mark recalled how Patrick had burned bright as a young man, but had then settled into a rather surprisingly orthodox domestic life. From time to time over the years, he had paused to think about this. It was an ironic fact that he, Mark, had been the conformist kid, a lower-middle-class grammar-school boy with a bad haircut, useless with girls, but very bright, very earnest. And there had been Patrick, a peacock, a super-bright shining light in the dull firmament of mid-1990s England, who had mocked everything that others had considered cool. He had laughed at what he called "the lumpen racket" of Oasis, had shrugged, bored when he heard Blur, had disparaged Damien Hurst, referred to Tracy Emin as a tedious old slapper, and claimed he preferred Chas and Dave to Gilbert and George. But then he took a teacher-training course and worked at a primary school.

Patrick was sitting up in bed pretending to watch TV, remote in hand. He looked up as Mark came in as though surprised to see him. He flicked off the TV and shook his head. "You look awful," he declared and broke into a smile.

Mark stared at him, and for some reason that eluded him he felt embarrassed. Then he sauntered over, leaned towards the bed and kissed Pat on the cheek. His friend's face felt hard, the bone lying barely a fraction of a millimeter beneath yellowy skin. Mark pulled himself back up and handed Patrick the book. Pat nodded as he read the title. "Very tasteful. Sit, Mark. Pull up that chair." He pointed to a repulsive early 1960s orange and green affair close to the bed.

Mark went to say something, but Patrick held up his hand. "Mark, no crap. Every second counts. That's something you realise when . . ."

Mark sighed. "Are you in pain?"

"No . . . well, no physical pain. Not now. I was. Fuck, I was. But, no, it's strange, just the past few days. They're giving me extra-strong something. Reminds me of our second year . . . that chap, Laughing Larry. He had all the good shit, didn't he?"

Mark smiled. "God, I'd forgotten him."

"But yes, Mark, I am in pain up here." Patrick tapped his head. "You see, I don't want to die. I did. Believe me, I did. In chemo. Holy fuck, I wanted to just . . . expire. But not now. Now, I actually feel better. I don't want to . . . But I imagine that's just, well, one of life's clever little fucking ironies, isn't it?"

"Is there anything . . . ?"

"Anything you can do for me? A new body would be nice. Even a new liver. But no. Just seeing you again is really something. But, Mark, I'm so bloody jealous of you."

Mark closed his eyes. When a second later he opened

them again there was a strange look on Patrick's face. Then Patrick started to shake his head slowly from side to side. He gasped, and his eyelids drooped.

"Pat!" Mark yelped, jumping from the chair and placing a hand on his friend's arm.

Patrick exhaled, opened his eyes. "Gotcha!" he said.

Mark took a step back and forced a smile. Then he tilted his head, sat down in the horrible chair and laughed. They both laughed. Their laughter knitted together. Janet could hear it from the kitchen, and she smiled.

"Okay, ice shattered," Patrick said and tried to pull himself up on the pillows. He winced, Mark stepped towards him and eased him up.

"You know, Mark, I've been through more emotional experiences in the last three months than in the rest of my waking days combined. It's another one of those weird ironies of life that, close to the point of death, you know more about yourself and the world than you ever have before . . . and you cannot *use* that knowledge. It's all entirely wasted, lost . . . forever. How sad is that?"

"Tell me."

"Well, there're the clichés . . . the prescribed stages of reaction to the dread news: denial, anger, bargaining . . . you know the routine. But, I dunno. Maybe I'm a freak. I was when I was younger, wasn't I, Mark? This time round I just felt bitter. How could the world go on without me? I kept thinking. But then, I suppose I always was a narcissist. I was ravaged by thoughts of Jan remarrying. I had visions of her stroking another man's hair, whispering in his ear her love for him as he penetrated her. I thought of my kids calling another man 'Dad'. It made me feel nauseous. Then I felt angry. I was furious with this revolting little mutation that was doing this to me, this piece of shit that was depriving me of my life, stopping me from seeing my children grow up."

"Those are natural feelings, Pat."

"I imagine they are." He looked down at his bony hands where they lay over the sheet. "Do you remember I once said to you that if ever I found Christianity, you must shoot me in the head?"

Mark smiled. "Yes, Pat, I do. Please don't . . ."

"No, don't worry. But I have had to wonder. You may be confronted with the same thing one day. What does a soldier feel as he calls for his mother on the battlefield? What does a mother cry as she hears of the death of her son? Is it all vanity? Is it all absolutely nothing? Is it simply us silly humans thinking we are so damn important that there has to be something bigger, something more? Or is there *really* something more? How can we know? Maybe it's not believing in a plan for Humanity that is the ultimate ego trip. What if denying the existence of God, turning away from any sense of meaning is actually the perfect vanity? Have you thought of that?"

"Yes, Pat, I have. But, look . . . I have no answers."

He smiled at that. "Okay," he said. "Then let's talk about you. How's your love life?"

Mark shrugged.

"Come on. I've known you for a very long time and I know what an incorrigible romantic you are. I can sense when you have a new someone in the wings."

"There's nothing . . . I've only met her a couple of . . ."

"Aha!" Patrick lifted his hand and wagged a finger at his friend. "There you go!"

"Okay, I met this woman called Abigail. She's a psychologist. It's all new, but . . . I don't know. There's something about her I can't describe it. I feel . . . I feel as though I've known her a long time, but we only met a few days ago."

Patrick studied Mark's face.

"What is it?" Mark asked.

"Nothing . . . Oh, I'm just . . . I'm really pleased for you. She sounds wonderful."

"Oh, come on! I hardly know her."

"But you just said . . ."

"You're right, Pat. I'm an incorrigible romantic. But we're scientists, we don't believe in hocus-pocus." He couldn't bring himself to say anything about Abigail's work on rebirth. It seemed somehow completely inappropriate. Mark had his hands up. "My rational self regrets what I said earlier . . . There!"

"Always suspected you were bipolar!"

"Look," Mark went on in spite of himself. "Abigail is great-looking, intelligent, interesting; of course I'm going to be smitten. It's been a long time since Jill and I . . ."

Mark caught an odd look in Patrick's eyes. He couldn't define it precisely, and the moment passed quickly.

"So," Pat said, forcing a smile. "What new bands are you listening to?"

Chapter 8

Mark walked along the gravel driveway to the car, knowing that he had left Patrick for the final time. He felt as though he was stepping away from his past and he could not shake off the belief that he could have done more, that he could have consoled his friend better. They had spoken for three hours. Most of it had been trivia; just what was needed. But some of it had hooked into his soul, cut into his inner being, whatever that might have been. As he had stood up and walked toward the door to leave, Mark had turned back to look at his dear friend. It was his final look; they had both known that. Mark had scanned his face, trying to distance Pat from his sickness as though he, Mark, were some kind of alchemist or shaman who owned the elixir of life, with the power of resurrection at his finger-tips. Then he had pulled down the door handle, walked into the hall, and the twenty-first century had returned with all its pain and anger.

Now the car felt like a malevolent object, an artificial thing that offended against the organic world, his world in which things lived and things died. Plastic and metal were seemingly eternal. The crushing machine at the scrapyard merely reconfigured them. Organic things—they rotted.

He stared at the house, and at that moment the memory of Professor Abigail Marchant's office came into his mind. It tugged at him. It brought some semblance of hope—didn't it? He took a deep breath and stared around at the foliage, the tarmac beyond. "FUCK OFF!" he shouted at the windshield, his spittle spraying the glass. Exiting the driveway, he drove twenty yards along the road before he was forced to pull over and stop. The tears were cascading down his cheeks, blurring his vision, stinging. He put his head down on the steering wheel, his body heaving. He sobbed and kept saying: "Oh." A low-pitched mournful word of defeat, submission, guilt, anguish.

The sixty-minute drive back to Heathrow and the airport hotel passed unnoticed. Mark checked in, traveled in the lift to the third floor, ran the plastic card through the security slot and stumbled into the room, the jet lag finally kicking in. He threw his shoulder bag onto the floor, flopped onto the bed and fell asleep.

He was in the large white car again, the American automobile with the huge fins at the back, the sweeping red dashboard. This time he was driving the car. He raised his eyes to the right and saw that the motorcade was approaching a low-rise brick building. He glimpsed someone moving high up in one of the windows. Then came a cracking sound. He swiveled round in his seat, slowing the car instinctively. Patrick was in the back seat, clutching his chest. Then came another crack.

In spite of the jet lag, Mark had slept for only a few hours. By ten that evening he found himself in an empty hotel bar nursing his fifth Scotch on the rocks. The bar closed a few minutes later and he returned to his room to contemplate the contents of the minibar. Seated in a chair watching Sky News with the sound off, he was startled when his mobile rang.

The first thing he heard were sobs, then a woman's voice breaking on every other word. "Mark—he's dead. Patrick's dead."

Mark swallowed hard and tried to breathe, but he could find no air. He stared fixedly at the lampshade, a horrible piece of cheap shit from Ikea. He tried to draw breath again, but nothing came. On the third attempt, the air reached his lungs. He suddenly realized he hadn't made a sound. Janet was speaking again. "Mark?"

"Jan." He took two deep breaths. "Is someone with you? The kids?"

"My mother is here. It happened two hours ago. They've just taken Pat's . . ." She broke down. "I can't talk now, Mark. I just wanted you to know."

He started to reply but the line was dead.

He walked over to the window. The clock said it was 10.34 p.m. but the sky was bright from the endless glow of the runways, the terminals and the hangars, the thousands of kilowatts from floodlights, the pinpricks of light from the insides of taxiing planes. Heathrow was a city, a place that never slept, a place that kept going. Mark watched, numb, as a plane came in to land. He could visualize a curved path, an imaginary ribbon in the sky arching up to the clouds and linking half a dozen aircraft, each on final approach.

He heard a loud crack, followed by another bang. He

spun round to face the empty room. Then came a screech of brakes. For a second, he thought that the sounds had come from outside, but he realized quickly that nothing could have penetrated the triple-glazed windows made of sound-proofed glass to block out aircraft noise. But there was nothing in the room that could have generated the sounds.

He smelled something odd. Rubber, burned rubber. He glanced at the kettle where it sat unplugged. A tremor of fear ran down his spine. "No," he said aloud. "No."

Mark ran his fingers through his hair and lowered himself onto the bed. He was soaked in sweat. The front of his shirt was sticking to him. He looked down and saw patches of wetness. "Am I going mad?" His words were sucked into the air around him. "Am I going mad?" He shouted it this time and vaulted from the bed, stumbled to the bathroom and leaned on the handbasin, staring at his reflection in the mirror. He looked as though he would never smile again.

He heard Professor Abigail Marchant's voice as though it were coming from the end of a long plastic pipe. She was repeating something she had told him the other night in the restaurant in New York. "There is actually nothing about rebirth that contradicts the accepted laws of physics. Nothing at all."

Seated on the edge of the bed, Mark looked down at the inexpensive beige carpet. What should he do? One part of him wanted to stay in England, go to Pat's funeral, grieve, be with old friends and Pat and Janet's families, to join the lament. But another, louder voice was saying something different. It declared that seeing his friend lowered into the ground was pointless, that others better qualified would be at Pat's graveside to comfort his widow. The second voice grew louder, more strident: move on, go forward, it was saying. Leave the dead flesh behind— there is something vital to learn from Professor Abigail Marchant, something Earth-shatteringly important.

Crossing the room, he picked up the phone and punched in Abigail's number. It rang and rang. He was just about to hang up when he heard her voice.

"Hi, Abigail."

"Mark!" She sounded genuinely delighted to hear from him.

"Look, I'm sorry about . . ."

"Don't be silly. Where are you? It's a terrible line."

"Heathrow Airport. I . . . I flew over to see a friend who is dying. Terminal liver cancer."

"I'm so sorry."

Mark could not speak for a few moments. Abigail seemed to sense it and said nothing.

"You still there?" he asked, his voice croaky.

"I'm here, Mark."

"My friend has just died."

Abigail went quiet again.

Mark could hear her breathing. "Abigail?"

"Um, I'm . . . I'm sorry to hear that."

"I was thinking. What would you say if I told you I wanted another go at being regressed?"

There was a pause. Abigail cleared her throat. "That would make me very happy."

"You okay?" Mark asked.

"Yeah, of course. Why do you . . . ?"

"You just sound flat suddenly."

"Been a long day," she sighed. "So—er—when do you get back?" She was clearly making an effort to inject some brightness into the tone of her voice. Mark wondered about that.

"About six in the morning. How about if I drop in around nine?"

"You'll be shattered!"

"I can sleep when I'm dead," Mark retorted.

PART 2

Everything has changed.

Chapter 9

"You look exhausted."

"Haven't slept much during the past forty-eight hours," Mark said as he stepped into Professor Marchant's office.

"A very strong coffee, please, Julia," Abigail said to her secretary as she retreated closing the door behind her. "You were very vague on the phone. Mark. What's happened?"

"The evening I regressed I got a call from the wife of Patrick Clifton, my oldest friend from Oxford days. She said Pat didn't have long to live, and that if I wanted to see him alive one last time I had to get over to the UK pretty damn quick. So I got the first plane out."

"You must have been very close."

Julia appeared with a coffee, placed it on the table in front of Abigail's sofa and withdrew.

"We were. I still can't quite . . . Anyway. I was at Heathrow and, I don't know, something happened. It was as though the tumblers fell into place. I started to think about what you had told me about rebirth and I realized that I had been resisting because I was scared."

"Scared of what?"

"Being led into the abyss of the irrational."

"Sounds very grand!"

"Look, as I said at the restaurant, if I was to believe in rebirth then I would have to discard everything I've been taught, everything I've understood to be true: the bedrock of my intellect, if you like. I wasn't able or willing to face that conflict."

"You're talking in the past tense."

"A slip!" Mark took a gulp of coffee.

"But you're now more open toward the concept of rebirthing?"

"Let's just say I'm not so dismissive as I was. I'm ready now to address the issue. Don't get me wrong—I still hold true to the maxim of Richard Dawkins: By all means be open-minded but not so open-minded that our brains fall out."

Abigail smiled. "And this change was precipitated by Patrick's death?"

"I guess so. It makes me no better than the sort of people I've always considered to be irrational wishful-thinkers, those who cling to religion to give them hope. I've always believed that these people simply chase rainbows, unable to face the stark, rational truth of life. For me the core reality of the universe was: that the whole shebang is chaotic, nothing but randomness; that we are just a chance creation in the great swirl of time; and that there was no meaning to existence."

"And you're using the past tense again!"

Mark laughed, then took a deep breath and was serious once more.

"Pat's death has opened a crack in my mind, Abigail. I'm not going to block it. I can't pretend it isn't there. I want to prise it open—and see what it reveals."

"Well, in that case we'd better get started. You feel up to regressing again?"

"It's the only way to find out more, isn't it? And besides, I'm still due to deliver an article on you and your work. What better way to research it?"

Abigail walked over to the recording equipment "Get comfortable, Mark. We'll do exactly what we did before. Just tell me what you experience—every detail. Just talk to me as though you're seeing a movie that I can't see and you're describing everything that happens on the screen, yeah?"

Mark nodded, and lay back.

Chapter 10

White. Then a smudge of pink. Everything out of focus. I lift my head and see the back of my hand on the sheet, pick out the dark hairs. From this range they look like burned corn sprouting from pale soil.

The room is very quiet. A pallid light breaks through a small gap in the curtains. I pull myself up, lean my head back against the headboard and hear it creak. It is a comfortable bed and I feel rested, but I could do with just a little more sleep. I peer at the alarm clock. It is one minute to seven. Rubbing my eyes, I throw back the bed covers and sit up.

There's a black telephone on the bedside table, and beside that a pad set into a tray with a pen across the top. The notepaper is headed with the name of the hotel: "The Texas". The decor is not exactly what my interior designer wife Ruth would consider chic, but to my eye it is warm and comfortable, pure Texan, with a bison head on the wall opposite the bed and lots of chintz.

Before running a shower, I arrange my clothes on the bed: a black suit, my best, a crisply laundered white shirt and a dark green tie. I think back to the previous day: one crazy whirl, as these trips always are. A short flight here from Houston. I had managed to get a call through to Ruth. It had to be quick—I was on a tight schedule. The president's party, all thirty-seven of us, had arrived quite late at the hotel. Jack and Jackie had gone to bed, but I had stayed up for a few drinks in the bar, chewing the fat with a couple of the team. I guess I must have drunk too much because my head is hurting a little this morning and my mouth is dry.

I stick out my tongue and stare at the reflection in the bathroom mirror. The shower water beats against the curtain.

I just manage to hear the doorbell over the noise of the water. "Okay," I yell and turn off the taps, grab a robe from the back of the bathroom door.

"Who is it?" I ask as I reach the door.

"Dave?"

It is my boss Malcolm Kilduff, Acting Press Secretary. "Need you in Jack's suite in ten."

"You got it."

I make it out of the room in five and almost crash into John Maclaren, one of the Secret Service guys I had been up drinking with last night. He's a big, muscular guy. I'm not sure how old he is but he looks very young for an agent.

"Steady," he says, gripping my shoulders. "You okay on those feet, David?"

I look at the smirk on his face and grin conspiratorially. "Mouth's as dry as old boots," I say.

"Busy fucking day ahead, Davey. The boss is driving us all mad. Insists on an open car. Won't allow any of the guys on the running boards during the motorcade. Fucking well determined to meet and greet." This last he *offers with a sneer. "The man's just asking for trouble, but no one can tell him."*

"Well, he is the president, John," I say.

"Yeah, he is. Anyways, don't let me hold you up. I hear there's a bit of a shit storm going down." And with that he turns and walks away. I'd like to ask what he means, but conclude that I'll find out soon enough.

And I do; just as soon as I step past the guard into Suite 850. I only have to see the faces of the three men seated around the coffee table in the lounge to know that there has been some sort of a hiccup.

"Dave. Sit down," John Fitzgerald Kennedy says. He is seated like the others in casual chairs upholstered in a heavily checkered orange and black woolen fabric. The president, dressed immaculately in a gray two-button suit, dark blue tie and crisp white shirt appears to be rested. His eyes sparkle with energy. I consider his profile and sense again that weird feeling I've had ever since I started working for the White House two years ago: that my job is a surreal one. How is it, I always think, that I ended up working with the Leader of the Free World? How did I land a job where I could sit next to President John F. Kennedy and he would address me by my first name? Sure, I had done all the right things. I had worked hard and delivered on my parent's efforts and struggles to get me through Harvard where I had excelled both in the lecture theater and on the sports field, and I had networked, becoming a good friend of Teddy Kennedy's. Yes, I had done all the right things, said the right things, kissed a lot of ass. But, fuck, how did I land up here? It feels good. It always feels good,

even when Jack turns a face frowning with frustration and irritation toward me.

"You seen the papers, Dave?"

"Er, no, Mr. President . . ."

"Here."

The headline screams: "Storm of Political Controversy Swirls Around Kennedy on Visit". I speed-read the first two paragraphs of the Dallas Morning News. *The paper is staunchly Republican and it is doing its level best to pour cold water on the president's visit to Texas, making as much capital as it can from rumors of infighting between Democratic senators.*

"Sir, it's nothing more than you'd expect from them. They're just preaching to the converted."

The president picks up another paper from the table. The headline reads: "Nixon Predicts JFK May Drop Johnson." "And what about this, Dave? You're supposed to be my Press Liaison. You shouldn't be allowing this sort of thing to happen. Where do they get this crap, anyway? Who's even suggested dumping LBJ? Certainly not me."

"Must be a really slow news day, Mr. President," I respond. "I really wouldn't take any of it at all seriously. The thing is, these guys are out to sell newspapers. They know, sure as Hell, we're not going to sue 'em."

"Might not be a bad idea. Give the bastards the shock of their lives."

I glance at Kennedy and then at the other two men at the table, Kennedy's personal assistant, David F. Powers, and Brigadier General Godfrey McHugh, the president's Chief Military Aide, and I can't decide whether or not

Kennedy is being serious. Then he produces a faint smile and motions with his head toward the window. "Okay, Dave, relax. Looks like we have a pretty good crowd outside the hotel. So we can't be in too much trouble with the people."

I know that he has every reason to feel jittery. He is here to garner support for the '64 election. His civil-rights policies have been received terribly by many of the more conservative of his supporters in Texas. One local magistrate told me in private at the bar last night that: "The boss's pandering to the niggers came like a turd in the mail." And that was from someone who was supposed to be a grass-roots party worker. But to make this worse, there are also genuine conflicts within the higher reaches of the party. It is no secret that JFK's younger brother Bobby, the Attorney General, cannot stand the Vice-President, Lyndon B. Johnson, and that the feeling is mutual. I recall how Pierre Salinger, the most senior Press Officer at the White House, had told me once that "Bobby can't do anything that could please Johnson—except commit suicide." It is also public knowledge that two of Texas's most senior Democrats, the state governor John Connally and one of the state's senators, Ralph Yarborough, despise each other so much that they can barely stand being in the same room. Meanwhile, Yarborough has even less affection for Vice-President Johnson.

To be honest, I can't abide Yarborough or Connally. When the thin layers of civility are drawn aside, each of them is exposed as a silly schoolboy, a man with an overinflated ego: petty, small-minded little men with way too much power.

"Yes, Mr. President," I say. "I think the people do love you, even if some newspaper editors don't."

Kennedy stands up, and I catch the briefest grimace of pain. It is another secret restricted to insiders that the president is not a well man. He has suffered chronic back pain for years and takes a cocktail of drugs that keep him functioning in the most demanding job in the world. This is a fact I have been made privy to only since I accepted my job at the White House and signed documents to keep my silence official. It has been explained to me that as JFK's Press Liaison there is no more important job than to prevent anyone outside the inner circle having even the vaguest suspicions that Jack is anything other than the epitome of good health and vigor that the public assume him to be.

"Sir," David Powers says, placing a palm in the small of the president's back. "Time for the gala breakfast."

"Is Jackie ready?"

"She'll be making a grand entrance about ten minutes after we're seated."

"Is this your idea, Dave?" Kennedy says, regarding me seriously.

"Yes, Mr. President. Well, it was O'Donnell who first suggested it, but I implemented it."

"I like it," Jack responds. "The people may claim they love me, but they really do love Jackie. I sometimes feel I'm the one on tour with her!"

We all laugh and the Brigadier General leads the way to the door.

The Grand Ballroom where the breakfast is to be held

is an impressive, if overbearing, room. Lined with dark wood paneling, it has huge windows along one wall that face onto a courtyard. Six massive crystal chandeliers hang from the ceiling. This morning the place is packed to the rafters. Two thousand wealthy Texans, mainly from the business sector, are here with their wives. These folks are the great and the good of Texas and some of them have paid up to $100 a ticket just to be in the same room as the First Couple. Two Secret Service agents lead the way into the Grand Ballroom. LBJ and his wife, Lady Bird, follow. Then come Jack Kennedy and Ken O'Donnell. Behind them walks another Secret Service agent, then two more advisors. They are followed by Brigadier General Godfrey McHugh. I walk in immediately behind McHugh, a fourth agent behind me. Everyone rises from their seats and applauds loudly as we enter the vast room.

Jack is all smiles. And why shouldn't he be? This break-fast crowd is made up entirely of party supporters. Many of them come from old Texan families who have donated to Democrat coffers for generations. They know that the state is a troubling one for the administration. Jack only just scraped home in the 1960 election; and yesterday, as the president's party left Houston, we all saw protesters lining the street and ugly placards: "IN 1964 GOLDWATER AND FREEDOM" and "YANKEE GO HOME". I even spotted one that said "KENNEDY: YOU'RE A TRAITOR".

Jack waves and then sits, the Texas Boys Choir strike up a rousing rendition of "The Yellow Rose of Texas", and I can feel an expectant hush descend on the room. The choir finishes to warm applause and the toastmaster, Raymond Buck, gets a nod from a Secret Service agent named Clint Hill who is standing at the doors to the huge kitchen on the far side of the room from the podium. The toastmaster stands as the audience falls silent. "And now," he says in his deep Texan drawl, "an event I know you have all been waiting for!" He sweeps a hand towards the kitchen and heads turn. The gathering erupts into applause as Jackie advances gracefully into the room and walks to the front, escorted by two security men.

As the applause dies down, Jack steps up to the microphone. "Two years ago in Paris, I introduced myself as the man who accompanies Mrs. Kennedy." There is a cheer and Jack smiles. He glances at Jackie, then at LBJ a few seats away on his other side, and adds: "Nobody wonders what Lyndon and I wear . . ." The crowd roars with laughter. I find myself smiling as I consider the adoring supporters and think to myself that this might just turn out to be a really good day after all.

Chapter 11

Breakfast lasts almost an hour and then the president's party is led from the Grand Ballroom, back into the elevator and up to the eighth-floor suite. Jackie seems to be in a light-hearted mood. I know that deep down she's a rather shy woman who in private professes not to like the spotlight. But for years now she has been an object of attention and, more recently, adoration bordering on the obsessive, so that she has had to learn to deal with such exposure. There is a steeliness to her that can only be put down to breeding. As First Lady, she is very aware of what is expected of her, and she never fails to rise to any occasion.

Today, Jackie is dressed exquisitely. Jack had specified that she should look elegant on the tour of the South. As if he needed to! How could his wife ever be anything but elegant? I catch her eye as I follow her into Suite 850. She is wearing a rose-pink Chanel suit with a navy collar over a blue silk blouse. Her hair is pure raven and immaculately styled into a bob. Atop this, she wears a pink pillbox hat to accessorize her blue purse and gloves.

In the room, Jack's mood seems to be the exact opposite of his wife's. He is angry again at the Press coverage of the trip. My boss Malcolm Kilduff has just shown the president another negative front page. "Christ, I come all the way down here and make a few speeches," Kennedy declares. "And this is what appears on the front page."

Fortunately for me, before he can point a finger Roy Kellerman, the head of the Secret Service detail on the tour, comes in. He is saying something into a walkie-talkie, but I don't catch his words. He gives a sign to one of his men on the other side of the room and takes two steps toward Jack Kennedy. "Mr. President," he says. "The cars are here; they're at the back of the building. Mr. O'Donnell says the area is sealed off. We should head for the airport."

Kennedy rounds on him and for a second the anger is still there in his face. Kellerman stares back blankly and Jack's expression changes. "Very well," he says. "Let's move on, get this thing over with."

At the insistence of the Secret Service agents, we take the back stairs. I've made similar journeys with the president's entourage before, but it never ceases to amaze me that, as a security precaution, the most powerful man in the world is regularly forced to take the tradesman stairs and to skulk around like some sort of lowlife.

Ken is indeed waiting for us as we emerge into the unseasonably warm morning, and it becomes immediately apparent to me that some decisions have been made during the past half-hour, none of which I've been made privy to because they have no bearing on my job. Jack has been absolutely determined the arch enemies within his camp would sit in the same car. So, in order to present a public face of unity, the contrarian Senator Ralph Yarborough is forced to share a car with LBJ.

The president's limo stands on the tarmac directly

ahead of us with a dozen more cars in a line behind it. I see Jack break away and take a couple of steps towards O'Donnell. "Ken," he says. "I thought I told you to keep the roof off the car."

"But Mr. President—"

"No buts, Ken. No buts. I want the roof off for the motorcade."

Ken stands his ground. Jack is forever upsetting the Secret Service by insisting that he have maximum access to "his people". He wants to be what he calls "hands-on". He does not like to put up barriers between himself and the public and he hates the idea that a US President cannot go freely into any American city. So today—a nice, sunny Texan winter morning that speaks to him of freedom and liberty—is perfect for lowering the barriers. "Sir, I have to insist," O'Donnell says.

"Look, Ken." Jack has his hands on his hips. "It wouldn't be difficult to shoot the President of the United States. All you'd have to do is get up in a tall building with a high-powered rifle with a telescopic sight, and there's nothing anybody could do."

Ken looks at him. The two men go way back, and although Jack is in the No.1 job and Ken is a few rungs down the pecking order, there is a huge degree of mutual respect and genuine affection between them. Ken keeps staring for several seconds. Then he says quietly. "Very well, Mr. President. Have it your way."

Fort Worth is a dull, featureless place. Low-rise buildings line its straight wide roads, and the drive to the air base is totally uneventful with just a few people close to the road waving flags and cheering on the motorcade.

We see no unpleasant placards, hear no slanderous comments. And, although Jackie has been a little perturbed about keeping the roof off the limo because she is worried that her hair might be messed up, she has acquiesced without a fuss, and waves to the spectators as we head towards Carswell Air Force Base just a few miles outside the city.

I ride in the back of a small tour bus with a two-way radio linking me with my boss Malcolm Kilduff who is ahead of us in a Cadillac, two back in the motorcade from the president's limo. As we take the turn into the Air Force base through a gate guarded by four heavily armed marines, I see the lead car cut across the tarmac straight to Air Force One sitting at the edge of the airstrip. The car carrying Johnson, his wife, Lady Bird and Senator Yarborough peels away towards a second, identical aircraft, Air Force Two. Our driver takes the bus along a strip of tarmac and pulls up a short distance from the steps leading up to Air Force One and I watch Jack and Jackie being escorted up the steps of the modified Boeing 707. I glance along the slate-blue and cyan fuselage, the presidential seal embossed close to the cockpit and the capital letters along the side: THE UNITED STATES OF AMERICA in the same font used in the Declaration of Independence. This last, I know, is a nice detail suggested by the ever-stylish First Lady.

I hook up with Kilduff at the door into the main cabin and follow him into the midsection of the plane where the Press and Staff Area is located. The First Couple are already installed and buckled up, and within a few minutes the pilot is given the all-clear for take-off.

I watch through the window as the stretches of criss-crossing black tarmac slip away beneath us. A young stewardess pours me a coffee and hands me a pile of newspapers. I don't really feel like looking through them. Sometimes I detest the Press. I have to work with them, of course, liaise with them, but some editors and some senior journalists are utter bastards; and many of the younger reporters are trainee bastards. But another part of me cannot resist and I pick up the top paper. Thankfully, it is the "New York Times" and has nothing about the trip to Dallas on the front page. I glance up and notice Air Force Two carrying the vice-president and his wife overtake us so they can reach Dallas's Love Field early to receive the Kennedys officially.

I inspect the papers. Anything exciting seems a little thin on the ground in today's editions. Which, I'd expected. As I had rightly told Jack, it was one of the reasons the local papers went with what they consider to be a hot political ticket. On the front page of the Times, *the main story is the death at the age of seventy-three of Robert Franklin Stroud, the "Bird Man of Alcatraz". I remember the movie starring Burt Lancaster. I took Ruth to see it only a few months back. I start to read the piece and feel the plane begin its descent.*

I knew it would be a quick hop, but this has to be the shortest flight I have ever taken. I look at my watch and calculate that we have been in the air for less than eight minutes. Dallas is only thirty miles from Fort Worth, but Ken O'Donnell vetoed driving there. He wants the motor-cade to start at twelve noon on the dot, giving us time to reach the Dallas Trade Mart in time for lunch at one o'clock. Making the trip by car would have put his schedule out of whack.

Five minutes later, we are on the ground and taxiing to a halt close to the control tower. From my window I can see the crowd gathered outside the base perimeter. Literally thousands have traveled here just to catch a glimpse of the First Couple.

I'm at the top of the steps long after Jack and Jackie have reached the tarmac where they are being shown towards a line of dignitaries headed by Johnson and Lady Bird. It is a glorious morning. The sky is a peerless blue, not a cloud to be seen; and for late November it is unseasonably warm. From the top of the stairs I can see the swell of people at the perimeter and a few hundred privileged members of the public inside the base, watched over by dozens of local police. I can also hear the sound they make, a joyful buzz of anticipation and excitement. People are waving handkerchiefs. There are dozens of placards, all of them welcoming; I see a "We Love You Jackie" and a "Please Come Over and Say Hello". I hear a voice behind me say: "God, the First Couple really do look like Mr. and Mrs. America." I turn to see Malcolm Kilduff, a big grin across his face.

I hold back as the presidential party walks over toward the main building a hundred yards away from where Air Force One has stopped, but even from across the airstrip the roar of the crowd is almost alarming. Strangely, I have no fear, the mood is so convivial. The Secret Service are not so relaxed, though. As Jack pulls away from the column of guards and dignitaries and approaches the gathered public, he seems determined to be seen as the mere mortal he is. He shakes hands, accepts gifts. Jackie walks behind him. I know her well enough to tell that she is nervous about all the attention.

For a second, I lose focus and remember something I saw on TV only a week ago, just before leaving for Texas. I had been watching a news bulletin with Ruth. A piece came on about a new English pop group, The Beatles. To me, they looked like a bunch of scruffy long-haired delinquents, but the Brits seemed to love them. Every time they played a show, hordes of girls would scream hysterically so no one could hear a word they sang. "Probably just as well," I had said to Ruth. She laughed. But she added. "I think they're rather cute."

The Kennedys have no screaming young kids mobbing them, but the fanaticism is not far removed from the reaction generated by the British beat group I had seen. Perhaps I'm jaded by such daily close proximity to the First Couple, I reason, but I cannot help thinking these besotted people are being undignified. What is missing in their own lives, I think, for them to have to worship other flesh-and-blood human beings? I have seen Jack wince with chronic back pain, watched as Jackie giggled like a little girl at some silly joke. The Kennedys are just like any of us. They cry and laugh and they feel jubilation and they feel pain. They were born from a mother and they will die.

A shove from a Secret Service guy snaps me out of my reverie and I realize the men in black are getting really edgy. I round on the agent and tell him to watch it. He ignores me and I decide to get out the way. Leaving the First Couple to press the flesh and smile, I walk over to find my boss. I spot him leaning against the car he is to travel in for the motorcade. He views the scene, fascinated. We have seen stuff like it before, but maybe it is because we thought this trip was turning to shit that we are now surprised by the positive reception. "And the lesson today, Davey Boy," Malcolm says, "is don't take any fucking notice of what the papers say." And he gives me another of his Cheshire-cat smiles.

Chapter 12

It takes Ken O'Donnell's personal intervention to persuade Jack and Jackie to step away from the well-wishers and to get them into the limo where Senator Connally and his wife Nellie are waiting. I start toward the tour bus, way back in the motorcade, but Kilduff touches my elbow. "Got one more space in here," he says, pointing to the lead Press car, a white Chevrolet, only five cars back from the president's limo. A few minutes later than O'Donnell had planned, the motorcade, totaling twenty-two cars, sixteen police motorcycles and three large Press buses, moves out through the gates and onto Mockingbird Lane before swinging southwest onto Lemmon Avenue, the main highway into downtown Dallas.

I catch sight of the lead car. This is followed by eight police motorcyclists in formation. Behind them is an unmarked police car. This, I know, carries the Dallas Police Chief Jesse Curry and two Secret Service guys. And as we take a turn in the road, I see the president's limo, a dark green armored Lincoln convertible. It is a huge vehicle with three rows of seats. In the front sits Jack's regular driver, Bill Greer. Bill, who is fifty-four and the oldest Secret Service man at the White House, has been with Jack for years. He is an experienced driver *whom the Kennedy's trust implicitly. In the front beside him is the Chief Secret Service agent on the tour, Roy Kellerman. Behind these two men sit Senator Connally and his wife Nellie, the latter directly behind Greer. In the back seats sit the First Couple. Jackie is on the left behind Nellie Connally and Jack is on the right, behind the senator. Cruising along beside the limo are four Dallas Police bikes, two on each side. Jack has insisted that there should be no security men on the running boards or on the back of the car where there is a platform capable of carrying two armed agents. O'Donnell has been protesting about this all morning, but Jack has gotten his way.*

Lemmon Avenue is a drab road lined with low-rise industrial units and warehouses, but within ten minutes we hit the outskirts of downtown and the spectators start to appear; people who have streamed out of their offices, factories and stores to glimpse the motorcade. By the time we reach the business district the crowds have swelled and fill the sidewalks on each side of the road. It is an awe-inspiring sight. As we weave through the streets I occasionally glimpse the presidential limo and spot an arm extended to the side of the car as Jack or his wife wave at the adoring hordes. Whole families have gathered at the roadside, kids lifted aloft to see the great man and his beautiful wife. Wheelchairs line the curb, and for a minute the motorcade stops so that Jackie can step out of the car and say hello to a group of wheelchair-bound devotees. Then we are off again, taking a sharp right, then left, cutting a path along the highway into the heart of the city. Here there are taller buildings. Flags hang from office windows, secretaries lean out precariously, waving and screaming their enthusiastic welcome. I hear: "Jackie? Hi, Jackie" and "Mr. President, we Love You."

Soon we are on Main Street and it seems to me that the entire population of Dallas has left work on an early lunch break and taken to the streets. Police have to clear some over-enthusiastic locals and the motorcade is forced to slow. We soon pick up speed again and approach the Criminal Courts Building on our left as we emerge into Dealey Plaza. It is a pretty green space encircled by squat buildings. A road runs straight ahead and forks left and right. We take the right fork.

That is when I hear a strange sound. At first I think it is a car exhaust backfiring but then I'm uncertain. I have absolutely no experience with guns—have never touched one, in fact. I hear another crack. This time I know it is not an exhaust but the sound of a bullet being fired, the noise slamming around the Plaza, ricocheting between the buildings. Then comes a third identical bang. I turn to Kilduff beside me and he has a shocked look on his face. I feel all my nerve endings spark—a spasm passes through my body.

"Holy shit! What was that?" my boss screams.

The car slows. Kilduff goes for the door handle but our driver, another Secret Service agent, Neil Juffie, spins round. "Don't!" he yells. And Malcolm complies. The car stops, the motor still running. The agent leaps out.

I hear screams, a clamour of voices. I cannot tell what anyone is saying. Then Kilduff whirls round and stares at me. "Damn it—that was definitely a gun. There's a fucking shooter."

I'm about to reply when Juffie jumps back into the car and slams the shift to "drive". We lurch forward as the agent grabs a two-way radio. "Juffie here," he yelps. "Rider Three? Do you copy?"

Nothing.

"Rider Three?"

"This is Rider Three. Head straight off. Do you read me? Straight off. Follow the president's car."

"What's happened, Rider Three?" Juffie shouts.

Silence for a moment. "Lancer's been hit." Lancer, I know, is the code name for Jack Kennedy.

"Did you say 'Lancer'?"

"Affirmative. Follow president's car. Out."

I see Agent Juffie shake his head and the full impact of what has happened begins to register. I swivel round to face Malcolm Kilduff. He stares ahead and seems unable to meet my eye. I swallow hard.

"God help us," I whisper.

Chapter 13

"Mark . . . Mark . . . Open your eyes. How are you feeling?"

He blinked and leaned up on one elbow, bringing his other hand to his head and rubbing his temples. "Okay, I guess."

Abigail handed him a glass of water and he drank half of it in one gulp.

"I got everything you said on tape." She was buzzing with excitement. "It's amazing."

Mark sat up. "I feel utterly disorientated."

"Of course," she replied. "That's perfectly normal. But I can honestly say I've rarely known a subject to go back so deeply."

Mark raised his eyebrows and forced a smile. "Glad to help."

"Look, Mark. This is really something. With a few exceptions, my subjects see flashes, fragments. They 'feel' rather than 'live' through the eyes of their previous incarnations. You were *so* graphic. What was it like?"

Mark paused for a moment to gather his thoughts. "I was there," he said emphatically. "I didn't tell you, but I've been having dreams. Dreams in which I'm in Dallas on November 22, 1963. But they are always surreal, jumbled. But this was completely real. It was as though I had just woken up as David Ashcombe. It felt as 'normal' as my life as Mark Bretton feels."

"But you were a passive observer?"

"Yes. Well, no. I was David Ashcombe. It wasn't as though I were two individuals. I wasn't observing. I *was* him."

"With no concept of who you are now, of course."

"No. There was no part of me there. I was as David Ashcombe must have been."

"And you therefore had no control over anything that happened? You could not alter what David Ashcombe did in any way?"

"It never crossed my mind. I was him. But I'm certain I could not have altered anything."

"Okay."

"So," Mark said. "If you subscribe to the rebirthing idea, in my last life I was a White House Press Officer and I was there when JFK was shot."

"*If* you subscribe, yes . . ."

"But it could have all been an extremely vivid dream."

"That is a possibility. But you just said yourself . . ."

"I know. But also, if this was my past life I was killed by an FBI agent I knew, John Maclaren."

"From your first regression?"

"Yes, and he was there at the Texas Hotel." Mark paused and took a deep breath. "I'm finding this hard to deal with."

Abigail put her hands on his shoulders and looked into his eyes admiringly. "It's always difficult at first, Mark. It'll get easier."

"I'm still not convinced. But then, maybe I don't want to be!"

"We can, of course, do some checking." She wandered over to her desk and Mark pulled himself off the couch to follow her. Abigail sat and peered at the screen of her Mac, which was showing the Google homepage. She typed in "David Ashcombe Press Officer Kennedy". A page of links appeared. The first few consisted of several David Ashcombes with links to the Press, but all of them were contemporary. There was a David Ashcombe who had edited a book on the Kennedy family, a blogger into political satire, and a musician named Dave Ashcombe who had worked with a band called The Kennedy Plot. She scrolled down and the pair of them read the single-line synopsis of each site, but there was nothing about a David Ashcombe who had worked for the White House in the 1960s.

"Doesn't mean much," Abigail said. "No offence, but he probably wasn't well known enough."

"Put in 'Who's Who in Kennedy Assassination'," Mark suggested and watched as Abigail typed it in. Then she clicked the first site in the list and it revealed a table with the names of those linked to the assassination on the left, listed alphabetically. On the right was a brief description of their roles.

"Everyone knows the key players," Mark said. "Connally, LBJ, Lady Bird. Look up Kilduff."

Abigail scrolled down to stop at the Ks and there was Kilduff, Malcolm. They both read the piece about him. "Acting Press Secretary on November 22, 1963. Press Secretary Pierre Salinger was abroad at the time of the trip."

"How would you have known that?" Abigail asked.

Mark looked away from the screen for a second and shrugged. "Maybe I read something when I was kid, or saw a program about the assassination."

Abigail said nothing, went back to the Google home-page and clicked on "images". After she'd typed in "Malcolm Kilduff Kennedy Assassination", a series of pictures appeared. Close to the bottom of the page there was a black and white picture of a man with vaguely Italian good looks, wearing a dark suit and tie.

"That's him," Mark said. "But of course I'd recognize him. He was the one who made the official announcement of Kennedy's death. I've seen him in old clips."

Abigail was nodding. "You're right."

"The same will go for anyone, won't it? The president's driver Bill Greer, Ken O'Donnell. I would have caught sight of all of them on TV, in newspapers, magazines. I might have remembered them subliminally."

Abigail pushed back her chair and stared at the screen in silence. Mark pulled a chair over from close by and sat beside her. "Okay," she said, after a moment. "I have an idea."

"What?"

"I'm not going to say. Just do what I ask."

"Okay," Mark said, feeling slightly uneasy.

Abigail leaned in and called up YouTube. Then she typed in "Dallas, November 22, 1963." "I want you to watch as many clips as it takes," she said.

"As it takes for what?"

"Not saying."

She opened the first video, a piece lasting six minutes

and fourteen seconds covering the arrival of the presidential party at Love Field, the Dallas airstrip where the White House planes had landed before the start of the motorcade.

The screen showed a color film taken by a professional; probably one of the local networks, Mark surmised. There was Air Force One glistening in the bright sunshine of that November morning. Jack Kennedy shakes hands with a long line of dignitaries as Jackie descends the steps from the aircraft. She joins her husband on the tarmac and someone hands her a bouquet of red roses. The camera pans round to show the crowds of well-wishers: at least a thousand people behind the perimeter fence and a few score more, specially selected to share the same air as the Kennedys. The glamorous First Couple walk over and start to talk to the people and to shake hands with a few of them. The Secret Service is there in force. The agents look worried and agitated. Their body language and facial expressions betray the fact that they were not only wary of the public but nervous, frustrated. They just want this show to be done with and to get their precious charges out of harm's way and into the limo.

"Okay, what was I looking for? Mark asked as the clip ended, "I've seen films like this before. We all have."

Abigail said nothing, just tapped at the keyboard until she had a second clip ready. "Again," she said simply.

This was a film of the president in the Grand Banqueting Hall of the Texas Hotel in Fort Worth. But for three minutes it showed nothing except Jack and the First Lady at the table, concluding with JFK stepping up to the microphone to make a few comic remarks about how no one was ever interested in what he or the vice-president was wearing.

"Same problem, Abigail," Mark said, twisting in his seat to face her as the clip ended. "We've all seen it before."

"Another one," she said. "Yeah?"

Mark sighed. "Fine."

The third film picked up immediately after the end of the first clip. They both watched Jack and Jackie walk towards the dark green Lincoln. Senator Connally is there in the middle row of seats. He stands up and Ken O'Donnell opens the offside door. Jackie is led around to the driver's side and JFK pulls himself onto the seat in the back row of the car. The camera pulls away then pans round to the left taking in the other cars. There is a black Cadillac and behind that the vice-president's light blue Lincoln. And, just for a second, the camera focuses on a white Chevrolet. The rear door is open and a slender figure in a black suit smiles at Malcolm Kilduff who is sitting inside the car. Kilduff is beckoning to the man. The figure shifts round toward the camera and seems to recognize the person shooting the film. The slender man has a long, narrow face, black greased-back hair. He seems to be about thirty, good-looking in an aquiline way.

Mark froze. Abigail could sense it and studied his profile. She had clearly been hoping for this reaction. He was staring fixedly at the screen, the blood drained from his face.

"Someone you know?"

Mark took a deep breath. "It's still not proof," he said slowly.

Abigail searched his face for a second. "No," she said after a long pause. "No, it's not. But you have to admit that the odds are stacking up, Mark."

"Damn it!" he exclaimed loudly and jumped up. The chair fell backward and he suddenly felt embarrassed. "Sorry," he mumbled and picked it up, placing it carefully upright. He brought his right hand to his mouth and started to bite on the cuticle of his thumb.

"Bad habit," Abigail said lightly.

"What?"

She nodded towards his thumb and he took his hand away from his mouth, sighed and shook his head slowly. "If I believe this, I have to abandon everything I ever learned, everything I've ever had faith in. I can't . . ."

"No, you don't, Mark. I've told you before. It's just pure arrogance to think that conventional science can explain absolutely everything."

He fixed her with a stare and said nothing.

"You know who that was, Mark. You know it was you. You as you once were in a past life—presumably your last life before this one. Can you deny that?"

Mark shook his head again, and, unthinkingly, he brought his thumb back to his mouth. "I need time to think this through," he said, almost to himself.

Chapter 14

It was early evening in Massachusetts—sticky, of course, with mosquitoes swarming over the water's edge where the Atlantic Ocean met the land. But inside the grand house, built on an escarpment and set back a hundred yards from the sand, the air was cool and fragrant.

The two men sat in sumptuously cushioned wicker chairs on a wide balcony girded by a white-painted wooden balustrade. The elder of the two, the octogenarian Orlando Steinheiser, was wearing a tux and had squeezed in this meeting before boarding a chopper that would take him to a gala dinner in Manhattan. Steinheiser had a good head of hair so white that it was translucent, each strand like a fiber optic. A man who had grown thinner with age, he had a hard, almost skeletal face with prominent cheekbones. But his most striking feature was his incredible icy blue eyes. He loved his eyes more than anything else about himself. Few others found them pleasing, though. Indeed, most people were frightened by them. During the eighty-one years in which he had viewed the world through them they had, in many situations, given him an instant and powerful advantage.

The other man, Christopher Trafano, was fifty-five years younger—for some, a lifetime. He was of Italian extraction and extremely handsome, with jet-black hair and brown eyes. He was wearing a finely tailored Armani suit, a white shirt with a buttoned-down collar and a gold Cerruti tie. To Trafano, Steinheiser was a god, an Olympian who had done everything, been everywhere. Now one of the richest men on the planet, he was more powerful than the president. But the old man would not live forever, and Trafano was still young. He looked at Steinheiser with a confident stare.

A table stood between the two chairs. A pair of gin and tonics in tall tumblers were the only things on the table. Mansfield, the seventy-two-year-old black servant who had worked at the house for fifty-seven years, took his leave after he had deposited the drinks, and the two men sat silently contemplating the waves as they rolled in.

"You've seen the new footage?" Trafano asked. He lifted his drink from the table and took a sip, eyeing Steinheiser over the rim of the glass.

The older man had lived in this house for more than half a century, ever since he'd married into one of America's wealthiest families. It had really been his wife's house. As had been the Fifth Avenue penthouse and the Bel Air acreage. She had died eleven years before. But long ago he had worked his way into the heart of her family's generations-old business empire and was now the real power and authority behind what had become a many-headed beast with interests in the arms industry, pharmaceuticals and oil.

"Yes, I finished watching it just before you arrived," Steinheiser replied. "You were right about what you said in your phone call. It is fascinating. During the six months since we first learned of her work she has continued to make great advances. This new subject of hers, though— he represents an exponential leap forward. Installing the camera and bugging the professor's phones near the start has reaped rewards aplenty. I have you to thank you for that suggestion, Christopher."

Trafano gave a faint smile. "Professor Marchant is a very determined and resourceful woman."

"Yes, she is. But I think even she has been surprised by her latest discovery. Who is he?"

Trafano leaned down and plucked a file from a leather briefcase resting against one of the table legs. It was a slender document encased in a clear plastic folder. "One of my people has done some digging, asked around, spoken to the guy's associates—discreetly, of course. It didn't take much—the man's an open book. Name's Mark Bretton. A Brit, naturalized. Regular guy. He's not exactly a secretive type."

"Does he need to be?"

"Well, no. He's rather ordinary in many ways. Lived here for twelve years. Journalist at the *New York Courier*. Seems to be pretty good at his job, well respected. Plays guitar in a blues band."

Steinheiser raised an eyebrow at that.

"As I say, a pretty regular guy," Trafano added.

"Anyone interested in him before?"

"Not in the slightest. Been on nobody's radar. Divorced. Lives in a small apartment in the Village. According to my man, Mr. Bretton drinks a bit too much, smokes a little weed, but has no criminal record."

"And how does he know the lovely Professor Marchant?"

"According to everything we have unearthed, he only just met her. Interviewed her for his paper."

Steinheiser laughed, a harsh bark. "How amusing. I imagine our man fell under the influence of the professor's inimitable charms."

"Quite possibly."

"And he had no idea that he had any special . . . 'gift'?"

"I don't think he had a clue. He has a background in science—physics at Oxford, no less. Something of a skeptic. I have a film from the professor's office recording their first meeting four days ago. He was initially dismissive, but seems to be coming round."

Steinheiser lifted his glass and took a sip. Then he replaced the tumbler and stared out to sea again. "There has been no one in Mr. Bretton's league. Not since . . ."

"No, he really is a class act."

"And a skeptic. How ironic. You know . . ." Steinheiser shifted to face Trafano. "My old professor at Harvard once said that journalists were only worth warm spit. I've always subscribed to this view, but having seen Mr. Bretton—or David Ashcombe—on this film, I'm beginning to change my opinion."

"So what now?" Trafano asked and drained his glass.

"Now? Now we keep observing, of course. Your live feed will be monitored twenty-four-seven. I want a man on Bretton and I want you to keep an even closer eye on Professor Marchant. I have a feeling we may have struck gold here, my friend. The trouble is, Marchant and Bretton will realize soon that they too have struck gold. Doubtless, the very clever Abigail would have already reached that conclusion. The Kennedy assassination, indeed!" Steinheiser shook his head slowly as he scanned the distant horizon. "Had to happen sometime, I guess. Very fortunate we saw it coming."

Chapter 15

To Mark, the apartment seemed filled with ghosts and shadows. He had never felt so disorientated. Even the break-up with Jill, the death of their baby and Patrick's passing had not jarred him so much. They had been tragic, life-altering events, but they'd been changes to his regular life, the life he knew he had, the single life he had believed to be his allocation. He had never conceived that he might have lived before, or indeed that he might live again after this existence was over. But the experience in Abigail's office—that was something so shattering that it reached to the very core of his being. It shifted everything, mutated the raw facts of "normality" that he had taken for granted all his life.

A part of him knew that the idea was an amazing, exciting revelation, something that could be viewed in a very bright, shiny, optimistic light. He would live forever, albeit as different personalities. But there was more, of course. Now he not only knew this astonishing thing, he knew there was a way to *communicate* with his previous selves. He could break through the barrier of loss between each of his incarnations. He could go back, almost as a time traveler might, to inhabit his old lives.

It was exciting, but it was also terrifying. Everyone liked to think they were special, Mark thought. But when some weird type of specialness was thrust into your face, it came as a shock. Why had his experience been so much more intense than for anyone else Abigail had studied?

He could feel his mind starting to race and forced himself to stand back, to get a grip. He had a gig in a couple of hours at Johnny J's in the Village, and he had invited Abigail. Now a large part of him was hoping she would not show up at the club. He wasn't so sure he wanted to show up himself.

He showered, changed, restrung his guitar, tuned it and left the building to walk the three blocks to the venue. The equipment would already be set up—he just needed to show up with his guitar.

By the time The Gondoliers took to the stage to play, Mark was feeling considerably more relaxed. Through long experience he knew just how much he could drink and how many tokes on a joint he could allow himself. The band were regulars at the club. They had been playing the same set there for almost two years and they had a loyal following. Tonight there was a good turnout. The place had efficient air conditioning, always an attraction at this time of year.

Mark had first taken to the guitar when he was ten and his uncle had bought him a cheap second-hand acoustic. He had started off learning a few chords from a book. When his father heard him making some progress he booked him onto a course of six lessons with a local teacher. They were as dull as dull could be, and at the time Mark believed that he had gained nothing at all from them. In fact, it was a miracle he had not been put off playing altogether. But by this time he had heard The Smiths, had posters of Johnny Marr on his bedroom wall and a video of one of the band's early shows. He was hooked and there was nothing some crusty old classical-guitar tutor could do to dampen his enthusiasm. It was only years later, as he began to branch out and found an idiom that really suited him—steamy blues in the style of B.B. King—that he realized the value of those six lessons because they had provided him with a foundation, the essential basic rules of a musical language.

It was not until they had almost finished their set that Mark spotted Abigail at the back of the club. She was standing close to the bar, nursing a cocktail. Their gazes met and she smiled. Then she shook her head slowly and made a face that meant she was incredibly impressed. The last notes of the band's encore, B.B. King's *Sweet Little Angel*, faded out to warm applause and Mark leaned into the microphone to thank the crowd. He put his guitar on a stand and left the tiny stage.

"What can I say?" Abigail declared leaning close to make herself heard over the volume of the DJ's deck. "You are a man of many talents, Mark."

"Too kind, too kind," he said, twirling his hands and bowing. "But no . . . Thank you," he added. He caught a whiff of her perfume. He had no idea what it was, but he liked it.

They had a couple more drinks at the bar, then Mark went back to the stage to put away his Gibson. A few moments later he was back beside Abigail, having entrusted his guitar to the safe keeping of the bass player, James. "Hungry?" he asked.

Abigail looked at her watch. "It's one a.m.!"

"Almost breakfast time," he replied, with a grin.

"I'll have a black coffee and watch you eat."

"A deal. I know a great all-night diner a block away—Frankie's. I'm convinced they do the best burgers on the East Coast. And their coffee isn't bad, either."

It was a classic diner that had stood there since at least the early 1960s. The irony of Mark's choice was not lost on either of them. "Wonder if this was here when my friend David Ashcombe was alive?" Mark said as they settled into a booth. The seats were red plastic, the table was topped with sparkly Formica. An expanse of glass offered a view onto the street. This part of town was still busy even this late. Mark watched a yellow cab cruise past and leaned towards Abigail. "I'm beginning to come to terms with it all," he said matter-of-factly.

"Really? I'm impressed."

"Oh, you shouldn't be, really. It's just good old working-class stoicism," he retorted. "What's a previous life or two?"

She studied his face earnestly.

"It's okay—I don't need the shrink looks."

Abigail smiled. "You've obviously been thinking a lot about the whole experience."

"Of course I have. And I'd be the first to admit that it takes some mental recalibrating, to put it mildly. I still don't know if I believe it is reincarnation."

"Rebirth."

"Whatever. But, at the very least, it's, well . . . interesting."

The waitress arrived and Abigail suddenly found she was hungry. Mark ordered the house specialty, something called a '59 Chevy, a massive burger with all the trimmings. Abigail appraised the menu, quickly realized that all the dishes were vintage-car-themed and eventually settled for a Soft Top—a slice of apricot cheesecake.

"So why are my memories so vivid?" Mark asked as the waitress left with their order.

Abigail leaned her elbows on the table and rested her chin on her interlinked fingers. "To be honest, I'm not sure. I've been working on a theory that if someone experiences an intense or traumatic event in a past life, they tend to have a more vivid past-life recall or what I call a 'Returning'."

"But you said that my 'experience' was one of the most vivid you had ever witnessed."

"It most certainly was. But even with the vaguer regressions of most of my subjects, there are degrees of immersion. I have one subject who keeps returning to a three-minute-long event in which he is a soldier in the First World War. He is horrendously explicit about what he lived through. That obviously left a deep impression on the part of him that passes from life to life."

"What is that?" Mark asked, his old skepticism stripped away for a moment.

"I'm not at all sure, Mark. As I implied the other day, I have no answers to questions that go beyond the bounds of science. I appreciate that, because of the research I'm involved with, you might not view me as a 'real' scientist, but . . ."

"Oh, Abigail, come on. I think we've moved beyond that! To me, the jury's still out on what we are dealing with here, but I have the utmost respect for your intentions . . ."

"How nice!"

The food arrived just as Mark was about to ask another question. They fell silent as the waitress placed the plates on the table. Mark surveyed the order.

"Could I have a knife and fork, please?" he said to the waitress.

She looked at him askance. "It's a burger, dude!"

"Humour me, I'm British."

Abigail brought a hand to her mouth, barely able to contain her amusement as the waitress retreated.

"What?"

"Nothing."

"The one and only time I ever went to a McDonald's I asked for a knife and fork. They thought I was mad too!"

"I don't think you're mad. It's cute."

"Ah!" Mark exclaimed. "I hate that word!" He could not have failed to notice Abigail's dilated pupils. "Anyway," he went on seriously, "the main idea about rebirthing is that there is a part of us that continues to exist after our body has perished, yes?"

Abigail nodded.

The knife and fork arrived. Mark cut into his burger and took a hungry mouthful, waving his fork in the air as he chewed and adopting an appreciative expression to indicate his pleasure. "You really should try this," he said and offered Abigail a forkful of meat and bun.

She leaned forward and took the food into her mouth, nodding appreciatively. "Good."

"I guess that has to be the case. Some part of us is eternal," she said after a moment. "But I don't know how that could possibly happen."

"And how many lives do we have?" Mark asked.

Abigail, with a mouthful of cheesecake, lifted her hands to indicate she had no idea.

"You don't know much really, do you, Prof?"

"I know this is good cheesecake!"

"But that's the point, isn't it, Abi?" Mark said.

She was a little taken aback by his familiarity but didn't let it show. And she wasn't unhappy about it, either.

"You like the cheesecake because it's a sensory 'real-life' pleasure. What we're talking about with . . . rebirth goes far beyond the bounds of what we have ever experienced before. It transgresses what we have both been trained to accept as the rules of science. Christ! It even goes against what the Church has attempted to make us believe."

"Which means, Mark, that the only thing we really have is observation, experiment and an attempt to formulate a theory. In other words, regular science."

Mark leaned on the table and rubbed his eyes. "Man, I'm tired."

"Not surprised. You've lived two lives today."

"And played a lightning set."

"Indeed."

Out on the street it was still stifling.

"Abi . . ." Mark called.

She turned and he had his phone ready. The flash went off.

"Oh! That's bound to be a horrible one," she protested.

Mark clicked the appropriate buttons. "Nope. It's perfect." He turned it to show Abigail.

She shrugged "Okay, I guess, for . . . what? . . . two a.m. Lordy."

"So, what now?" Mark asked as they walked through Tompkins Square Park and emerged onto Avenue A.

"Well, I need a cab, and I don't mind working on a Saturday if you feel like seeing what happens next in Dallas."

"I know what happens next in Dallas."

"But do you really?" Abigail asked and lifted her arm to hail a cab.

Mark helped Abigail into the taxi and waved as it pulled away from the curb. He watched the car merge with a stream of traffic on Avenue A and thought how much things had changed during the past week. He had lost someone very dear to him, his old friend from the days when both of them had been kids with hopes and dreams and ambitions, and now here he was beginning to feel that he might have acquired a new character in his life, someone who had the potential to change things dramatically.

He started to walk uptown. It was only a few blocks back to his apartment. He knew a short cut and he took a right into East 7th Street. About fifty yards on, there was a well-lit alley that cut through to Eighth. He turned along it. The alley was deserted, backs of buildings standing either side. He picked up the pace as he reached the far end and could see lights. Just as he emerged into the street, a car pulled up to the curb directly in front of him. It was an inconspicuous green Ford Territory four-wheel drive. Mark started to head east along the sidewalk. The Ford's rear door opened. He saw a flash of movement to his left and a man rounded the back of the vehicle, shoving him inside and sliding into the seat after him before slamming shut the door. Mark felt a sharp pain close to his left ear and collapsed unconscious as the car accelerated away along Eighth Street, east towards FDR Drive.

He had no idea for how long he was out, but as he came round he heard muffled sounds. There was the throb of the car's engine as it accelerated and then braked. He could hear voices but could make out nothing of what was being said. He tried to open his eyes, but for several minutes he found the effort too much. His head was throbbing and the pain stretched down his neck and across his shoulders. He was beginning to focus on the back of the seat in front of him as the car came to a halt. The engine stopped. He felt hands pulling him upright and managed to find his voice.

"What the hell is this?" he groaned. He moved his head slowly as the man who had pulled him into a seated position, a beefy, square-jawed specimen, stepped out and held the door open for another man to get in. Mark could see two others outside the car. One was smoking a cigarette. The guy who had just got out of the car joined the other two, accepted a cigarette from his friend and turned his back to the vehicle.

Mark struggled to find some clarity. His head began to clear slowly and he could now see properly. Outside, it was dark. The man in the seat beside him was about mid-fifties, in an expensive-looking suit, powder-blue shirt and Windsor-knotted tie. He had a shaved head, a pale wide face, large dark eyes and thin lips.

"Mark Bretton," the man said, "please allow me to apologize for the rather crude methods I was persuaded to adopt by my American friends. But, you know how it is—when in Rome and so forth." He had a cut-glass British accent and Mark was left with little doubt about the man's pedigree: he wore Eton, Oxford and the Guards on his sleeve.

Mark said nothing, just stared at the man.

"My name is Hubert Elton-Hornsby."

Mark couldn't help smirking. "Well, of course it is."

He looked into Mark's eyes blankly. "I work for a British government department. I need you to answer a few questions."

"A British government department? And you couldn't have just popped over to my place for a cup of Darjeeling?"

"As I said . . ."

"Yes—when in Rome. What on Earth does British Intelligence want with me? I'm a journalist at the *Courier*, for God's sake! It's hardly Woodward and Bernstein territory."

"It's nothing to do with your work, Mr. Bretton." Elton-Hornsby paused for a moment. "You were very close friends with Patrick Clifton."

Mark couldn't hide his surprise.

"You seem startled that I should mention the man."

"Patrick? What . . . ?"

"What is my interest in Patrick Clifton? Well, let's just say my colleagues and I are concerned about something your old friend has done."

"My old friend is dead."

"We are aware of that."

"So why should you . . . ?"

"Mr. Bretton," Elton-Hornsby said slowly. "Please stop wasting my time. We believe Patrick Clifton passed a package on to you shortly before he died."

"A package?" Mark looked incredulous. "You are kidding, right?"

Elton-Hornsby simply stared at him without expression.

"No, you're not, are you? Jesus! I feel like I'm in a Le Carré novel."

"Are you claiming you know nothing about this, Mr. Bretton?"

"You have me, I'm afraid." Mark looked out of the window and saw that the men had finished their cigarettes. One of them glanced furtively at the car. "I don't have the first clue what you're talking about."

"You're either a very good actor or—"

"Listen," Mark snapped. "I don't know what the hell this is about."

The man held his stare then looked down with a sigh. "Patrick Clifton worked for a secret science department within the British military."

It took a moment for the words to sink in. Then Mark laughed . . . and laughed. Elton-Hornsby just watched him with Zen-like stillness, his face expressionless.

"Okay," Mark said. "That's very funny, actually." And he took a deep breath to recover. "It *almost* makes up for the fact that you've had me whacked over the head and dragged out here in the middle of the night. But not quite. I'll be on the phone to my lawyer first thing." He made a move for the door.

"No, you won't," Elton-Hornsby said, his voice brittle. He reached out to grip Mark's arm. "You won't do anything of the sort, Mr. Bretton. In fact, you will not breathe a word about our meeting, nor will you mention to anyone Mr. Clifton's involvement with the British military. If you choose to ignore what I'm saying you'll not just be brought to a piece of waste ground such as this." And he nodded towards the bleak exterior. "You will find yourself in a shallow grave *under* a piece of waste ground. Do I make myself—?"

"Oh, for fuck's sake!" Mark spat. "What is this shit?"

But Elton-Hornsby ignored him and Mark heard the sound of the car door opening.

"Wait!" Mark yelled as someone gripped his shoulder. "Christ!"

Elton-Hornsby pulled himself out of the car. Mark tried to resist the man yanking him through the open door, but another arm reached in and found his leg. He was dragged roughly from the back seat and gripped about his upper arms. Elton-Hornsby's face hung in the half-light a few inches from his own. "We'll talk again," the man said.

Mark landed hard on the rutted concrete and earth, and a stab of pain shot up his right arm as he made contact with the ground. Twisting his head, he caught a glimpse of Elton-Hornsby sliding into the front passenger seat. He heard a crunching sound—feet on parched soil—and saw a boot swing towards him a fraction of a second before it smacked into the side of his head.

Chapter 16

Abigail's apartment was on West 88th Street, an over-priced but relatively spacious one-bed place on the twelfth floor, with a coveted view over the Jacqueline Kennedy-Onassis Reservoir.

All the way back from the Village she had been thinking about Mark. She had felt an immediate attraction toward him four days ago when they had first met in her office, but she had pushed the feeling aside. The last thing she needed now was a relationship. She was far too busy for that. But her feelings were growing stronger every time she saw him, every time she thought of him. Sure, he was handsome and talented and somehow vulnerable— damaged, even—but it went further than that and now she was beginning to wonder. Could she have stumbled upon something extraordinary?

Alighting from the cab, she paid the driver and stepped quickly into the foyer of the apartment block. On the scale of things the area was a safe one, but she was always cautious. A good friend had been mugged three months ago, an attack that had taken place near here at six in the evening on a well-lit street. It had shaken her up. She said "Good morning" to the doorman and he escorted her to the elevator. A minute later, she was inside her apartment and kicking off her shoes.

Abigail felt as though she should be exhausted, but she wasn't. She had gone through the invisible barrier of tiredness and out the other side. There was no need for her to be in her office early tomorrow, so there was really no point in trying to force sleep now. Instead, she grabbed a bottle of Evian from the refrigerator and swigged at it as she walked along the hall to a tiny room located before the door to the living room-cum-diner. It was a minuscule study, just large enough to contain a small metal-framed computer desk and a chair. A Mac sat on the desk. She lowered herself into the chair and placed the bottle of water on the glass top beside the monitor. Then she switched on the computer.

She watched the screen light up and her wallpaper appear: a farmhouse nestled in a field of corn. Then she nudged the mouse and clicked on a program called "Regress".

Abigail had first decided that she needed this piece of software some four months ago and had, by good fortune, met just the person to design it: one of her subjects, Gareth, a computer boffin who had worked for over a decade in Silicon Valley before relocating to New York. "I need to be able to auto-regress," she had told him in strict confidence one morning after a session in her rooms. "Would it be possible to design a program to do that?"

It had taken Gareth a month of evenings and weekends to devise the system but, after the bugs had been eliminated, it did actually do the job. It provided a complete autohypnosis system made up from a series of programs that could relax the subject staring at the screen and slowly induce a hypnotic state indistinguishable from one created by a professional hypnotist. Using the webcam and digital recorder built into the Mac, Abigail could film and sound-record herself. Two safety devices had been added to the set-up. The first was a timer so that the hypnotic state could be reversed and terminated by the computer at any given point preset by the user. The other was a "keyword" or "key-image": something that the subject memorized and could conjure up in their minds if they needed to snap out of the hypnotic condition suddenly. It could be anything: a color, a name or a symbol. A voice-recognition device added to the Mac would detect the uttered word and break the connection.

Abigail had practiced with the device for three months and now she was so skilled with it that she could hypnotize herself in little more than sixty seconds. But most significant was the fact that she had explored her own past lives more than she had studied those of any of her subjects, and she had documented everything in detail. From these regression experiments she could delineate between six different "past lives".

The earliest memory was of Eleanor, the wife of a Lancastrian baron. Abigail was not sure of the date, but from studying the video and audio of the regression she thought that most of the memories came from about the 1350s. Following Eleanor there had been Magneilla, a Spanish woman who spent her entire long life in a tiny Basque village nestled at the foot of the Pyrenees. Magneilla lived to be almost ninety and was followed by Nadia, a Portuguese noblewoman who during the 1760s traveled to Goa where her family established a spice plantation. The following life consisted of mere flashes. Abigail was not even sure of the name of this previous self, and the life had ended abruptly before her first birthday.

By contrast, she could recall her two most recent incarnations with great clarity. They were filled with detail and she found that she could most readily return to them. Two lives ago, Abigail had been Hannah, a waitress in Los Angeles who had died of breast cancer at the age of forty-two. She had married and had a child, a boy she named Gregory, who was six when she passed away in 1927.

Abigail's final life before her present existence, the one she had visited most frequently, was her time as a young married woman in the early 1960s. It was her most clearly recalled previous self and the past life she could relate to most closely.

It was to this life that she now needed to return. That afternoon she had spent three hours studying Mark Bretton's regression tapes, the recordings of what Mark had said and film of him lying on the couch in her rooms. Then she had written up detailed notes on what he had described. It had been at once an invigorating, thrilling and, at times, frightening experience. She could barely believe what Mark had reported on the recording. It was confirming everything she had hoped for. More than that, it made sense of so many things that she had not really understood before now. The potential of what she had witnessed was barely conceivable. Indeed, as she had watched and listened and written and thought, she'd had the oddest feeling that even she was still not yet realizing the power of what she had succeeded in unleashing.

Now it was time to return herself, time to fit together a few more pieces of the puzzle. Abigail set the parameters of the program, checked that the camera and the voice recorder were working, gave the Mac her keyword, clicked the mouse and stared at the screen.

It is late evening and I'm looking through the window onto the street below. I'm on the sixth floor of our apartment block in Silver Spring, Maryland, a fifteen-minute drive from Washington DC. Wayne Avenue, the street below, runs through downtown. Our one-bedroom place is five stories above a shop. The road is lit up by neon signs and headlamps. I draw closed the curtains and step back into the room.

I feel lonely, but when I settle onto our cherished Eames sofa, a wedding present from my parents, I start to relax. Alice, our Siamese cat, jumps up onto my lap and makes me feel wanted. I gaze around the room, and although I feel a little lost without David here I get a warm glow inside as I survey our tiny fiefdom. I love this sofa I'm sitting on and adore the vibrant shade of orange that Mum and Dad chose, a color which, to my eye, contrasts perfectly with the Rotaflex pendant lamp hovering directly over the coffee table.

Even though it's a chilly late-November evening, it feels cosy in the apartment. When we had been shown around by the agent a week before the wedding last year, I had been immediately attracted to the place because of the fact that it had the very latest central heating system. I suffer in the winter and feel the cold more than most.

I think about switching on the TV. But I cannot bear to. I'm still in shock, still reeling from the news that President Kennedy has died. It's too much to assimilate and I'm feeling drained of emotion. David, of course, was right there, right there at the scene. For a time I was verging on hysteria. I loved Mr. Kennedy, and the one time I had been introduced to him I had been so proud. But when I saw the report on TV about the shooting in Dallas my first thought had been for my husband. I had not known if he was safe or not. I told myself he was fine, but without any evidence. Gradually, though, news seeped out that only the president had died and Senator Connolly had suffered serious injuries. Then, around six-thirty, David had managed to get a call through to me and I found I could breathe properly again. He'd said he would be home soon.

I look at the clock on the wall and realize that almost two hours have passed since David's brief call from Bethesda Hospital. I feel powerless and small and I watch the phone, expecting it to ring at any moment.

I desperately need it to ring. I stand up and walk into the kitchen to fetch a glass of water and that is when I hear the familiar trilling sound and can barely believe it. I dash back into the living room, grab the receiver and start to speak: "Ashcombe resid—"

I hear David's voice. "Ruth" he says, interrupting me.

I babble a response and he interrupts again. He sounds terrible, even though he is trying to disguise his anguish. "Listen, I gotta be quick," he is saying, an edge of panic in his voice.

"Why?" I say, feeling his anxiety infecting me down the line.

"Ruth, get out the house," Dave urges. "Go to your Aunt Joan's in Missouri . . . tonight . . . Right now."

I feel a stab of terror in the pit of my stomach. I'm confused. "Aunt Joan?"

"I can't explain," Dave snaps. Then, more gently: "Just do what I say, please."

There is something I really want to tell David, something I've been keeping as a surprise for when he got home. "But Dave—" I begin. He cuts across me. "No buts, Ruth . . ."

I stare around the room, focusing for some odd reason on the bowl of plastic fruit on the sideboard. Beneath it, the shutter door of the TV is half-closed and the big gray screen is blank. I can hear the faint rumble of cars drifting up from the street, but traffic is light for this time of the evening. David is speaking but the words pass over me.

"Look, Ruth . . . This is life or death."

I'm acting on autopilot. I stare at the blank TV screen bisected by the shutter and then my eyes drift up to the photograph of Dave and me on our wedding day. It is in a silver frame, standing proudly at one end of the sideboard.

"Is it to do with . . . ?" I ask.

"Of course. Now, please . . ."

I feel the tears welling up and the view of our lounge grows blurred. I grip the receiver and feel my nails cut into the soft flesh of my palm. I start to sob. David says a few words, trying to comfort me.

"Dave, I have to tell you something," I gasp. I hear

some strange noises and he starts to breathe heavier. He mumbles something: "I love you." The words sound desperate. The connection snaps.

"Dave? Dave?" I feel sick. I lower the phone and look at it in disbelief, hardly noticing the narrow line of blood running towards my wrist. I pull the phone back to my ear. "DAVE?" But there is nothing from the other end except a steady burr.

For a few moments I don't know what to do. I feel numb, paralyzed. I slump onto the sofa and I want it to swallow me up, dissolve my body, spirit me away. Then I seem to snap back to reality. I'm suddenly aware, for the very first time, that this is not just about me. It's not about David, either. I'm pregnant and I have another life to consider. I must act.

I rush to the bedroom, throw some clothes into a suitcase, half of them mine, half Dave's. I run into the bathroom, scoop up some essential toiletries and toss them into a washbag and throw that on top of the clothes in the case. Back in the living room I pull open the top drawer of a cabinet under a small bar. Inside the drawer I find a metal box. I flick the numbers of the combination lock and the lid lifts. Inside is a bundle of cash, about two hundred and twenty dollars. I stuff the money into my purse, run back to the bedroom, close the case and pull it through to the living room. Then I spend a moment scribbling a note asking the neighbor to feed Alice while I'm away for a couple of days. I stuff the note along with a five-dollar bill into an envelope that I find in the same drawer under the bar. I hurry over to Alice. She is stretched out on the sofa. I give her a hug, kiss the top of her head and let her go back to sleep.

Twenty seconds later I'm in the hall with the suitcase. I walk to the neighbor's door along the hall, stuff the envelope into their mailbox and run back to the elevator as I hear it arrive on our floor. The doors open, I rush in and stab at "B" for the basement garage. Feeling the elevator plummet through space toward a future that has suddenly turned to jelly, I catch my anguished reflection in the mirror and I know everything has changed.

PART 3

"I'm not scared anymore. I'm home."

Chapter 17

May 1963

CIA Assistant Director Orlando Steinheiser slipped out of the shade-striped mid-blue Buick, pulled down the front of his gray suit jacket, straightened his tie and stretched his neck. The flight over from Washington and the drive from Las Vegas airport had played havoc with his lower back. He spun on his heel as his assistant John Maclaren came round the finned trunk of the massive car, carrying a black leather briefcase. The agent had hung up his regulation black suit in Langley and was now undercover, wearing a trilby and a check jacket which Steinheiser thought looked faintly ridiculous.

It was at least a hundred degrees in the shade, the heat dry, nothing like the East Coast humidity that Maclaren was familiar with. He was sweating profusely. It amazed him how people could actually live on the edge of the desert. It seemed somehow primitive, but he said nothing. The chief hailed from New Mexico and at that moment seemed irritatingly comfortable with the Nevada climate.

"It's through here, boss," Maclaren said and nodded towards a plain wooden door that led into the Sundowner

Hotel. "Back stairs. Howard Devline got the plans over to us just before we left. Leads up to a fourth-floor emergency exit. From there we get into a service corridor, takes us to the conference room."

Steinheiser said nothing and followed his assistant. Maclaren shut the door behind them and wiped his brow.

The others were already there, seated around a small table. Richard Nixon and J. Edgar Hoover looked up at Steinheiser as he walked over, shook their hands and sat down opposite them.

"Good afternoon, gentlemen," said the CIA man. Two men stood behind Nixon. Steinheiser recognized them as the politician's regular henchmen, Nicky Cutler and Elory Grange. They had their arms folded, their faces sweaty in spite of the air con. Maclaren took up a similar stance behind Steinheiser's chair.

"I take it you have everything in place," Nixon said, his drawl familiar from a thousand TV broadcasts during the election campaign three years ago. Pitted as he had then been against the handsome and photogenic JFK, he had come across so badly through the new medium that most viewers thought he had lost the election months before polling day. Nixon's face was lined, his forehead huge. He looked older than his fifty years and probably would have looked older still, Steinheiser mused, if it had not been for the hair-dye bottle.

"We are almost there," Steinheiser replied and stared into Nixon's face before turning to Hoover, a podgy man who had also hit the hair colorant. His skin was waxy and from across the table Steinheiser could smell the FBI Director's halitosis. The CIA man loathed Nixon and

Hoover in almost equal measure. But whenever he recalled images he had seen of Hoover, dressed in a black dress and make-up, fellating his assistant at the Bureau, Clyde Tolson, Steinheiser always experienced an extra frisson of disgust.

And what of Nixon? What could not be said of the man? Steinheiser wondered. He would be the first to admit that he, Orlando Steinheiser, was no saint; he had broken almost every law in the land, including those against murder, theft and blackmail. He had tortured and abused, and knowingly destroyed the lives of innocents. But Nixon? Nixon was in an altogether different league. There was one golden principle that separated Steinheiser from the former vice-president, which was that he, Steinheiser, had done those things for the sake of America, for the greater good. Richard Milhous Nixon's every evil deed had been done for nothing but the furtherance of one purpose: the advancement of Richard Milhous Nixon.

"Tell me everything, please," Nixon said. He leaned forward, his forearms flat on the table, his long fingers intertwined.

Steinheiser turned to Maclaren as the agent handed him a file from the briefcase. The CIA man opened the document without putting it down on the table.

"We now have the presidential schedule for the coming months. The European tour in June effectively dominates the calendar until July. We certainly won't want to touch him in Europe. But he'll be in San Francisco on August 14 and Dallas on November 22. Each presents an opportunity."

Nixon said nothing for a moment.

"I would go for San Francisco," Hoover commented. "Plenty of subversives we can pin it on. Commies on every fucking street corner."

"But they're everywhere," Steinheiser replied.

"More of them in California—per square mile."

"Yes, but Edgar," Nixon said, "although I have nothing against pinning the blame on a Communist, we also agreed that we liked the 'act of individual madness' angle."

"Nothing madder than a Red."

"I agree," Nixon replied and then produced one of his unctuous smiles. "But I think that on balance we can weave a better backstory in Texas. The place hates Kennedy. They see him as a nigger-appeaser."

"A precise description," Hoover growled.

"True, and the Southerners were solidly behind *me* rather than *him*. They haven't forgiven him for a list of things. Frisco's too liberal; all the faggots and the bleeding-heart liberals will come out of the woodwork."

"I would have to agree," Steinheiser said. He shifted his gaze from Hoover to Nixon. "We need to keep our network restricted to the smallest number of people possible, but we will still need some support. It will be easier to get that in Texas. There will be fewer questions asked."

Hoover rubbed his chin with a porky hand. Steinheiser noticed his jazzy opal cufflinks. "It puts it all off for a further three months. Tongues may wag in that time."

"Well, it's up to all of us to make sure they don't, isn't it, Edgar?" Steinheiser replied, casting his steely blue-eyed stare Hoover's way. "And if they do, they'll have to be cut out."

"So what's the plan?" the FBI chief said resignedly. He leaned back in his chair, hands folded on his gut.

"We have a patsy," Steinheiser said. "This guy." He laid a photograph on the table. It showed a thin man with receding hair and small eyes. He shifted the picture round so the other two men could see. "Former Marine. His name is Lee Harvey Oswald. A good marksman, Communist sympathizer, malcontent, gets into trouble at every turn. Last month he tried to assassinate a retired Major-General in Dallas while the old man was at home watching TV. One Edwin Walker." Steinheiser glanced at the file. "Bullet fired from a moving car. Hit a window frame instead of the man's head."

"Not *that* good a shot, then," Hoover observed.

Steinheiser gave him a withering look.

"This Oswald obviously got away with it," Nixon said.

"Yes, but we have a fat file on the incident."

"You've approached the man?"

"Not yet, but he'll work for us. He has the motive, the skill, and we know he is fearless. He also hates Kennedy for interfering in Cuba."

Richard Nixon laughed suddenly. "Fuck me. *Interfering?* The sonofabitch didn't go nearly far enough. Made us look like idiots!"

"Yes, well, anyway," Steinheiser said icily. "He's our man."

"And the plan?" Hoover asked.

"Details have to be confirmed. I suggest we get Oswald in an elevated position. There will be a cavalcade through

Dallas. Kennedy has made it clear to his staff that he wants to engage with 'his people'."

Nixon exhaled noisily through his ample nose.

"But I assume you will not be relying on a single shooter?" Hoover asked, his stare locked on Steinheiser.

"Of course not. We'll assign a CIA man we can trust," Steinheiser replied curtly and moved his head back a little to indicate Agent Maclaren standing behind him. "Maclaren has been decorated for his skills as a marksman."

Nixon's two associates glanced at the CIA man with faintly contemptuous looks.

"And what about this Oswald character? You can trust him to keep quiet in the lead-up?"

"His wife is pregnant with their second child."

"Good. And afterward?" Nixon said, peering down at his intertwined fingers.

"Oswald will be dealt with," Steinheiser said.

"Very well. It is agreed, then." Hoover slowly stood up.

"We should meet again before the event," the CIA Assistant Director remarked. "And we can remain in touch through the usual channels." He left with Maclaren a step behind him. Hoover said nothing and followed the agent out. Two FBI men stood waiting at the emergency exit.

A short time later, Richard Milhous Nixon slid into the back seat of a black sedan in the parking lot of the Sundowner Hotel. He leaned back, catching the eye of the driver in the rear-view mirror; he was a short man with a thick neck and a scar running from his right ear to his lower lip. "You get all that, Jerry?"

The driver opened the glove compartment to show a small tape machine, the spools still turning, a radio receiver next to it.

"I fucking hope so," Nicky Cutler spat, undoing his shirt and ripping at a lead stuck to his abdomen. "These damn wires itch like fuck."

Chapter 18

Six Months Ago

Senator Roger Gates had insisted that he send a car to pick up Professor Abigail Marchant each Tuesday at two p.m. and take her from her office on 47th Street down to Bellevue Hospital at 462 First Avenue.

Abigail had spent a year at Bellevue as part of her training. It looked precisely the same now—a massive sprawl of buildings, one of the biggest public hospitals in North America and perhaps the most famous one. More than a dozen years after she'd been there as an intern no one she had known remained working there.

It was the same driver every Tuesday. Martin was a man who kept himself very much to himself. In fact, he barely said a word and drove carefully, with a classical music station playing low on the car stereo. Every Tuesday, he dropped Abigail at the same spot outside the main doors of the Psychiatric Wing, held the car door open for her, touched his cap and was gone.

It was a chilly February afternoon with a peerless blue sky and the temperature hanging around freezing point. Abigail loved days like this. They reminded her of family holidays at their farm in Utah and the cold breeze from the mountains there. In her memory, the Utah sky went on forever. Sometimes, when she had taken herself off to the lake where the sky touched the water, she would lie in the grass and imagine she was floating at the centre of a gigantic sapphire.

She took the steps two at a time and checked the top for Roger Gates. He was always there to meet her. But today he was nowhere in sight. Abigail reached the doors and there was still no sign of him.

At reception she showed her pass. The woman behind the counter knew her and waved her toward security. She checked in her briefcase and walked through the detector arc.

"Professor Marchant," one of the guards said and nodded.

Abigail stepped toward the guard. "You haven't seen Senator Gates, have you, Joe?"

"No, professor. You want me to call through?"

"It's okay." She passed into the brightly lit corridor. She had been coming here at this time every Tuesday for the past twelve months and this was the first time that Gates had not met her at the entrance.

Abigail took the elevator to the fourth floor. The doors opened onto the secure ward. Directly ahead stood the Attendant's desk. Ursula was on duty, just as she was every Tuesday afternoon. She was a hard-faced woman with beefy arms, a crucifix hanging in the "v" of her blue shirt collar. Abigail had discovered a while ago that Ursula's facial expressions ran through a very limited repertoire. Today she had her usual stern look, edged with tiredness. As she took the three paces to the desk, Abigail could hear the usual medley of sounds: a TV from the first room on the left, a phone ringing in another corridor. A nurse pushing a trolley flashed past, almost running into her.

"Professor," Ursula said, "Senator Gates is expecting you."

Abigail was about to answer when the woman went on. "I'll get James to go with you. There's been some trouble."

"What kind of trouble?"

"Not my place to explain, Professor Marchant." She spoke into a walkie-talkie at her collar. "James, front desk, please—asap."

The orderly, James Kalaski, must have been close by because he appeared at the end of the corridor within seconds and ambled over. Abigail headed toward him. He was a short rotund man in a blue one-piece. He swung round without a word as she approached and she followed him along the passage, took a left turn, a right and then passed through a set of double doors. This was the private ward reserved for those who could afford long-term individual care.

Two armed guards patrolled a corridor from which three rooms led off on each side. All the doors were closed and locked. They had names on them. Abigail knew them off by heart. The patients behind these doors were all in for the long haul: they had been here twelve months ago when she had first been invited by Roger Gates, and many would still be here in twelve months' time.

Stopping at the last door on the left, Abigail stood a

foot behind James Kalaski. From inside they could hear crying, muffled sobs and, low in the auditory range, a man's voice saying something in somber, soothing tones, the words impossible to distinguish.

James rapped on the door. After a moment it opened. Roger Gates saw James first, then Abigail. His expression of deep anxiety lifted a little when he saw her.

"We'll be okay, James," Gates said quietly.

"I'll be right here, sir," the orderly replied, indicating a chair across from the door.

Gates shifted his gaze back to Abigail. He was a handsome older man who looked at least a decade younger than his seventy-three years. He had a narrow face, pepper-and-salt cropped hair, and a deep tan, the kind that seemed settled into his skin for good. He was wearing a seersucker jacket and a crisp white shirt open at the collar. He leaned forward and pecked Abigail on the cheek.

"We're having a bad day," the senator said and ushered her in.

It was a large room with a hospital bed, a sofa, an armchair, and in one corner a big-screen TV inside a shallow perspex box. The floor was carpeted in beige, the walls colored a calming cream. One wall was covered with a child's drawings and watercolors. A locked cupboard against the wall opposite the window was, Abigail knew, filled with books, DVDs, a computer and an easel with painting materials, paper, crayons and chalk. The window itself was covered with a sturdy grille and looked out onto First Avenue four stories below; the noise of afternoon traffic was just a distant hum.

On the sofa sat a young girl with striking red hair and dark eyes: Abigail's special patient Peggy Gates, the senator's granddaughter. Peggy, now ten, had been in Bellevue's High Security ward for three years. Most of the time she was passive and mild-mannered but, seemingly without reason, she would sometimes fly into hysterics, become uncontrollably manic, destructive, suicidal. On these occasions she was impossible to communicate with and so far removed from reality that it was impossible to break through the barriers around her mind.

Medication helped, a cocktail of drugs that had made her face puffy. But these provided only a partial remedy. They simply took the edge off the worst times.

Roger Gates had agreed to commit his granddaughter after a particularly violent attack three years ago, the month after the girl's parents, Gates's son Howard and his wife Beatrice had died in a boating accident. Peggy had smashed up her room. Then she had made her way to the kitchen, found a bread knife and had just begun to scythe into her left wrist when the cook walked in on her. Peggy had turned the blade on the poor woman and cut her face before Roger Gates's personal assistant Jerome Newson had heard screams, dashed in and overpowered the girl.

Peggy was sitting rocking backward and forward, humming. A shoulder restraint kept her on the sofa. She was staring blankly at her hands, palms up on her knees. She looked up as Abigail came into the room.

"Professor!" the girl squealed and her face suddenly became animated. She glanced at her grandfather and beamed. "Thank you, grandpa. Thank you. You've got the professor here to take me back."

Abigail stepped forward and settled herself onto the sofa next to Peggy. She saw Gates lower himself into the armchair, cross his legs and interlock his fingers in front of him.

Abigail had first met Peggy twelve months ago. Roger Gates had come to see her after reading about her work in the *New York Times*. He'd simply dropped into the office uptown expecting to see the professor straight away. But Abigail had been run off her feet. When Gates was still in the waiting room two hours later, she knew he was serious. Her assistant Julia had left, she was tired but had agreed to go to a café nearby to chat. And as Gates had explained his story, Abigail had begun to realize just how important Peggy could be to her research.

When she was four Peggy had started to talk about her friend Harry. Her parents, Howard and Beatrice, knew no Harry and had put it down to a childish fantasy. Some kids had imaginary friends, they'd reasoned, maybe Peggy had one too. But the girl soon began to elaborate, to fill in detail after detail, and the strangest thing about all this was the consistency, the fact that Peggy's tales about what she began to call her "other family" and about their neighbors—Harry's parents—never broke their internal narrative structure.

Then, when Peggy was seven, her parents had been killed. Roger had concocted some explanation, one that satisfied neither of them. The terrible mood swings and the violence quickly followed; and next came the incarceration, when Roger, bereft and overworked, could find no other way to cope.

In hospital, Peggy had deteriorated. She went for weeks without speaking. Then at other times she would become aggressive, hurting herself and attacking those around her. She was put in a padded cell and heavily sedated.

Abigail had first met Peggy on a chill day like this one, hoar frost on the windows, the heating ratcheted up too high. Peggy had been sullen, coiled in upon herself. Abigail had seen patients like this girl many times before and it was clear to her that Peggy was suffering terribly from what the professor had defined as "Split-Lives Syndrome" or SLS. Much to the irritation of her colleagues in the psychology fraternity, she had recently published a paper on the subject in the *Chronicles of Para-Science*, a journal considered way beyond the pale by orthodox scientists.

In this paper Abigail had suggested that some individuals, almost exclusively young children who managed to connect with some aspect of their past lives, were unable to understand it or were not allowed to process it properly and became psychologically imbalanced. In some cases this led to a severe form of bipolar disorder.

Peggy, Abigail had realized quickly, was a textbook case. Although the girl could not rationalize it, she knew instinctively that she was now living a different life from the one in which she had a close friend called Harry. And then, when her mother died, the loss multiplied her inner sense of disconnectedness with her present life. At the edge of her conscious mind, Peggy realized her mother was now in a different world. Perhaps a different life, a baby maybe, younger than her.

It had proven to be phenomenally easy to regress Peggy. Roger insisted upon being there with a nurse on hand. He was understandably anxious and demanded that the regression should be conducted in Peggy's hospital room, not in Abigail's office. To everyone's surprise, it had been the most peaceful, gloriously happy returning that Abigail had ever witnessed. Part of Peggy, a very strong part, was anxious to get back to somewhere else, to learn and to understand what had been happening to her. She loved her grandfather but she was desperate to find Harry.

It did not happen, of course, not during that first regression. Instead, she had returned to the seventeenth century when she had lived in a remote Scottish village. She described her husband, a simple man named Barclay. She was seventeen and recalled how the English attacked her home, raped her and killed her husband.

Then the regression shifted to what turned out to be nineteenth-century Switzerland. Her name in this life had been Fran and she was part of a wealthy family who owned a hotel in the Alps. Then, with another shift, she was in the ancient world in which she was a slave girl from Gaul called Anais. It was as though Peggy was searching, trying to find the life she wanted. After twenty-five minutes, Abigail had called her back.

Peggy had opened her eyes and showed her disorientation immediately. Abigail, Roger and the nurse could see the girl's facial expressions shift with alarming speed: anger, frustration, then melancholy.

"Please take me back," Peggy had pleaded, tears streaming down her cheeks.

Abigail had been unsure what to do. She had never experienced a subject so attached to her past lives before. Usually, those whom she studied were rooted in the present. The past was a totally alien place at first and going there was disorientating. But with Peggy the reverse was true.

With Gates's approval, Abigail took his granddaughter into another regression. Peggy returned to the Scottish village, to a time shortly before the English raid. She was dancing in a village festival, the sun was shining, there were flowers in her hair. Peggy smiled as she lay back on the sofa. She was happy. But then the smile faded, as though something was jogging her mentally, telling her to keep searching.

That was when she first found Harry.

She was an eleven-year-old named Constance living in New York in 1898. Harry was sixteen. Her parents had died from pneumonia during their first winter in the New World. They had arrived on Ellis Island so full of hope, the three of them, and now she was alone. Harry was a neighbor who had just started work. He was not earning much but he brought her food and eventually persuaded his parents to take her in. To Constance, Harry was an Olympian, he could do anything. They loved each other. He protected her, they were inseparable.

Peggy lay hypnotized and laughing, a look of unalloyed joy on her face. She seemed, just for a moment to be a normal kid again. Abigail had shifted in her seat and caught Roger Gates's expression, and in that moment it told her everything. He was relieved, that was clear; but he could not hide a deep existential hurt. Abigail had understood that. The man had always thought of Peggy as his little girl. Yet she was an ancient being, just as he was. But his granddaughter was in touch with her ancient self and she could slip in and out of lives, other lives, lives in which he was not her grandfather, lives in which they did not even know each other. It was a horribly painful thing to come to terms with.

At first it had been hard to drag Peggy back. But there seemed to be an immediate rapport between her and Abigail. The professor could keep her calm, guide her and soothe her all at once. They had shared a remarkable and instant bond, and Abigail took pains to include Roger Gates in the psychic embrace.

During the twelve months that followed, Abigail grew close to the senator. He was a warm man, very different to the image of politicians that she had cultivated in her mind. She was estranged from her own father and had not spoken to him in over a decade. Her mother Gwen had died from a brain hemorrhage eleven years ago, and so Abigail could identify with Peggy on many levels. Subconsciously, she began to consider the girl to be a much younger sister, Roger almost a replacement father.

Peggy's Split-Lives Syndrome was deeply entrenched, and although being able to regress had given her a sense of meaning and partial calm it also exaggerated some of her feelings of disconnectedness. She knew she could not go back to her old lives except during those short sessions. She also found it difficult to steer her regressions, even with Abigail's help. She would often go weeks without returning to become Constance in New York, and she could not find Harry.

In one regression, in which Peggy returned to the Swiss hotel and her life as Fran, she met a child named James Turner, who was to become Harry in a subsequent life. He was only two years old. He had only recently learned to walk and could say no more than a few words. But Peggy, through the eyes of Fran, knew instinctively that James was Harry, or would be Harry, even if Fran herself had no idea. It was a painful experience. It came as a shock to Peggy that Harry could be there, but at the same time not be there; be there, yet out of reach. The experience had so upset her that when she emerged into her twenty-first-century hospital room at Bellevue she could barely speak. Roger too had been shocked and had almost canceled the following session. He had only relented when Abigail explained that Peggy needed to resolve this incongruity or it would cause serious psychological damage.

It was soon after this that Peggy found Harry again. During six successive weekly sessions she had managed to find her old life in New York a century earlier. And each time she emerged from the Returning calm, smiling, relaxed, a normal child again.

But then the therapy moved into a new phase: Harry was murdered.

The trauma almost pushed Peggy into a catatonic state, and it had taken all Abigail's expertise and personal empathy with the girl to bring her back from the edge.

"He had to die sometime," Abigail had tried to explain to Peggy. "You must realize, Harry would have gone on to another life, just as you did, just as we all do."

Such talk helped . . . eventually. But the shock remained. Abigail and Roger could see it in the shadows under Peggy's eyes. And, for the following three months, the girl found a new mission: to investigate her friend's murder, to track down his killer. That was what the plucky young orphan Constance had done a century ago. Now Peggy could see it all through her eyes. She could not change a thing, she could not exert the slightest influence on the past, but she could observe and she could bear witness.

"Your grand-daddy tells me you've been upset, Pegs," Abigail said and took the girl's hand. Her skin had a waxy texture, another side effect of the drugs, Abigail knew.

Roger leaned forward in the armchair. "Better now, though, yeah?"

Peggy gave her grandfather a nod. "Yes . . . better. So can we start?" the girl asked impatiently.

"Sure." Abigail positioned a pillow under Peggy's head, untied her restraint, and eased her back. "Make sure you're comfy, Pegs."

A faint smile played across the girl's pale lips. Abigail leaned over and began to speak quietly.

"Oh, this isn't it," Peggy muttered as soon as she had regressed.

"Relax, Peggy."

"But . . ."

"Sshh . . . go with it," Abigail said and started to whisper softly in the girl's ear, taking her further under. She could feel Peggy sink down deeper into the regression. She kept whispering, sending her on, down through the layers of separation, nudging Peggy away from herself, away from Constance, into whoever she was in whatever time and place.

Peggy screamed.

Roger sat up, jolted. "What's . . . ?"

Abigail lifted a hand. "Roger . . . please."

The girl screamed again, a horrified burst of noise. Then she moaned, shivered . . . "Agh!"

"Abi . . . you sure?"

She rounded on the senator. "Please!"

He nodded, but came over to the sofa and sat a couple of feet from his granddaughter's head.

"Peggy, listen . . . Talk to me."

I'm Rachel.

"Okay, Rachel."

Abigail scanned Roger's face. He looked puzzled. Peggy/Rachel was speaking in English but with a strong East European accent.

Oh . . . the stink! It's terrible. I'm in a crowded place. It's dark. I feel the press of bodies against me. I can't tell what I'm wearing, but it's itchy.

I remember . . . I was pushed onto the train. I'm in a cattle wagon. It's coming back to me. I lived with my family in Warsaw. The Jewish ghetto. And then they came for us . . . my parents . . . blood on the snow . . . drip, drip from the gaping wound in my father's head; his blank eyes, ice crystals on his lashes, melting, water running into those dead eyes. The German guard kicked him in the face, dead teeth smashed in. And mother . . . she was raped in front of us, her legs pushed back so far that her hips dislocated. She'd screamed and screamed, and the soldiers laughed as they staved in her head with their rifle butts.

The door is opening and the cold wind rushes in. It's twilight, a slither of orange spilling through the wire fence directly ahead. Voices, shouts. I feel the press of people release as we spill out of the cattle truck. A soldier grabs a woman by the hair pushing her to the ground. He is stamping on her face.

I sense the fear all around me, inside me. It's like the stink, it's clawing at my throat, choking me.

I jump down to the snow, receive a kick to my ribs, the pain drills into me and up my spine. A flashlight is pointed at us. I shield my eyes and look around. I see snow, concrete, metal-gray uniforms, ragged skeletal humans. I peer down at my striped trousers, striped jacket, touch the rough fabric, catch a waft of excrement and sweat.

I'm knocked hard in the back and I trudge forward. Voices all around. It's starting to snow, and as crystals land on my face and dissolve I'm reminded of my father's eyes, his icy lashes and the fact that he has gone, forever.

We're passing through a gate. I catch my arm on the barbed wire and the metal slices through the fabric and cuts my flesh. I suppress a yelp. The butt of a rifle slams between my shoulder blades. The air is filled with breath, cold breath, malodorous, the breath of starvation. My own breath is catching in my throat and I think for a second that I'm going to die. And, for all the pain, even now in this black, black incomprehensible moment, I don't want to die. I want to be free. I want to live and love and be me.

I think of making a run for it, but I know I'm too weak. And besides, I know I cannot go two steps before a bullet finds me.

We stop. More shouts, more rifle butts, a kick. A face appears in front of me. A young man, about my age, nineteen maybe. He is shouting at me, his nose an inch from mine. His spittle hits my skin. I smell his well-fed breath. He grabs me, shoves me to the side. I fall into line behind a long row of others. They all look the same, all look the same as me, striped, starving animals.

Through gates. Marching boots. Shouts. More shouts. Through a door into a large room. I'm squeezed in, pressed against other bodies. I cannot tell how many people are here, but I can sense them, hear them, smell them. The door slams shut. A light comes on. An old man in front of me starts to crumple at the knees. He slips down and I can see those behind where he had stood. A child, an old woman, two small-boned teenage girls. Behind them, more crushed bodies, gasping for breath as their ribs are compressed.

Who is that? I see a young man. He's about the same age as the guard, about the same age as me. Like all of us, he is as thin as a bird, his head and eyebrows shaved to a dark stubble. He has cuts and bruises all over his face. His black eyes are huge with dark rings around them like a panda's.

Our stares meet. I know him and he knows me.

I hear a hiss. I look down, then back to the young man. I feel giddy. I know what this is. I've heard stories, but I did not believe they were true.

I'm screaming. We're all screaming. We all know, suddenly. I see the boy's face contort and I stretch out my hand toward him. He reaches out his skeletal fingers to me. HARRY!

Chapter 19

Present Day

Mark shivered. The temperature had dropped dramatically and sweat had dried on his skin. He pulled himself to his feet, wincing, a throbbing pain at his right temple. He flexed his fingers and rubbed his forearm.

"Well, this is fantastic," he said aloud.

He was under a concrete roof, an elevated freeway. He could hear the rumble of tires now, light traffic passing through the predawn. To the right he could see the water and, further on, familiar shapes: Brooklyn Naval Yard, a tangle of steel, cranes and concrete buildings, the warm glow of neon. Now he knew where he was: under the FDR East River Drive, near Rutgers Park. He turned away from the water to stare across the dusty waste ground. A track led off to an opened and rusty gate. Elton-Hornsby's car must have gone that way, he thought. Directly ahead stood a cracked concrete wall, uneven steps leading up to the elevated road. He started towards them.

The stairs stank of urine. A page of the *New York Post* flew up and spiraled in the air, over the wall and onto the expressway. Mark rounded a corner and stepped onto a narrow path beside the road, cars rushing towards him, headlights blazing. He saw a break in the traffic and ran across the wide road to a central island. A pause and then another sprint to the far side and more steps leading to South Street beyond.

His cell rang. He found it in the back pocket of his jeans, peered at the screen and saw that it was Janet Clifton calling.

"Jan."

"Hi, Mark, is this a good time? It's just . . . I need to tell you something."

He paused for a moment and looked around him, running a hand over his sore temple. The street was lined with dark houses. He suddenly felt anxious—the events of the past few hours were starting to catch up with him.

"Er . . . listen, Jan, let me call you back. You at home?"

"Yeah."

"Okay, give me five minutes."

Mark walked quickly. It was quiet, a downtime, no one visible on the street, the crack dealers resting for an hour or two. He picked up the pace a little and within a few minutes he was on the edge of Chinatown.

The street-cleaning vehicles were out. The black of night was beginning to lift, a humble glow edging its way in. In half an hour the place would be lambent with orange light, a new day dawning. He reached a payphone just off Grand Street. It stood in the shadow of a run-down brownstone building.

"Jan," he said after hearing the line connect.

"Hope it's not too early there, Mark."

He smiled. "Haven't been to bed yet!"

Jan was silent.

"It's Pat's funeral today, isn't it, Jan? Is that why you're calling? You okay?"

"I'm bearing up, Mark . . . Just. I have to for the kids. The funeral is this afternoon. But that's not the reason I called. Oh, look . . . I don't know what to think. I, um . . . I've found something for you."

"For me?"

"Well, I assume so. Oh, look, sorry . . . I, er, I was going through some of Patrick's things. He kept boxes of stuff . . ."

He heard Jan take a deep breath. He could picture her sitting in the hall of the house in Oxford. The crazy blend of pictures on the wall facing her. To her right would be the door leading off to where Patrick had been lying, the living room they had converted to a temporary bedroom as Pat had waited to die.

"That must have been hard," Mark said softly.

"Um . . . yeah, but it has to be done . . ." A long pause. Jan cleared her throat. "I'm sorry, Mark. I didn't think it would be so tough to talk about."

"You said you found something for me," Mark said quickly, trying to help Jan focus.

"That's right. A USB with the word 'Bob' written on the side."

Mark felt a tingle down his spine. Only Patrick had ever called him "Bob". Hearing it now jolted him. He saw in his mind Patrick standing at the bar of a club in Oxford called Back To Nature. They had just played a great improvised set around half a dozen blues standards, and Pat had said to him: "I'm going to call you Bob from now on."

"Bob?" Mark had to shout to be heard above the boom of dance music.

"Robert Johnson . . . Bob. You sounded like Robert Johnson tonight."

"Oh, come on! I wish!"

Patrick had been distracted by a girl they knew and hadn't heard him. Mark had grinned to himself, emptied his glass and knew that Pat wouldn't remember it in the morning. But he had, and for a while he used the nickname in private, just between the two of them. Mark had treasured it.

"So Pat remembered that, after all these years?"

"He told me the story. Look, Mark, it must be something important. Why else the cloak-and-dagger stuff?"

"You tried it?"

"No. It didn't feel right . . ."

"Silly thing," Mark exclaimed. "Honesty, Jan. It's one of the things I've always loved about you."

He made her laugh briefly. "So what should I do?"

Mark paused for a second and looked across the street. His head was aching. A newspaper seller was opening his kiosk, a beam of lemon light shining from inside as he lifted the shutter.

"You near a computer?"

"Just a sec."

Mark heard Jan cross the hall, open a door, the hinges creaking. Then came the click of fingers on a keyboard.

"Right. I've plugged in the USB. There's one file called 'Bob'. I'm going to open it."

A few taps, a sigh. More taps. "It won't open in Word. Just brings up a notice: ENCRYPTED DOCUMENT."

Mark bit his lower lip and watched the newsstand guy pulling a trolley of candy from inside the kiosk.

"Weird. Okay, Jan, send the file over to me."

He heard her take a deep breath. "It's just that it's obviously something Patrick thought was important enough to encrypt. I should read it asap."

There was a silence from the other end of the line.

"Jan?"

Nothing.

"Jan?"

"Mark, listen, I'm scared."

"Scared? Why?"

"I think someone was here. Someone has gone through the house."

Mark felt the hairs on the back of his neck stand up.

"It was this morning while I was out. Maybe I'm just being paranoid, but some things have been moved. No one else would have noticed, probably. But that's crazy, isn't it, Mark? Why would anyone do that?"

"Shit!" Mark exclaimed. "I should have stayed over there—for a few days, at least."

"Don't be silly . . . you have a life." Mark heard Jan inhale deeply again. "So do you think I'm being paranoid?"

He didn't want to alarm her. "I think you're probably super-stressed, Jan. Which isn't at all surprising. Have you thought of taking a break after the funeral? Maybe you should go off somewhere with the children. It's still the school holidays, isn't it? Take them to Disneyland Paris or something."

Jan fell quiet again. "God . . ." she muttered after a moment. "Will this nightmare ever end?"

Mark could think of nothing to say.

Then Jan was suddenly speaking again, her voice jagged as though she was commanding herself to get a grip. "I'll email that file over to you, Mark."

He gave her his email address. "What are you going to do?" he asked as Jan noted down the address.

"Oh, I'll cope."

"You remember, Jan. I'm only across the Pond. If ever you need me . . . I'll be thinking of you and the kids . . . and Pat. I hope it all goes well."

"Thanks, Mark. I'll be fine. I have to be . . ."

Chapter 20

Mark took a cab to 55th and Sixth, then walked a half-block west.

At the offices of the *Courier*, the night shift was close to finishing up. There was no big breaking story so everyone seemed pretty relaxed, feet up on desks, sleeves rolled back, the umpteenth cup of coffee on their work-tops. He knew a few faces but hadn't worked nights here for a couple of years.

Mark strode over to his workstation, pulled up a chair and woke the computer from its hibernation. He tapped the keyboard, brought up the mail inbox and there was the message that Jan had sent twenty-seven minutes earlier. It contained an 84KB attachment titled "BOB".

Mark hovered the cursor over the file symbol, was about to open it but then changed his mind. He pulled open a drawer, searching for a USB or a blank CD. He found a drive, slipped it into the back of the computer and moved the file over. It downloaded in a few seconds and he had just deleted the original when he heard someone call his name. Spinning his chair round, he saw the editor, Sam Helmer, bursting through the door.

"Mr. Bretton!" the huge Texan boomed. "Thought you'd drop by, hah?"

Mark gave him a smile which was not returned. Helmer strode over to his office at the back. "Get your ass in here, Mark," he called. "Shut the door."

The editor lowered himself into his specially designed chair and nudged the mouse of his computer as Mark pulled up a much smaller chair. For a few seconds the big guy ignored him and focused on his flat screen, scanning the lines of text that only he could see. Mark understood that it was a deliberate move to make him feel uncomfortable. He knew Helmer well.

"So, Mark. I have to say I've seen you looking better."

Mark glanced down and only then realized how disheveled he was. His shirt was filthy—there was a patch of blood at the right elbow. He ran a hand across his stubbly chin.

"Looks like you've been at Fight Club before work."

Mark sighed wearily. "Much more mundane." He nodded towards Sixth Avenue. "Fucking cab driver pulled away as I was half out the car."

Helmer said nothing. Mark watched him, and with his left hand fingered the USB which he had managed to slip into his pocket.

"You wanna talk to me?" the editor said, his face expressionless.

"About?"

"Mark, what's going on? You haven't delivered the piece about the reincarnation woman . . . what's her name?"

"Abigail Marchant."

"Yeah, right, Marchant. I know you had to go to the UK for a couple of days but you were given the assignment three days ago." He flicked his gaze toward the wall clock.

"It's 6.15 in the fucking morning and you look like you've been sleeping rough."

Mark had his hands up. But Helmer hadn't finished. "We go back, Mark." He fixed him with a hard look. "That's why I know I can trust you. But you need to talk to me, man."

Mark took a deep breath. "I think this is a much bigger story than we originally thought."

Helmer sat back with his arms folded.

"Be honest, Sam, you thought it was a simple kook story, right?"

Helmer said nothing, just considered Mark seriously.

"You wanted an intelligent piece. Well, I can give you one."

"Please don't tell me you're a convert, 'cos I won't believe it, Mr. Science Guy."

"Give me some credit."

Sam shook his head and sighed.

"Professor Marchant is an interesting woman," Mark went on. "She's clearly a flake, but she's photogenic and, most importantly, she believes utterly in what she is researching. I think we have a major story here."

"A major story, Mark? You okay?"

"Look, it has all the ingredients. She's a good-looking woman, and reincarnation is all about wishful thinking. Deep down everyone wishes it were true, that we could live forever."

Helmer was clearly still skeptical. "You sound like you're quoting from some crackpot website!" Then he looked down at his folded arms. "You know about her problems with the American Psychiatry Association, right?"

"Yeah, of course. They don't like her. Don't you think that adds more spice?"

"All right, Mark. What do you want?"

"Time."

"You've already had time!"

Mark stayed quiet, staring Helmer out.

"You don't think you're being strung along?"

"Meaning?"

The editor held back, but Mark knew what he meant.

"You think I'm indulging in wishful thinking—is that it, Sam?"

"I didn't say that."

"Didn't have to."

"Okay, Mark. You want both fucking barrels? You got 'em. Yeah, I wonder, as your boss, whether you might be getting personally involved for three reasons. One: You lost a child. Two: Your best friend has just died. And three: Professor Marchant is hot."

For a second, Helmer thought Mark was going to explode. He had never seen him lose his cool and part of him was curious. But the Englishman simply laughed and the tension evaporated.

Mark stood up slowly. "So, you going to give me more time?" he said, putting his hands in his pockets. He could feel the USB again.

Helmer leaned forward, elbows on his desk. "Two days, Mark," he said. "And your copy had better be fucking good."

Chapter 21

One Year Ago

They tried to make her room as comfortable as possible, but whatever they did nothing changed the fact that she was their prisoner. She had lost track of how many years she had been kept here, and just lately her lives seemed to be overlapping, merging so that there were many moments when she was in this life physically but felt that part of her still existed in a past incarnation. At other times she would become immersed in a regression and elements of her life in the twenty-first century would infiltrate and confuse her.

She contemplated the wall. The men would be here soon. They always came at this time. She would hear the slap of their boots on the concrete of the corridor beyond the locked door to her room. It was dark outside, a cold desert dark that spared no illumination except for the artificial light pouring outward from the windows of the Institute. Yes, she knew a little bit about where she was. She knew a little about who she was and where she had been. Funny, though, she thought, she knew far more about *who* she had been.

From hints and clues, overheard words, slips of the

tongue and fragments of memory, she had pieced together a few facts. Her name was Elizabeth, but here the men often referred to her as "Patient E": an epithet she did not much care for. She wasn't sure, but she thought she was fifteen years old now and that she had been here for three years. But the problem was that the days all merged into one, so she accepted that she might be fourteen or sixteen and she could have been here for two years, or perhaps four. She also knew she was in some sort of research complex in a desert region of New Mexico at least thirty miles from the nearest town. She had a strong sense that dozens, maybe hundreds of people worked here, but she only encountered the same handful of them each day.

For the first year, they had forbidden her any form of contact with the outside world. They had tried to explain to her that they wanted to "turn off the noise" to keep her regressions pure and uncluttered by the present. She hadn't really understood what that meant and she had been desperately unhappy. Eventually they had changed their minds and a TV had been installed in her room. When the stimulus seemed to have no effect on her ability to regress she had been allowed to keep it. Now she spent most of her time watching TV. Some things confused her, some made her happy, others made her very sad.

She remembered faded snatches of her life in Chicago. Her parents were very poor. The roof of their tiny top-floor apartment in Bridgeport leaked and they had no air-con, no central heating. Her father hadn't worked a day in four years.

Elizabeth had been experiencing confusing regressions

for at least two years before she had told her mother about them. That had been when she was six. She knew her age because she had not been at school for very long. Her stories were kept in the family for a long time, but then, soon after her eleventh birthday, a strange man had come to the house to talk to her. She had spent hours with him and his friend, a short man with a gray beard and small black eyes. She'd had to answer lots of questions and agree to do some tests. Then her father had persuaded her to be hypnotized by the small bearded man. He assured her, they all assured her, that everything would be all right.

She had been hypnotized and she had returned to one of her favorite lives. She was a teenage girl living in Paris. It was late spring and the pansies were out in the window boxes on the balconies of the grand houses in her neighborhood. She was taking her baby brother out for a walk along the Left Bank. A car passed her. Its roof was down and it had a huge red bonnet and a chrome grille. It made an odd noise.

Later, they took her to another life. This was not so good. She was very skinny. She looked at her arms, and she had very black skin. She was terribly hungry. She touched her abdomen and it felt hollow. There was the taste of blood and salt in her mouth, her lips were parched, her eyes sore.

When Elizabeth had come out of hypnosis, the two men seemed to be very pleased with what she had told them. Her parents were seated in a pair of chairs close by. They had a haunted look about them. Her mother Emma's face was pale as milk.

She had no recollection of the journey here and she found that she could not bear to remember her parents' farewells. It almost seemed now as though the life she had shared with them was another of her previous incarnations and not part of this one. That made her sad.

She heard the boots. The door opened. One man in a uniform held it open, a second came into the room and stood very upright against the wall opposite her bed as the small bearded man came in. His name was Professor Nathan Morrow. He was wearing his usual white lab coat, a row of pens in his chest pocket.

Elizabeth knew the routine and did not need to say a word. She simply followed Morrow out into the corridor. The security guards fell in behind her. She had never resisted. She saw no point. Why would she? They weren't hurting her, at least as far as she knew. They looked after her. She had movies on DVD, she had good food and all they ever asked of her was to undergo regular regression. She did not mind this most of the time. There were some lifetimes she disliked and a couple she positively loathed. But she had learned a neat trick that she had kept to herself. She could control her destination, could steer herself to the past lives she wanted to go to.

The corridor twisted and turned and opened into a large windowless room with white walls and a high ceiling lit by powerful halogen spots. The floor was tiled and a comfortable reclining bed stood in the center of the room. Next to this were two chairs. At the end of the bed there was a remote-controlled video camera on a stand. A microphone hung low over the bed, a lead ran up into the ceiling along a conduit to a control room filled with recording equipment and computers manned by two men in lab coats. They were just visible through a large glass window.

As they approached the opened door to the room, Morrow turned to Elizabeth. "We have a guest today," he said and waved her in.

A very old, tall, thin man in an immaculately tailored suit, striped shirt and blood red, lightly patterned tie stood in the middle of the room. He had icy blue eyes and his hair was so drained of color that it disappeared against the perfect white walls so that, at first glance, it seemed as though the upper third of his head had been removed. Elizabeth recognized him immediately as the man who had visited her parents' house years ago. She had seen him here on a few occasions since then. His name was Orlando Steinheiser.

Elizabeth was asked to lie on the bed and to place her arms at her sides. Steinheiser stood across the room talking quietly to Morrow. A third man, Steinheiser's chief aide Christopher Trafano, joined them from the control room. Elizabeth could no longer see them, nor could she make out what they were saying.

"You have the new serum?" the scientist asked.

Trafano lifted a small metal case onto the bench in front of them.

"Any updates on the lab trials?"

"Just that everything seems to be working fine and there are absolutely no side effects—just as I predicted," Steinheiser replied.

Professor Morrow gave him a skeptical look. "Well, as long as you know I'm still not happy about this."

"Duly noted," Steinheiser said flatly and glanced back at Elizabeth reclining on the bed.

She looked up as Morrow walked over. "You okay, Elizabeth? The usual routine, my dear." He nodded to a figure in the control room adjacent to the lab and the cameras and recorders were switched to "on".

Elizabeth showed absolutely no reaction as the needle went in. She was used to it.

Morrow spoke softly, the same words he always used. His voice was soporific and Elizabeth saw no reason to resist him. Indeed, she was looking forward to returning.

The light is soft here. Mother is leaning over the cot, talking to me. She is smiling, touches my cheek. I feel her skin against mine.

Mother is moving away and I feel as though I'm falling. Colors rushing past. I'm confined, trapped. Something is enveloping me, pulling me. Ohhh . . . ohh.

I know this place, but I don't have a word for it.

And now I'm moving again.

I see a man wearing a suit, with a winged collar and a cravat. He is peering down at me, a scalpel in his right hand. I fall back . . . oh . . . oh. I taste blood. My chest is wet.

A fire. The flames play with the air. I'm transfixed by the flames. I see my tiny hairy fingers, feel the wolf skin against my cold, empty tummy. The fire starts to warm me. I touch the hair on my face, run a finger around the ridges above my right eye and across my broad nose to the other low brow.

Falling.

Sand in my mouth. I'm thirsty. I turn my head. I feel different somehow. I see colors again, bright lights. The sky is an endless blue. I see my arm, but it's not an arm. What is that? My skin is not skin. I don't know what it is.

Aggh, my tongue. My tongue is flicking out. I have something in my mouth. I swallow. I move my strange head again and see the scales. I'm gray, green. I hiss.

I'm falling again.

Bright light. Water. At least I think it's water. I only think that because of me . . . Elizabeth. There's another here, but it is a simple thing. I feel impulses, but no thoughts as such. Only Elizabeth thinks, and Elizabeth is an intruder. Light again, water, vibration, a tremor. I move, respond, but I don't think. Only Elizabeth thinks.

Falling. The familiar place again. I'm me, really me, just me. Elizabeth is here, Claudine is here; Samantha, Mambatu, Chi Nan, Shirley, Kinma and Joanna too. Some of them I know better than others. But they are all me.

Mother, I don't like this. Mother . . . I'm scared.

Mist . . . lights again in the mist now.

The other five are here. I see them. I'm not scared anymore. I'm home.

Chapter 22

Six Months Ago

She had been sound asleep when her cellphone trilled. "Abigail. It's Roger."

Instantly awake, she leaned over and saw the clock. 1.45 a.m. "Roger . . . what?"

"Please—come to the hospital. Now."

The senator's voice sounded tense. He was straining to keep it even. She knew not to ask. Knew she just had to go. The line went dead.

She took the elevator down to the second basement. It was cold. The car bleeped at the touch of the remote. She jumped in and sped away up the ramp, the heater on max.

The journey downtown passed in a blur of light and noise. Rain beat against the windshield and all the time Abigail was trying to imagine what had happened, trying to suppress her worst fears. The traffic around Broadway was snarled up as usual and she crept forward, tapping the steering wheel impatiently with her fingertips, leaning out the window to try to see what was happening: as though it would make any difference. She called Senator Gates back, but his phone kept going straight to voicemail. She left two messages giving him updates.

It was 2.14 when she finally reached Bellevue. She parked, ran to the main doors and flashed her ID at the guard. He stopped her. She had never seen him before. He was the night-shift guy and she had not previously been here at this time of night. He looked her up and down. She kept telling herself to stay calm.

"Can you tell me your business, Professor—" he studied the rectangle of plastic that Abigail had handed him "—Marchant?"

"I have a sick patient. Her grandfather called me. Said it was urgent." She emphasized the last word.

"Your patient is?"

Abigail looked around, exasperated, and took in the staff at the reception counter. There was no one there whom she recognized.

"Peggy Gates, granddaughter of Senator Roger Gates. He called me. He will be mightily pissed if you don't—"

"There's no need for that tone, professor."

"I do not mean to be . . ." Abigail began again as calmly as she could. She kept looking past the barrier.

"Your patient's number is?" the guard asked and tapped at a computer beside the gateway onto the wards.

"61213."

"Six, one . . ." The guard typed with one cautious finger.

"Abigail . . ."

She looked up and saw a face she knew, one of the doctors from the psych ward.

"What you doing . . . ?"

Abigail flicked a glance toward the guard and the doctor got it right away. He came over, his white lab coat flapping around his knees.

172

"McCain," he said stopping a few feet behind the guard. "I know this lady. Let her through, please."

"I'm still checking."

"No, you're not," the doctor snapped. The guard bridled but said nothing as he stood aside.

"God, thanks, Dr. Nelson," Abigail said as she darted into the corridor.

"Think nothing of it. Hey, how about we—?"

"Can't stop now. Emergency!"

Then she was through the door and racing along the next corridor. She could hear screams and recognized the sound instantly.

The light in Peggy's room had been dimmed. She was lying on the bed, restrained with leather straps wrapped around her calves and others holding her arms to her sides. Her wrists and ankles were bound to the frame of the bed. She was shaking, screaming uncontrollably. Two orderlies stood by the bed while Roger Gates and a doctor talked animatedly. The doctor was extremely agitated. As Abigail walked in, Gates spun round and saw her. A momentary flash of relief passed across his face. He walked across and guided her over to Peggy.

She stared down at the girl and ran a hand along her cheek. Peggy's face was crimson, her hospital gown soaked through with sweat, the fabric clinging to her skin. She peered up at Abigail, seeming not to recognize her for a moment, but then she stopped screaming.

"Sssh . . . there, there, calm down, Pegs," Abigail murmured. "What have you given her?" she asked the doctor.

"A mild sedative," the doctor replied. "105 mg/ml Valium."

Abigail twisted back to the patient. "What's the matter, Peggy? What has happened?"

"Harry," the girl rasped. "It's Harry."

"Harry?" Abigail said quietly and ran through the events of the afternoon in her mind: the returning in which Peggy had been in the gas chambers and seen her friend just moments before death. The girl had come out of the regression unable to speak, her face drained of blood. She had eventually calmed down. But it had taken all Abigail's skill to make Peggy believe that the returning was over, that it had happened more than seventy years ago. And, as she had left the hospital an hour later, Abigail had felt nervous, wary. She had never allowed a patient to immerse themselves so deeply. There was no way she could have known that Peggy would regress to a concentration camp, still less that the climax of the experience would take her to the gas chambers and a fleeting moment with her friend.

"You have to keep some distance from Harry," Abigail said softly, holding Peggy's stare. "You know how it works. You died, Harry died. But you both lived again."

The girl was staring up at her. She swallowed hard.

"Now . . . try to steady your breathing. Just as I taught you to—yes?"

Peggy continued to stare at her, her eyes huge, their pupils dilated. Rivulets of sweat ran down her cheeks. Abigail could see that the pillow under Peggy's head was sodden, her hair a tangled wet mess.

"Breathe, Peggy, breathe. Slow your heartbeat . . . that's good—steady breaths."

The girl did as Abigail instructed. And gradually Peggy's breathing became slower, steadier.

Roger Gates came over and held his granddaughter's hand. The girl didn't take her stare from Abigail.

"That's great, Pegs . . . great . . . Good girl."

"You and me," Peggy said, her voice shaky.

"That's right. You and me—we can do it."

"No," Peggy said. "No, I don't mean that."

Roger lifted the girl's hand and kissed it. She ignored him.

"You and me, Abi—I want to talk to you."

Abigail gave the girl a brief smile. "Okay." She leaned towards Roger Gates. "You okay, if I . . . ?"

He looked disturbed, a trace of hurt in his eyes. "Um . . . yeah . . . If that's . . ."

Abigail glared impatiently at the doctor and the orderlies. The doctor glowered back.

"I think it would be for the best," Abigail said.

"I'm not so—" the doctor began.

"It's what my granddaughter wants," the senator said matter-of-factly. "Please . . ." Gates pointed toward the door.

"We'll be right outside," the doctor told Abigail and nodded to the nurses to go ahead of him.

When they had all left, Abigail pulled up a chair beside the bed and held the girl's hand. "Well, you certainly know how to clear a room!"

Peggy squeezed her hand.

"So. We're alone, Pegs. I'm all yours."

"You know me, don't you, Abi?"

Abigail examined those big dark eyes. There remained

175

an edge of panic in them, some personal, secret fear. For a moment she was unsure what to say. Peggy often made strange remarks, but there was always a meaning to them. It was just that sometimes you had to work hard to understand her.

"Abigail." Peggy's voice was growing steady now. She sounded almost like an adult. "I *know* you. You *know* me. We have always known each other."

"Yes," Abigail replied. "I think we have."

"I know we have. I've seen you in regressions. I've seen you in the in-between place."

"The in-between place? What do you mean, Peggy?"

"The place we go to between lives. I've been with you there."

Abigail did not know what to say. She felt incredibly uncomfortable suddenly.

"It is a place that is everywhere and nowhere, infinity and nothingness; so unlike any physical life." Peggy sounded older, wiser; her face and her voice no longer seemed to be related, one to the other. "It is a beautiful place," she went on. "It's not Heaven like the Bible stories, no angels or fluffy clouds." She gave Abigail a challenging look almost as though she were expecting a response and had prepared for an argument. But it passed quickly and she stared off into space.

"There's no God there either, Abi. No God. None at all. No trace of God. Just people, but not people. Am I making sense? I am, aren't I? I am making sense. No God, Abi. No God. Just people, the essence of people, the spirits of us all. I feel whole when I'm there. I never do here. I feel incomplete here, as though only a part of me is living this life. You understand, don't you? You do understand?"

Abigail scrutinized Peggy's face. The girl seemed incredibly calm. Ironically, talking about the in-between place seemed to have quietened her frenzied mind, spirit, soul . . . who could tell from where the pain had come?

"Could you untie me, please, Abi?"

The professor looked at the straps holding the girl's feet and wrists to the bed, and the restraints around her upper arms.

"This place," Abigail said, ignoring Peggy's request. "This place you're talking about. How do you get there? How do you leave?"

"I don't know. In a way I'm always there. We are always there. It's home. I see Harry there, Patrick too. And David and Elizabeth. And you. All of us."

"All of us? What are you talking about, Pegs?"

"You are Ruth."

"Ruth? Who is Ruth?" Abigail sensed a deep existential anxiety. For a horrible moment she felt as though she was floundering, stumbling in the dark. What Pandora's Box had she opened? Even after researching rebirth for more than two years, she knew so little. This young girl had entered the void, had seen things that could barely be imagined, things so far beyond the normal everyday world of the senses, the nuts-and-bolts universe we accept as "reality".

"You were Ruth in an earlier life. You *are* Ruth. You are many others, too."

"And who are Patrick and Elizabeth?"

"They are the wisest. David is Rex. Ruth is Magneilla. But we are one. We are six, but we are one."

177

"You're not making any sense, Peggy."

"Please untie me, Abi."

The professor gazed at Peggy's face, saw her serenity, so different from the way she had been only a few minutes ago. She was breathing steadily now, her eyes bright and alive, their pupils back to normal. Then Abigail looked at the straps again. Leaning forward, she started to unbuckle them slowly.

"Patrick, he's started to call us the Oneness of Many Parts. But he is ill once more. He doesn't know it yet, but he will leave this life soon."

"And Elizabeth?"

"She is also ill, but she is strong. She is fighting. Elizabeth is Cathy and she is wise. She is the wisest. But they will not stop. They keep hurting her."

"Hurting who? Who is Elizabeth?"

The restraints were undone. Abigail helped Peggy to sit up and the girl let her legs dangle over the side of the bed. She was perfectly relaxed now. She gave a little shiver.

"Here, Pegs, you're cold," Abigail said and swung round to pluck a blanket from a chair behind her.

Peggy was off the bed and hurtling toward the door before Abigail was even aware that she had moved. She tugged at the handle, the door opened and she vanished into the corridor.

Abigail dropped the blanket and sped across the room, almost colliding with the doctor and Roger Gates as they turned round to see Peggy charge out. Abigail had the momentum to keep going even though her feet were slipping on the polished floor.

Peggy was nimble, incredibly fast, and she pulled ahead. Racing along the corridor, she dodged the guards, and twenty feet from the end of the passage she lowered her head.

Abigail realized what Peggy was going to do a second before she did it, and knew that she could do nothing to stop her. Peggy was sprinting, running faster and faster toward the end of the corridor and a tall window protected by vertical steel bars spaced a few inches apart. Peggy slammed into the bars head first, her skull shattering on impact, the sound like the crack of a whip echoing round the corridor walls.

Chapter 23

Present Day

Returning to his apartment, Mark felt as though he had been away for days but it was only just over twelve hours since he had left for Johnny J's. The place was stifling and smelled musky. Instead of turning on the aircon, he crossed to the windows, unlocked them and pulled up the frames. The noise from the street rose dramatically but it was a fair trade-off.

He returned to the main room, opened his laptop, and while it booted up he walked through to the kitchenette where he found the coffee-maker. He had left the glass receptacle for the espresso in front of the machine, dried coffee grounds all over it. He shrugged, flicked the device on and began to make a strong brew. He yawned and rubbed his eyes. "Shit! I'm getting too old for this," he said quietly to himself.

Five minutes later Mark was back at the little table where he always worked. There was no way he could focus on his article for the paper now. In fact, in spite of what he had told Sam Helmer at the office, he had completely lost any interest in or motivation for writing anything about Abigail—or anything else, for that matter. His world had been turned upside down. He had no time for anything as trivial as his job, the *Courier*, Sam Helmer.

He lowered the blinds halfway down the windows, allowing a smudgy orange light into the room. Then he pulled up his chair, straightened the laptop, extricated the USB from his pocket and slotted it into the machine. A few keystrokes and he had the file in the center of his screen.

He tried to open it. A message appeared.

ENCRYPTED FILE

He right-clicked the mouse and a box opened.

PASSWORD PROTECTED. DO YOU WISH TO PROCEED?

Mark clicked the mouse again. A line of text slid across the center of the screen:

THE NAME OF THE FIRST WOMAN WHO BROKE YOUR HEART

Mark stared blankly at the laptop and then smiled. "Typical!" he said and took a sip of coffee before tapping in more words on the keyboard.

TANIA BRAITHWAITE

Another box appeared.

WHO ONCE CALLED YOU BOB?

Mark tapped in:

PATRICK

WHO INTRODUCED ME TO JAN?

MY COUSIN, HELEN

INCORRECT

"Bugger!" Mark exclaimed. He took another large gulp of hot coffee.

HELEN BRETTON

NAME THE MOST INTERESTING PERSON YOU'VE MET THIS YEAR.

Mark was surprised. He leaned back, cup in hand, then lowered it to the table without drinking. He typed:

ABIGAIL MARCHANT

The file opened.

Hi Mark,
By the time you read this I will be dead, but not
gone. Oh no, not gone. I'm writing this document a

short time after you left the house. I wanted to talk to you about the things I'm about to relate, but it just didn't seem right. It has never seemed right.

You told me you had met Abigail, and she must be the most interesting person you've met this year, so you have of course opened the file. An ingenious encryption, yeah? Only you knew the answers to all the questions.

So you must be surprised that I know Abigail and you must also be confused about what this is about. I know I would be!

God . . . so where do I begin?

Okay, let's be very dull and start at the beginning because I think you're probably quite confused enough, dear boy.

I've lived before: many times . . . So there you have it.

But then, so have you.

I wasn't as young as some kids are when they realize that they are living through just the latest of their lives. I was about to hit puberty and started to have very disturbing nightmares in which I was dying in different ways. My parents were bemused when I started gabbling on about brothers and sisters they never knew I had!

They took me to a doctor, then a shrink, but they all thought it was just a reaction to hormonal changes, and after that, my parents, being typically middle-class and British, just tried to pretend that the problem wasn't there. They approached it all very stoically and put it down to a "phase".

But then a weird coincidence occurred. My father: you remember him? You met him a few times, years ago. Well, he went to Oxford too, if you recall. He had an old friend from Balliol who was now a research scientist, a man named Elton-Hornsby, Hubert Elton-Hornsby. They had stayed in touch in a vague sort of way, but then Mama and Pa had their fifteenth wedding anniversary and Elton-Hornsby was invited. He'd been an usher at their wedding back in the 1970s.

Anyway, to cut a long story short, Elton-Hornsby stayed with us for a couple of days and he realized there was something not quite right about me. Pa confided in his old friend over a bottle of brandy one night, and suddenly my life was changed.

Turned out that Hubert Elton-Hornsby was a big cog at a research institute that was part of DERA—the Defence Evaluation and Research Agency. His team was based just outside Cambridge and was a kind of advanced-ideas think-tank, if you like. They had a division that worked on what they called "Paranormal Notions Research". He was very interested in what my parents described as my "symptoms" and explained that he and his team had encountered a similar phenomenon with other kids, usually four- or five-year-olds. He wanted me to come to Cambridge for a few days to undergo some tests.

Obviously, Mama and Pa weren't overly keen. But, as I said, Elton-Hornsby was an old friend and they eventually went along with it. And that was the start of six years of being a lab rat. I was regressed hundreds of times, using hypnotic techniques. Everything I said was recorded and documented, filed and cross-checked.

They didn't tell me much and I don't think the researchers told my parents more than a fraction of what they discovered, but I made it my mission to unearth all the material gathered on me between the ages of twelve and eighteen, and I actually know far more about my rebirth history than the DERA researchers realize.

Just a few months ago, about the time my cancer returned, I succeeded in hacking into their files. I wanted everything they had on me from the years I had given myself over to their work. I felt I was owed it. I have all this material secreted away somewhere and no one will find it without my help. Much of it is mundane, but it also contains some startling revelations. At the end of this message I have attached an encoded link for you to see a sample of what I have. Suffice it to say, it is a veritable gold mine of research into rebirthing. The Cambridge team cataloged no fewer than fifty-one of my past lives dating as far back as 400 BC.

Now, you probably have a thousand questions and I wish I could be there to answer them. Perhaps the greatest regret of my present life is that I was never able to talk to you about this business. I kept arranging times to do so: you probably remember now. There was the weekend you came to stay at my parents in London while they were away and we sat up late, drinking cheap wine and listening to early Pink Floyd and Soft Machine. I remember you asking me what the problem was and I just side-stepped . . . I could never figure out the best way to bring the subject up.

Anyway, the fact is that even though I was studied by the DERA team for six years, and I've found out a great deal about rebirth, I still have many more questions than answers. And I'm sure some things will remain a mystery no matter how many times we are reborn.

There seem to be certain laws that apply to rebirthing. I do not know how these laws came about or what their final purpose may be, but they are there. One of them is that human beings group together in sixes. What do I mean by that? I mean that through the ages humans travel through their lives in three pairs, three "male souls" and three "female souls". The pairs are what people refer to as "soulmates".

I don't know why I didn't talk to you about all this. Oh look, I must have known why at some level. But, well, by the time we met at university I was feeling very disillusioned and unhappy with the course that my life had taken. I was resentful of the fact that before I was old enough to know what I wanted to do my parents and their friends had made life-changing decisions for me.

It was my cancer, you see. Yeah, you've probably guessed it. I was first diagnosed when I was seventeen, and it was a direct result of too many regressions. And why do too many regressions make you ill? It is another one of those questions that I cannot answer. I just know they do. I was regressed three hundred and seventeen times in six years. It took its toll.

Maybe that is why I didn't want to talk to you about it. You were nothing to do with all that. You were my friend and you were not involved with the whole regression business. I wanted it to stay that way. I wanted our relationship to remain pure.

So what is it with Abigail? I've known her for almost six months. She somehow heard of me through her own researches and made contact. I met her in London. I learned a great deal from her and I like to think that she gained something from me, too.

We've stayed in touch. A few days ago she told me about your first regression and how remarkably detailed your experience had been. I don't know what it will lead to, Mark, at least not in this life. I know instinctively that I only have hours to live. So I will not know what you will learn.

I'm so glad you came to see me. Everything I said came from the heart. Even though I know it is not the end, that I shall be reborn, I do not want to die right now. I love Jan and the kids. I wanted to see my children grow up. I wanted to watch *This is Spinal Tap* with them and for them to get it. Existence is cruel. I feel cheated: death has come too soon. But I want you to know that your visit means so much to me. I wanted you to know all this. I wanted to say, as I lie here close to death, what it was I still couldn't bring myself to say to you face to face, even though I had discovered from Abigail that you too were able to regress.

You will learn a great deal from Abigail. But I'm sure you already know that.

Goodbye, my dearest friend.

Pat

Mark stared at the screen for a long time. He had been so lost in Patrick's words that the world had seemed to melt away. But as he stopped reading, reality began to encroach: the noises from the street, a light breeze rattling the blinds. He focused on the monitor, saw the link that Pat had mentioned earlier in the letter, and clicked on it. A sentence appeared.

WHAT WAS THE BEST GIG WE PLAYED?

Mark tapped in: JAIMIE'S 21st

WHAT'S MY FAVOURITE SHELDON?

He shook his head. Sidney bloody Sheldon! Patrick had once tried to explain his fixation to him, but he never did get it. He just accepted it, like sweeping under the carpet your girlfriend's undying love for the Bay City Rollers. He typed in *The Sky is Falling* and the site opened.

Mark saw a panel of subheadings and clicked on one called "Regression Chronology". It was a two-hundred-page document listing all Pat's fifty-one chronicled lives. He flicked through, speed-reading a few paragraphs here and there. It was written in the form of a lab report with dates, experimental conditions and a list of chemical names. "The subject regressed to Bolivia, circa 1755," he read. A few pages on: "The subject experienced distress during the description of his death throes in what appears to have been a battle in the First Napoleonic War. He emerged disorientated. We calmed him with Valium and Alprazolam, 0.5 mg."

Mark moved the cursor to the bottom of the document. "This is consistently the final regressive destination," he read. "We have tried to guide the subject, but without success. Conclusion: There is an unusually long gap between this final recordable incarnation and the present one. Explanation: Unknown." Mark moved the cursor up the page. At the top it said: "Subject returned to March 1916, the Battle of Verdun. He was a private named Neville Sinclair. Describes experiences in the trenches in graphic detail. Became greatly agitated seventeen minutes into regression. Standard reaction to death experience."

Mark paused for a moment. He knew that Pat had been born in May 1976. He should have had at least one more life during the sixty years between 1916 and 1976. "Another mystery," he said aloud and shifted the cursor to a tab that read: "Video One". He clicked, and a list of clips appeared, each followed by a reference number. Mark chose one at random and the film opened.

It showed an over-lit room with stark white walls. A chair, like something from a dentist's surgery, was placed in the center of the floor. Two men in scrubs stood by the chair. A teenage Patrick—Mark guessed he was about fourteen—sat in the chair. Mark was startled to see that

189

the boy had hair—lush auburn curls. He had seen a few pictures of Pat taken before they had met at Oxford, but for some reason seeing him on film was different. Mark swallowed hard. This was more difficult to watch than he could have imagined.

One of the men placed a hypodermic against Patrick's forearm, pushed in the needle and depressed the plunger. Pat closed his eyes and started to talk straight away. With shocking clarity, his adult voice came through the speaker. Mark flinched involuntarily. "Okay. So, Mark," Pat was saying over the film, "this is me, June 1990. I'm fourteen and I had no idea what they were pumping into me. It was only later I learned that at various junctures they had used floroxinin, tipazamine, deoxydeprazone, mitophosphine and barium diglutonaphylharpinin. These were to calm me, to free my mind, to open neural pathways to repressed memories, and to increase the impact of the hypnosis techniques they employed. It was a carcinogenic blend, of course, which only exaggerated my body's negative reaction to such frequent regressions."

Patrick was silent for a few moments and Mark could hear what the boy in the film clip was saying. *The boom of the big guns . . . I 'ear it in me sleep. I 'ear it all the time. Sometimes I don't know if it's real or just in me head. The other day I couldn't shake the boom from me head. I thought me brain was gonna explode. And then I had an idea. I would get me head blown off. That would stop the fuckin' boom. I dropped my rifle at the dugout door, took off me helmet and started to climb up the mud.*

The fourteen-year-old Patrick paused. He seemed unable to speak for a second. His face had been without expression but now a look of contrition appeared. It was followed quickly by a nervous smile, then a look of shame.

I almost made it, too, but the mud . . . it stopped me, see. I couldn't get a grip. I couldn't reach the . . . The sergeant caught me, cuffed me around the ear, he did. Put me on report, the bastard.

"This was always the most recent life I could reach," Patrick said. The film clicked off.

Mark kept his hand lightly on the mouse and was about to move the cursor. The doorbell rang. It took a moment before he realized what the sound was.

He pulled himself up from the chair, walked to the door, peered into the spyhole and saw Abigail standing in the hall.

"I've been calling you all morning," she said as Mark let her in.

He picked up his cell from the table. The battery was flat. He held up the phone to show her.

"You look dreadful, Mark. What the hell have you been doing?"

"You're the second person today who has said that."

"It looks like you haven't slept. You're still wearing—"

"I *haven't* slept. Look, you want a coffee?"

Mark went off to the kitchen and Abigail nosed around the room, looking at the rows of books on the shelves that stretched across an entire wall of the apartment. On the floor stood boxes of vinyl. On a table in the corner sat a record deck and a top-end amp. Curios lined the mantelpiece over a disused fireplace filled with more books. She saw a terracotta warrior's head, a Venetian mask, a glass ampule on a wooden stand, a bird's skull.

Mark came in with two cups and handed one to Abigail. Abigail lowered herself onto the beaten-up old chesterfield opposite the wall of books.

"So what's happened?" she asked.

He told her about his British abductor. She looked suitably shocked. "Christ, Mark!"

"Yeah—I've been a journalist for a dozen years but never been abducted. Seems I'm keeping dangerous company." There was an edge to his voice.

She held his gaze. It was obvious that she didn't know quite how to react.

He took a gulp of coffee. "I got a call from the widow of my old friend, Patrick Clifton—remember I mentioned him to you?"

She nodded.

"Why didn't you tell me you knew Pat, Abigail?"

"I was going to. I just got swept up with it all. How do you . . . ?"

"He left me a message. It's on my laptop. Jan found it on a USB. It was password-protected. He directed me to a secret website that is also encrypted."

Abigail sipped her coffee.

"I'm pretty damn angry, actually," Mark said. He sat down heavily on the arm of the chesterfield. "You told Pat about me. You had no right." The sounds of the street seemed suddenly louder. Mark felt blood pounding through his ears. He hated conflict, avoided it at all costs, but he was riled. "Why have you been so secretive?"

"I'm sorry, Mark. It probably sounds lame to you, but

192

I wanted you to behave naturally. I didn't want to burden you with too much. When we first met you were so, well . . . so *defensive*."

"I was skeptical. There's a difference."

"Yes, I know, and I understand that."

"Oh, good!"

Abigail paused and looked around at the room. "If I've upset you, I'm truly sorry. But you have to accept the fact that I couldn't say any more than I did. What would you have thought if I had told you a couple of days ago that I knew Patrick? That your old friend—your closest friend—was a research subject for the British Secret Service? And a gifted regressor? You would have thought I was a nut!"

"My best friend couldn't tell me what was happening, either. He kept it from me all these years. What's wrong with everyone?"

"I think you're primarily angry with Patrick, Mark . . . and you can't do anything about it."

"That sounds like psychobabble to me. Seems to me you're trying to duck out of it."

She sighed. "I didn't mean it like that."

"So how did you mean it, then? I'm curious."

"I stick by my decision to say nothing about Patrick. It would have been a crazy thing to introduce into an already freaky-enough mix. You see that, don't you?"

Mark looked at Abigail, his expression lightening a little. "Well, Pat's story fills in the background and it explains the business with this Elton-Hornsby character. He kept asking if Pat had passed anything on to me."

"May I ask what Pat said in his personal message to you?"

Mark shrugged. "It was mainly private—an apology, really. He had wanted to tell me about his experiences for years but could never bring himself to."

"Did he say why?"

"He'd grown resentful of the way he had been treated. He was bitter that he had contracted cancer because of the experiments. Said he wanted to keep our relationship 'pure'. He told me he knew you, that you had met . . . in London. He said I could trust you, and talked about something he called 'groups of six'."

She raised an eyebrow at that. "Must have been confusing for you."

"I'm learning fast, Abigail."

She came over and sat on the sofa close to where he was perched. Looking up, she said: "I really am sorry I upset you by not saying anything. There's nothing sinister about it, I promise you. I guess my obsession with my work led me to tell Patrick about you. It was unprofessional of me."

Mark exhaled loudly. "Apology accepted. It's just . . . why didn't Pat tell me? I can accept his reasoning, but I thought there were no secrets between us."

"It must come as a shock."

"I'm getting used to shocks." Then he seemed to let it go. "So why are you here again?"

She laughed and the tension broke. "You *have* had a rough time of it, Mark. You said last night you wouldn't mind if we worked on a Saturday!"

"Ah yes, I did, didn't I? So what now?"

"How about we catch a cab to my office and see what happens when you regress. If you're still game."

Mark stared into her eyes. "Oh, I'm game, Abigail. I'm game."

PART 4

"Jack, Jack, Jack. Can you hear me? I love you."

Chapter 24

Oh fuck! The noise! What the hell is happening?

I hear so many voices, coming from all directions. We are accelerating away fast, the huge Chevy engine growling like a disgruntled grizzly. I'm thrown back in the seat and grab hold of the leather strap above the door to my left.

Outside the car, a kaleidoscope of movement and color; women screaming, people running. I see a man in slacks and a short-sleeved shirt gather up a small boy and cover him on the ground with his own body. A woman in a headscarf stands rigid, her hand to her mouth as though she has been frozen in time, her handbag about to slip to the grass from her fingers. Through the windshield I see the next car ahead of us in the motorcade, a white Ford carrying the Dallas Mayor, Earle Cabell, swerve right, then left and we almost plough into the back of it before it speeds away with a screech of tire rubber.

I catch sight of the president's car about forty feet ahead. Jack has slumped down. I can barely see him and Jackie has twisted in her seat and started to scramble back, out and across the trunk. Even from here I can see she is covered with blood. There are streaks of it across her pink jacket and dripping from her chin. For a second

I think she has been hit too. A man appears on the trunk. I recognize him as Secret Service Agent Clint Hill, assigned to protect Jackie. He's a well-built guy who had been on the running board of the car behind the president's. He has jumped from the car, sprinted to the Kennedys' limo and grabbed a metal grip on the trunk. Using the car bumper as support, he is throwing himself forward, guiding Jackie back down into the car. Another man leaps from the Cadillac immediately behind the limo and starts to run as fast as he can, but he can't catch up as the car accelerates away. It is Agent John Ready—I was drinking with him last night. He slows, swings round at a yell from his superior, and bolts back to the follow-up car. The agents there are waving frantically toward the vice-president's car, signaling its driver, the Texas state trooper Hurchel Jacks, to close the gap.

Through the radio we hear the cross-talk from the agents in the lead cars, their voices desperate, edged with panic. Roy Kellerman cuts through the others. "Lawson, we're hit," he yells, calling Secret Service Agent Winston Lawson in the Dallas Police car directly ahead of the limo. "Get us to the hospital immediately."

I hear in the background sounds from inside the president's car, screams, Kellerman bellowing: "Go!" to Bill Greer, Jack's driver, and faintly, from far back in the limo, comes Jackie's pathetic wail and eight words. "My God, they have shot his head off."

Immediately, the white police car and a phalanx of outriders swerve away to the left and tear ahead. I hear the police car's siren start up. Our driver, Neil Juffie, slams his foot down on the accelerator and I'm thrown back again into the rear seat. I look to my right. We are flashing past stunned witnesses. Some have barely started to react, others are running. The first bullet was fired only a few seconds ago but it seems like hours, seems like some of the people beyond the window are actors in a movie, the film slowed down artificially.

A dozen yards to my right is a small hill, a patch of green, a concrete wall, some trees and a wooden fence. Some of the bystanders are twisting round to look at something or someone at the top of the knoll. A motorcycle cop pulls over, jumps off his bike leaving the machine on its side. He rushes up the hill pulling out his pistol. I can just glimpse a man dressed in black, but we are accelerating so fast that I cannot make out any details. As we face away, I think I see him tug a rifle over his shoulder and vanish behind some trees.

Darkness. We're roaring under the triple underpass that takes the road beneath a railway bridge. I saw the layout of the area during the briefing last night. Now the lead cars tear past the cop car as they emerge from the far end of the underpass. The road under the bridge is only a couple of dozen yards long and we are screeching out the other side into the dazzling sunlight, our car still accelerating. We must be doing seventy, minimum. The driver is determined to get up there with the lead vehicles and we shoot past the white Dallas Police car as well. There are just four cars now pulling away from the rest, the president's limo, with Agent Clint Hill still clinging on for dear life, the Secret Service follow-up car with half a dozen agents inside and on the runners, the vice-president's limo, and us. And we are all still gaining speed.

I gaze back through the rear window of the Chevy and see a confusion of vehicles at the exit of the Triple Underpass. Scores of people line the streets, none of them seem to know about anything that has happened a few hundred yards back in Dealey Plaza. Bystanders are filming the muddle of cars.

"Where's the nearest hospital?" Malcolm Kilduff asks. His voice is still shaky and I can hardly hear him over the wailing of sirens and the roar of the powerful engine. I shake my head. I have no idea. Juffie takes a hard right and we follow the other cars onto Stemmons Freeway, heading north.

There are hundreds of spectators on either side of the freeway. This is the route the motorcade was scheduled to take. We are still on our way to the Trade Mart where Jack was due to attend a luncheon.

The car radio crackles again, more voices. All the radios are open. "We're going to the hospital," I hear. I think it's one of the guys in the lead car driven by the local Police Chief, Jesse Curry. "Parkland. It's about three miles ahead."

"Got that," comes another voice.

"Have 'em stand by. Get men on top of that there underpass. See what happened up there. Have Parkland stand by."

I flick my gaze toward the speedometer on the dash. We are topping eighty. Half a dozen bikes race on a few yards ahead of us. They're guarding the presidential car and the Lincoln carrying Johnson. I can just make out Clint Hill still grasping the handhold on the trunk of the limo. He's hammering the metal beside him with his right

*fist and shaking his head. Then I see him glare back, just
for a few seconds. He catches the eye of Ken O'Donnell
in the follow-up car and gives him a thumbs-down.*

*I turn as Kilduff looks round at me. He has seen it too.
Just at that moment everyone in our car picks out Jackie's
pitiful voice. "Jack, Jack, Jack. Can you hear me? I love
you."*

*I feel sick in the pit of my stomach and I think there
is no way I can throw up: not now, not as people are
dying and suffering, not as my friend slips away. For in
that moment, I think of Jack as my friend. In that moment,
we are all equals. Jackie's cry of pain and horror and
loss is mine too.*

*An outside transmission breaks through the intermittent
babble of cross-talk and it seems that everyone else
hooked up to the same frequency shuts up to hear what
is being said. "United Press International," a dislocated
male voice intones. "Three shots were fired at President
Kennedy's motorcade today in downtown Dallas."*

*Tires squeal as Juffie swerves to the left; another thud
and a grinding as the car protests. Two cops stand outside
the Trade Mart, looking bewildered. They start to wave
their arms. Immediately to our offside, a motorcycle cop
almost loses control of his bike. Dust powders the windshield, and for a second the view of the freeway is
obscured. Juffie puts on the wipers and it clears as we
pull off onto a smaller road and over a cattle grille. The
bump sends Malcolm sprawling half off his seat. I go to
grab him with my free hand and feel the vomit come up
into my throat. I keep it down, yank Kilduff back and take
several deep breaths, a medley of sounds break over me,*

203

the screech of tires, the wailing of sirens, the roar of the cars, and there, faintly in the background, the sound of Jackie in the presidential limo crying over the open radio microphone.

Chapter 25

When I open my eyes I can see through the dusty windshield a large modern concrete building rearing up on our right. A sign flashes past. It reads: PARKLAND MEMORIAL HOSPITAL.

Our car comes to a stop almost bumper to bumper with the limo carrying two Secret Service guys, Jacks and Youngblood, in the front, vice-president Johnson and his wife Lady Bird in the middle row, and Senator Ralph Yarborough in the rear.

Agents jump out of the other cars ahead of us. Youngblood leaps from the convertible that is carrying the vice-president. A second later Ken O'Donnell sprints from the follow-on car. Four Special Agents follow close behind. But Chief of the Secret Service detail, Roy Kellerman, who has been in the front of the targeted car, is first off the blocks and runs over to the doors to the emergency entrance. He arrives at the doors and bellows "Get two gurneys here . . . NOW!" Jack's driver stays at the wheel, the car's engine idling. Clint Hill finally slips down onto the bumper and then, a little unsteadily, he reaches the tarmac. He is the first to make it to the back seats of the presidential car.

But I'm not far behind. Everyone here knows me and

I'm wearing my pass for anyone at the hospital who doesn't. I'm considered one of the inner circle, with full access. I race from the rear of the Chevrolet and Kilduff half stumbles out through the other passenger door. Agent Neil Juffie is a few steps ahead of us. I turn as I pass the vice-president's limo. Johnson is sitting bolt upright, his face white as albumen. Beside him is Lady Bird, shrunken, tiny.

The president's car is swarming with people. Clint Hill is leaning in towards Jackie from the open door on her side. The First Lady is crouching over her husband, rocking gently and cradling his head. I can hear her whimpering. As I approach the door I almost expect to hear a familiar voice say, "Hey, guys, I'm all right," and for Jack to raise himself on one elbow. But instead I see something very different.

The inside of the car has been splattered red and gray. It looks like the work of some crazy artist, a Jackson Pollock disciple given free rein with an aerosol paint can. Jackie's clothes are splashed and soaked in places where she has been holding Jack's head against her.

And then there is Jack himself. He is lying slumped— half on, half off the seat. Jackie is trying to keep his head out of sight but in spite of her best efforts the damage is obvious. Half his skull has been blown away. I can see the gray of brain tissue on his cheeks, blood oozing over the rippled folds of his ragged cerebral cortex, the startling white of bone, the inside surface of his skull ripped aside and flipped back. I smell the president's blood. The stench is blended with that of sweat and urine. Jack's left eyeball is bulging out of its socket.

Congealing blood covers his face so that he is barely recognizable as the man I had seen and spoken to such a short time ago. And it is only then that I realize just five minutes have passed since the shooting started.

"Oh, my God! Mr. President, what did they do?" I say, shaking my head.

Jackie looks up at me. "Dave, he's dead."

Ken O'Donnell says something to Hill and the agent moves aside to let his superior through, but he stays close to the opened door. I hear Nellie Connally, the Governor's wife, yelling for help. No one seems to have noticed that her husband, who was sitting directly in front of Jack, has been grievously wounded. He is slumped in his seat, barely breathing, his wife clinging to him. "For God's sake, will someone help us?" she cries.

Two stretchers on wheels arrive at that moment, each pushed by an agent, and three doctors and a group of nurses stream through the emergency doors onto the tarmac. I hear the crunch of brakes and two more vehicles pull up—another Secret Service vehicle carrying four agents and a police car. Two state troopers leap out and rush toward us.

Kellerman appears at my elbow and pushes me to one side as he yells above the near-hysteria of the people crowding around the limo. Two agents help a doctor get Connally onto one of the stretchers. He is bleeding profusely, his jacket and shirt red, his face blue. He is gasping for air. Nellie is on the verge of hysteria, tears streaking her face as she tries to help but just gets in the way. One of the newly arrived troopers takes Mrs. Connally's arm and leads her along beside the stretcher, *allowing one of the doctors to get to work on the injured man as he is wheeled toward the doors into the emergency room.*

I whirl back to the car and see that O'Donnell has reached round to Jackie's side and is talking to her. "Mrs. Kennedy, you've got to get out," he says with uncharacteristic gentleness.

"There's no need," Jackie sobs.

O'Donnell leans in and tries very carefully to lift Jackie's arm from across Jack's face. But she won't move.

"Please, Mrs. Kennedy," O'Donnell is saying softly.

Jackie merely moans.

It is odd but I can hear every word in spite of the pandemonium.

"Please," Clint Hill says, leaning in behind O'Donnell. "We must get the president to a doctor."

"I'm not going to let him go," Jackie gasps.

"We've got to take him in," Hill says desperately.

"No, Mr. Hill. You know he's dead," Jackie snaps. "Let me alone."

Then O'Donnell realizes why the First Lady is resisting. It's because she cannot bear the thought of people seeing the state that Jack is in. She knows from experience that cameramen will have arrived by now. O'Donnell removes his jacket and places it over Jack's head and chest. Jackie looks up and moves her arm away.

Roy Kellerman rushes over to where the vice-president and Lady Bird are still sitting like wax figures in the light blue Lincoln convertible, and I know what this means. He is about to instruct the new leader of the nation what to do next.

I'm not sure why, but for all the clinical coolness of the action I accept that this has to be done. But there's something more—there's a deeper sense of acceptance building inside me.

As I stand and look around, there is panic and chaos all about me. Jackie is still moaning softly, but the sound is amplified in my ears and in my mind. People are rushing about. Doctors tear across the tarmac, shouting at nurses. Secret Service men, paranoid by nature, don't know quite what to do. For a while at least they have to hand over the reins of guardianship to medics. More cars screech to a stop behind the line of vehicles outside the doors to the ER. I hear the hospital doors crash apart as Connally's gurney goes inside.

But, for a moment, it is all hyper-real, like a dream. Everything is contorted. I look over to the presidential limo and I see a haziness around Jack's body. It is there for just a second, a shimmering—an effect of the light, maybe. But then I hear Jack's voice. I know it is him, even if it does not sound like the man's living voice, the slightly adenoidal warm voice I had come to know so well. I know this voice more intimately, although it is not really a voice at all, it's a vibration, a tremor in my chest, in my heart, a throbbing in my brain. It is the sound of a soul I have known forever and, although I cannot hear clear, definite words, I know what Jack is saying. He is saying: "It's all right. It's all right. I'll see you again soon." And I know Jack is "speaking" to me and only to me.

Chapter 26

Jack's gurney crashes through the doors of the ER. A doctor is yelling something I cannot make out. The pandemonium is amplified now in this confined space just inside the building as the sounds bounce around the concrete walls.

I run in, close to the gurney. Jackie has placed her hat and the bunch of red roses she was given at Love Field on top of Jack's body. At the end of the corridor I catch sight of the stretcher carrying Senator Connally.

A flash bulb goes off. It is the first I've seen since we were on Stemmons Freeway. Clint Hill turns to see who is taking pictures but he is swept along with the human tide flooding the corridor and heading for Trauma Room 1 directly ahead.

I catch sight of my boss Malcolm Kilduff a few yards back. I have not seen him since we all piled out of the Chevrolet. He starts to barge his way in. Then I feel an elbow hard in my side, turn round and see Merriman Smith, one of the Press guys I had met the day before in Houston.

He recognizes me. "How is he, David?" he asks.

For a second I lose it. "He's dead," I snap and immediately regret it as I see the man spin on his heel and battle his way toward a phone we passed a second ago.

Trauma Room 1 is a narrow room about twenty feet by twelve with gray tiled walls and an off-white ceiling. The gurney is pushed in and shoved against a rack of machines with tubes and wires dangling from them. There is just one doctor in the room waiting for us, a dark-haired guy who looks younger than me. In spite of his youth, he has an air of authority and the crowd breaks around him. Two nurses keep us all back in the corridor and the door is slammed shut.

There is a window onto the trauma room and I see the young doctor checking the president's mouth and shining a torch into his eyes. A group of medics run toward us along the corridor and race into the room. They spread out. Each of them obviously knows their role precisely.

Although the view is obscured by the doctors I can see there is blood everywhere. The sheet the president is lying on is stained red, with barely a patch of white cotton left, and the floor is slippery with blood. It seems to be oozing from holes all over Jack's body.

I hear a commotion behind me as O'Donnell tries to comfort Jackie. Then Johnson's wife Lady Bird arrives and pushes her way through the pressing bodies and pulls Jackie away to a couple of chairs a few yards along the corridor and out of sight of the window. There is no sign of Johnson. I guess he must have been whisked away by the Secret Service and put in another room for his own safety. I notice that Kellerman and a couple of his men are no longer with us in the hall.

I swing back to the window and see one of the doctors make a cut-down along Jack's left arm. Another doctor is leaning over Kennedy's head and beginning an emergency tracheotomy. Jack lies as still as a pebble on the beach. His chest is not moving. He is flat on his back, his eyes staring blankly at the ceiling. The doctors prod and poke and cut and slice and there's no reaction from him. I start to wonder why they are bothering at all: the man is clearly dead. But I know they have to do their duty: they have to make every possible effort to save the president, even if they too know that he is, without a doubt, deceased.

I hear Jackie's voice and look around. She is up out of the chair and shaking her head. Lady Bird is trying to calm her, but I cannot make out her words above the noise all around. Jackie moves quickly past me along the corridor. As she reaches the door of the trauma room a nurse emerges. I read her ID tag: Nurse Doris Nelson. She has a dreadful, mournful look on her face.

"I'm going in there," Jackie says very quietly.

Nurse Nelson is a big woman. She takes a step back and folds her arms. "You can't come in here," she says, her voice level, the same tone she would use for any relative of any patient.

Jackie lifts her head slightly. "I'm coming in and I'm staying." She walks forward and the nurse does not budge. Jackie puts out her hands to move the woman aside but Nurse Nelson stands her ground.

"I'm going to get in that room," Jackie hisses.

I'm beginning to wonder how this will conclude when Agent Clint Hill appears at the corner a few yards away. He marches over and demands to know what is happening. The nurse gives him a hard look.

"I want to be in there when he dies, Clint," Jackie says pathetically. A tear spills from her right eye and runs down her bloodied cheek.

"Do you think you should take a sedative, Mrs. Kennedy?" Clint asks gently.

Jackie whirls on him. *"No! I just want to be with Jack!"*

Hill takes Jackie's elbow and moves her forward. Nurse Nelson starts to move to block them and Clint gives her such a deadly look that she backs off. *"It's her right,"* the agent says forcefully and they sweep past the woman into the room.

The nurse walks away towards an admin room, presumably to complain to her superior, and I slip into Trauma Room 1 along with Malcolm Kilduff, O'Donnell and an agent I know only by sight.

The room is packed now. A throng of doctors and nurses surround the gurney. I stand back and watch as Jackie squeezes her way toward where Jack is lying.

One of the doctors, a man in his early forties, is clearly in charge now. He is calling out instructions to the others. He swings round as Jackie appears at his elbow and remains admirably calm. He pauses for a second, his gloved, bloodied hands out in front of him. *"Mrs. Kennedy,"* he says.

I can see the side of Jackie's face. It looks like a blood-flecked porcelain sculpture, her exquisite profile framed by dark waves of hair, large eyes staring fixedly at her husband lying motionless under the harsh bleaching bulbs. His skin is blue, his flesh smeared with blood. More blood drips off the edge of the gurney and pools at the surgeon's cotton-covered shoes. Jackie brings a hand to *her mouth, turns slowly and walks straight toward where I'm standing close to the wall. She gazes up and recognizes me. I can feel tears on my face and my skin is cold. I feel not a trace of shame as I let the tears tumble.*

I take a step toward Jackie. She is moving in a daze. She stares down at her right hand. It is clasped tight. I stop and watch her as she moves a few more steps toward me, her arm outstretched. I take the thing in her hand and she walks past me. I peer down to see a piece of Jack's brain the size of a golf ball.

Chapter 27

Air rushes from my lungs and a pain stabs my chest. Acting on autopilot, I step to my right, see an empty surgical dish on top of a cabinet and place the piece of Jack into it. Hearing a new sound, I look back and see that Jackie has fallen to her knees. She is facing the corner of the small, crowded room and is praying quietly.

Without thinking, I bring my palm to my face. I can smell the president's brain tissue on my hand and quickly pull it away. I see the soles of Jack's feet a yard ahead of me, a glimpse of his bare upper half. One of the doctors starts to give him heart massage. Then, for the first time, I notice a monitor on a spindly metal stand close to the end of the gurney. It bleeps unsteadily, a white trace flicks up and then down leaving a ghost of light in its wake. As I watch, the flicker stops, a single line swims across the screen, blinks out and starts again. Straight line, ghost image, blink . . . straight line, ghost image, blink.

"Somebody get me a stool," the doctor snaps. A nurse sees one a few feet away and pulls it over. The doctor leaps onto it so that he can find a better angle to massage the president's heart. I see his forearms push and pull back. Again . . . and again. After five more pushes, he stops, leans back and lowers his surgical mask. "It's too

late," he says. He steps down from the stool and tugs off his latex gloves, sighing heavily. Another doctor to his left, a short man with a receding hairline, leans in and pulls the sheet up over Jack's head.

Jackie appears at my left and I move away to stand close to the door that leads out to the corridor.

"Your husband has received a fatal wound," the chief medic says.

"I know," Jackie whispers.

I count eight people in the passageway, including Lady Bird and Roy Kellerman who looks flushed as though he has been running. I shake my head slowly. Lady Bird jerks away and her shoulders shake. Through the door, I can hear her wail.

The room starts to empty. I feel Kilduff's hand on my shoulder. Two nurses disconnect the tubes and the wires to the monitors. Soon I am out in the corridor, staring at the tiled floor as I walk away from the open doorway. I gaze back through the large window into the trauma room and see that only Jackie and O'Donnell are left in there with Jack. O'Donnell is weeping openly.

Jackie walks over to the gurney and starts to kiss her husband's body through the sheet. She begins at his feet and moves slowly up to his shattered head. All around her nurses are mopping up the puddles of blood and ooze on the tiled floor.

There is a sound from the end of the corridor. A priest stands there. He is wearing a black robe and a purple and white stole around his shoulders. In his left hand he holds a small black box and there is a Bible in his right. One of the Secret Service guys opens the door to the trauma room and the priest hurries inside. Those of us gathered in the corridor look on as the priest leans over Jack, pulls back the sheet and anoints the dead man's forehead with holy oil. We cannot hear what he is saying but the Catholics among us would recognize the words used as the priest administers the sacrament of extreme unction and an absolution.

The priest pulls back and O'Donnell says something inaudible, then bows his head as the priest offers a prayer. The nurses have all stopped cleaning up and stand motionless, looking at the floor. One of them wipes a moist eye, another brings a hand silently to her mouth and I see her shake with barely suppressed grief.

I know that Jack left his body before we were even inside the hospital. I saw him go, or at least a faint glimmer of his leaving, some resonance of a soul, or whatever. I can't explain it. I've never been a religious man but at this moment I know there is some otherworldly connection between the spirit that had resided in Jack Kennedy and the one that resides in me.

The door opens. Jackie is the last to leave. She looks like a bleached-out photograph: the colors—the red on the pink dress and jacket, the red on her almost translucent skin, her raven hair about her pure white throat—all are faded. She walks unsteadily toward us. Lady Bird grabs her left arm before any of the Secret Service guys can move an inch and she helps her to a chair where she slumps like a sack of grain.

I spin round to my left and see my boss Malcolm Kilduff. He has a cigarette at the corner of his mouth and indicates with a flick of the head that I should follow *him. He leads the way to the end of the corridor where it joins the main passageway from the entrance. Three state troopers are blocking anyone from coming any closer to the trauma room. There are at least twenty Press men in the corridor. I hear shouts, protests. One of the men in the group spots us. I know him from the Texas TV network. He calls over, but I ignore him. A flash bulb goes off, and for a second my vision is flooded with intense white. I feel angry. "Hey!" I shout at the photographer, but the sound is lost and I'm being pulled away along another corridor. Then we stop. Malcolm is gripping my forearms and staring at me. I feel his thumbs through the fabric of my suit.*

"You okay, kid?" he asks, staring into my eyes.

I nod and take a deep breath. "I guess."

"Good," Kilduff replies. "The day has only just started!"

We walk along the corridor, turn left and see two of the agents from the motorcade standing together, an open door behind them. They step aside and we walk into a large room with four beds, curtains drawn back. Sunlight spills in through a window across from the door. Lyndon Johnson sits on the edge of the nearest bed on the left. Agents Youngblood and Bill McIntyre from the presidential follow-up car stand close by, while Roy Kellerman, the Secret Service Chief, is trying to get a point across to Johnson. Kellerman stops as he sees us enter.

"He's gone," Kilduff says as we step into the room.

All four men stand gaping, like automatons from some ridiculous science fiction movie with their plugs pulled. Johnson is the first to react. "Oh my God!" he exclaims and steps down from the edge of the bed.

"I know this might seem like a terrible time to mention it, sir," Kilduff goes on, "but the world has got to know that President Kennedy is dead."

"Don't they know it already?" Kellerman says, confused.

I study my boss's face. It is drained of blood and he seems to have aged ten years in the past hour. "I haven't told them," he says slowly.

Kellerman nods to Youngblood and the agent walks to the door with Malcolm following close behind. "You wait here, Dave," Kilduff says over his shoulder.

Kellerman clears his throat. "Mr. President?"

Johnson jolts and jerks his head up. It seems to have only just struck him that he is now the thirty-sixth President of the United States. He turns quickly to face Kellerman. "What'll we do, Roy? What'll we do?"

"You'd better get the hell out of here," Kellerman replies, "and get back to Washington straight away. Take Air Force One."

"What about Mrs. Kennedy?"

"She will not leave the hospital without her husband."

"I don't want to leave Mrs. Kennedy like this."

"I'll stay with her until she is ready to leave, sir."

Agent McIntyre steps away toward one of the other beds and is talking into his radio. I catch the words "unmarked car" and "side entrance omega".

Johnson fixes Kellerman with a hard look, shakes his head slightly and heads for the door, escorted by Agent McIntyre and the two men who had been posted in the corridor. He stops as he reaches the door. "You take good care of that fine lady," he says and turns right, away from the main corridor.

Halfway back to the reception area Kellerman peels off and heads for the main doors. I can see past the growing throng that more cars have crowded into the parking area outside the hospital. I count a dozen uniformed policemen and guys in black suits whom I don't recognize. I check my lapel to make sure I still have my White House Press Corps ID and I almost crash into Nellie Connally who is being comforted by Lady Bird as the two women approach the foot of a flight of stairs from the second floor. I suddenly feel a pang of guilt because, in all the time I've been in the hospital, I've not given a single thought to the seriously wounded senator. But I can tell from Mrs. Connally's expression that her husband is still alive. "Mrs. Connally," I say gently and extend a hand to help her take the last step to the corridor. "How is he?"

"David . . ." She looks like she's about to cry. "He's terribly injured . . . but they think he's going to survive."

I exhale. "That is good news."

"He's in surgery," Lady Bird adds.

I escort the two women away from the baying crowd of journalists and photographers. More flash bulbs go off, and in a few seconds we round the corner into the corridor leading to the two trauma rooms.

I let the women go and cross the main hall to find a water fountain. I suddenly realize I'm parched and cannot remember the last time I drank anything. As I slot the paper cup under the tap and watch the water tumble, I look left and see that a man is pushing against the far side of a service door leading from a courtyard. Behind him stand three other men, all dressed identically in black jackets and overcoats, black ties and white shirts. They are trying to navigate something through the opening. I walk over to help with the door and see that the men are funeral workers. A black casket on a trolley stands between them.

I press back against the wall and let them by. The last man through nods gravely as he passes. I stare back after them and then away to the corridor the far side of the main hall where, some hundred feet away, Jackie, O'Donnell, Clint Hill and a couple of other agents stand in a small huddle. Jackie looks up and sees the men and the casket coming toward her.

I scoot down the passage and across the hall into the corridor that leads to the trauma room and the dead president. Hill and O'Donnell are trying to persuade Jackie to come with them, to sit in another room so that the funeral guys can get on with it. But she's not listening. She is staring at the black casket as it rattles toward her. The four men in black overcoats look everywhere but directly at the widow. They go into the trauma room and Jackie follows them. O'Donnell makes a half-hearted attempt to stop her but lets his hand fall to his side. Clint Hill steps back. I reach the door to the trauma room. Seeing that O'Donnell has gone in, I edge through the door very quietly.

Two of the men maneuver the trolley carrying the coffin parallel to the gurney and open the lid to reveal a sump-tuous padded white satin lining. The leader of the team walks over to a cupboard, and without a word he removes a pile of sheets and towels. He hands these out and the men line the coffin with them, creating a well-protected

221

area where Kennedy's head will rest. They remove the sheet covering Jack and lift his body. He is covered in gore still and his head wound gapes horribly, a red and gray crater, his hair drenched in blood. It's a struggle but they manage to get Kennedy into the box.

I've been standing back against the wall. O'Donnell is by Jackie's side. She walks over to the casket and the men step back. She looks down at her dead husband and slips off her wedding ring. Then she leans in and places it on Jack's finger.

"Did I do the right thing?" Jackie asks, suddenly anxious, scanning O'Donnell's face.

"You leave it right where it is," he says.

"Now I have nothing left," Jackie mumbles.

The casket is wheeled through the door right behind us, and as I leave the trauma room, Kellerman and four secret service agents come quickly round the corner from the main hall.

"We're going out through the rear entrance," Kellerman says firmly and nods toward the funeral workers. "The area has been cleared." Clint Hill falls in behind Jackie and we start to move off back along the corridor. I hang back, the last of the group.

Twenty yards along the main hall, just short of the rear exit, the whole party stops. I move forward to see what is happening.

A slender man in a dark suit and black tie is standing with his right hand up, palm out. His face is so narrow that it looks almost surgically altered. He has a pipe stuck in the top pocket of his jacket and just beneath this rests an ID tag. I read: "Earl Rose: Dallas County Coroner".

"You cannot take the president from this building," Rose says. His voice is confident, each syllable precise. "The homicide has occurred in this state, so the body must undergo an autopsy here."

Kellerman shakes his head very slightly. "My friend, I'm the Special Agent in charge of the White House detail of the Secret Service. This is the body of the President of the United States and we are going to take him back to Washington."

"No, that's not the way things are," Rose declares and folds his arms across his chest.

"The president is going with us."

"You're not taking the body anywhere. There's a law here. We're going to enforce it!"

A couple of the Secret Service agents bristle and shift their footing, ready for action.

Kellerman is implacable. "This part of the law can be waived," he says and stares straight into the coroner's eyes.

Rose glares back undaunted and shakes his head. I feel concerned for the man.

"You'll have to show me a lot more authority than you have now," the Secret Service chief retorts.

"Sir, President Kennedy's body is staying here."

There is a pause. To me, it feels like at least a minute but it can be no more than a second. "Fuck it—we don't have time for this," Kellerman snaps. He reaches inside his jacket and pulls out his pistol so fast that the gun is leveled before Earl Rose can even flinch. Kellerman automatically slips into the power stance: arms outstretched, weapon gripped in both hands. Two of his agents react *almost as quickly. They fan out, stepping to left and right of the hapless coroner. "Move aside, sir," Kellerman barks.*

Earl Rose is utterly shocked but tries his best to retain some dignity. He doesn't raise his hands, just unfolds his arms slowly while staring fixedly at Kellerman's gun. Without another word, Kellerman steps forward and Rose is shoved to one side. One of the Secret Service agents tugs at the door and we all pass through into a sour lemon daylight.

Chapter 28

It is hard to imagine that Love Field is the same airstrip where Air Force One landed just over three hours ago. This cannot be the same day, can it? The same afternoon? How is that possible? The adoring, cheering crowds have gone to mourn in their homes and workplaces. Save for a heavy police and army presence the place is now almost deserted. The gate onto the airstrip is manned by state troopers and I see half a dozen Secret Service agents among them. They are immediately identifiable in their black suits, black ties, white shirts and aviator sunglasses.

Jackie and Clint Hill are seated in the back of the hearse and O'Donnell is beside the driver. I'm in the first car behind them. Kellerman sits to my left and on the other side there is an agent I recognize only vaguely. We have left my boss Malcolm Kilduff behind at the hospital to deal with the clamoring newsmen. We pause for a moment at the gate and then we are waved through.

We pull up close to the steps leading up to the Boeing 707. I see the four funeral men jump from the hearse in front and I follow Kellerman out onto the tarmac. We run over with the other agent from our car to help with the casket. O'Donnell, Hill and half a dozen men cluster round, and between us we manage to get the incredibly heavy coffin up the stairs.

Inside, a space has been cleared for it by removing a couple of rows of seats at the rear of the aircraft. I see Jackie disappear into the Presidential Suite and I'm just about to head for the front of the plane when LBJ marches out of the suite, clutching a briefcase and looking flustered. He is followed by two male assistants, each with folders bursting with papers.

The main cabin is cramped and hot and filled with cigarette smoke. I suddenly realize I haven't smoked since the motorcade and think how odd that is, considering how stressed I have been. But then I think that perhaps I have been so preoccupied with what has been going on that I have forgotten about so many things. I suddenly experience a guilty pang as I recall that I haven't given my wife Ruth a thought, either. She is probably out of her mind with worry. I should call her, but I realize the chances of that are slim: all the lines will be taken up with urgent business. Domestic matters will have to wait.

I find a seat and flop into it, draw on a cigarette and watch the smoke float up. I think how it looks like a ghost, a spirit, and my mind flashes back to the moment outside Parkland Hospital and the vision of Jack leaving his body. What was that? Was it an hallucination? Something stress-related? Or was it a trick of the light? But then I remember the sensations running through me as I watched that mysterious vapor hover over the dead man, and I can hear his voice again.

Johnson and O'Donnell stop in the aisle close to my seat.

"I think we should leave immediately, sir," O'Donnell is saying.

At almost six-four, the new president towers over the adviser. "I will not take off until I've been sworn in."

O'Donnell lets out a heavy sigh. "Has someone been called in to do it?"

"Judge Hughes is on her way."

"Can no one here swear you in, Mr. President?"

"No one here knows the wording," Johnson replies brusquely.

O'Donnell is about to respond when we all hear voices from the door of the plane. An elderly woman in a black judicial gown is snapping at a young agent. Johnson sees her and strides over.

"Sarah," he says, more animated than I have seen him since the shooting. The agent steps aside and Johnson and Judge Sarah Hughes embrace.

"It's been a while," LBJ says. "And I sure wish it was under different circumstances, but it's good to see you, judge."

The woman nods, giving her old friend a wan smile.

"All right, let's get this over with," Johnson tells O'Donnell. "Get as many people as you can into the stateroom of the Presidential Suite. And will someone please help Mrs. Kennedy and ask her to be beside me for the oath?"

I do my bit and squeeze through to the front of the plane where some of the men who had left the hospital with Johnson a while earlier are helping to pack away boxes of state papers. I spot one of the White House staff whom I know a little talking to a young woman who is

227

at the telephone station. She is trying to get a line to Washington but is not having much luck. I see Roy Kellerman and tell him what is happening at the rear of the plane. Then I follow him past a couple of agents into the slightly less crowded part of the aircraft where the coffin stands opposite the door of the Presidential Suite.

As we arrive at the open door of the stateroom we can see the place is packed and I glimpse the judge facing us. In front of her, with their backs to us, are Johnson, flanked to his right by his wife and to his left by Jackie. In the middle stands a microphone and I notice one of the White House team operating a tape recorder in the corner.

Neither Kellerman nor myself can get any closer so we just stand still in the doorway and listen as Judge Hughes reads a line from the oath. This is repeated by LBJ until the whole short promise is recited. A camera flashes twice, then a third time as the oath is almost completed. And in the silence I feel again an almost overwhelming sense of otherworldliness. I know I can rationalize that in years to come I will reflect upon this day and see it in relation to all the others of my life. It will stand out as perhaps the most significant day, of that I am sure, but it will become just another memory. Only, right now, I am living the moment and the moment seems unreal. Everything has happened too damn fast. It isn't possible—is it? How could it be that just a few hours ago I was sitting on this plane en route to Dallas, sharing the same air as President Kennedy? And now he is lying not ten feet from me, his head smashed to pieces, his life-force gone, just his battered mortal remains stuffed *into a casket. And how can it be that here, in this room, ten feet away from me in the other direction stands Lyndon Johnson being sworn in as the thirty-sixth President of the United States?*

And then it is over. Jackie and Johnson shake hands, Lady Bird kisses the former First Lady on the cheek and the group file out. It's stiflingly hot and everyone is sweating and panting for air. The air con is off because the plane needs to be airborne for the system to work and the jet has been sitting in the sun for three hours, soaking up the heat.

But as I return to the corridor and step aside to let the others by, I hear the engines of the giant aircraft start up and I see people exiting from the rear of the plane. Jackie is nowhere to be seen. I surmise she has stayed in the suite and returned to the bedroom.

"Buckle up, David," I hear O'Donnell say close to where I'm sitting. "I want to get this fucking thing in the air asap."

The engines change note, the rear door of the 707 is slammed shut and sealed. Johnson and Lady Bird are escorted to a private room near the front of the plane and I catch sight of O'Donnell swinging himself down into a chair and tackling his seat belt as Air Force One finally taxis toward the runway.

I see a flash of green, then tendrils of cloud. The plane rolls a little in the turbulence and the pilot swings us round north as we climb.

Then we are leveling out and people are already up and out of their seats, rushing around the confines of the plane. Apart from the Presidential Suite, it is incredibly cramped and today it is even more crowded than usual. There are twice as many people as normal on the aircraft, and Jack's casket takes up three rows.

The door to the Presidential Suite opens and Jackie emerges. She has redone her make-up but has not touched the Chanel suit she has been wearing.

"Mrs. Kennedy," I say, "do you want a change of clothes? I'm sure—"

She shakes her head. "No, David, thank you." Then she fixes me with her dark eyes, her face drained of emotion. "Let them see what they've done."

O'Donnell is walking toward us and behind him come some of Jack's oldest colleagues, Dave Powers, Larry O'Brien, the former president's campaign manager, and Brigadier General Godfrey McHugh. O'Donnell is holding a bottle of Irish whiskey in each hand. He pulls up a metal document box and straddles it in the aisle. Dave Powers squeezes past, headed for the galley. He reappears a few moments later with glasses clutched in each hand. He starts to pass them around. Ken slops whiskey into the tumblers and raises a glass, "To the best man I ever knew," he says softly.

I look at Jackie and see how she is struggling to keep her composure. Ken nods at her glass and Jackie knocks it back, then contemplates her lap and the empty glass.

The lights are lowered in the cabin. I hear the voices of the small gathering who sit around Jack's casket. They are chatting and reminiscing. I let the sounds drift over me with the taste of the whiskey still on my tongue. Larry O'Brien is talking fondly of Jack's visit to Ireland just a

few months ago and how he charmed everyone he met.
I stay silent, letting the alcohol soothe my troubled mind,
but knowing that it will take a lot more than a glass of
whiskey to do that properly. Slowly, the voices fade and
I fall asleep.

Chapter 29

There is a moment, isn't there? A moment just as you resurface from a dream and you lie in a state of blissful ignorance. Then reality floods in, memory ripples across your consciousness, and you recall the dread facts. I rub the sleep from my eyes and look around me.

The plane has landed in Washington and we are taxiing along the runway. I check my watch. It is a minute before five p.m. but then I remember we have crossed over to EST and it is really just before six o'clock.

The rear door of the plane opens almost immediately the engines stop and I see Bobby Kennedy charging through the opening into the aircraft. He freezes as he sees his brother's casket and stares at it for a second, his face unnaturally pale in the overhead lights. Then he glimpses Jackie and stumbles toward her, arms outstretched. He embraces her. "Hi, Jackie. I'm here," he murmurs.

"Oh Bobby," she sobs against his shoulder.

He kisses her on the forehead and examines her face as though she is about to crumple. And no one would be too surprised if she did. I notice a Marine in the doorway of the plane. He salutes as Brigadier General Godfrey McHugh stands up.

"Sir, we have come for the president," the young officer says stiffly.

"We'll be taking him down," O'Donnell snaps, moving forward between the brigadier and the Marine. The officer steps back and Larry O'Brien, who has been sitting next to Jackie and who is closest to the casket, unlocks the clasps and braces that have held it in place throughout the flight. Eight of us, including Bobby, then lift the coffin to the aisle and on toward the rear door.

Outside, the air is cold and windy. We maneuver Jack's casket into position, and from where I am standing I see a ten-foot-deep metal container rise on a mechanical lift. Its bright yellow walls and top look utterly out of place. O'Donnell and one of the agents lead the way and in a few seconds we are all inside with the coffin resting on the floor.

The area around the plane is swarming with people. As we are lowered to the tarmac I can see dozens of uniformed men, and at a respectful distance stands a film crew and a group of photographers. Powerful floodlights have been erected close by and the area is awash with glaring white light. I can see that Bobby is about to lose his cool with the spectators. Jackie touches his arm and he swallows back his anger in order to concentrate on getting the coffin out of the container.

A gray Navy ambulance has nudged up close to the container and we accept the help of a couple of cadets who step forward and put their arms under the casket of their fallen president. I glance to my left at one of the Marines. He is just a few feet from me. He is very young— no more than eighteen or nineteen, I guess. Tears are streaming silently down his face. We edge along the tarmac, shuffling sideways, and manage to lever the box into the rear of the ambulance before securing it in place.

I run to a car, a black Oldsmobile parked a few yards away, its engine running. O'Donnell and a couple of his men are already in the car. I recognize Agent John Maclaren at the wheel. I haven't seen him since leaving Dallas and surmise he must have been on Air Force Two or the cargo support plane that took off with us a couple of hours ago. Maclaren indicates that I can jump in the front next to him if I want to. Closing the door, I watch Jackie and Bobby slip into the back seats of the ambulance carrying Jack. Kellerman and Burkley climb into the front. I recognize Bill Greer, the Kennedys' regular driver. I have overheard someone say that the poor guy is eating himself up because he believes he could have done more to save his president in Dealey Plaza.

We pull away slowly toward the freeway. It is silent in the car, each of us lost in our own private thoughts, all of us drained. I peer out at the night. I know this freeway leads to a Naval hospital called Bethesda.

There are many people lining the streets, two, three deep in places. Most of them have their heads bowed.

Bethesda Hospital is a dull collection of irregular concrete boxes. I've been here once before, about three months ago. An old friend from college had been in town to give a talk at the hospital.

Now—God—there are thousands of people here. I cannot believe it. How did they know to be here? Then I realize that so few things are beyond the view of the public now. There must, I suppose, have been news about the destination of Air Force One on TV. Information about where the casket would be taken must have been broadcast to the nation. I feel a sudden welling anger, an irrational resentment that Jack can't be left alone even a few hours after he has had his brains blown out. But the painful thoughts fade quickly. It is inevitable, I reason. Fame in life, fame in death. And besides . . . why shouldn't the people of America know what has happened in every detail? Why shouldn't they be here to express their grief and their love for the man?

But the strangest thing is the silence. I can barely hear a sound from the watchers. A few naval officers and a line of cops are holding back the near-silent crowd from the driveway immediately in front of the main doors of the hospital but, as the ambulance and the car I am traveling in pull up, the onlookers surge forward: mute, grave. We all stay put for a few seconds to give the police and navy personnel time to move people back.

Jackie and Bobby emerge from the ambulance, the agent who had been with Kellerman springs from the front-passenger side, holding a sub-machine gun. Half a dozen Marines appear from the doorway of the hospital to form a wall around the Kennedys and Kellerman as they are bustled into the hospital. I can just make out a figure in a black suit and white clerical collar—a naval chaplain, I guess.

Then our car starts to move again.

"The morgue is round the back," Agent Maclaren says.

The ambulance takes a left turn and heads slowly down a narrow service road to the rear of the building. It is darker here away from the lights of the main entrance.

I see the ambulance's brake lights come on and we stop abruptly. A group of men in surgical scrubs are standing around a trolley. I stay in the car and watch as they pull the coffin out of the ambulance onto the trolley and turn it slowly to face the rear doors of the hospital. As they enter the building, I jump out of the car.

I've never been inside a morgue before and the first thing that hits me is the stink. It smells like nothing I've ever known, a blend of cleaning fluid and raw meat, and there is a bloody, iron-tasting tang to the air. There are two autopsy tables. One of these has been pushed to the back, close to a tall metal cupboard; the other is positioned almost centrally.

As I stand in the open doorway of the morgue, I hear a sound from the corridor. A group of four naval officers armed with sub-machine guns approach and take up position. Two stand each side of the door of the morgue and the remaining pair stop with their backs to the far wall, staring fixedly ahead.

Inside the room two men in green surgical gowns are waiting for the casket to be opened by a pair of technicians dressed in blue boiler suits. They watch as the latches are unfastened and the lid lifted. There are at least fifteen people in the room, and as I enter I turn to see Bill Greer, Paul Landis and another agent I know quite well slip in beside me. They walk to the right side of the room and watch solemnly as the technicians lower their hands into the coffin and carefully lift Jack's body, shuffle to their left and lower him onto the mortuary slab.

The dead president is wrapped in bloodied sheets. Those around Jack's head are scarlet as though dyed. The doctors slowly remove the sheets exposing Kennedy's color-leached body. His head rests back against a small wedge. One eye is open, staring at the ceiling and its strip lights. Jack's hair, sticking up in spikes, is rigid with dried blood. There are lines of red down each cheek and running along the left side of his neck.

"Gentlemen, could you all please go through to the anteroom?" one of the doctors says. "We need to take X-rays."

I watch the others troop out through a glass door into a small room adjoining the morgue. But I don't want to follow them. I cannot stand being in this place another second. Instead, I light a cigarette and walk past the guards into the hall. I enter a long corridor and go round a corner to my left. At the far end the corridor merges with the main thoroughfare near the hospital reception area.

I spot a payphone across the way and realize again that I haven't spoken to my wife Ruth. I find a coin in my pocket, and in a moment I'm through to home. It is so good to hear Ruth's voice even if it is heavy with dark emotions. Like everyone else, she is shell-shocked. But she is so relieved to hear from me and for a moment I choke up. And then, after a few more words, the call is over. I hang up and start to walk toward the main thoroughfare. Ten yards on I hear whispering voices coming from the other side of a door a few feet ahead of me. The door is almost closed, but a crack remains between it and the frame. I can't make out what is being said, but I think I recognize at least one of the voices. I stop and strain to hear. Curiosity overtakes me and I step quietly to my left toward the source of the sound.

I creep up and lean back against the wall. Part of me is wondering why the hell I am doing this. It is ridiculous. Why am I eavesdropping on a private conversation? What has got into me? But then another part thinks: So what? You used to be an investigative journalist, didn't you, David? Isn't this what investigative journalists do? This voice wins out and I strain even harder to pick out what's being said.

"They've definitely caught Oswald?" one of the men asks.

"Not only do they have him, they're convinced he's the only shooter."

The first man produces a noise through his nose. "Fucking idiots!"

"Nixon must be cock-a-hoop, sir."

"And why shouldn't he be?"

"I imagine Hoover is wetting himself with glee."

"Not a nice image, Maclaren, but yes, I guess he probably is."

A shiver of raw fear runs down my spine. Maclaren? John Maclaren? I thought I had recognized that voice. Agent John Maclaren? What the fuck? I can't believe this. Is it a sick joke? What in God's name is going on?

"And Jack Ruby is prepped to dispose of Oswald?"

"Champing at the bit, sir."

"So, mission accomplished. That useless sonofabitch has been removed—permanently."

"Mr. Nixon will now have a clear run in the '64 election. That limp-wristed fool Johnson doesn't stand a chance. Dream ticket, Mr. Steinheiser: Nixon and Hoover."

"Sure, now we've blown that nigger-loving,

commie-sympathizing fucker's brains out we'll soon get this country back on its feet."

Another spasm: terror, fury, nausea. Did Maclaren say Steinheiser? I know only one Steinheiser: Orlando Steinheiser, the Assistant Director of the CIA. What madness is this? Are they really saying they had Kennedy assassinated? No, it cannot be.

I start to pull back. A face appears a foot in front of mine. It's Maclaren. He is so close I can see myself reflected in his pupils. He grabs my collar. I wrench back and the agent's grip tightens. A few feet behind him in the shadows stands Orlando Steinheiser, his angular face bisected by darkness. I react instinctively, bring my knee up hard and fast straight into Maclaren's balls. He tries to stifle his agony but loosens his grip just enough for me to tear myself away. I seize the tiny chance of escape, swerve, duck, pull myself round to the agent's side and run as fast as I can along the corridor towards the main thoroughfare.

Chapter 30

Fuck! This is terrifying. I've had dreams like this. Dreams in which I am running and running and someone vile is chasing me. Sometimes they have a gun. Sometimes they have a knife. In those dreams, I run and run and I get nowhere.

But this is no dream. I risk looking over my left shoulder and catch Steinheiser and Maclaren running toward me, the agent pulling his gun from inside his jacket.

I swing right and emerge into reception. It is a scene of mayhem that reminds me of Parkland. Naval officers with their rifles held in a ready position are watching over a large group of people who have spilled into the main lobby from outside. One corner, closest to the doors, has been roped off.

Next to the counter the pressmen have gathered; at least a dozen photographers with their cameras at their chests, men with notebooks at the ready and a couple of reporters clutching the latest portable dictaphones. Behind the counter, nurses and receptionists run back and forth. An elderly black porter with white stubbly hair pushes a trolley laden with fresh, crisply laundered sheets. He gawps around him at the extraordinary scene.

For a moment I am at a loss what to do. I feel panic

welling up, but I sense that it is a benevolent force driving me on. I cannot let the panic possess me, though. I have to stay rational, think about what I am doing. But what am I doing? Those men plotted Kennedy's murder. They will not let me live, not now. That much is certain. There is nowhere to hide.

I head for the doors, out to the horseshoe of tarmac under the high sloping canopy at the front of the hospital. The area is packed with people, members of the public who have flooded here after hearing the dread news on the radio or from their TV sets. I risk another look back and I can see Steinheiser and Maclaren. They have reached the edge of the crowd in reception. Steinheiser pauses for a second to say something to a uniformed cop. The policeman nods, pulls out his gun and the three of them head my way. Maclaren catches sight of me. I duck low and barge a way to the main doors against the tide of people still coming into the foyer.

Then I am out in the open and the freezing air. But I'm barely conscious of it and feel my face wet with sweat, my shirt sodden. I spin to my left and run as fast as I can to the end of the tarmac horseshoe. I keep going. I glimpse faces as I speed past them. They all seem preoccupied. They hardly notice me. A kid, a small boy wearing a buttoned-up red overcoat with a black velvet collar and holding his mother's hand, steps in front of me. I swerve as the mother yanks the boy back and she shouts something at my receding back.

Two seconds more and I am close to the edge of the building. I don't want to risk a glance back, but I can't resist it. I see no sign of the men chasing me. But these guys know what they are doing. I reach the corner and tear round it. It is quieter here. I spot a doctor fifty yards ahead as he runs from the parking lot toward the main building.

I career round another corner close to the rear of the building. I can see ahead to the spot where we parked no more than twenty minutes ago. The ambulance and the Oldsmobile have gone, the sidewalk is empty. A dim light comes from a window high up in the wall of the hospital, but it is pretty dark here—the nearest street light stands a dozen yards away.

I know I must not stop running, but I don't know where the hell I am running to. Then I notice a car across the street. Its lights are off. I recognize it. It is one of the cars that followed us from the Air Force base. I see the driver. He is sitting in the darkened car, smoking a cigarette.

I cross the street quickly. The driver sees me and lowers the window.

"Hey, Davey," he says and I recognize the voice. I shift to one side and let light fall on the man's face. It is Special Agent Frank Taylor who I have not seen since The Texas hotel early this morning.

"Frank," I say, as calmly as I can.

"Shitty business," he says and flicks a glance at the hospital.

"I still can't . . . Look, Frank, can you help me?"

He gives me a puzzled look. I have known him for a couple of years, we've gotten drunk together at least twice, but there is an edge of suspicion in his eyes as he looks at me. He is, after all, an FBI agent.

Before he can respond, the radio in the car crackles and a voice spills from the speaker. "Agents B12 and C45." It is Maclaren. He sounds a little out of breath. "10-33," he spits. "Repeat: 10-33. We have a 187. Suspect David Ashcombe, Press Liaison. Shoot to kill."

I know these codes. I have heard them so many times. 10-33, an emergency. 187, homicide. Frank Taylor goes for his gun, but I'm too quick for him. With all my strength, I send my fist through the opened window. It engages with the man's temple and a sharp pain ripples up my arm to my shoulder, making me gasp.

I don't know what I've done but Taylor crumples, falling to his right onto the shift, out cold. I open the door, drag him across the seat and out onto the road. I check to see if he is still breathing. He's unconscious but has a steady pulse. I move him away from the car onto the sidewalk, jump in the car and twist the ignition key.

Before I can pull away I'm dazzled by headlights. A vehicle heads straight for me and slows. As it stops, I see that it is the Oldsmobile. I put my foot down hard on the accelerator, swing round a yard to the left of the car and catch sight of John Maclaren at the wheel, another agent in the passenger seat. Maclaren sees me, yells, and pulls away. I race past along the service road, screech around the bend and slow as I see people crossing in front of me, headed for the hospital.

I ram my hand down on the horn and the people scatter as I speed through a gap, spin to my left, the tires screaming, and accelerate toward the open gates. A guard watches me approaching fast and the idiot steps out onto the road, his hand up. I go straight for him and at the last moment he jumps back and I pull onto the highway, slam my foot down again and roar away.

Where am I going? I'm no good at this sort of thing, but I suddenly think how amazing it is that we can snap into flight mode, just like that. It is fight or flight, and I know I cannot fight these guys. But where do I fly to?

I am on Interstate 95, heading west. I know this road well. The traffic is quiet on my side of the freeway, but lights head toward me, cars shoot past traveling east toward the dead president. I'm aware that I am driving fast, really fast, my foot flat to the floor.

I catch headlights in the rear-view mirror, but I have no idea if it is my pursuers' car or just some random guy traveling home late from work. The car gets closer. I can just make out two men in the front. It is the Oldsmobile. The passenger leans out of his window. I see his arm swing out of the car, his gun hand rise.

I swerve the car and hear the crack of a bullet. My side mirror shatters. I'm charged up with adrenalin, barely thinking about what I am doing, just reacting. I swerve again and try desperately to make the car go faster, but it won't. I'm already driving flat out.

I see a sign, a turn-off a hundred yards ahead. I leave it to the last second and then screech over to the exit lane and up the ramp. I look in the rear-view mirror again, hoping that my simple trick has shaken off my pursuers, but of course it has not. Their car is closing the gap between us on the off-ramp.

I spin the wheel hard left and roar around a bend, jerk it the other way and skid across the road, just making it into a side street on the right. I can hear the other car.

Headlights rush toward me. I'm swaying across the road like a drunk driver. A car blares its horn. I peer in the mirror. The passenger in the Oldsmobile leans out of the window again. I swerve and almost plow into an oncoming car. The driver overcompensates and mounts the curb. I can see in the mirror that the poor man has lost control. His car spins, but miraculously it ends up back on the road facing the right way. I see it shudder and sway, but eventually the driver brings it straight. He pulls to the side of the road and stops, his brake lights blazing red as I speed off.

I cannot shake off the Oldsmobile. I career around a corner, just managing to keep the car from rolling. We are in a residential street lined with comfortable, average suburban homes, living-room lights ablaze. I suppose everyone is still glued to the TV or listening avidly to the radio. I accelerate along the street, topping sixty. For a second the Oldsmobile vanishes from my rear-view mirror. Driving like a madman, I put some distance between us.

I hurtle left into a side turning and see weatherboard houses, blue paint, white paint, a picket fence, willowy late-fall trees looking bedraggled. I flash past evenly spaced street lights. I'm only vaguely aware of where I am now. Still steaming ahead, I take a sharp right, then another and I feel more confident. Ahead, I see a narrow track running between two houses. I guess it is an access road to a rear garage. I pull into it, flick the headlights off, kill the engine and wait.

Ten seconds pass, twenty. Then, just as I start to feel I cannot wait a second longer, in my rear-view mirror I *see the Oldsmobile flash past the end of the alley. I leave it another thirty seconds, a minute. Then I twist the key, reverse out, face the way I came and floor the accelerator.*

I'm speeding down another residential street and I'm trying to think straight. I tell myself I must formulate some sort of plan. I have bought a little time, that is all. Now I have to use that advantage. The lights of a gas station appear up ahead. I pull onto the forecourt, then take the car round the side of the building as a man in overalls, a smear of grease across his right cheek, appears in the doorway. I get out of the car and walk round, see a payphone. I ignore the guy, who looks me up and down and then ducks back into the building.

At the phone I struggle to find a coin in my jacket pocket and only then realize just how much I am shaking. I must have looked odd to the mechanic, I think, but I can't do much about that.

I fish out a dime, slip it into the slot, wait for the tone and dial. It rings and rings, and then, just as I'm about to give up, I make the connection.

"Northgate residence."

"Sis," I say, trying to keep my voice as level as possible.

"Davey—what's up? You sound . . ."

"I was in Dallas today."

"You're okay?"

"Yes, of course, Cath."

I hear a sigh. "I'm sorry. It's just . . ."

"Yeah, I know. Look, I need to see you."

"What?"

"I can't explain, but it's—"

I hear a man's voice calling her. It's Cathy's husband,

Kerry. She shouts back. "It's David." Then she returns. "Are you in trouble?"

I don't know what to say for a few moments. Then I realize I should just be blunt. "Yes, Cath, I am. I'm in desperate trouble. I need to see you right away, but I can't risk going to your place."

"What about home?"

"No, out of the question."

"For God's sake!"

I fall silent again and Cathy seems to suddenly under-stand how serious I'm being.

"Okay, Davey. Where? When?"

My mind is in turmoil. I haven't really thought this through. "Ah . . . there's an all-night diner in the CBD, on G Street, the Treasury Building end. I think it's called Macky's."

"I know it. It's Marco's. What time?"

I look at my watch and move my wrist into a shaft of light reflected from the canopy over the gas pumps. It is almost eight. "Half an hour," I say and hang up.

Chapter 31

As soon as I put down the phone I think maybe I have just made the worst possible decision.

There was some sense to it, I guess. My sister works for the CIA. I don't know what she does exactly, but I know she has moved up through the ranks and is now an important cog in the machine. We have a family joke that's wheeled out almost every year when we go to our parents for Thanksgiving. Although we each work for the government in DC, our jobs are in very different departments so we cannot divulge to each other what we do. Mom and Dad think it's hilarious.

This runs through my mind as I dash back to the car. Apart from the garage guy, I am alone. I reverse out and can just make out the man at the counter.

I still don't really know what I'm doing. I still don't have a coherent plan. The traffic is light on the Beltway as I head west and then turn off north towards the CBD. I keep flicking my gaze to the rear-view mirror, and although I see nothing suspicious, I know this is merely a reprieve.

I remember a parking lot a short walk from the diner. I pull into it and find a space. Then I just sit there for a few moments trying to calm myself, trying to work it all out.

I feel sick to my stomach and suddenly realize I haven't eaten since breakfast. The thought of food just had not occurred to me all day. I don't feel hungry now, just sick. I have never been so scared in my life. "Fuck!" I say aloud. Fuck—why did I have to be the one who overheard Maclaren and Steinheiser? Why couldn't I have just minded my own business for Christ's sake? Dad used to always tell me that my nose would get me into trouble one day. But then I'd become a journalist and I had ribbed him that my nose was now earning me a good salary. But Dad had been right all along, hadn't he?

Just for a second I am almost . . . almost able to imagine I'm safe, that everything will be all right after all. I'm here, anonymous, out of sight. I could just stay here forever, let the world move on without me. Or I could just vanish. But then I think of Ruth. I think of my parents, my sister. Fuck it—I think of myself, the career I've built up. And, yes, I think of Truth. I think of Responsibility. Those men were complicit in the murder of my president. They killed Jack—and today I learned something I still don't quite understand about Jack— about Jack and me.

God! Am I going insane? What am I saying? Has it all gotten too much? I must be cracking up. But no, that is not reasonable, is it? How can I ignore what I experienced? I can't disregard that moment outside Parkland. I saw Jack go. I heard his voice in my head.

I feel dampness on my cheek and realize that tears are slithering down my face. I think of brushing them away but a more dominant part of me stops my hand moving.

I want to feel the warmth of the tears, just as Jackie had wanted to keep Jack's blood on her clothes. I've wanted to cry all day, but except for that brief moment in the trauma room it has been impossible. Now, here in the dark in this secret, silent place, a wire fence a foot from the end of the car's hood, somehow the sound of my own sobs fit. They are a proper response.

Running out beyond the shelter of the parking lot roof, the cold cuts into me and I pull my jacket hard against my chest, turn up the collar and walk quickly. I turn west, my head down, scan the street furtively. In a moment I am on G Street, heading toward the Treasury Department. Ducking left into a narrow passage between a pharmacy and a tailor's store, I see the lights of a diner. A man in an apron emerges from its door. He looks up and sees me approach.

"Still open?" I ask.

"Sure thing, buddy. Be with you in one moment. Get warm!"

I give him a brief smile and walk into the diner. It is deserted. I pick up the menu, look at it without really seeing it and light a cigarette. The owner comes through the door and right behind him is Cathy, who hurries over and gives me the sort of hug I haven't had from her since we were kids. "'Oh, Davey,'" is all she can say.

I pull her away and hold her elbows. Tears run down either side of her nose. She wipes them away and throws herself into a chair, snapping back to grown-up Cathy, CIA agent Cathy.

I stare at her silently. Cathy is too thin, her face almost gaunt. Our mother is always telling her that she will dissolve like a snowflake if she doesn't eat, but Cathy takes no notice. She looks tired and drawn, but then I guess this evening almost all of us do. She meets my gaze. We have almost identical brown eyes. People have wondered if we are twins.

She glances around and sighs heavily. "So tell me, what's this all about?"

I look down at the check tablecloth and decide I'll just tell it how it is. "I was with JFK today—in Dallas."

She frowns. "Yes."

The owner suddenly appears from behind the counter and comes over to us, a pad in his left hand. "What can I get you folks?"

"Just coffee for me," I say. "A large black."

Cathy nods at the man. "Same."

I get the feeling that the owner wants to stop and chat, but he quickly senses the vibe and retreats to his kitchen without another word. I watch him go and see him pass behind a cupboard. I look toward the door and through the window.

"David! You're as skittish as hell. What's . . . ?"

"I know who killed Kennedy," I say quietly.

Cathy pauses for several beats. I cannot read her face at all. She takes a deep breath. "It came on the news," she says. "They've arrested a guy."

"I know. I heard that too, at the hospital. But I don't mean that, Cathy. I mean I know who is behind the assassination."

"What!" Cathy blanches, and now it is her turn to clock the room, the kitchen, the door, the window. "How, David? Christ!"

251

I put my hands on the table, covering hers. She seems surprised. "I overheard something I shouldn't have at Bethesda Hospital."

"Please don't tell me that they know you know . . ."

I just stare at her.

"Oh God." She pulls a hand away and brings it to her mouth. I have never seen my sister so scared. Then she does the same trick of suppressing her emotions. She is CIA Cathy again. "Okay. We have to get you away."

"Cath." I twist in my seat as the owner steps from the kitchen, carrying two cups of coffee. We say nothing as he places the cups on the table and retreats diplomatic-ally. He probably imagines that we are lovers heading for a split.

"I have to consider Ruth." I think about saying, ". . . and you," but realize that need not be said.

"Yes. I understand." Then she pauses and leans forward. "You have to tell me."

"I know. I know I do. Someone has to get the truth out there because my chances are slim, sis."

I'm shocked when she does not contradict me, and I think: What is it you do at the CIA, Cathy? What horrible secrets do you know? I tell her what I heard. She listens: no interruptions, never breaking eye contact. Then she shocks me a second time.

"Makes perfect sense."

"What?"

"Look, I loved Jack, just the same as you, David. But the man was making enemies every way he turned. And his brother is doing the same. If you had told me it was

252

Castro, or the Soviets, or LBJ himself I would have been no more surprised."

"And the CIA? Steinheiser is your boss."

Cathy tilts her head to one side. "You've already learned too many dangerous things today, big brother. You have covered your tracks? How did you get away?"

"I stole a car. They chased me. I shook them off."

Cathy gives me an admiring look.

"So, what now?" I ask.

"I will get proof."

"How?"

"Leave that to me. I'm assuming that's why you called me." She does not mean to sound brutal. I know my sister. I know how she changed when she was trained by the CIA and she gave her life to the job like a nun joining a nunnery. "But you have to get away. You have to get Ruth to disappear too, but not with you."

I flinch at that.

"David, think. Don't go near your home. Don't go near Ruth. She has to get away from Washington NOW . . . or they will kill her."

I don't know what to say. I must look desperate.

"But where do I go?"

"You can't stay in the States."

"What!"

"David, they will hunt you down and they will kill you without a thought. Even abroad, they will chase you. Believe me. These people have a very long reach. Orlando Steinheiser is evil—evil and very, very powerful."

Cathy stands up. "I'm going to stay here for a moment. You must go."

She hugs me again. The same desperate hug. And we each know that we will never see one another again.

I kiss my sister on the cheek. "Expose the truth, Cathy."

She looks at me, silent. I turn and stride to the door and the alleyway beyond.

Chapter 32

I reach the end of the narrow passageway and emerge onto G Street, keeping to the shadows, and start to walk toward the Treasury Department. I have to warn Ruth. I have to warn Ruth, that is all I can think about. But I'm not thinking straight. I'm so confused, so scared. I hear a sound, spin round and see Agent John Maclaren and the other guy from the Oldsmobile emerging from a building ten yards behind me. Maclaren spots me, goes for his gun, and I run.

The street is almost deserted. I am a fast runner but I'm not at my peak anymore. I'm not as fit as I once was. Ruth has been feeding me too well. Too many TV dinners. I hear the two men pounding along the pavement. I pull into another alleyway, running as fast as I can. I feel my chest pounding. I cross the street, zigzagging as I go. The men haven't fired their weapons. I'm consoled by that for a second.

I'm sprinting so fast that I'm terrified I'll slip on the sidewalk, but I'm more terrified I'll feel a bullet slam into my spine. I keep going, taking deep breaths, barely conscious of where I am or where I am going. Then I see the Press Building directly ahead. I've acted like a homing pigeon, I think as I race along the sidewalk. I pull in at the main doors and realize I've put some distance between myself and the two men.

I lunge into a gap in the revolving doors, willing them to spin faster, but they circle at their own sweet pace. I can see Maclaren less than fifteen yards away along the street. He is passing the entrance to the neighboring building, the other agent at his heels. I enter the Press Building.

I survey an over-lit reception area and flash my ID at security.

Howard, the duty officer, knows me. I reach the closed elevator doors and notice, out of the corner of my eye, that Howard has picked up the phone. He glances over at me and I know that he's been told something I didn't want him to hear. I see Howard lower his hand to his gun and I rush away from the elevators and bolt for the staircase ten yards ahead along a corridor. He shouts: "Mr. Ashcombe. Stop, Mr. Ashcombe."

I ignore the man and reach the first step. My heart is thumping harder now. I feel sad. I'll never survive this, a voice yells inside my head. I'll never see Ruth again. And then a wave of anger. Damn them. Damn this. I'm not a fighting man. I'm no hero. I'm a White House Press Liaison, for Christ's sake.

And then something else. A nagging thought. A sensation. I'm not sure what it is, but it's digging into me, eating at my mind. Something about this situation . . .

I'm halfway up the stairs and I hear the front door of the building open. Then comes the slap of leather soles on the marble floor. Then voices. I recognize Agent John Maclaren's baritone. It's like sandpaper. The Secret

Service guy sounds a little out of breath. *Perhaps you won't get me, you bastard,* I think. I run faster, my own breath coming now in gasps. I feel my chest hurting, stabbing pains like knives cutting through my lungs.

I reach the top of the first flight of stairs, grasp the metal rail and yank myself round, keeping tight to the wall, faster that way. And then up the next flight, ignoring the pain, driven on by raw fear. As I reach the second-floor landing I hear a wonderful sound. The ting of an elevator. The sound comes from overhead, and I know that the elevator is coming down from the third floor. I dive for the call button, stumble and fall forward, just managing to stab the plastic disk. The elevator stops, the doors open. I ram my finger against the "door close" button, hearing the rush of feet on the stairs growing louder, closer. I glimpse a black jacket, and then the doors shut. I let out a deep sigh and lean forward, head against the wall.

A loud bang reverberates around the inside of the elevator. One of the Secret Service agents has fired his weapon at the elevator door. I can barely believe this display of violence. Then I realize I still have my finger pressed on the "door close" button and haven't touched the other controls to tell the elevator where to go. I leap forward as another bullet to the doors makes the enclosed space shudder. I hit the button marked "Level 6".

I take long, deep breaths. *I have to control my heart rate or I'll go into cardiac arrest,* I think. And the weird thoughts start to cascade into my mind again. I'm trying to understand . . . there is something about this situation . . . I lean back against the metal wall, straining for some clarity. I catch sight of myself in the mirror to the left.

Rivulets of sweat run down my lean ashen cheeks. I look like a wet cadaver. My black hair is disheveled, my suit sweat-soaked, white shirt filthy, tie askew. I check my watch. It's almost nine.

The elevator stops abruptly. I hit the "door open" button and run out onto the landing. This too is over-lit with fluorescent strips running along the empty corridor. I count a dozen doors, six a side interspersed with panels of opaque glass. A strip of brown carpet runs along the center of the corridor. There's no one around. I head straight for my office, third door along on the right. A small sign reads: "David Ashcombe, Press Liaison." I unlock the door and dive inside.

The room is small. On the desk sits a telephone. I switch off the light. The view of the room collapses into darkness. I walk back carefully to the desk and reach for the phone.

Wait . . . I know this. I know this. I've been here before. No, I couldn't have . . .

It feels like an eternity as I wait for someone to pick up. Three rings, four, five. I begin to despair. I tap my fingers on the desk, strain to hear anyone approaching. The Secret Service guys will be here any second. I feel the panic growing. Ruth picks up.

"Ashcombe resid—"

"Ruth."

"Dave, darling."

"Ruth, baby. Listen. I gotta be quick."

"Why?"

"Ruth, get out of the house. Go to your Aunt Joan's in Missouri . . . tonight . . . Right now."

"Aunt Joan?"

"I can't explain. Just, please, do what I say."

"But Dave . . ."

"No buts, Ruth. I'll make my way to your aunt's, meet you there just as soon as I can."

"I don't understand."

I take a deep breath and close my eyes for a fraction of a second, feeling the cold Bakelite of the receiver against my cheek. "Look, Ruth. This is life or death."

"Is it to do with . . . ?"

"Of course. Now. Please."

She starts to sob.

"Please, honey . . ."

"Dave. I have to tell you something."

I'm only half-listening. I hear a sound . . . scraping. Then the whine of a creaky hinge as a door is opened along the corridor.

"Ruth, I have to go. I love you."

In the blackness I tiptoe over to the door, straining again to hear. I think I discern voices, but I can't make out anything. I open the door a crack and peer along the corridor. A man, Maclaren's sidekick, steps through a doorway into the office two along from mine. Agent Maclaren is already inside. I can hear him rifling through the desk. I slip out into the corridor. I don't dare look behind me as I fight back the dreadful thoughts, the panic, the terror. Any second I expect a raised voice to yell out my name, followed by a shot and the sharp sting of a bullet.

I reach the end of the corridor and the emergency exit. I push on the bar and risk checking over my shoulder. A man emerges from the office, sees me, raises his gun and I fall forward onto the bar across the door.

"Stop, Mr. Ashcombe. Stop."

A second later I'm picking myself up from the cold concrete and a bullet smashes against the wall, sending chunks of brickwork over my head. A sharp fragment hits me in the neck and I feel a stab of pain, pull myself to my feet and rush for the stairs, grabbing for the metal rail.

I stumble down the stairs, panting. And I'm talking to myself, panicking. "Oh fuck! Oh fuck!" I keep repeating it aloud. I hit the wall and bounce back. The door to the emergency exit slams open above me and the two men crash into the stairwell. I duck away from the opening in the center of the staircase, keeping to the outside wall. I see a flash of black cloth.

"Stop," Maclaren yells. "David—we will fire again if you do not stop . . . now."

I ignore him. I know I'm dead meat if I stop. My only chance is to run. But I don't really know what I'm doing or where I'm going. They have such an advantage. There are two of them, they are armed pros. I'm a glorified office grunt, a pen-pusher, as my cousin Tom calls me. And the dread thoughts try to intrude again, but I don't dwell on them, don't allow them in.

I reach the second floor of the stairwell. The floor is wet. I rush round the concrete curve, keeping to the outside wall. A bullet smashes into the wall behind me and I feel my stomach flip. The sound of the shot is horrendously loud, a boom from the gun and a crack from the shattered brickwork.

I twist round and see Maclaren's gun pointed straight at me. And then . . . and then . . . I know. I suddenly know. I've been here before. I see it all. I visualize Maclaren raising his gun, watch as the bullet leaves the barrel.

The Secret Service agent pulls the trigger. The gun jerks upward slightly, a burst of light from the tip of the barrel, and I dive forward. The bullet thuds into the wall, sending more debris and shrapnel into the air.

I'm on the ground level, a door in front of me. I run at it. It falls away from me and I trip forward, landing heavily on the concrete outside. A stab of pain rushes along my jaw and my teeth hurt. I pull myself up, trying desperately to draw air into my lungs. I hear another bullet crunch against the wall of the stairwell and I'm away along a dark alley. I stumble into a trash can, sending it clattering across the dirt, spilling garbage as it goes. I feel faint and my muscles are spasming. I almost fall but just manage to stop myself. I see a narrow opening to my right and veer off toward it.

I stop, struggle for breath and feel the brick against my face. My eyes are filled with tears.

"David." The voice comes from behind. I twist round and see a flash of light. I'm thrown backwards as the bullet slams into my head. I hear a crack of bone, the thud of the bullet rocketing through my brain, the squelch of organic matter as a chunk of it splatters against the bricks.

The right side of my vision has clouded over, a dark veil of blood slithers over my eyeball and I can see nothing on that side. Maclaren crouches down, peering into my

face and I feel a loosening in my bowels. I start to gurgle,
feel warm blood on my neck. It flows down under the open
collar. I feel drunk, stoned. Nothing works anymore. The
view through my left eye fades to nothing.

PART 5

The Oneness of Many Parts

Chapter 33

"Christopher, we have a situation," Orlando Steinheiser said into his cell. He was standing on the balcony of his Massachusetts home overlooking the Atlantic Ocean. The air was hot and sticky. He sipped some San Pellegrino.

"What sort of situation?" Christopher Trafano, Steinheiser's aide, asked.

"The live feed from Professor Marchant's office. Nathan Morrow's people down in New Mexico have just alerted me. It's getting dangerous. You need to deal with this problem right now. Understood?"

"I'll get Cantril onto it."

"He's in town?"

"Flew in this morning. We've been on alert for a while, remember?"

"Good. Call me the second that Cantril's done."

Chapter 34

Mark opened his eyes. Abigail's face came into view. She helped him sit up. He was sweating, his skin cold.

"You're shaking," she observed. "Just give yourself a second."

"I'm fine." Mark raised a hand to his forehead and started to stand. "Whoa! Actually . . ." He lowered himself back to a seated position. Abigail sat close to him and put an arm around his shoulders.

"So it was Hoover and Nixon in cahoots."

"And this other guy, the CIA man, Steinheiser."

Abigail nodded.

"You look pretty shaken yourself, Abi."

"Well, it's not every day you learn the truth about the Kennedy assassination," she retorted and handed him a bottle of water. He gulped it down then, took a deep breath. Color began to return to his face. "But nothing is provable."

Abigail studied his face. "I know. It never has been."

"My sister, Cathy. She knew. I told her. She must have been killed before she could . . ."

Abigail picked up her iPad from a side table close to the couch, slid a finger over the screen and called up Google. She tapped in "Catherine Northgate". Nothing

266

useful appeared, no one linked to the CIA or the Kennedy killing.

"She was definitely CIA?"

"Yes," Mark replied. "As David, I knew very little about what my sister actually did. But I do know she was working her way up."

"All right, let's try something different." She tapped the screen again. A new page appeared.

Mark read the heading. *Deaths linked to Kennedy Assassination.* "It's some crackpot conspiracy site."

"Maybe it is, but the basic facts are the basic facts." She scrolled down, and there at No. 54 was the name Catherine Northgate. Mark read the entry. "CIA operative. Unknown rank. Found dead. November 23, 1963, Washington DC."

Abigail laid the iPad on the couch beside her.

"I caused my sister's death," Mark said quietly, staring into space. "If I hadn't . . ."

"Mark, it happened fifty years ago, in another lifetime. Don't beat yourself up over it."

He contemplated her earnest expression. "No, you're right. But it was all a waste. It's obvious she was killed before she could let anyone know the truth—or before she'd decided never to pass on the secret." His eyes were watering.

"You look all in, Mark," she said gently. Mark took her hand, leaned forward and brushed his lips against hers. Her lips parted, then she pulled back. "There's something I need to tell you about all this."

Mark was about to answer when he saw Abigail's expression change. She'd seen a red dot of light playing over his forehead. "Get down!" she screamed and pulled at his shoulders.

They fell to the carpet and a loud crack came from the wall above the couch. A chunk of plaster shattered, sending powder and bits of brickwork into the air. Abigail spun round toward the window high up in the opposite wall. There was nothing to see except the grey concrete of a building across the street.

"What the fuck!" Mark exclaimed.

There was another crack. A second lump of wall smashed to fragments that cascaded down on them.

They kept low, made it to the door and out into the reception area.

"What is going on, Abigail?"

"Not now. We have to get out." She plucked her bag from where she had left it on her secretary's desk less than two hours ago. "They'll expect us to dash to the first-floor exit. If we do that they'll pick us off."

"Who will? Who are 'they'?"

"No time, Mark. Just trust me."

They ran out into the hall. Abigail punched the elevator call button. The light above the doors clicked through the stories of the building, reached twenty-four and the doors opened.

They ran in and Abigail stabbed at the button marked four.

"Why four?"

"Random decision."

The elevator descended, the doors opened and they sped out into a carpeted corridor. It was late on a Saturday afternoon and there was no one else around. They saw to their left a pair of glass doors, the words ENDOVER INSURANCE written across them. To the right, two more doors, a pair of brass plaques. Between the elevator and those doors stood an emergency exit, a green illuminated box mounted on the wall above it. Abigail grabbed Mark's hand. "Come on."

Beyond the exit door they dashed round a bend, down a flight of stairs, took another bend, clinging to the rail, panting. Ahead was a pair of double doors marked LEVEL 3. Abigail pushed on them and they ran out onto another empty landing. This had a concrete floor—no doors, no companies. She turned right, Mark close behind. Ahead was another emergency exit. Abigail pressed against the metal bar and they were outside, the late-afternoon sun an orange haze, the air humid, sirens squealing, everything normal.

A black metal staircase descended the final two floors to the ground.

Mark leaned forward, hands on knees, wishing he'd kept up with his running fad from a few months back.

It took them no more than ten seconds to reach ground level at the back of the building. Ahead stretched a narrow, noisy alleyway, a row of huge growling air-conditioning units stretching thirty yards along the eastern side.

They took a convoluted route along another alleyway leading away from the building and emerged onto 46th Street, stopping to catch their breath under an awning of an upmarket deli, Rodrigo's. It must have been ninety degrees still and about eighty-five percent humidity. Mark's T-shirt was sticking to his skin and Abigail's cheeks were wet with perspiration, strands of blond hair plastered against her face. She waved over a cab and it pulled up to the curb.

"Downtown," she told the driver. "West 24th, Phoenix Car Rental."

Mark just caught the end of it. "So what's this all about?" He slammed shut the door and sat down close to Abigail.

"I've been worried for a while that my office was under surveillance."

"By who?"

"I don't know. I've even had the place swept—twice, actually; the most recent sweep was last week. Nothing. They must have been using remote devices, top-end stuff."

"Abigail, I'm about three steps behind here."

"Look, Mark, don't you think that what we are finding out from your regressions is, well . . . sensitive?"

He frowned. "Yes, of course it is. I'm sorry. I'm just . . . a little disorientated. That nice man Elton-Hornsby was after something he thought Pat had given me. Pat's wife in Oxford was sure someone had gone through their house." He ran a hand over his forehead. "What a fucking mess! But we can't prove anything. Whoever is eavesdropping on our sessions, whoever shot at us, can only be disappointed. All right, so I learn who killed Kennedy. Who's going to believe us? Imagine it: So, Mr. Bretton, how exactly did you establish who assassinated JFK?" Well, you see, I was regressed under hypnosis—"

"Mark!" Abigail put her hand up. "That's not the point. We've learned a very important secret. It might only be a matter of time before we get proof. The people

270

behind the surveillance, the people employing the gunman, they're not going to risk us finding out something they want kept secret, are they?"

"But it was fifty years ago, Abi."

"So? I know for a fact that one of the people you saw in the regression is still alive."

"What!"

"Steinheiser. Orlando Steinheiser. He is an incredibly powerful, phenomenally rich man, the patriarch of a highly respected family. If he was in part responsible for the crime of the twentieth century, I don't think he would want anyone to know about it, do you?"

"There's a lot that you're not telling me, Abigail."

Buildings and people flashed past, unnoticed by either of them.

"Abigail?"

"I worked for Steinheiser."

"What the hell!"

"It was just for a short time, five years ago, before I started my own research programme. He had established a state-of-the-art facility near Albuquerque with huge funding, and he was studying regression."

Mark noticed the driver turn his head slightly. He'd obviously picked up the odd word.

"You worked with the CIA?" Mark hissed.

"He wasn't CIA then. That whole thing was half a lifetime ago, for Steinheiser. The place in New Mexico is a private institute. He's a multibillionaire. I left because I did not agree with his ethical code, if you could call it that. I didn't agree with the experiments he was conducting and the ones he was planning."

Mark was shaking his head. He looked hurt. "Why didn't you say anything? I'm so sick of all this secrecy."

"I didn't think it was relevant—"

"Not relevant?" Mark snapped a little too loudly. The driver flicked them a glance in his rear-view mirror. "Of course it was fucking relevant, Abi. What the hell have you got me into? I've been beaten up and dumped by some British guy who was involved with abusing Patrick. I've just been shot at! And now you tell me Orlando fucking Steinheiser—the man who . . ."

"Ssh!" Abigail gave him a furious look. "Mark, I know you've been—"

He had his hands up. "You can't imagine . . . I've lost my best friend . . . learned that I'm a—"

"Mark!"

The cab jerked sideways as the driver pulled to the kerb and stopped, leaving the engine ticking over.

The driver twisted round. "Hey, lady!" he called through the grille separating him from the passengers, his voice brittle. "I can do without this, okay? This is where you get out—both of you!"

"What?" Abigail retorted.

"Look, I'm not a well man. My shrink, right? He tells me I can't expose myself to conflict."

"You're a cab driver in Manhattan for Chrissakes!" Mark shot back.

"I gotta feed my family, smart-ass. And it ain't just conflict—it's other people's conflict . . . that's what I can't stand, capeesh? I lock myself in here all day, I don't talk to no one, don't get involved. But you guys—so . . . out, scram. After you've paid . . ." he read the meter . . . "six-eighty."

Mark was about to lose his temper, but Abigail was already getting out on the traffic side. A driver leaned on his horn, forcing her to dash for the sidewalk. She gave him the finger as she went. Still barely comprehending what was happening, Mark fished out a five and two ones from his pocket and tossed them between the bars of the grille. "Keep the change," he spat.

Brimming with rage, he stepped onto the sidewalk, looked up and saw that Abigail was grinning.

"Oh, yeah! Really fucking funny!"

Her eyes widened and her grin gave way to a loud laugh. She brought her hand to her mouth, but still couldn't contain herself. Mark just stared at her as though she were mad, and the more he maintained his hurt expression the funnier Abigail found it.

He shook his head, the pained look dissolving to a smile. Then he laughed and they fell into each other's arms. Passers-by gave them a wide berth.

"My life is just getting stranger by the second," he stated, gripping Abi's arms, the anxiety and bewilderment returning. He felt giddy suddenly. "Why exactly were we heading to a car rental, anyway?"

"We have to get out of the city. Our apartments will be watched. The next most obvious place for us to go to would be one of the airports. After that, the train stations."

Mark nodded. "But where are we going?"

"New Jersey."

"Why?"

"I know someone there, someone who can help us."

"But . . . ?"

"No buts, Mark. You just have to trust me on this."

"Why? Why, Abigail? I hardly know you."

She smiled. "Because we are soulmates."

Mark felt as though all sense of reality was slipping away. He was standing on Fifth Avenue. Looking up, he realised they were at the junction with 36th street. A trickle of sweat ran down his spine. The noise of the busiest metropolis in the western world had muted to almost nothing. The car horns, the rush of people, a fire-truck siren, the bleep of the traffic lights, it all seemed to be filtered through cotton wool. All he could hear was Abigail's voice. He gazed at her and only her face stood in sharp relief; everything else was a blur. Her face slid to one side and Mark's field of vision filled with blue sky.

Chapter 35

He had known it. Of course he had known it. He had known it since the moment he had first set eyes on Abigail. But something in his mind had suppressed the knowledge. He had known it all, every bit, subconsciously. But none of that, not a fraction of it, had filtered through to his conscious mind. Not until that moment on the sidewalk, standing at the corner of Fifth and 36th. Then it was all completely and utterly obvious. He had always known Abigail. She was his soulmate.

The sense of motion came first, then the hum of the engine, the feel of the soft leather seat, Abigail's scent. Mark opened his eyes and saw trees slide past, evening summer sun piercing the spaces between the foliage and leaving halos on branches that melted away behind them.

"Hey! It's alive!" Abigail smiled at him from the driver's seat. He still could barely differentiate the dream world from what might be reality. What had happened recently? Had he been to England? Had Patrick died? Had he been regressed to 1963? Had Abigail said what she had said? But then he felt an incredible warm feeling, an astonishing, deep security and an intense, almost unbearable happiness. She had said what she had said and he had known it all along and he had never felt such love for another human being.

"We're almost there."

Mark pulled himself up, rubbed his eyes. His mouth was dry. For a second, he couldn't speak.

Abigail filled him in on what had happened. She had bundled him into a cab on Fifth Avenue. This time, the driver had driven them to West 24th Street without incident and Abigail had convinced him that Mark had drunk a glass of wine at a late lunch when he was already taking Vicodin for a bad back. She even managed to persuade the guy to wait while she organized a hire car, and he had then helped get Mark, drowsy and mumbling incoherently, into the passenger seat. There Mark had slept for the entire two-and-a-half-hour journey, through the traffic of Union City and out onto the I-95. She had ditched the SIM cards from their cellphones so they could not be traced, used an ATM in Manhattan to pay for the car hire so no credit-card transactions could be followed, and withdrawn enough cash to last them for a while. They were now a few miles short of Princeton.

"What you said back there, Abi. Something in me already knew it. I can't believe I'm saying this. If a week ago you had told me this would happen I'd have thought you were insane, but some part of me was aware that we had known each other for much longer than the brief time we've spent together in this life. Somehow, though, it never filtered through."

"And then it seemed obvious?"

"Yes, utterly. So obvious that any other suggestion would have sounded mad. But what do you know about it,

Abi? You've been involved with this stuff for years. I'm a newbie."

"Oh sure, I'm the oracle of all knowledge!" she laughed. "Okay . . . I've been piecing things together gradually. And this is just half-guesses, right? A smattering of facts, speculation; but it seems that all human beings have lived hundreds, maybe thousands of times and we go through those lives in groups."

"Pat mentioned groups of six, three pairs of male and female 'souls'."

Abigail nodded, keeping her attention on the road.

"But why?"

She shrugged. "I told you, I'm just piecing it together. Remember, I told you when we first met that I'm pretty bad with the 'whys'."

"All right. But with these 'sixes': sometimes members of the group must get out of sync with the others."

"Well, yeah, definitely. We don't all live the same length of time. Nor are we all born on the same day, or sometimes even during the same decade."

"Which means we don't always find our soulmates," Mark said.

"That's right. But, more often than not, we do."

"So . . ." Mark paused and drew breath. "You and I . . ."

"I have no idea how many lifetimes . . ."

"You must be getting sick of me!"

She laughed and shook her head slowly.

"And Patrick is one of our six, isn't he?"

"Yes."

"Who are the other three?" Mark asked.

"I only know one other."

"Who?"

"You'd read about the affair at Bellevue Hospital by the time we met for the interview, hadn't you? It was the spur for the American Psychology Association to suspend me. But the media twisted the facts and Peggy Gates, the girl at the center of the horror who committed suicide, she was not insane, as the papers implied; at least, not in the conventional sense. She was one of us, Mark, and she had experienced the most horrible things."

Abigail told him about Peggy's regressions. Mark sat listening without saying a word, seeing but not seeing the main highway give way to a narrower road, fields each side, the sun lowering on the horizon. After she had finished he barely knew what to say. There were just too many questions and he suspected that most of them were unanswerable. Eventually he said: "Peggy's grandfather, Senator Roger Gates. He did not hold you responsible in any way?"

"No. I told you at our first meeting, he completely understood. He knew there was nothing I did that pushed Peggy into killing herself. In fact, she and I had an incredible bond, as you would expect. But she was dislocated from this world, unable to cope with this existence. For her past few lives she had what people in the 1960s might have called a 'bad trip'. She couldn't go on. She needed to get away to . . . wherever it is we go . . . the Oneness of Many Parts, she called it."

Mark nodded, lips pursed tight. "And so where are we heading now?"

"To see Roger Gates. He's no longer a senator. He's retired from politics, but he's the wisest man I've ever met."

"And you obviously think he can help us."

"I *know* he can."

Abigail pulled the Honda off the road onto a gravel track, the dust kicking up. Mark spotted a figure standing at the open front door of a large old house. He was a slender man wearing a short-sleeved pale blue shirt, linen chinos and brown loafers. Abigail had told him that Gates was seventy-four but from here the man looked at least fifteen years younger.

The car stopped close to the door and Roger Gates stepped onto the driveway. Mark climbed out and saw Abigail and the elderly man embrace. The backs of the former senator's hands showed his age, his fingers a little gnarled, skin speckled with liver spots.

"This is Mark," Abigail said.

The two men shook hands.

"Abigail has told me much about you. She called earlier from the car. Come in. You both look exhausted."

Gates led them through to a spacious high-ceilinged lounge. It had a large bay window looking out to the drive and the fields and the trees beyond. Two walls were lined, floor to ceiling, with mahogany bookcases. The remaining wall was covered with framed photographs, a miscellany of snapshots from Roger Gates's life: portraits of Peggy, Senator Gates with Obama and Clinton, black and white graduation photos and images of his deceased wife Molly and their two sons, Howard and Truman. Howard had been Peggy's father. Truman had been killed in the first Iraq War in 1991. Mark and Abigail sat close together on an old subtly patterned sofa. Gates drew up a chair.

"Let me fix you a drink. Do you like wine, Mark? I have a few nice reds in my modest cellar."

"That would be great."

He was back in a few moments handing out a bottle. Mark read the label.

"A Shiraz from the Napa Valley," Gates said. "A little family-run vineyard that my wife and I loved. A 2005, a particularly good year." He opened the bottle and poured. Lifting his glass, he offered a toast: "To old friends and to new friends." They clinked glasses. He took a sip and made approving noises. "Now, down to business." He turned to Abigail. "You did exactly the right thing, my dear. Apartments or airports—not good options under those circumstances."

"Abigail told me she thinks Orlando Steinheiser is behind it," Mark said. "I'd never heard of him until today."

"Until your most recent regression?"

Mark glanced at Abigail.

"I hope you don't mind," she began, looking concerned. "Roger is, well, like a father to me. I haven't broadcast our discoveries to the nation, but we three should have no secrets from each other."

Mark took a sip of wine. "How much do you know, Mr. Gates?"

"Please . . . it's Roger. Abigail told me that you had regressed to November 22, 1963. That in your last life you were a White House Press Liaison named David Ashcombe. She had regressed you to the point where Kennedy was shot. She said she wanted to take you back there again. I assume you did go back—just before you were attacked in Abigail's rooms—and that you have found out something truly astonishing. Do you feel comfortable talking about this?"

"I guess. So this guy, Orlando Steinheiser; he must be ancient."

"He's eighty-two in October this year. I shan't be sending him a card! Okay, so where to begin with him?" Roger looked past Mark and Abigail to stare at one of his magnificent bookcases packed tight with leather-bound volumes. "I worked for him when he was Assistant Director of the CIA."

"You were CIA!" Mark and Abigail said in unison.

"1962-67."

"I had no idea."

"Why should you, Abi? Former operatives don't wear signs around their necks."

"So obviously you were working for Steinheiser at the time of Kennedy's assassination," Mark said.

"Not only did I work for him, I was in Dallas on November 22. Just a very junior officer. I played a small part in finding Oswald."

Mark whistled. "I'm sorry, but this is getting weirder and weirder."

"The weirdness is just beginning, young man! One of my closest friends in the CIA was Catherine Northgate. She had a brother called David."

"What happened to her? Do you know?" Mark asked, feeling slightly queasy.

"You're going to have to bear with me, both of you. It's an odd tale. Catherine was very dear to me. In those days it wasn't usual to have close friends of the opposite sex, not real platonic friends—that's quite a modern phenomenon for the most part. But Cathy and I were buddies. I loved her as a dear friend and I was devastated when she died.

"We went on many operations together. She saved my life once. Anyway, to cut to the chase. On November 22, I was working very late in the Washington office. I'd flown back about seven o'clock. Reached Dulles Airport about nine and went straight to the office. I didn't want to watch TV or listen to a radio. I didn't want to talk about it. I needed to close off, pretend it hadn't happened. You'd understand, Mark. Anyway, I was at my desk on the main floor and Cathy turned up."

"That would have been just after I . . . David saw her; told her."

"She had her own office. I went in to see her. She was agitated, a little paranoid. At first I put it down to the events of the day. We were all . . . shell-shocked. But then . . ."

"She told you?"

"Yes."

"What!" Mark exclaimed. Abigail placed a hand gently on his arm.

Gates was startled for a moment. "Mark, she died that night or early the next morning. After we talked I trudged to the bus station and home. The next morning I got to work about nine. The office was abuzz. I sat on my own for a while. I couldn't focus. I don't think many of us could. I had loads of stuff to do in connection with Oswald's arrest. I knew I'd have to get back down to Dallas for his trial in a day or two."

It was very quiet. The ticking of an old clock, the

282

rustling of leaves beyond the window. The light had faded outside and the room had fallen into its own dusk. Gates stood up, walked over to the door and switched on the light.

"So, you've known all this time?" Mark said.

"I've known, but I could not prove a thing—big difference."

"Couldn't you have dug a bit? Found out more?"

"I wanted to stay alive," Roger Gates replied gently.

Mark shifted his gaze toward Abigail who was watching Gates silently.

"And so you've never found out any more?" she asked.

Gates shook his head. "I served four more years under Steinheiser. He was my boss's boss's boss's boss. I only ever met him once. He wouldn't have known me from Adam. I had no access, no 'in' on anything. I was an office grunt." He chuckled. "I returned to college to take a doctorate in law and then, later, I went into politics."

Gates offered them some more wine. Mark accepted with a quiet "thank you". Abigail declined.

"I'm sorry to disappoint you, but it was all a very long time ago. I was a kid."

"We didn't expect anything from you, Roger," Abigail said. "Just maybe shelter for the night if that's . . ."

He laughed. "That goes without saying! But, look, actually I do have something more. A little while after Peggy died I had all her things from Bellevue brought here. I wanted to keep them somewhere private. There were drawings, poems she'd written. She kept a load of photographs on her laptop. The nurse had taken some of us in Peggy's room on my iPhone and they had gone into the hard drive." He paused for a moment and took a sip of wine. "Ah, anyway, Peggy kept a sort of diary on her laptop. At first I felt I was intruding upon her privacy when I read it, but then I had to remind myself that the dear child was dead, and who else would ever get to read it? Maybe, I supposed, she had kept the diary for me to see one day. I know . . . it sounds like a feeble excuse."

"Why didn't you tell me, Roger? It could have been useful in trying to understand what happened," Abigail said.

Gates shrugged and drank a little more. "I don't know, Abi. I think maybe I wanted to keep something for myself. You know, I felt a little jealous of the bond you had with Pegs."

"That's silly, Roger . . ."

"Is it?" Gates looked distressed. "I know from what you've said that Peggy was one of your 'six'. I don't think you could ever understand the pain of exclusion that produced in me. I was only Peggy's biological relative— a blood link, not a 'soul connection'. But you and her . . . Anyway . . ." The elderly man waved a hand in front of his face. "That's all my personal baggage."

"But hang on," Mark said. "Who's to say how much of our 'souls', our personalities are embedded in our physical DNA? Abi and I have discussed this and from our admittedly limited knowledge of the mechanism of rebirth, we've begun to think of it in terms of a quantum-level manipulation of our genetic material—an interaction between a force we call 'soul' and our material bodies. So how do we know if some element of our 'spiritual' selves, the bit that moves from life to life, is not linked in some way with the DNA that we pass on to our children, our grandchildren?"

Gates was concentrating hard on what Mark was saying. "I can't pretend to understand quantum mechanics," he answered. "But do you really think there might be something in this theory? Abi?"

She raised her eyebrows. "As far as the scientific community is concerned I'm Public Enemy Number One so I'm hardly one to pooh-pooh the notion!" she laughed. Then, suddenly serious: "Neither of us has studied the matter deeply enough, but I know for certain that rebirth is a fact. But in spite of the way my more orthodox colleagues view me, I am also a scientist and I have not abandoned my training or my empirical reasoning. Science could not begin to explain rebirth right now; but who knows? One day we will and I'm convinced that the explanation will fit some understanding of quantum mechanics and genetics more advanced than we have at the moment."

"There's so much we don't know," Mark interjected. "For all the many advances in the past few decades, both quantum theory and genetics remain areas of study that have barely been explored. For a start, geneticists know that something like ninety-seven percent of DNA is 'non-coding'. They call it 'Junk DNA'."

"What on Earth is that?" Roger looked a little lost.

"It means DNA for which we cannot yet assign a function," Abigail said. "It's more than likely that in the future we will learn that this DNA has some subtle role in the natural scheme of things, but it would be unscientific to say that all of it will be ascribed to mundane biochemical processes. Maybe the answer to how the soul migrates from life to life will be found in this so-called junk DNA." She looked contrite. "I should have realized how you felt, Roger. Of course you would conclude that although Peggy was your flesh-and-blood granddaughter it ended with simple biology. I'm so sorry . . ."

"I did think that, Abi. You two had such a natural closeness, and when I came to accept the notion of rebirth and to embrace it I was left with a terrible emptiness. When I said earlier I was a little jealous, I was underplaying it. I was almost overwhelmed by a sense of loss. For a while I lost all faith in the value of my own existence. In a strange way I felt I had already lost Peggy before she killed herself. I fact, I drove myself to believe she was never 'mine'. And there were times when I resented you. I can admit that now. But I never blamed you. It was merely a fact of life."

"The thing is, Roger," Mark said, "Abigail is right: science will explain it one day and a mechanism will be understood and I'm convinced we will learn that 'simple biology' is nowhere near as 'simple' as it appears to be."

"Few things ever are, my friends," Roger replied. "But look, enough about my feelings. The real point is the diary."

"Yes," Abigail said and held up her glass. "I think I will have some more, after all, if I may."

Gates poured the wine and returned to his seat. "In her diary, Peggy wrote about a recurring dream. She hadn't told me about it. I had no idea. But, reading it, I began to piece a few things together." He paused and leaned forward. "Peggy said she had been visited in her dreams by a young woman called Elizabeth. She said Elizabeth was one of her 'six'."

"What!" Abigail exclaimed.

Gates continued: "Elizabeth was being held prisoner somewhere—somewhere hot, somewhere remote. She'd been there for something like four years and was simply called 'Subject E'. She was being regressed, forced to regress, pumped with drugs . . . Abigail, what's wrong?"

Her face had turned the color of alabaster and the hand holding her wine glass had frozen a few inches from her mouth. In her mind she could visualize Peggy moments before her death telling her about the mysterious Elizabeth. "Nothing," she said. "Nothing . . . go on."

"In Peggy's recurring dream, this imprisoned girl kept telling her about her past lives and . . ." Gates paused a moment, drew breath. "In her last life Elizabeth had been Catherine Northgate."

Chapter 36

It had grown cold and Roger made up a fire in the ancient grate with wood from the forest behind the house, logs he had chopped himself that spring. Then he had shown them their cosy small-windowed rooms on the top floor, given them towels and spare blankets, and returned with them to the living room. He gave them a second bottle of the Napa Valley Shiraz, along with bowls of olives and potato chips from the kitchen, and wished them goodnight.

Mark and Abigail sat on the rug in front of the blazing fire with the lights off. The orange and red of the flames were reflected in their eyes and on their skin.

"If I stop, even for a moment, to think about all this I'm lost. It could drive a man insane!" Mark commented. Abigail leaned her head on his shoulder. "So we obviously have to get to the place Steinheiser is running. Did you ever know an Elizabeth when you worked there?"

Abigail sighed. "No, but Peggy mentioned the name."
"When?"

"Just before she killed herself, six months ago. She said Elizabeth was the wisest of us and that she was being held somewhere. She also said Elizabeth had been Cathy, but I didn't put the two together until Roger . . . I just pray she is still alive."

"What the hell are they doing there? What were *you* doing there?"

"It is very much like the place where Patrick was studied. Except that facility was run by DERA, a British government organization. Steinheiser set up his own research institute."

"For what?"

"To find out as much as possible about the mechanism of rebirthing, of course."

"But why? People like Steinheiser aren't interested in knowledge for its own sake. He's after something."

Abi gazed into the flames. "I was never entirely sure myself, but I think he had many objectives. For a start, he wanted information—secret, lost information. If he found research subjects who could regress or who could be guided to regress to certain key points in recent history, he could gain information that has been lost to us."

"What else?"

"He could get useful information on living people, enemies, and use it to blackmail them."

"What? How?"

"Well, think about it. Under the right conditions anyone can be regressed. Some people are more susceptible or open to hypnotic procedures than others, but using certain drugs and techniques that Steinheiser's people have developed over the years and perhaps also with research he has stolen from the British—he is a powerful man with many resources, remember—he could have hand-picked candidates who would be the most useful to him."

"What . . . you mean he has sent people back to gather

information that he could use both as espionage material and against his personal enemies?"

"I told you, I'm not sure. But in the past five years I've had a lot of time to dwell on the man's motivations. He is an ex-Assistant Director of the CIA so he has many enemies. He's a man driven by a lust for power and money that never seems to be sated however much of each he acquires. Put all that together and I think my assessment is pretty accurate."

Mark nodded thoughtfully. "Roger is a good man."

"He is. He's living proof that not all politicians are evil. He's the anti-Steinheiser."

"So how did you learn that we are soulmates?" Mark asked, tilting his head to look into Abigail's dark eyes.

"I had a patient who was a computer nerd. He helped me set up an auto-regression system."

"You are kidding me!"

"No. I have auto-regressed to at least a dozen previous lives. And in my last life . . ."

"You were Ruth!"

"Yes, I was Ruth. I regressed to the time when I was in our apartment and you called me from Bethesda Hospital."

"No!"

"I ran, as you told me to."

"You made it. You got to your Aunt Joan's?"

"Yes, I did. And do you remember when you regressed and you called me, I kept saying, 'Dave, I have to tell you something'?"

He nodded. "Yeah."

"I was pregnant, Mark. That's what I wanted to tell you."

"God! So what happened?"

"I left the apartment and drove to Missouri. It took me almost two days. I stayed overnight at a motel in Charlottesville, tried calling your office, the apartment. I was half out of my mind with worry. I arrived at Aunt Joan's the morning of the twenty-fourth, certain you would have gotten a message to her, but she was shocked to see me. That was when I really started to panic.

"Now I know why, of course, but it wasn't until the following day that I learned you'd been killed in an 'accident'. I finally managed to get through on the phone to Malcolm Kilduff. He said he'd been trying to reach me for days! He was genuinely horrified when he realized I hadn't been told. He explained that you and Cathy had died in a car crash near Baltimore. He didn't know any more. He asked me where I was, and I lied."

"Christ!"

"Aunt Joan was a wise old owl. She knew you were a White House Press Liaison and your sister was CIA. She understood right away that something was going on and forced me to stay put, wouldn't let me go to your funeral, and she looked after me."

"So . . . so how did you die? You're thirty-four now, right? You must have died within, what? Sixteen years—by the late 1970s?"

"It was a month after our daughter Helen was born. Hit and run. Helen was unhurt, miraculously. I died at the scene."

Mark looked suitably stunned. "Something of a coincidence!"

"I'm sure it wasn't. They took a while to trace where I'd

gone. But after Cathy was murdered they must have begun to wonder if you'd tried to pass a message on to me before they'd killed you in the stairwell of your office block."

"Jesus!" Mark exclaimed. "I'm responsible for two deaths because of what I overheard."

Abigail shrugged, then pecked him on the cheek. "Hardly your fault, Mark. And besides, it's ancient history."

"And our baby was orphaned."

"Joan took care of her for a short while, but then she put her up for adoption."

"How on Earth do you know that?"

"I did my research. I couldn't resist. About four months ago, when I began to auto-regress, I was drawn to my last life as Ruth and I suddenly had this desperate need to go and find Helen."

"You what!" Mark pulled back, shocked.

Abigail put a hand on his shoulder. "I know it sounds flaky but I couldn't help myself."

"And what? You found her?"

"I tracked her down to a suburb of Kansas City. Her adoptive parents had lived there. She had married a schoolteacher; she's a mum, has a son in college. I didn't speak to her. I just stopped outside her house. I felt like a stalker! I saw her leave for work one morning. She is fifty. A lot older than me. I was looking at a woman who was my daughter but not my daughter and she was seventeen years my senior!"

Mark watched her lift her wine glass to her lips. She looked tired but excited.

"It was the kookiest thing, but really spiritually uplifting at the same time. I can't really explain it."

Abigail rested her head back on his shoulder and for a moment they both considered the dancing flames. Then Mark turned slowly and kissed her. She slipped back onto the carpet and he leaned into her, their mouths locked together.

As they made love they each felt the same sensation, a blending of the incredibly familiar with the unknown. It was the sort of sex that a devoted couple might experience after a long separation, but a thousand times more powerful. Physically it was almost overwhelming, but at a deeper, completely non-physical level, on the plain of "the spirit", "the soul", the immortal elements of their being, things that had no adequate name, it was the single most intense, joyful, liberating experience of their lives. In some silent, wordless way it was an apotheosis, the ultimate gestalt, a resolution. They felt a oneness, which for them—for Mark, for Abigail, for Ruth, David, Eleanor, Magneilla, Jerome, Ashkii and all the others they had been—could exist nowhere else.

Chapter 37

Away from the isolation of Roger Gates's country house, hidden as it was in the woods outside Princeton, Mark felt a creeping sense of paranoia. Every face he saw had a suspicious cast: people were assessing him, holding his gaze just a little too long. He experienced it in the lounge of Philadelphia International Airport and, later, on the plane packed with people. It wasn't as though he was a complete stranger to danger. He had been mugged within a month of moving to New York, but it felt that during the past few days his life had morphed into the plot of a Hitchcock movie. He'd been snatched, assaulted—shot at, for God's sake! And now here he was with Abigail, heading straight toward the nexus of the danger and with any number of people working for Steinheiser or Elton-Hornsby after them.

Emerging from the arrivals area of Albuquerque Sunport it seemed as though they had flown to another country, the steamy humidity of New York giving way to a dry, crisp heat that touched lightly on the skin. It was late afternoon, the sun high, the temperature about ninety in the shade, an unblemished blue sky floating over the yellow and the ochre of the landscape that was dotted with white and gray low-rise buildings.

They picked up another hire car and headed off in the direction of a Radisson that Mark had booked that morning en route to Philadelphia. Abigail had lived here for two years and knew the city well: she drove.

Ten minutes later they pulled off the highway. The hotel stood directly ahead behind an expanse of lush lawn, sprinklers twisting and spraying.

Their room was on the third floor. It was large, but its 1980s decor was in urgent need of a makeover. The main window offered a view onto Central Avenue, with its colorful canopies and sunshades over restaurants and bars, people on the sidewalks wearing shorts and T-shirts, the sun blazing.

They were traveling light. Everything had been bought at Philadelphia Airport—an overnight bag each, a couple of changes of clothes from Gap, toiletries, and Mark had also bought a pay-as-you-go SIM and a Wi-Fi card. Abigail had her handbag from her office and Mark had his wallet, which had been in the inside pocket of his jacket. They sat in a pair of low-slung chairs at a coffee table in the bay of the window. Mark had a notepad to one side and a map of New Mexico opened out on the glass top.

"Okay, let's think. How on Earth do we get into the facility? You're the expert."

"The facility is here." Abigail pointed to a spot in the desert. "It's not marked on the map, but you take Highway 40, the main road running east out of the city." She traced a line across the paper. "Here is a little town." Her finger hovered over the word "Moriarty". "It's about thirty miles from here, tiny place. From there you take a dusty track north."

"How far along this track? Looks like, what? Five miles?"

"About that."

"So, the security?"

"I left there five years ago, so it could have changed, of course. But even then it was pretty tight. They operate officially as the San Miguel Research Institute—after the name of the region—and are listed as a 'Mental Health Research Organization' with a government license. But they are highly secretive—obviously. There is a perimeter fence which is patrolled by guards and dogs. On the southern side there's a secured entrance into the complex for which you need an electronic pass card. The same card gets you around the inside of the building and access is dependent on your status. I had very high clearance, but naturally my card was returned to them when I resigned."

"So, even if we could somehow get inside the perimeter and into the main building without being caught, we couldn't do much without an employee pass card and I'd imagine if we are to have any chance of finding the girl Roger mentioned—Elizabeth—it would need to be one with a high security rating."

"Yes, it would."

Mark inserted the new SIM into his phone and hooked up to the hotel's Wi-Fi to get online. He put in "San Miguel Institute" and placed the iPhone on the table so they could both see it. The place had a small and pretty straightforward website, the home page showing the building a few miles north of Moriarty. There were headings across the top of the page: "History", "What We

Do", "News" and a contact page. Mark tapped the headings and they read the carefully worded text of the scrupulous cover story. He moved across to "News". It contained mostly dull insider material about promotions and profiles of "employees of the month". A few photos of staff members flashed by as they scrolled down the screen.

"Looks like there've been a few changes in personnel," Abigail noted. "I don't recognize half these people—wait. That's it!"

"That's what?"

Abigail pointed at the phone. "Most of the senior researchers live in a smart estate on the edge of town and travel in and out of the facility. Only the junior staff and the techs live in."

"So?"

"That guy." She tapped the screen. "Graham Truro."

"The classic science nerd with the big head?"

Abigail laughed. "Yes, actually . . . he does have a big head, doesn't he? And it says here that he's just been promoted so he's still working there. He had a real thing for me."

Mark smirked at her and she shoved his shoulder playfully.

"Ah, right. And Dr. Truro has a good security rating to go with the big head?"

"He does!"

Chapter 38

Abigail stepped out of the hire car and made a show of not noticing Graham Truro climb from the black BMW 528i parked outside his apartment. It was growing dark and for a nasty moment Abigail thought that the man had not spotted her. But then she heard a familiar Texan twang and Truro saying: "My God! Is that really you, Abi?"

She looked up, pretended not to recognize him for a fraction of a second and then flashed him an enchanting smile. "Graham?"

He nodded and his own round face lit up with delight. He had small green eyes, cropped black hair and a head out of proportion to the rest of him. "What the hell you doing here?"

Abigail put on an Oscar-worthy performance. "Oh, just visiting the old city."

"It's been, what? Five years?"

"Almost to the week, Graham. You're still here." She waved a hand toward the luxury condos. "Still at San Miguel?"

"Yep."

"Looks like you've had a promotion, too." Abigail feigned admiration and nodded toward the car.

Truro beamed. "Head of Department A."

Abigail exhaled loudly. "Wow, Graham . . . that's . . . that's, well, fantastic!"

"So, where you headed to now, Abi?"

She lifted her arms, let them slap against her sides and shrugged. "I've just left an old girlfriend's place over there." She pointed at one of the smaller buildings beyond a stretch of well-manicured lawn across the street. "I had no idea you were still here," she added by way of an excuse for not looking him up.

He waved a hand between them. "Don't be silly. Hey, you fancy a drink? It's been a pig of a day and I'm gasping for a margarita. I make a killer cocktail . . . apparently!" He gave her a wolfish grin that was so absurd Abigail almost laughed. But instead she simply raised her eyebrows.

"Better not be too strong," she responded. "Gotta drive." And she followed Graham towards the complex of low-rise Mexican-style homes.

Truro was so excited that it made Abigail feel guilty and she had to keep reminding herself why she was here. She stood admiring the sumptuous interior of the scientist's house even though the decor was the opposite of her own taste, and she made cooing sounds over the huge TV and the gaming console as Graham strode into a kitchen so white it was almost dazzling. The overhead spots bleached out the counter and the pearlescent-veneer cupboards so much that when Truro opened the door to a massive refrigerator to reveal a row of eggs, a lettuce, some lemons and a yellow squeezy mustard bottle, the brief flash of color came as a welcome relief.

Truro lifted down a blender from one cupboard,

plucked a bottle of tequila from another and set to work. Abigail wandered across the stone floor of the lounge, her high heels (specially purchased for the occasion) clicking as she went. Coming up behind her former associate, she brought a chloroform-soaked handkerchief round swiftly, pulled it up hard against Truro's mouth and nose and kept it there as the man struggled for a few seconds before crumpling in a heap.

She immediately felt dreadful, thrust the cloth into her pocket, walked back into the lounge and took several deep breaths. She had not realized how damaged she would feel after attacking another human being, even if she had only put him to sleep for a few hours. Earlier, in the hotel room, she had told Mark that she thought the difficult bit would be obtaining the chloroform and sweet-talking Truro, but that had not been the case. Her medical license made the first easy, while the second came natur-ally. What had not come so easily was acting on the need to hurt someone. She was astonished to see her hand shaking as she punched in the speed dial for Mark's cellphone.

Abigail was still a bundle of nerves when she heard a faint tap at the front door. She walked over, checked through the spyhole it was Mark and let him into the apartment.

"Neat work, Abi," he said. He was wearing a smart suit, shirt and tie.

"I feel awful about this."

Mark looked into her eyes. "Abigail . . . Dr. Egghead here will be fine. He will wake up feeling as if someone has hit him with a hammer and he probably won't even

300

remember what he was hoping he was going to get. But there'll be no permanent harm done."

They walked through to the kitchen. Truro was out cold, lying on his back and snoring quietly. Between them, they managed to turn him on his side into the recovery position. Then they returned to the lounge, found the man's jacket, his wallet and his pass card. Mark plucked the BMW keys from where Truro had left them on the ultra-white kitchen counter. Before joining Mark at the door, Abigail gave the scientist one final check to make sure his airway was clear and that he hadn't hurt himself when he collapsed.

Abigail drove the hire car and Mark followed close behind in Truro's 528i. The traffic was light, mostly families returning from church, heading home after trips out to the desert or visiting relations and friends. Ten minutes after leaving the condo the two cars were out on Highway 40, the last glimmers of light snuffing out as the sun set behind the mountains. Cacti lining the road cast distorted silhouettes across the dusty tarmac.

Ten miles out they passed an eatery called The Taco Place. A solitary white beaten-up truck was parked outside. Following this stretched twenty miles of nothing but darkened desert, and far off to their left the purple slopes of the southern side of the Santa Fe Mountains.

Just beyond Moriarty and half a mile along the track leading north to the facility they stopped. Abigail took the hired Toyota a couple of hundred yards off the road so that it was out of sight. She had a briefcase on the passenger seat. She picked it up, ran over to the BMW and jumped into the back. Mark had the pass card. Ten minutes later the gates and the perimeter fence of the San Miguel Research Institute appeared in the beams of the car's headlights. Abigail lay down between the front and rear seats and covered herself with a sheet taken from Graham Truro's place.

Mark pulled up to the gate. Next to it was a machine similar to one at the exit point of a standard car park. A uniformed sentry sat in a booth close by. He was watching TV, the light from the screen playing irregular patterns across his face. Bored, he scanned the car, recognized it and looked away again as Mark ran Truro's pass card through a slot and drove slowly into the facility's grounds.

They stopped in the shadows at the rear of the building. Abigail sat up, brushed fluff from her dress and picked up the briefcase. Mark climbed out, stepped round and opened the rear door for her as though she were an important visitor to the Institute. They sauntered over to the back entrance. Mark slid the pass card along a sensor groove and the door opened.

A schematic of the complex was attached to a wall just beyond the entrance. Abigail checked it to see if there had been any changes made during her five-year absence, but it looked exactly the same as it had during her tenure.

"So, where now?"

Abigail pointed to the diagram. "This end of the Institute, the north side is where all the research labs are kept," she said. She pointed along a corridor to their left. Mark could just discern a row of doors toward the end, and beyond these a T-junction. "Over that way," she turned and pointed to the front, "the upper floors are all residential."

"How many research subjects are here?"

"In my day, it usually varied between twenty and twenty-five."

"So, what? We just head on over and see if we can find her room?"

"I'd prefer to find out a bit more about her first, Mark."

"How many staff work here?"

"I can only go by my own experience. I was one of ten psychologists. There was a team leader. That would be Graham Truro now. The Chief Scientist of the whole Institute is a man called Morrow, Professor Nathan Morrow. He was in his late fifties when I knew him. I noticed him in the staff picture on the website, so I imagine he's still here. He was a big fish—set the place up with Steinheiser over a decade ago."

"And what about Steinheiser? Is he here a lot?"

"He comes and goes. Stays for a day or two, disappears for weeks. He's a multibillionaire, remember. I always had the feeling this place was a sort of folly or a hobby for him, but one that he took extremely seriously. Nevertheless, he has no technical knowledge that I'm aware of, and he left the running of the place and the welfare of the subjects to Morrow and his team."

"All right. So, info on Elizabeth."

Abigail thought for a moment. "We have a problem with access. Everything is on computer, of course, but it will be protected, very carefully protected—obviously."

"We don't have a hope, then. Any passwords or access codes that you knew five years ago would be obsolete."

Abigail nodded but was not paying much attention.

"Are you listening to me, Abi?"

"Oh, sorry. I just thought of something. Professor Morrow is a pretty old-fashioned guy. He is up with the program because he has to be, but deep down he's a closet Luddite."

"So?"

"It was a running joke here that Morrow always wanted to keep paper copies of everything in a special archive room. People grumbled that it took up space that could be used for . . . oh, I don't know, more recreation rooms, or a larger canteen, but . . . well, he wouldn't listen."

Mark raised crossed fingers. "Let's hope he hasn't suddenly joined the twenty-first century, then. Where is this room?"

Abigail led the way, walking at a sensible pace as though they were here on official business. At the end of the corridor they turned left. There was a bank of three elevators. They went up four floors and stepped out into a carpeted corridor. The walls were painted cream and fluorescent strip lights ran the length of the ceiling.

"It's quiet," Mark commented.

Abigail glanced at her watch. "It's almost nine-thirty on a Sunday evening. What do you expect?"

A man came out of a door on the right a few yards ahead. He was wearing a lab coat and holding a long roll of paper, a printout. He ignored them completely.

On the wall were a number of metal signs. Mark read labels with arrows beneath them: "Labs 1-4", "Isolation Room B", "Administration Division C" and such mundanities as "Cafeteria" and "Toilets" with their own appropriate arrows. Two labels up from the bottom, he saw "Archive Room".

The door of the room opened with the pass card. The lights were off, but even with barely a sliver of illumination from the corridor Mark sensed that the room was cavernous—and overcrowded. Abigail flicked on the light and closed the door behind them. It was exactly as Mark had pictured it.

"Jesus, it *is* a waste of space," he exclaimed. "And paper. It almost makes me want to go hug a tree!"

A central aisle ran between racks of storage containers. There seemed to be no order to them, but then at the far end of the room they found two lines of tall gray metal filing cabinets. Their drawers were labeled chronologically, starting from 2006 for the top drawer of the first cabinet on the left and leading up to the present day on the right of the room.

"Looks like they keep the modern stuff here and then send it to the racks over there as more paper arrives to take its place," Mark said.

"I remember coming in here once with a clerical assistant to put some files away," Abigail replied. "The chronology is based on when research subjects arrive. Then they just add material to their file. If they leave the Institute their file is relegated to the racks as well."

"And you don't remember a 'Subject E' or Elizabeth when you were here?"

"No. But she must have arrived just after I left because over six months ago Peggy was writing about Elizabeth being here for four years."

"Okay, so that would mean her file should be about here." Mark pointed to the second and third cabinets on the left. Abigail went for one, Mark the other. They were stuffed to overflowing with papers. Lifting a file sleeve each, they started to flick through their contents in silence.

"Nothing about Elizabeth," Mark commented. "But this is to do with a guy called Hugh Fallon who arrived in 2008, so we can't be that far off."

Abigail returned her file and they moved along to the third one in the row. Mark opened the top drawer, lifted the sleeve closest to the front and pulled out the papers. The first words he saw were: SUBJECT E: ELIZABETH SOMERS. UNIT C. Room 14.

"Bingo!" He lifted a couple more sleeves from the cabinet and took a pace back.

Abigail moved in and flicked through the hundreds of sheets in the file sleeves of the top drawer. They were all about Elizabeth. She tugged open the second drawer, trawled through and pulled out a file at random. The heading read: SUBJECT E: ELIZABETH SOMERS. REGRESSION No: 566A. Hardly able to believe what she was seeing, she plucked another folder from the third drawer. The title page declared: SUBJECT E: ELIZABETH SOMERS REGRESSIONS Nos: 800-900, SEQUENTIAL SUMMARIES.

Abigail turned to Mark, who looked up from what he was reading.

"Elizabeth has been regressed almost a thousand times." She waved a hand at the cabinet. "This entire unit holds files just on her!"

Chapter 39

The moment Mark first saw Elizabeth she reminded him of an acquaintance from university days, a girl called Simone Lancaster, who had been bipolar and had been institutionalized during the Hilary Term of their second year. He had hardly known her, but out of some still inexplicable sense of duty he had visited the girl a couple of months after she had been committed. Simone had been drugged senseless and had looked as though her flesh could barely cling to her frame.

Abigail stood next to Mark by the door into C14, which they had opened by using Truro's pass card. Elizabeth was barefoot and dressed in a baggy pale green top and trousers. Although her body appeared to be at the limits of physical survival, her hazel eyes were alight with life and energy.

"What do they call you here?" she asked, her voice little more than a whisper. "Last time you were Ruth." She scrutinized Abigail. "And you . . ." Elizabeth inclined her head slightly toward Mark and produced the faintest of smiles. "You were my brother, my darling brother . . . David."

Mark felt a shudder pass through him. He recognized her immediately . . . loved her immediately. He took a hesitant step forward, then two more, and Elizabeth fell into his arms. She felt as light and as hard as a papier-mâché human, and she smelled of diluted blood and polluted flesh, an odor that he had encountered only recently, in Oxford when he had held Patrick close to his own body for the last time. It was not the smell of death but its precursor, the scent of cells and tissues fading, losing their grip, barely held together by tenuous fraying threads.

"Very touching." It was a man's voice and it came from behind Abigail. None of them had heard the door open. Orlando Steinheiser, dressed informally in slacks and an open-necked button-down shirt was clapping slowly, mockingly, his cupped bony fingers and palms creating a hollow slap.

Mark spun round. There were three men with Steinheiser. To his left was a very handsome dark-haired man in his late twenties, with a revolver held close to his hip. A little further back in the corridor stood a small bearded man wearing a white lab coat. Next to him the third man was dressed in a lightweight linen suit. He had a shaved head and dark eyes. Mark recognized him immediately as the British researcher who had abused the teenage Patrick and had snatched Mark himself on Eighth Street a couple of days ago: Hubert Elton-Hornsby.

"I've heard so much about you," Steinheiser added. "Mark Bretton, 'Regressor Extraordinaire', former press aide to John Fitzgerald Kennedy, no less. We met—sort of—a long time ago." He turned to Abigail. "And Professor Marchant. It's so good to see you again. I've been following your latest resea—"

"Who are you?" Elizabeth shouted, startling everyone and pointing a finger at the young man with the gun.

Steinheiser smiled very calmly. "Sorry, Elizabeth. This is my right-hand man, Christopher Trafano."

Elizabeth glared at him. He responded with a sheepish grin.

"Why are you keeping this girl imprisoned?" Mark snapped.

"Well, that's really none of your business now is it, Mr. Bretton? And besides, Elizabeth is not being kept 'imprisoned'. She is a volunteer."

Mark turned to the girl. Her stare was fixed on the man with the gun, Christopher Trafano.

"I don't believe that," Abigail said.

"Well, again, with respect, professor, that's none of your business. However, the fact that you have broken into my institute with what I presume is a stolen pass card *is* my business. And you will understand that I'm not particularly happy about it." He looked into Abigail's eyes, then gave Mark a cold stare. "We assumed you would turn up. You managed to slip away from Manhattan and we knew it was only a matter of time before you learned about Elizabeth here. Abigail, your rooms were bugged months ago; yours, three days ago, Mr. Bretton. We know as much about your remarkable regressions as you do. And, of course, we are familiar with your poor deceased friend Patrick Clifton."

"So, what now?" Mark asked. "I suppose you plan to imprison us, pick our brains?"

"Well, yes, naturally I do. My colleagues here would be very interested in interviewing both of you. I'm sorry.

I've been very rude." Steinheiser half turned. "This is our Chief Scientist, Professor Nathan Morrow." He pointed to the small bearded man. "You know him, of course, Professor Marchant. And this is Professor Hubert Elton-Hornsby. He works closely with Professor Morrow. In fact, Abigail, Professor Elton-Hornsby was your immediate successor here. He transferred from his position working for the UK government to take over after you left us."

Mark glanced back toward Elizabeth. She had stopped staring at the young man with the gun and had lowered herself to the edge of her bed, placed her hands in her lap and was now peering into the middle distance.

"So, if you would please follow me?" Steinheiser said. "I would like to take you to your quarters. You will find them very comfortable, of course. They have been prepared for your arrival. We plan to reconvene at eight a.m. tomorrow." He held a hand out toward the door.

Mark caught Abigail's eye, then gave Christopher Trafano a malevolent look.

It was obvious that they could do nothing but acquiesce.

Chapter 40

Mark awoke to silence; a silence so profound that he was aware of his own heart beating. Checking his watch, he saw that it was 3.34 a.m. He had been asleep for less than an hour. Before that he had spent a long time lost in thought and staring around the sparsely furnished room, wondering how he and Abigail might escape. But in the short time he had been unconscious his mind had been filled with strange images, voices, sights and sounds—things that had once been real and things he could not fully understand consciously; places constructed from pure instinct, primal places with no names.

He had dreamed of Patrick, but his friend's face kept changing. Then the dreams had altered. He was with Abigail, but she was not Abigail, she was Ruth, she was Imelda, Anna; and he was not Mark, he was Gerald, Vitnu, Omagha. In one vision he was wearing a white robe stained with blood and sand, and a goat's head lay at his sandaled feet. In another, he saw a man on horseback charge toward him and heard the loud clank of metal against metal, the sky all awhirl as he stumbled backward. And then he had returned to the present moment and the dim glow of a lamp at the side of his bunk.

Mark's head ached, he felt extremely tired, and for a

moment he struggled to accept that only a few days ago his world had been so normal. During the past week everything had changed, every preconception, everything he had modeled in his mind, the constructs of his universe; they had all transmuted to the point where they were now barely recognizable.

And then there was Abigail. He could not quite understand still why it had taken him so long to realize who she was, who they were. But then he recalled that the same had been true of Patrick. It was as though his mind had put up a defensive barrier to the concept of rebirthing, soulmates, sixes and the precipice beyond which lay the terrifying notion of eternity. No mind could consciously welcome a rewiring of itself. He remembered a talk given by a prominent radical neurologist, Francis Hamlin, that he had attended in New York. The lecturer described what he dubbed "mind maps", personal neural constructs. According to his theory, every person had a self-customized model of the universe in their head. When something truly life-changing happened to us, the model was shaken. Sometimes it was shattered beyond repair and we went insane. If we managed to salvage enough of our own mental self-image to keep functioning we could go on in altered form, our mind maps reconfigured.

He heard a sound from the door and pulled himself upright on the edge of the bed. The handle turned and the door opened inward. Professor Hubert Elton-Hornsby stood at the threshold with Abigail and Elizabeth immediately behind him. They all came in and Elton-Hornsby closed the door quietly. He put a finger to his lips.

Mark stood up. "What the hell?"

"Sssh, you idiot!" Elton-Hornsby hissed. "Don't you understand the universal gesture for keeping quiet?"

Mark turned to the women. Elizabeth was dressed in jeans, a sweatshirt, pumps. She still looked like an emaciated wreck but at least she was wearing something that made her look less like a patient in a psych ward. He surveyed Abigail's face and she gave him a brief reassuring smile. "Let the professor speak," she whispered.

"Why should—?"

Elton-Hornsby took a deep breath. "I'm here to help."

"How?"

"I'm getting the three of you out of this place." He raised his pass card.

"And I'm supposed to believe you? Last time we spoke you told me you worked for the British government. That was just before one of your gorillas kicked me in the head."

"Do you have any better offers?"

"How do I know this isn't some game? Some psychological test?"

"You don't. But as I said—"

"Yeah, yeah, all right. Well, if this isn't some bullshit game, why would you be so helpful as to get us out of this place?"

"Until four years ago I did work for the British government—for DERA, the Defence Evaluation and Research Agency—and I did come here to replace Professor Marchant." He shifted his gaze toward Abigail for a second. "When you and I met recently in New York it was under rather unfortunate circumstances, I agree. And, indeed, I was being economical with the truth. I was not ready to cut ties with Steinheiser and was simply doing his bidding, trying to find out what had happened to the information that Patrick Clifton acquired from us in the UK."

Elizabeth stood motionless. It seemed as though she was barely breathing: just observing the three of them, taking everything in, absorbing everything, but saying nothing, expressing nothing.

"I came here because the division of DERA for which I worked—the Department of Paranormal Notions Research—was winding down. Professor Nathan Morrow, the Chief Scientist here, and Orlando Steinheiser persuaded me to cross the Pond."

"I know about you," Mark said, his voice harsh. He avoided Abigail's gaze. "I know what you did to Patrick. You more or less killed him."

Elton-Hornsby sighed. "And I'm very sorry about that."

"Yeah—so is Pat's wife Jan and their two fatherless kids."

Abigail walked over to Mark and they sat on the edge of the bed together. Elizabeth didn't move an inch. The English scientist took a couple of steps toward Mark and Abigail.

"Before I agreed to come over here to New Mexico, Morrow and Steinheiser told me some of what they knew about Elizabeth." Elton-Hornsby gave the young woman an affectionate smile. "It was the clincher that pushed me into taking on the job. I realized that Elizabeth was another Patrick, maybe an even better subject."

"Who you thought you could abuse!" Mark snapped.

Abigail placed a hand on his shoulder and squeezed gently. "Hear the man out, Mark."

"Why should I?"

"Because he has some useful things to say." She squeezed Mark's shoulder a little harder.

"It wasn't like that, Mr. Bretton. In fact, it was the very opposite. I did not want another great mind to suffer."

"So why is this poor girl such a mess?" Mark pointed to Elizabeth. "Look at her!"

"I quickly learned that I had no real say in what experiments were conducted on any of the subjects here, especially Elizabeth, who has been Morrow's and Steinheiser's prize lab rat."

"So why didn't you leave?"

"Two reasons," Elton-Hornsby responded, and for the first time he showed some anger and resentment himself. "First, this institute is the only one in the West still conducting serious research into regression and rebirth." He nodded toward Abigail. "With no disrespect to you, professor—you are a one-woman show with limited resources.

"Second, I thought that by being here and working with Morrow and Steinheiser I might put a brake on their ideas, moderate them; which I think I have succeeded in doing to a limited extent. Elizabeth here has been administered an enormous range of experimental drugs and undergone many hundreds of regressions, but I can assure you that if I had not been here she would have died long ago."

"And so you are telling me," Mark said, "that you are springing us from this place because you have finally come to accept that you cannot slow Morrow and Steinheiser forever and that their research will kill Elizabeth."

"It is too late for that." They were all startled by Elizabeth's voice and turned to look at her. She still had not moved. "I have very little time left. Professor, you do know this to be fact," she said to Elton-Hornsby. "There is no point lying about it. I think we have moved beyond that."

"Very well," Elton-Hornsby said resignedly. "I won't lie. You are right, Elizabeth. I'm much too late to save you, and it is not the main reason I am here. Morrow and Steinheiser have picked my brains for over four years. Not in quite the same fashion in which they have picked yours, Elizabeth. I admit that. But they have bled me dry and they refuse to give me any credit for the work that has come out of this place; work which I'm sure you at least, Professor Marchant, will appreciate as significant, whatever nefarious and unethical methods my superiors may have used. For that I cannot forgive them, and for that I wish to seek repayment."

"Well, at least that sounds honest," Mark commented.

Elton-Hornsby seemed drained, as though the very act of confession had taken everything out of him. He had a hunted look and it was this which convinced Mark that the man was telling the truth. The scientist might have possessed a grain of altruism somewhere in his soul, but it was not that which had brought him here with Abigail and Elizabeth. He had been driven to it by anger, frustration, a fury that had festered into hatred. Those emotions could be trusted.

"Follow me," Elton-Hornsby said. He strode to the door, opened it a fraction and scanned the empty corridor.

"Won't they see us on CCTV?" Mark asked.

"I've dealt with that. Steinheiser only visits sporadically, which makes me effectively second in command here, remember? There is only one man on duty in the monitoring room. He watches a set of screens linked to two dozen cameras positioned strategically around the complex. But he is not doing that at the moment. When I popped in to see him about half an hour ago he was as respectful and attentive as I would have expected right up to the moment when I injected him with a powerful sedative. He's now snoring, happily prostrate on the carpeted floor of his observation centre. Now, hurry."

They passed through two straight corridors, the second running perpendicular to the first. They saw no one. Mark checked his watch again. It was 4.09 a.m. They saw a line of closed doors on the left, then, to their right, the open door of a laboratory. Two men in white lab coats had their backs to them. The taller of the two was holding a flask containing a glutinous green liquid. They were studying it intently up against the light coming from a fluorescent strip in the ceiling.

Directly ahead stood a set of double doors. Elton-Hornsby used his pass card to open them and suddenly they were out in the crisp, cold desert night. The only sound was the faint hum of the light in an EXIT sign.

A dark green SUV stood on the gravel a few yards in front of them.

"It's ready to go. It's got a full tank. There's food and water in the back, plus some basic medical supplies."

Mark looked into Elton-Hornsby's dark eyes, the light from the exit sign reflected in his pupils. "Where are we supposed to go?"

The scientist put his hand on Mark's shoulder and guided him away from the two women. "I had a chance to explain this to Abigail earlier. We collected Elizabeth together before we came to you back there. Elizabeth is very close to death. She . . ."

"How close?"

Elton-Hornsby shrugged. "Days . . . at best." He lowered his head. When he looked up again, Mark could see the strain in the man's face. He had suffered a great deal. It was clear now through the bravado, the carefully modulated British stoicism. His life's work had been brought to an ignominious halt, doubtless by some ridiculous government budget cuts. Then he had fled across the Atlantic and straight into a snake pit where his ideas and knowledge had been plagiarized by crooks and charlatans.

"I really am sorry about your friend, Mark. Patrick Clifton was a great kid and I know he grew into a fine man. We honestly had no idea what the side effects of too many regressions would be. We still don't fully understand why it happens."

Mark's expression remained blank. "You didn't answer my question. Where are we supposed to go?"

"You can't go back to Albuquerque and you can't return to New York yet. Steinheiser has eyes and ears everywhere. Well, almost everywhere." He gave a thin smile. "I have a small place out in the desert. Soon after I relocated here I realized I needed somewhere to get away to sometimes, somewhere far from anyone. I told no one about it, so Steinheiser and Morrow are totally unaware that the place even exists."

"How do we get there?"

"Drive back to the main road, turn left, away from Albuquerque. Precisely fifteen point six miles from the junction there's a track off to your right. It runs directly south. Then there's nothing for over eighty miles. Eighty-one point seven miles south of Highway 40 you'll find another track east. Two miles along there lies a disused quarry. My cabin is close by. You couldn't get more isolated."

Mark nodded and started to turn back to the car.

"And, well . . ." Elton-Hornsby said. "Good luck, old chap."

Chapter 41

Through the window of the SUV, Mark surveyed the clear, moonless sky, its black expanse pinpricked by countless stars. There had been no need for an ID check or pass cards on the way out as the guard had seen Elton-Hornsby drive the vehicle in earlier in the day. Elizabeth lay asleep in the back, stretched out across the seats with a pillow under her head and a blanket wrapped around her frail body. It was cold outside and they had the heater on in the car.

Away from the lights of the Institute it felt as though they were floating in space. The twin beams of the car headlights cut through the darkness, but beyond their edges the world dissolved to nothingness. They could be anywhere, anytime. Mark felt oddly comforted by it, almost as though they had been cast adrift, set free from the world and all its troubles. He knew it was irrational, but for a while at least he could convince himself that the void offered protection.

Following Elton-Hornsby's instructions and watching the odometer, half an hour from the Institute they reached the turn-off from the highway onto the dirt track south. The eastern sky was beginning to brighten. At first it appeared as nothing more than a thin mauve radiance that transformed the cacti and the withered, leafless trees to spectral figures, but as the lemon rays of the morning's first light splayed skyward, the nightscape gave way to an expanse of almost preternatural bleakness: sand, scrub, succulent plants and dust.

They drove in silence for a while. Elizabeth slept, barely breathing; Mark and Abigail were each lost in their own thoughts. The isolation—the void, as Mark had thought of it—was alight now. It no longer felt as though they were floating in space, but with the sun came a freshness, the hopefulness of a new dawn. For sure, they were hiding, running, but now they each sensed there was some tangible purpose to this journey. They were fleeing to protect Elizabeth, to get her away from the place that had made her so gravely ill.

"You know, Abi," Mark said quietly. He gazed at her profile, the early-morning light playing across her cheeks. "I've been thinking a lot about my last regression and trying to square the fact that the ending, as I was murdered by Agent Maclaren, was slightly different to the first time I experienced it. I couldn't work it out."

"Couldn't? Sounds like you've solved it."

"Well, yes and no . . . maybe!"

He saw her lips twist into a grin.

"I realized that the second time in the stairwell things went differently because, during that regression, I had started to remember my first time there. I distinctly recall a sense of déjà vu as I was running down the stairs. A feeling that I had been there before."

"I heard you say that, Mark. It'll be on the tape."

"So I influenced the outcome."

321

Abigail nodded.

"But that struck me as ridiculous because, if that were the case, either my regression was nothing but a fantasy, a dream I made up as I went along, or I'm able to change my own history. What's more, if I could do that, what was to stop Patrick changing the outcome of November 22 by altering what happened in his regression? If he went back and agreed to the roof of the car going on, he wouldn't have been shot."

"By the same token, what was there to stop Peggy going back and changing the outcome of the SS raid when she was Rachel? She could have saved her parents and escaped the gas chamber."

"Precisely. But there is also the fact that it would cause a time paradox."

"And you've been taught that that isn't possible, right? It's a staple of time-travel stories." Abigail uncapped a bottle of water, offered it to him. He took a swig and handed it back.

"Okay, that's the received wisdom," Mark said. "But I think I have an answer, because actually, in theory at least, it *is* possible to change your past without causing a paradox. How good is your theoretical physics, Abi?"

"Rusty."

"Have you kept up with things at all since college?"

"I read *A Brief History of Time*."

Mark gave her a withering look. "Have you heard of the many-worlds interpretation of the universe?"

"Er . . . nope."

"We all go through life thinking there is only one history, one present, one future, one universe. But if the many-worlds interpretation is to be believed, this isn't actually the case. Suppose that every time anything happens, the universe splits into two—a universe where it happened, and another in which it didn't."

"And by 'anything happens', I take it you mean a major event?"

"No," Mark said emphatically, "the exact opposite, actually—which is the whole point. Anytime *anything* happens, the universe splits into two."

"But that would mean there is an almost infinite number of universes being created all the time."

"Exactly. Every time an event on a subatomic level occurs, two universes are produced."

"So taking that idea to an extreme, there could be universes that are only one subatomic-level transition different from ours—in other words, identical all bar the shouting . . ."

"And there would be others that are so alien as to be unrecognizable to us because they have constantly followed different paths," Mark interrupted. "There could be universes in which our solar system, our galaxy doesn't even exist."

"All right, but what does that have to do with your regressions being slightly different?"

Mark paused and rubbed his forehead. "The old idea of time travel was that you couldn't go back and alter the past because that would distort the present; and that even if you changed things in only a tiny way you could create a huge effect—the sliding-doors idea—you remember the movie?"

Abigail nodded.

"For example, suppose I went back to a time before my grandparents met, and I scared a cat so that it ran out into the road in front of my grandfather's car, causing him to swerve, hit a wall and be killed. I would never have been born. But then, the paradox would be: If I had never been born, how could I have gone back in time to scare the cat?"

"And you're saying that this idea isn't actually correct—that there is no paradox?"

"Correct."

"Because of the many-worlds interpretation?"

"Yes. If I go back in time and scare the cat, that sets in motion a chain of events that would not happen if I did not go back in time. Two separate universes are created spontaneously—one in which my grandfather dies and I don't exist, and one in which I don't scare the cat, my grandfather doesn't die before meeting my grandmother, and I am born."

"So, although by regressing you're not actually travelling in time, your awareness of the previous regression altered things and those two realities—one where you, as David Ashcombe, were killed in the stairwell and the other one in which you, as David Ashcombe, died in the alleyway—can co-exist without causing any paradox."

"And the same would apply to any regression by any of us."

"So Patrick could have gone back to his life as Kennedy and changed what happened that fateful day in Dallas. He could have agreed to the roof staying on the car, or he could have pushed through a last-minute change to the schedule and taken a different route that didn't pass the book depository. Those changes would have each created universes different from the one we know, the one we live in right now."

"Go to the top of the class, Prof!"

Abigail turned to face him and rolled her eyes. "You know . . . this all comes as a relief."

"Yeah?"

"Remember at Roger's house you were asking me what I thought Steinheiser was hoping to gain from the research he was funding? Well, I did wonder if . . ."

". . . he thought he could change history, like some science fiction character using a time machine? Yes . . . well, that's understandable. We all grew up with *Back to the Future*, but real physics doesn't work that way. And I'm sure Steinheiser's been made aware of it. So you can stop worrying about that."

"Good!"

"The universe is random, Abi. There's no such thing as free will. No one can control their own destiny. Karma is a nonsense. Life, the universe, everything is simply chaotic. We try to imprint some sort of order upon it, but we can only do that in tiny, temporary and personal ways."

"That's a pretty bleak vision of life, isn't it, Mark?"

"Maybe, but who said it would be rosy?"

"What about rebirth? Hasn't what you have learned recently cut through any of this existential desolation?"

"To be absolutely honest, Abi, I really don't know. All my adult life I have held the belief that there is absolutely no meaning to existence. That we are just an accident of Nature, a blip in the continuum. That we are born, lead our biochemical lives, see through our allotted time and then we die. End of story. Learning that we reincarnate, or that we are reborn many times, hasn't led me to God."

"I'm not suggesting it should, Mark. But doesn't it imply that there is more to human existence than just physical, material beings living a life as part of the ecosystem, then withering away to nothing? We are eternal beings. There is a lot more to being human than the sum of our physical parts."

Mark nodded. "I guess so. Maybe I just need more time to take it all in." He caught a glimpse of a building to their right and pointed east. "Hey, look . . . 'civilization'!"

They pulled off the track and the SUV bumped over rough terrain until Abigail found another path, ruts in the soil created by Elton-Hornsby's many visits to his isolated property. Fifty yards on they passed along the top of a shallow quarry, the strata of sand and earth and the occasional freckles of ore still visible. Skirting the pit, they turned left and directly ahead stood a tiny stone cabin, as rustic and primitive as could be imagined; a place that was the very antithesis of the sophisticated urbane man who owned it.

Chapter 42

"It's beautiful being with you," Elizabeth said. She was sitting up in bed in the single small bedroom off the living area. She had slept for twelve hours and some of the pallor had gone from her cheeks. She had eaten a little soup but seemed to have no appetite. Mark knew that any real hope the girl would survive was nothing but sentimentality.

"I will die soon," Elizabeth went on matter-of-factly. Mark and Abigail were seated in identical chairs that had been taken from the kitchen and placed each side of her narrow bed. "And it holds absolutely no fear for me. Neither should it for you, my loved ones."

Looking at her propped up on a pile of pillows, Mark was reminded of pictures he had seen of saints with their large God-filled eyes turned to heaven as they lay on their deathbeds, arms limp at their sides, palms upward over the coverlets.

"Are you in any pain?" Abigail asked, and Mark suddenly felt a jolt. It was a question he had asked Patrick less than a week ago.

"A little, but it is nothing. You know, I feel no resentment toward Mr. Steinheiser or Professor Morrow. I have lived a very full existence, even if I have not spent many years in this incarnation. I know their intentions were impure: Steinheiser is a man driven by selfishness and greed, while the professor simply has an overzealous thirst for knowledge and cares nothing for anything or anyone blocking his way, but they have actually done me a great favor."

"How on Earth can you say that?" Mark complained.

"Because, although they have harmed my body, the hundreds of regressions they forced upon me and the drugs they have used have educated me, enlightened me. What I have gained during one short existence would otherwise have taken many lifetimes to acquire, and for that I'm grateful.

"Loved ones," she went on, seeing Mark and Abigail's doubting looks. "They took me to many hundreds of different past lives. I experienced vague memories of times so far in the past that they were never even written about— there is no record of them except those to be found in the rocks and the stones of the Earth. I was regressed to times before I had human form."

"But I assume you never once mentioned your most recent life before this one, or else Orlando Steinheiser would have known who you had been and done everything he could to force your secrets out of you."

Elizabeth nodded and produced a faint, conspiratorial smile. "I am stronger than him, older than him. He suspected something, of course. He was there, he was responsible for the death of President Kennedy. He knew I held a secret from my last life, but I would never reveal it, no matter what he did to me. Patrick did the same. You two are the only ones alive to whom I may relate that part of my history."

"What do you mean, Elizabeth?" Mark asked.

"Patrick . . . he was your dear friend. I know he died a short time ago. He is one of us."

"Yes, I know that he was one of our six," Mark replied. "I read some of the reports of the experiments Elton-Hornsby performed. But I could find no records of any regressions of Patrick's after the First World War when he served as a private in the British Army and died at the Battle of Verdun in March 1916. Pat was born in 1976. In the notes and reports I read there was no explanation for the long gap."

"As I said, Patrick refused to allow himself to be regressed to the lifetime before his most recent incarnation."

"Why?"

"For the same reason as me. He knew they were particularly interested in it."

"Because . . . ?" Mark enquired.

"Because, after he was Private Neville Sinclair, Patrick was John Fitzgerald Kennedy."

Mark experienced the same sensation that he had felt twice before during the past few days; a shock that was not a shock. A jolt that rattled his consciousness, shook the model of the universe in his head, the personal mind map he had drawn. But, on a deeper level, he had known all along. Of course Patrick had been Kennedy. He remembered the sensations he had felt as JFK had died, recalled the experience of sensing the man's soul, his spirit leaving his physical body outside the hospital in Dallas.

He noticed Abigail staring at him from the other side of the bed. "I'm getting used to shocks," he sighed. "And, of course, a part of me knew. But does that mean Jackie Kennedy was one of the six? Was Peggy Jackie?"

"No," Elizabeth replied softly. "The soul who was Jackie Kennedy is not one of us. We do not always find our soulmates, even if we are born at the right time, but with Patrick's two most recent incarnations he has gone through his lives with other women who were not The Ones."

Mark shook his head slowly. "Of course: Patrick's widow Jan isn't one of the three females in our six."

"I am Patrick's soulmate," Elizabeth replied, a fleeting sadness in her eyes. "We were not together when Patrick was Jack Kennedy and I was Catherine Northgate and we have not been together this time. But I will be with him very soon."

"I sort of realized that too," Mark replied. "As soon as you and I met, Elizabeth . . ." He glanced across to Abigail. "There's so much I've known without it ever breaking through."

"We each know everything there is to know about the others in our group," Elizabeth remarked. "It's simply that, for any number of reasons more often than not, we suppress things. Or we have not yet woken up enough to understand what our soul knows."

"What do you mean, not woken up enough, Elizabeth?" Abigail asked. She leaned forward, her elbows on her knees, her chin resting in the palms of her hands.

"We're all waking up, little by little. It might not seem like it when you consider what horrors are perpetrated in the world each day, but we are. We are all learning as we move from life to life."

"It's the Buddhist concept of rebirth, and one of the central tenets of Hinduism and Sufism," Mark commented.

"Yes, some religions embrace the principle of rebirth. It's an ancient idea. There are records describing the concept dating back to 600 BC. But each religion has a slightly different take on it—as you'd expect."

"But you're saying that we are evolving through reincarnation," Abigail said and stared straight into the girl's eyes. The light in the room was beginning to dim, the sun lowering in the sky. It was a primitive house without electricity, and they had been drawing water from a well outside. It was clear that Elton-Hornsby had wanted a place as far removed from the hi-tech world of the Institute as he could possibly get. "Why are we evolving, Elizabeth? Do you know?"

"I have begun to understand only in this long, long lifetime," the girl replied, her eyes lighting up with excitement. "I know this body," she glanced down at the shape of her legs under the blankets and her skin-and-bone torso dressed in one of Elton-Hornsby's woodman's shirts that Abigail had found in a cupboard, "is only sixteen years old, but I have played out many lives during this one.

"I've only glimpsed things, but I have learned that all human beings are linked. We are six, my loved ones." She reached out and took Mark's hand in her left and Abigail's in her right. "But all intelligent beings share a bond, and by that I do not simply mean just the human beings who are born and reborn and live solely on this world. I mean all intelligent life everywhere—the universe is teeming.

"But, Abi, you ask: what is the purpose?" Elizabeth

peered into the middle distance for a moment and then turned slowly to Mark. "Loved one, in this lifetime you have learned a lot about physics, haven't you?"

He nodded. "A bit, but I think we believe that we understand a lot more than we actually do. I've learned nothing more profound than what has been revealed to me during the past week."

"But you understand the idea of the expanding universe?"

"Yes," Mark said. "It's pretty much a proven fact that the universe began about fifteen billion years ago with the Big Bang, when a singularity expanded spontaneously. No one knows how or why, of course. But the universe is still expanding and will continue to do so for maybe another fifteen or sixteen billion years. But then it will reach a point where the expansion stops."

"Then what happens?" Abigail asked.

Mark shrugged. "No one knows. One theory suggests that it will just dissipate to nothing so that all activity stops and the vaguest remnants of energy will bubble away. Other theorists suggest the universe will start to contract again and maybe everything will run in reverse. Thirty billion years will have passed and the universe will begin to squash itself into a singularity again—the Big Crunch, they call it!"

"The truth is actually amazingly simple," Elizabeth replied.

Mark studied her gaunt face. Dusk had fallen and shadows were splayed across the bed, along the walls.

"We, the intelligence in the universe, evolved from the singularity just as did stars, planets, everything. And we, the intelligence in the universe, will keep evolving until we become what religious people call 'God'."

"I don't understand," Abigail said.

"The universe is infinite and lasts for an infinite time, but it goes through a cyclical process beginning with what the authors of the Bible called Creation, what scientists describe as the Big Bang. Stars form, planets cool, life develops, life evolves, intelligence grows from increased complexity. Intelligent beings continue to learn. We go through technological stages, many races destroy themselves. The fittest survive and evolve further. We shed our bodies, we become spiritual entities, we coalesce, the whole is so much greater than the sum of its parts. We have a taste of this when we die. 'The in-between place' as our loved one Peggy called it. The place we go to when we leave behind our bodies, the place in which we reside before we are reborn, this gives us a sense of the coalescence that intelligent beings eventually achieve.

"And after eons we become 'God'. And what does 'God' do best?" Elizabeth giggled and squeezed Abigail and Mark's hands. "'God' reverses the expansion of the universe and we start again, compression, singularity, Big Bang, new life, new intelligence, new 'God'. Isn't it beautiful?"

Mark glanced at Abigail. By now it was almost too dark in the room to see her, but he could sense that she had turned toward him.

"Elizabeth," he said quietly. "Not so long ago I would have said you were high on something. Now I know Truth when I hear it."

He could see the white of Elizabeth's smile through the gloaming.

"Well, that's good, Mark. And I think that's quite enough philosophy! Don't you two want to know what Cathy did next?"

Chapter 43

Mark and Abigail had found a few kerosene lamps and a barrel of fuel earlier in the day while Elizabeth had slept. Now they set up a pair and lit them, one each side of the bed, and placed a third one on a table at the far side of the room. The lamps produced an oddly comforting warm glow, the sort of light that modern people had forgotten existed.

Elizabeth closed her eyes and her breathing became shallow.

I wait a while in the diner after David goes. I'm really not sure what he is planning to do—all of this has come so suddenly. I've told him he must get away, far away, as soon as possible, but I can't make him do anything he doesn't want to do. I leave a dollar on the table, turn up the collar of my coat and walk out into the alley outside Marco's.

My initial shock has passed. I'm in professional mode. I've been very well trained and I've dedicated the last six years of my life to the Central Intelligence Agency. I know how to respond in almost any situation, but even I have to admit this one is straining my limits. Like almost everyone else, after what has happened today in Dallas

I feel stressed and emotional; and now this, another huge jolt to the system. And I know that my beloved brother is in mortal danger. I know how the CIA and the FBI operate. I know Steinheiser is a powerful man. And as for his co-conspirators . . . well, everyone knows them, even if they don't know the real them.

I had parked in a nearby street and I'm soon heading west out of the CBD and onto the I-495. The traffic is very light. Actually, I see almost no one in the center of DC and then out on the interstate I catch sight of perhaps half a dozen cars during the time it takes me to drive to our new HQ at Langley.

The car park behind the new building is surrounded by trees. Indeed, the entire vast complex is secluded from the world in woodland not far from the Potomac River. The wind rustles the leaves, and it is chilly. There are quite a few cars here, but that's nothing other than I would have expected. Today has been a massive day for the CIA. I had only just reached home myself when David called me some ninety minutes ago. And now here I am again.

It's an impressive building. It was opened officially a couple of years ago by none other than Jack Kennedy. My department had only taken up residence here about eighteen months ago, so everything is sparkling and gleaming new. We're in Building M, second floor. I'm feeling tired so I take the elevator, watch the light for the second floor flash by, feel the deceleration and step out through the opened doors into a carpeted corridor. I hear people chattering, telex machines chomping and the clatter of typewriters. A woman I know, Irene Cosova, totters across the corridor, carrying an armful of files to an office on the right.

The fourth door on the left leads to my little room. I just reach my desk when Roger appears in the doorway. He has a cigarette dangling from his lips. I give him a wan smile and beckon him in.

"How you feeling?" he asks.

"Oh, you know . . . same as everyone else, I guess. You?"

He shrugs. "I just got back from Dallas."

"You were there?"

He tilts his head, sits in the chair across the desk from me, taps his cigarette on the edge of my ashtray.

"Sorry; dumb question!" I say. "Were you . . . well . . . there?"

"No. I was way back behind the convoy. Then I was sent across town to track down the shooter. He killed a cop after he shot JFK. Did you know that?"

I nod and look into Roger's eyes. He is my best friend. I'm married, but I'm not happily married. My husband, Kerry, is a decent enough man but we have no real connection and most of the time I wonder why on Earth I married him. Every day I thank God we do not have children, because I have an instinctive feeling that our marriage will not last. Having said that, Roger is not my lover. Sure, he's an attractive man and very bright, great personality. I love him as a dear friend. And you know what I love most about him? He feels the same way about me; I know that for a fact. We're, well, buddies. I've never known that with any other man.

"Yeah, I heard about the guy being arrested," I say.

337

"What's up, Cath? What you doing here?"

"Why are half the people I see here staying over?"

"Okay, but you seem upset."

"Aren't you?"

He raises both hands, and starts to get up, leaning down to stub out his cigarette.

"Hey, look, I'm sorry, Rog," I say and he sits back down. "Okay . . . something has happened."

He looks at me, puzzled.

I pull over a sheet of paper and write on it: "I don't know if the room is bugged" and show it to him.

He raises an eyebrow and pulls the paper across the desk, writes and swivels the paper back so I can read it. "Play safe."

I add: "Roof, five minutes."

"Okay, Cath. Look, maybe you should just go home. There's nothing more you can do here," Roger says. "I may have to head back down to Dallas early tomorrow, but you know, it's chaos, absolute chaos. We think we have contingencies for everything, but we're kidding ourselves, aren't we? Who would have dreamed . . . ?"

"Yeah, you're right. I just feel, well, useless. I feel I need to do something."

"Cathy, it's not your department. Just go home. Keep the damned TV off!"

Roger eases out of the chair and walks toward the door. "See you tomorrow."

Up on the roof it's freezing and drizzling. I have on an overcoat, but Roger is in his regulation suit and trilby. We find some shelter behind a heating conduit but I know the poor man is suffering. He takes out a packet of Marlboros. Offers me one. I take it and he lights the cigarettes with a silver Zippo.

"So tell me," he begins. "What's happened that sends us up here, Cath?"

I scan the roof, all senses alert, and find I can't actually come out with the words. Roger looks at me, confusion spreading across his face.

"I've never seen you quite so—"

I lift a hand. "It's my brother David."

The skin on Roger's forehead creases, but he doesn't interrupt, gives me time. His patience is one of the many likeable things about him. So different from my husband Kerry.

"David was there today . . . right there. And then he came back on the plane with the coffin."

"No shit!"

"He followed the White House team to Bethesda, and, well, he overheard something." I swallow hard. "Orlando Steinheiser talking to Agent John Maclaren about a conspiracy hatched between himself, Nixon and Hoover. A conspiracy to kill JFK."

Roger stays very still, his cigarette poised an inch from his lips. He closes his eyes for a couple of seconds. "Okay," he says eventually, clears his throat as though he is struggling to speak. "Okay." He draws on his cigarette, then grinds it under the sole of his right shoe.

"Could your brother have been mistaken?"

I shake my head "No. I've just left him in DC. He was chased from Bethesda by Maclaren and another agent. They know he knows."

"Holy crap! Where is he now?"

"I told him he had to get the hell out—go abroad."

Roger lights another cigarette, offers one to me. I shake my head.

"So what now? I take it they have no idea that you know."

"Not unless they saw me meet with David, which I very much doubt. But . . ."

"But what, Cathy? You're not thinking what I think you're thinking, I hope."

"I'm going to get evidence. It's David's only chance."

"What!"

I put a finger to my lips and immediately realize I'm being silly. There's no chance that anyone else would be up here in this weather. Roger is shivering and has wrapped his arms around himself.

"What can you possibly do?"

"I haven't had that much time to think about it," I reply. "But it seems obvious I have to get something to lead me to some hard evidence. I'm going to see John Maclaren."

"But that's insane, Cath!"

"It's the only thing I can do. I can't go to Steinheiser now, can I?"

"No, but you could just walk away, keep schtum."

"And leave my brother without a hope?"

Roger's expression is hard. "He has no hope anyway."

"I'm not willing to accept that."

"Cath, please! Think about this. I understand, but . . ." He puts a hand on my elbow. "You're going to get yourself killed too."

"I'm a big girl, Rog."

"I know. But these guys are much bigger. They—"

I put a finger to my friend's lips. "I appreciate . . ."

"Do you?"

I gaze down at the concrete. When I look up, Roger has an imploring expression on his face. "Wish me luck," I say and start to turn. He grips my elbow, hard. Our gazes meet. Roger purses his lips. He lets go of my elbow and I walk away toward the door and the stairs that lead me back down from the roof.

Chapter 44

I know Agent John Maclaren vaguely. He's a few years younger than me. In fact, at twenty-two, he is really young for an officer. I know there's been lots of gossip at Langley that he has been promoted too fast and that his "special relationship" with Steinheiser is down to the fact that the Assistant Director had been close to Maclaren's late father and John is being fast-tracked.

Whatever the truth of that, one thing I know for sure is that John Maclaren is a very wealthy young guy on a big allowance from a family trust. He is only in the CIA for the action and the glamour and certainly not for the annual salary of $4,586.95. The guy lives in a very smart apartment in Georgetown: the entire top floor of a brownstone on Wisconsin Avenue.

It isn't a long drive from Langley to Georgetown and the roads are clear all the way to the Beltway, but then suddenly I hit heavy traffic and I realize it must be because of all the people driving back from Bethesda Hospital. Before I can take a different route I'm caught up in a three-mile tailback almost within sight of the George Mason Memorial Bridge over the river.

It takes almost two hours to cover the next six miles, and as I pull up on the other side of the street from

Maclaren's place I'm more tired than I can ever remember being. It's five to midnight, Wisconsin Avenue is almost silent and the restaurants are closed and blacked out. I can see no one on the sidewalk, but I notice that a light is on in John Maclaren's apartment.

We've chatted a few times, shot the breeze at the water cooler once or twice. I've got a cover story for why I'm calling on him at this time of night on this particular day, and from the passenger seat I pluck up a file that had been in a cabinet in my office. But I still find it hard to actually make myself get out of the car and step into the lion's den. I know I'm taking a huge risk, but I have a plan of sorts. I'm a professional and I will certainly not underestimate Maclaren. He is a conspirator, a traitor, a murderer, and for all I know he could be the one leading the hunt for my brother. I've had a lot of time to think things through while sitting in my car on the freeway.

I cross the street quickly, take the stairs to the third floor of the old building and face a door with a brass letter "B" positioned at eye level. I ring the bell on the wall to the right of the door. There is no response. I try again. Still nothing. I tap on the door. "John?" I strain to listen but hear nothing coming from the apartment.

From my handbag I withdraw a nail file. It has been ground down to half its normal thickness and width, almost a stiletto. I've used it before to gain entry through locked doors. It's a trick you learn during the first week of Basic Operations Training at Camp Peary. I turn the file left, back, left again, back, right, and hear a faint click, turn the handle and ease the door inward. I deliberately leave it ajar. Another lesson from Camp, gives you an easier escape route if you run into trouble.

There is a wide hallway, old parquet flooring brought up to a high shine. In the dim light coming from a room at the end of the corridor the walls are a dusky gray.

I reach the end of the corridor, the folder in my hand. The door to the room stands half open. There's a faint sound: piano music that I can't identify. I tap on the door, hear scrambling, a man's voice mumbling something, then a crash, a curse. I walk in and Maclaren is pulling up a lamp by its cord and trying to balance it back on a side table. He sways, very drunk, turns, sees me but doesn't recognize me, starts to mumble something more, then seems to comprehend who I am and staggers over.

"John," I say. "It's Catherine. Catherine Northgate."

"How did you . . . ?" he slurs, and nods in the direction of the hallway.

I half turn. "The front door was open," I lie.

"What the hell do you want?"

"May I?" I indicate that I would like to come into the room properly. He does a rather comical imitation of a gentlemanly wave of the hand and I move closer, holding out the folder. "You mentioned this yesterday before you went to Dallas. It's the Franklin Report."

He looks utterly bemused and I realize he is really, really drunk. I notice an empty bottle of whiskey on its side on the floor. There is another, half full, standing on a side table that is a twin of the one with the lamp on it. I see that next to this bottle is his standard-issue Sig P210 pistol.

Maclaren manages to shake his head slowly and raise

344

a hand to his forehead. He rubs the skin and looks at me without focusing terribly well. "Today . . ." he says. "Today? How can you care about . . . ?" And he waves vaguely toward the file.

"Actually, I don't," I say, flinging the empty folder to the floor and pulling out my gun.

Maclaren reacts incredibly slowly. He steps back and again falls over the table with the lamp, landing in a tangle of limbs, his head hitting the floor hard. It seems to bring him some awareness. He looks up and I see that he is fractionally more coherent.

"What the fuck?" he gasps.

I step forward, pull him up with my left hand gripping his shirt, and he half falls, half staggers onto the sofa. I lean over him, the gun pointed directly at the center of his forehead.

"I know what you've done."

He gives me a bleary-eyed look but I can tell he is sobering up pretty fast and has understood what I said. Then he does something really strange. He lets out a low moan, almost a gasp of agony, and starts to cry.

I'm not easily fooled, and I'm certainly not fooled now. Knowing what I have recently learned about this man, I wouldn't trust him as far as I could spit a goat. I hold my gun perfectly steady and just watch him. He weeps and weeps, gasping for air. His face is as pale as that of a corpse. His hands cover half his face, but I can see tears slithering down his cheeks.

"Maclaren!" I snap. "Stop the pretense."

He keeps weeping.

"Maclaren!" I yell it this time and his hands jerk away

from his face. His eyes are red, bloodshot, his cheeks moist.

"I didn't want to be sucked into this."

He looks into my face. His vision seems clearer, his eyes a little more focused.

"Oh, right! You're suddenly filled with remorse."

He peers down, lets out a sob, then wipes his mouth with the sleeve of his shirt. "I need a drink."

"No, you don't." And I shift the bottle across the table.

"I was there when they planned it." Maclaren says. His voice is almost normal, just a slight slur and an occasional hesitancy. I have the impression that he is really struggling to pull himself together, as though it's very important to him to be clear about this. It makes me even warier and I move the gun forward a fraction of an inch.

"Steinheiser has taken me under his wing. He trusts me. There were two meetings. One in Vegas, the other in New Mexico. Details were settled at the second one on August 10. But I never felt comfortable with it. I hate Hoover, I hate Nixon. I dunno about Steinheiser—he was my dad's buddy, not mine. I've cooperated with him, I've done everything he's asked . . . But now, today . . . fuck, Catherine. I feel . . . Look, I recorded the second meeting. No one knew."

"You what!" I scream but manage to calm down quickly. The last thing I want is for someone to overhear us. "You taped it?"

He nods.

I sigh heavily. "Why did you do that?"

"Protection, maybe?" He sounds a little slurred again and is once more losing focus.

346

I lean forward and smack him across the face, very hard. He falls sideways before slowly pulling himself up. He gives me a venomous look, blood running from his right nostril.

"Oh, fuck this! Screw you . . . Why should I . . . ?"

I take a step forward and shift the gun to his left temple. "Because," *I say crisply,* "if you do not tell me everything I will splatter your brains all over that wall." *I nod at the white space behind the sofa.* "You know I will, Maclaren."

"Okay, okay! Fuck!"

My nerves are on edge, all senses ramped up. I recall my training, steady myself. I'm aware that he could go for his gun, but I'm pretty convinced his reactions would be much slower than mine. And there's actually something else, something very strange. I almost feel sorry for him. I almost feel bad about holding a pistol to his head. I feel some unfathomable connection with Maclaren which I've never even begun to sense before. At the water cooler he was just a guy at work. We'd passed each other on the stairs, in the car park, but there was nothing. Now, suddenly, I have this really odd sensation. I know he is feeling terrible about what has happened. The man is riddled with guilt.

"Look, Catherine," *he says, eyeing my gun at his head.* "I don't trust Steinheiser. I wanted some insurance. That's why I taped it."

"Where is the tape? Here?"

He brings his hands to his face and starts to cry again. I nudge the barrel of my gun against his skull just enough for it to hurt, and he snaps his head back, his eyes watering.

"Of course it's not here! I hid it."

"Where?"

"It's my insurance. I can't—"

I push the gun in harder and he squeals. Pulling the revolver back a fraction, I see I've pierced his skin with the muzzle leaving behind a red circle.

"In the desert."

"Whereabouts, Maclaren?"

"Okay . . . It was like this. Steinheiser is megalomaniac, right?"

"No kidding!"

"He detests Nixon and Hoover and he wanted to put on a bit of a show, yeah? Steinheiser comes from Albuquerque. He's sort of proud of it too, for some fucking reason." Maclaren belches. It stinks. *"Anyway, he decides to hold the second meeting in the middle of the New Mexico fucking desert at the Trinity Site."*

"Trinity? Where they tested the first atomic bomb?"

Maclaren nods, a suggestion of a sardonic smile around the edges of his lips. *"It's a military base, a missile-testing range. Steinheiser has access, of course, and he claimed it would be a super-fucking-safe location, no chance of anyone eavesdropping."* He pauses to gather his thoughts. *"But, you know, he actually just wanted to show them who was boss and to get them to the most uncomfortable place he could—the middle of the desert in August! A hundred and ten fucking degrees. Steinheiser insisted they couldn't sit in the cars because they might have been bugged. It was actually really funny seeing Nixon in his shirt and tie, eyebrows wet with perspiration, and you can imagine what a mess that pig Hoover was in. He looked like an oiled hog ready for basting." Maclaren gives a drunken giggle. "I had a cassette recorder from work."*

"A what?"

"A cassette," he slurs. "Fuck, doesn't matter . . . new recording device. Not public yet." He takes a deep breath. "So, after the chat, we stayed in some shithole called Las Cruces that night; Hoover and Nixon got away, scuttled back to Washington as fast as they could. I snuck out of the hotel at two a.m., drove back to Trinity, buried the tape directly under the remains of the tower that held the test bomb—the government have preserved the damn thing. It'll probably be a fucking tourist attraction one day!"

"Where, precisely?"

"Why should I—"

"Because . . ."

"Yeah, all right, you'll . . ." His eyes roll up and I think for a moment that he's going to pass out. Instead he vomits in his mouth, keeps it in. A trickle of spew escapes through his lips.

Maclaren swallows and struggles to speak. "Can I have some water?"

"No. Here . . . take a swig." I hand him the whiskey bottle, never shifting my stare from him.

He knocks it back and hands it to me.

"There are four half-buried stumps in the sand," he says slowly. "I dug down about three feet, a small hole right next to the north-eastern stump, close to the inside corner."

I study his face and obviously I do not look totally convinced by what he has said because he lets out a heavy sigh. "I'm telling you the truth," he gasps. "And I want to wash my hands of the whole—"

"Oh, do you now, Maclaren? And you think you can do that, yeah?" I just manage to catch myself. This is an irrelevance . . . I have to let the fury go. "Okay, so the conspirators were just Nixon, Hoover and Steinheiser?"

Maclaren swallows hard. A line of sweat runs from his hairline. "They planned everything. There were two shooters plus a backup. Oswald was the patsy. There was a CIA guy on the grassy knoll. Steinheiser wanted me to do it. I have a 9.9 for marksmanship." He stops, swallows again. "But I got out of it. I couldn't do it. They got some other guy on the knoll."

I'm about to ask another question when I hear a sound from the stairwell outside the apartment: footsteps, one man moving purposefully, the leather of his shoes slapping on the marble.

I dash across the room. A large cupboard stands against the north wall, directly opposite the window. Maclaren reacts predictably slowly.

"Where're you?" he begins. He hasn't heard the sound from outside. "Catherine? I want to tell you everything . . . I feel so . . ."

I reach the cupboard. Under my breath, I thank God it's unlocked and empty and squeeze inside just as the door at the end of the hallway creaks open. The sound of footsteps grows louder. I manage to pull in the doors silently, leaving a crack through which I can watch the room. I try to quieten my breathing, keeping as still as possible. I hear a man's voice. "John?" The leather soles slap on parquet flooring, and I hear another "John?" Through the narrow opening between the cupboard doors I see that Maclaren is still unaware of any strange sounds or voices. Then a man passes by the cupboard. It's Orlando Steinheiser. John Maclaren jerks his head up, stunned for a moment.

"Been a rough day," Steinheiser says with an edge of mockery to his voice. He can tell instantly that Maclaren has hit the bottle hard. "Don't blame you for getting smashed, John, but I was going to ask one last job of you. I can see there's no point now, though. By the way, did you realize your front door was ajar?"

I level my gun at the opening. Any moment now I expect Maclaren to tell Steinheiser that I'm hiding inside the cupboard.

But he doesn't. He starts to get up from the sofa, but Steinheiser motions for him to stay put. Maclaren's face is bathed in sweat and he looks petrified. Steinheiser stares at him, puzzled. "What's up, John?"

Maclaren cannot find his voice. His eyes search the room. Something more than alcohol is affecting him, and Steinheiser can sense it.

"Maclaren?" the older man says very slowly. "What is wrong with you? Where's the bravado? You were so pleased with yourself."

"I've obviously drunk too much, haven't I?" Maclaren bellows.

Steinheiser is startled for a second, but recovers amazingly quickly. "And . . . ?"

"What do you mean: 'and'?"

Then Maclaren bursts into tears.

"Fuck me!" the Assistant Director blurts out. "Please don't tell me you've lost your nerve."

The younger man is trying to speak as he weeps, but

the words are all mangled. I can understand no more than the odd syllable. After a moment, he seems to realize he sounds ridiculous, forces away the sobs and wipes his mouth and eyes with the back of his right hand. His gaze starts to drift toward the cupboard, but then he swings back to Orlando Steinheiser.

"I wish I had never gotten involved with this!" His eyes are bright, clear, the drunkenness forced aside. "You!" and he points at Steinheiser's face. "It was wrong! And now I've had to kill again—David Ashcombe."

The shock hits me with a ferocity that is almost physical. I actually experience an involuntary spasm of my muscles. The barrel of my revolver taps the edge of the door, but Steinheiser doesn't notice. I feel vomit rising up in my throat but manage to force it back and steady my hands. I'm a pro, I tell myself. I'm a pro. And I force away the sudden horrible awareness that my beloved brother is dead.

Steinheiser sniggers. "You fucking baby! It's a little late now, isn't it, Johnny boy? A little fucking late!"

"No," Maclaren retorts with sudden conviction. "I have insurance."

I see Steinheiser flinch. "Insurance?"

"A tape. I recorded the second meeting." He sounds triumphant. "It's hidden somewhere you will never find it."

Steinheiser brings his left hand to his chin and nods slowly. "Admirable, I guess. The sort of thing I would have done." As he is speaking he reaches into his jacket pocket with his right hand and pulls out his Sig P210, a silencer screwed in place.

352

"Now, John, you know how strict I can be, don't you? You've seen what I can do to other human beings, haven't you?"

Maclaren starts to pull himself up, but Steinheiser merely has to poke him with a finger and the drunken man falls back against the cushions. "I'll tell you what I'm going to do, okay?"

Maclaren stares at him, his face drained of blood.

"Okay?"

Maclaren nods.

"Good. Now, I'm going to give you three seconds to tell me the precise location of that tape or I will start shooting off bits of you, beginning with . . ." He waves his gun around, then points it down to a spot between Maclaren's thighs. "Your balls."

John Maclaren starts to reply and I fire my weapon. A bloody circle appears between the man's eyes and his head jerks back. The wall behind him looks as though the contents of a can of red paint have been tossed at it. I smash open the cupboard doors, crash out and fire straight at Steinheiser. The shot misses by an inch and punches a hole in the far wall close to the window frame.

Shocked for a second, he recoils, but he is a consummate professional and he has an incredible reaction time. I fire again as he brings his gun round to point at my face. The bullet hits his left arm and I see a spray of red fly up close to his elbow.

I spin on my heel and run for the door to the hallway. I've stopped breathing. I realize I haven't drawn breath since I burst from the cupboard. A medley of sounds reaches me: a scream from the apartment below, my shoes

*pounding on the parquet floor. I'm a few feet from the door.
I reach out my left hand to grasp the handle and sense
a strange dislocation in my back. My legs give way and,
as I fall, I realize my spine has snapped in two. I collapse
to the floor, completely paralyzed, my head slamming
against the wood. I hear leather soles approach, then the
soft thud of a gun close up, firing through a silencer.*

Chapter 45

Mark lifted his head from where he had been gazing at the floor. Elizabeth's eyes were closed. He glanced at his watch. It was almost eleven. The kerosene lamps now provided the only illumination. Through the window the night was pitch black.

Abigail stood and took Elizabeth's hand. "Wakey-wakey." She squeezed the girl's bone-thin fingers lightly and shook her gently. Elizabeth did not respond.

"Is she still under?" Mark asked and got up from the chair.

Abigail ran her hand along Elizabeth's slender wrist to find a pulse point. Mark saw Abigail jerk.

"She's dead, Mark!"

"No! She can't be." He came round the bed and stood there, peering down at the tiny emaciated body. Only a couple of days ago, as David Ashcombe, he had stood, equally powerless, beside the bed upon which the dead president lay.

"She looks at peace," Abigail said very quietly. And it was true. The dead girl lay with her head tilted back slightly, lips and eyes closed. The lines of strain had gone, her brow no longer furrowed, her skin a perfect white. She could have been sleeping the untroubled sleep of a baby or a saint. Abigail gently pulled up the sheet to cover Elizabeth's face.

Out in the kitchen it was cold. Mark made a fire, using wood from a pile of logs stacked on a narrow porch to the side of the front door. Then he walked back into Elizabeth's room to retrieve the lamps. He stopped at the foot of the bed and looked at her shape under the sheet. The fabric of the sheet had settled over her face. He leaned over the bed and kissed her forehead through the material.

There was a simple stove in the corner of the kitchen, the fuel supplied from a gas bottle. Abigail found a couple of pans, heated some tinned soup and sliced a loaf of bread. Then they sat at the small rough wooden table, eating in silence with just the pallor of the lamps and a brighter glow from the fire casting light around the room.

"So we have to get the tape," Abigail said.

Mark nodded. "I suggest we leave very early. Steinheiser is no fool and he has eyes everywhere, it seems. We can't waste a moment."

"And the tape will give us the proof."

"If it has survived the past half-century."

"It was a clever decision on Maclaren's part. Untraceable, a dry, warm location. He wasn't a fool either. He would have done his best to save the evidence for posterity. He didn't owe Steinheiser any favors, did he?"

"No." Mark gazed into the middle distance.

"What is it?"

"Oh, it's just that I'm beginning to remember things. Just fragments, almost like feelings of déjà vu." He stared intently into Abigail's eyes and she smiled.

"What do you remember?"

"Mostly Ruth."

"Makes sense."

"I can return to the moment I met you . . ."

"At Tim and Hilary's apartment in Baltimore."

"Yes. You were with some guy."

"Charlie, I think his name was." She laughed.

"And before that, before Ruth, you were Hannah."

Abigail looked down at her clasped hands. "Yes, I was. And you were Rex. I left you a widower."

"Cancer."

She nodded.

"I have flashes of how LA was in those days. It was the 1920s, wasn't it? It was such a small place then, the film studios just starting out. I remember you wanted to get into the movies."

Abigail laughed. "I nearly did, too. But I died a waitress." Her expression became more solemn. "What happened to you and our boy, Gregory?"

"I don't know, but I guess Rex didn't last that long. David Ashcombe was born in 1931. I was thirty-two at the time of Kennedy's death—my death.' Mark took a deep breath. "I saw him, you know."

"Saw who?"

"Pat . . . Jack. I saw his soul leave his body."

"Tell me, Mark."

He described what he had seen and what he had felt outside Parkland Memorial Hospital. "I think he was brain-dead for quite some time before the doctors got to him, even if they did record a faint response on the heart monitor in the Trauma Room. In fact, I think Jack was clinically dead within seconds of being shot but, for reasons I cannot begin to explain, his 'soul', if you want to call it that, hung around for a while. Perhaps it's different for different people."

"I didn't sense Elizabeth leaving," Abigail said.

"No, me neither."

"Same with Peggy." Abigail's expression had frozen as she recalled the trauma of the girl's suicide. "I was first to her. She was alive for a few moments, but the shock to her brain . . . There was only a flicker of life left in her. She died as Roger held her to his chest. But I saw nothing like you've described."

He shrugged. "Just another of the many unanswered questions."

They moved over to an old sofa closer to the fire and lay down together. Mark put his arm around Abigail's waist, smelled her hair. He felt complete for the first time in his life.

They fell asleep and stayed asleep until the sky lightened and the room filled with morning radiance, dust motes floating in the air and caught by the rays of the sun, the fire reduced to ash.

Mark found tools in a small shed to one side of the cabin. He walked out to the rear of the property, carrying a shovel, and looked back. He could see Abigail through the window of what had been Elizabeth's room for a short time. She was removing the bedding and creating a shroud from a sheet that she had taken from a high shelf in a wooden cupboard to the right of the bed.

Abigail had not noticed Mark staring at her and he reveled in the way she moved, the way her wavy blond hair caressed her shoulders. She was a beautiful woman, but he knew it wasn't really about that. As he watched her—she was totally unaware of him—he could see her as she had been during the past, all the different versions of her, Abigail, his soulmate. He saw Hannah, the wannabe actress who had withered away in an LA hospital ward. He saw Ruth, darling Ruth. He remembered how much he, as David, had adored her. But he also saw, faintly, the woman Nadia. He could not place where or when that was, but he recalled her lips on his. He remembered, very vaguely, their wedding day, lotus flowers at their bare brown feet. And from some time even more distant came diaphanous images of Abigail as Eleanor. He had a sudden flash, a memory of her with a coronet of flowers in her dark hair, hair that tumbled to her waist, her ruby lips and slender fingers. Then another recollection. They lived in Venice, a grand palazzo. Eleanor's fingers were caressing the wrinkled skin of his face as he lay dying in her arms, his beard white as the snow falling to the canal beyond the palazzo walls; her old, old, loving eyes searching his. Mark remembered her whispering something: "I will see you again, my love . . ." even though she could not possibly have known the truth.

He watched Abigail leave the room and strode a few paces away from the cabin where he found a patch of ground that somehow felt instinctively right. And there he began to dig.

It was a simple grave. No headstone, no marks to indicate who lay under the sandy soil, and somehow that seemed fitting. Elizabeth knew who she was, who she had been. And now she was in a place where flesh and bones had no meaning. As a young man, Mark had failed to understand why people seemed to feel an attachment to the dead bodies of their loved ones. He knew that in ancient times people believed in an afterlife to which they could take their worldly possessions. He'd learned at school how the Victorian obsession with tombs was partly a show of wealth and partly a way in which the living could boost the importance of their family. It was only later that he intellectualized it as a basic human need to cling on to something cherished, lost. Aside from the frail artifice of memory and the coldness of photographs and films, the bones and the rotting flesh were all that remained to allow the grieving to convince themselves that their loved ones had ever lived.

Now he understood why he had never shared this desire. Some part of him had known that he and all human beings were eternal, that the bodies we inhabit are mere shells, as durable as a computer or a car, as frail as a flower, as fleeting as lightning. That did not mean they were without value; for without those shells there could be no physical life. He certainly had no sympathy for ascetics who denied the importance of the flesh. He was well aware of Abigail's physical beauty, but to him her true beauty, her grace went much deeper.

They stood together close to the patch of ground beneath which Elizabeth's dead body lay, and they were silent, each thinking their own thoughts. They did not pray, nor did they offer up any form of farewell because they both knew that Elizabeth was no longer there. Instead, they knew she would be in the "in-between place" that no one understood, the place they would return to sometime and the place they would leave again to take up a new physical form, to travel a new path; to learn more, and to evolve—as Elizabeth would have it.

Chapter 46

Back in Elton-Hornsby's SUV, they had the air conditioning on full blast. Mark noticed the digital thermometer on the dash reading 81 degrees outside and it was only 7.37 a.m.

The track from the house took them directly south to Highway 380. They crossed it and found another dirt road. It was rutted and rocky, and three miles from the highway they were forced to stop. An eight-foot-high gate stretched the width of the track and a wire fence ran east and west as far as they could see. A metal sign had been clipped to the top of the gate. It read: *Property of the United States Government. DANGER: White Sands Missile Range. Strictly NO ADMITTANCE.* Under this, in smaller writing, was a warning about it being a federal offence to go beyond this point.

They had expected something like this. According to the official Trinity Site web-page they were now at the perimeter of a government-owned expanse of over three thousand square miles of land that was strictly off-limits to the public except for just two days a year—the first Saturdays of April and October when officially organized tours were allowed inside.

"Only one way to get in there," Mark declared as they

pulled up a few yards short of the gate and stared through the dusty windshield.

He put the SUV into reverse, retreated a hundred yards. "Keep your belt on but bend right over. Here." He found the blanket that Elizabeth had used on the back seat and handed it to Abigail. "Put it over you . . . glass."

He revved the engine and put his foot down. The SUV was a powerful four-wheel drive and Mark got it up to close to sixty as they slammed into the gate. At the last second he ducked and let the vehicle take over. The gate flew off its hinges, somersaulted diagonally over the car, thumping twice on the roof as it went. The windshield shattered into thousands of glass pellets that cascaded into the car. Mark took his foot off the gas and blindly found the brake, bringing the car to a juddering halt.

"You okay?"

Abigail lifted the blanket. Pieces of pulverised glass trickled to the floor and around the gear shift. She looked back through the rear window and saw the mangled gate on the road, the edges of the fence twisted and buckled. "I'm in better shape than that."

Around them was pure, smooth, almost featureless desert: the sand white, barely a cactus to break the uniformity. To the east and south stood the Oscura mountain range, while the view to the west and north resembled abstract paintings daubed by Nature.

They followed instructions from the satnav and headed due south as a few dark shapes began to appear slowly in the whiteness; a stubby fence, a couple of signs and a stone pyramid about a dozen feet tall.

They stopped the car and walked over to the pyramid. On the south-facing side, at head height, a square brass plaque had been screwed into the stone. Mark read: *Trinity Site. The location of the testing of the first atomic bomb. July 16, 1945.* Abigail glanced to her right and saw, a few yards away, four uniformly spaced metal stumps partially buried in the sand.

"The remnants of the tower that held the bomb," she said.

It was incredibly quiet, just a light breeze ruffling their hair. The front of Mark's white shirt was already stained with sweat and lines of perspiration ran down his face.

"Maclaren told Elizabeth he'd put the tape under the north-east stump," Abigail said and started to walk over. Mark opened the back of the SUV, retrieved the spade he had used to dig Elizabeth's grave and joined Abigail. In the silence and the blazing heat they stared down at a rectangle of steel about a yard across.

"Close to the inside corner, Maclaren said, didn't he?"

Abigail nodded. "So that's here." Mark thrust the edge of the shovel into the sand a few inches from the corner. He dug down about a foot and hit concrete.

"Shit! Okay . . . the four corners of the tower would have been sunk into concrete footings."

They moved a few feet toward the center of the arrangement of stumps and Mark tried again. Three hard stabs at the sand and he hit concrete again, cursing. He began a third time a foot further in away from the stump. This time he just clipped the edge of the footing. He whistled and kept going, sweat soaking his shirt and lathering his face. After a couple of minutes, he stopped, took several deep breaths and wiped his face with his sleeve.

Abigail ran over to the car, found a bottle of water in the passenger footwell, snatched it up and started to run back to Mark. She stopped abruptly. In the distance she could see a cloud of dust and a dark object moving fast across the sand towards them. "Oh hell!" she gasped and raced over to Mark, calling to him as she went. "Someone's coming."

Mark was on his knees, the upper half of his body in the hole he had just dug. He did not hear her. She ran up to him and shouted again. This time he jerked up, his face smeared with dirt, a line of sand running across his forehead. In his hand was a metal container. He twisted round to where Abigail was pointing.

The car was driving incredibly fast across the flat, smooth surface, and by the time Mark had straightened up it had almost reached them. He made to run for the SUV, but Abigail caught his arm. He looked down at her hand. "What you doing?"

"There's no point, Mark."

He closed his eyes for a second. As he opened them again a black Mercedes with darkened windows screeched to a halt a few yards away. The driver's window came down and they saw Christopher Trafano wearing aviator sunglasses, the barrel of his pistol, an M9 Beretta, pointed straight at them. The passenger door opened and Steinheiser climbed out of the car, walked round the bonnet and stopped a few paces in front of them.

"How did you know we were here?" Abigail asked. Her voice was calm.

"Oh, some useful technology. We only learned yesterday that our British friend had betrayed us after we spoke to a very unhappy technician in the monitoring room and watched some scraps of CCTV footage from cameras that had continued working. Plus, Elton-Hornsby didn't turn up for work at the Institute as scheduled. For the moment he eludes us, but not for long. We worked out that he would have encouraged you to stay at the cabin he thought we had no idea about. We then tracked you via satellite; I have a wide range of resources at my disposal." He paused for breath. "Where is Elizabeth?"

"She died last night," Abigail replied, her voice still calm.

"I see."

Christopher Trafano stepped out of the Mercedes and walked towards them slowly. He stopped a few feet behind Steinheiser, his gun at waist height and pointed directly at Mark. Abigail gave the man a contemptuous look and noticed a fleeting spasm of panic pass across his face. There was something not quite right about his body language.

"So, what is it that has brought you all the way out here?" Steinheiser asked. "What's that in your hand, Mr. Bretton?"

"Why should I tell you?"

Steinheiser smiled. "Because my friend Christopher here has a gun pointed at your heart. That's a bit of a dumb question for such an intelligent man, isn't it?"

Mark looked from Steinheiser to Trafano.

"Please?" Steinheiser said and put out his right hand. Abigail watched as Trafano shifted position slightly.

Perspiration ran down his face. As the older man grasped the metal box, Trafano removed his shades and took a step closer.

Steinheiser ran his fingers over the top of the container. It had been sealed with tape around the edge, but this had rotted away almost entirely. He slid a couple of fingernails under the rim of the box and prised off the lid. Inside lay a small rectangular object wrapped in metal foil. Steinheiser lifted the curious thing from the box, placed the container on the sand, straightened up, ripped away the foil and lifted a cassette tape from the crumpled wrapping. Holding it up to the light, he squinted at the tape, sighed and shook his head.

"I remember that meeting. It was hilarious," the old man said. "Fifty years ago almost to the day. Nixon and Hoover, both useless assholes. And I outlived them, outdid them. Even then, I showed them who was in charge."

Abigail studied Christopher Trafano's face. It seemed as though several intense emotions were struggling for dominance in his mind, but she could not begin to understand what it was that he was feeling.

"What is it, sir?" Trafano asked, standing two paces behind Steinheiser.

The former CIA man held the tape and shook it slowly up and down. "This . . ." he replied. "This is a recording that a man called John Maclaren made of a meeting that took place at this very spot half a century ago."

Trafano came up beside Steinheiser, studying the tape silently.

"It was a meeting to finalize the details of the assassination of John Fitzgerald Kennedy. Maclaren was one of my closest aides. He betrayed me and recorded the meeting."

"But how come?" Trafano began, the sweat running down his cheeks. He looked scared. "If you knew it was here, why didn't you destroy it long ago?"

"I didn't know it was here until just now," Steinheiser retorted. "Maclaren died before he could—"

Trafano gasped.

"What is it with you?" Steinheiser snapped. "You've been behaving strangely ever since we left the Institute."

Trafano's mind was in turmoil. At that moment, it seemed to him that he was existing simultaneously in two different realities. There was the scene playing out in front of his eyes: the couple standing in front of the eighty-one-year-old Steinheiser with the memorial pyramid a few yards away, the ex-CIA boss holding up a cassette tape. But there was another reality. It was the same spot on Earth, but it was a different time. There was no memorial—that had not yet been built. To his right stood a row of three cars, museum pieces, at least fifty years old. Beside the cars, a clutch of five men. A much younger Steinheiser, the politician Richard Nixon, and the FBI Chief, J. Edgar Hoover. Close to them were a pair of bodyguards.

He glanced down, saw the pants of his gray Armani suit and his black Italian loafers, but superimposed upon these were black trousers and highly polished lace-ups. He lifted his head and could see Steinheiser's mouth moving.

"Snap out of it, Trafano!"

The words crashed through his head like a siren going off.

He managed to pull himself together. "I'm sorry," he said. "It's the heat."

Steinheiser laughed. "Northern pussy! Fuck! I feel as cool as a cucumber . . . my homeland . . ." And he swept a hand round, taking in the desert and the mountains and the blue, blue sky. His stare snapped back to his aide. "What you waiting for? Kill them."

"You have the tape," Abigail cried. Her previous calm had slipped away.

Mark put an arm around her and pulled her close.

Steinheiser tilted his head. "What a lovely couple you make. Shame you have to die prematurely. But . . ." He looked from Abigail to Mark. "You signed your own death warrants back in Manhattan. I have always adhered to the principle that the past should be left well alone. Picking over old wounds, sticking your nose into other people's business . . . bad idea, really. Very rude."

Christopher Trafano stepped forward, raised his pistol.

Trafano's hand was shaking. Mark readied himself to pounce. He knew he would die, but maybe, just maybe, he could live long enough to kill the men and save Abigail.

"I can't," Trafano spluttered. "I can't . . ."

Steinheiser pulled his own weapon from a holster under his jacket, a vintage Sig P210, lifted it and fired two bullets in quick succession. The first grazed Mark's shoulder. The second slammed into the side of Abigail's head.

Chapter 47

"No!" Christopher Trafano bellowed, the sound sucked in by the dry, dead air.

Steinheiser spun his gun round with surprising agility for an octogenarian. But Trafano had almost half a century on the old man and was much faster. He grabbed the gun from his boss's fingers, hearing a digit snap. The ex-CIA boss yelled in agony and Trafano brought the handle of the gun round, smacking it hard into Steinheiser's left temple.

The old tape flew into the air as the old man fell back. Steinheiser and the cassette landed in the desert sand a few yards apart. Trafano snatched up the tape, then froze for a second, looking down at Abigail's body. A long streak of red stretched away behind her head.

Mark lay sprawled on the ground, blood flowing from his shoulder wound. He pulled himself upright, turned and saw Abigail. A shudder passed through him and his face contorted as he fell to his knees beside her.

There was a red and black hole the size of a dime to one side of Abi's forehead. A line of blood trickled from it, rolling down the side of her skull to her hair. Mark lifted her head and felt it almost fall in two. There was so much blood that it had started to pool. On the ground behind her lay pieces of bone and brain, a spray of red staining the white powdery sand.

She was still alive, gasping for air, her eyes rolling, unable to focus. Mark leaned over her.

"Abi." The word caught in Mark's throat, his voice breaking between the syllables.

Her eyes focused on him. A tear ran down Mark's cheek and landed on her lips. "Abi . . . Abi . . . You're going to be all right. This isn't over . . ."

Abi's eyes were moist. A drop of blood appeared in the corner of her right eye and spilled over the lid.

"Mark," she managed to gasp. "I'll see you again. We'll always be togeth—"

He lowered his head and sobbed. Christopher Trafano stood a few feet away, his gun lowered, unable to say a word. He watched Mark's shoulders shake. Then, with stunning speed, Mark stood up and took two steps over to where Steinheiser lay unconscious. He kicked the man in the head with all the force he could muster, then he fell on him, smashing his fist into the former CIA chief's face. A guttural animal sound came from Mark's throat.

Trafano pulled on Mark's shoulder and grabbed his arm. "Stop!" he yelled. "Stop!"

Mark completely ignored him and pulled his arm free. Trafano yanked him backwards and he sprawled on the sand, whirled round, got to his feet and went for Steinheiser's sidekick.

Trafano had his hands up. "Mark . . . Mark, listen. You don't want to kill him. You want him to be disgraced, exposed, don't you? Sweet fucking justice, man!"

There was a madness in Mark's eyes. He'd seen too much, lived too much during the last few days.

"We have to get the story out. Tell the world."

Mark stopped, closed his eyes for a second. "And why the fuck do you care? You work for that bastard." He spun on his heel, stabbing a finger at the unconscious Steinheiser.

"I did," Trafano said. "But then I realized."

"Realized what?"

"That I'm one of you."

"What?"

"I've known for a long time. Or a part of me has. It's just that I couldn't accept it." Trafano nodded toward Orlando Steinheiser. "He thought I was behaving strangely on the drive here. And I was, I guess. From the moment we left the Institute I was gripped by a disturbing sense of . . . God, I don't even know what to call it. Déjà vu, maybe?"

"And you expect me to believe that?"

"No, probably not. But it's true, Mark. As we pulled up just now I felt as though I was passing through time; the past and the present were . . . one. I saw things, Mark. I suddenly knew who you were."

"Of course you knew who we were—you met us at the Institute and you probably saw the films from the cameras that you or Steinheiser must have installed at Abi's workplace."

"I don't mean that," Trafano said. He took a deep breath. "I suddenly really *knew* you. That was the moment I understood you were two members of my 'six'. How could I not have known it before?"

"Yeah, and what about Elizabeth? You've met her before. How come you didn't realize who she was?"

"I honestly don't know," Trafano replied, shaking his head slowly. "But it all came flooding back. Just now, just when I saw you and Abigail. I was John Maclaren. I was there in Dallas on November 22, 1963."

"Yeah, right! You've seen the tapes from Abi's rooms, Trafano. You're lying."

"Why would I do that? I have the gun." He held his hand out, the pistol in his palm, let it drop to the ground between them. "Why would I make it up?"

Mark kept his stare fixed on the other man.

"Listen, Mark. Believe me, you must know how weird this is for me."

Mark could see that Trafano's face was lathered with sweat. A line of perspiration ran down his jaw.

"I remember other things," Trafano said suddenly. "Other incarnations. I lived in New York a long time ago—late-nineteenth century. My name was Harry."

"Harry?" Mark exclaimed. He recalled Abi telling him about Peggy Gates's past lives and the young man she had loved in 1890s New York.

"Yes. I knew a girl—Constance. I loved her. I was murdered, strangled close to water, at the docks in New York. Then there were other lives. I was a tailor in Russia, a merchant in China. And . . . yes, yes . . . the smell . . . a horrible smell, noxious fumes and a young emaciated woman. Constance . . . but no, it couldn't be Constance because she was a young girl when I died in New York. No . . . her name was Rachel."

Mark simply stared at Trafano, aware of his own breath,

373

the scorching air, the pains from every part of his body, the stab of agony in his shoulder. And then the smell of Abigail's blood.

Christopher patched up Mark's shoulder with a bandage and tape from a first-aid kit from the glove compartment of the Merc. The bullet had just cut away a chunk of tissue, but the wound had bled copiously. He lifted the back door of the SUV and found a length of rope, tied Steinheiser's hands behind his back and put a gag over his mouth. Between them, the two men dragged the still unconscious man across the sand and dumped him in the space behind the rear seats. Mark then returned to Abigail's body. Feeling no pain from his shoulder, he lifted her carefully and paced over slowly to the car.

His mind was utterly numb, pushed beyond pain, beyond fear, into a place where nothing mattered anymore. But he knew that he had a few final duties to perform before the curtain could fall on the play. Even if he no longer cared about what happened to him, whether or not the sun would rise tomorrow, he owed it to Abigail to finish what they had started . . . could it really have been only a week ago?

Trafano had found the sheets and blankets in the SUV, the ones that Elizabeth had slept in as she, Abi and Mark had fled the Institute. He had laid them out across the back seat and now he helped Mark to lower Abigail's dead body onto the seat.

A few minutes later, Trafano was driving them away from the stone pyramid commemorating the site of the first atomic-bomb test and Abigail's fresh blood had begun to dry black in the white sand.

They headed directly north, almost retracing the path that Mark and Abi had taken less than ninety minutes ago. Mark watched the sand flash past the window, the distant blue and gray of the mountains. He could see Abi's face, hear her voice, her laugh. The fact that she was dead seemed so impossible that he could not contemplate it. In this incarnation he had known her for such a terribly short time. It was almost as though creation, the universe, whatever, was mocking him. "Here," God was saying, "have your soulmate, start to contemplate a future together, cherish the one you have traveled through so many lives with. Then . . . poof! I'll snatch her away—just like that." What a great cosmic joke . . . fucking hysterical.

They made it to the perimeter fence and drove maybe half a mile west, following the wire until they reached the gate that Mark and Abi had demolished. Pulling up, they saw a plume of dust rising above the scrub: the telltale sign of a vehicle approaching.

"Hell!" Mark exclaimed.

"I was half expecting this," Trafano replied. "Steinheiser covers all bases. He would have had a backup prepared to follow us if he didn't call in within a certain time frame."

"So what now? We can't go back."

"Follow my lead. They won't know what's happened back there."

A black sedan kicking up dust came into view around a bend a hundred feet ahead.

Trafano stepped out of the SUV and waved his arms above his head. The other car slowed and came to rest a few yards away. Two men in dark suits and aviator shades got out of the rear of the car while the driver and a passenger in the front stayed seated.

"Jaimie," Trafano called. "Sure glad to see you."

"What's happened? Boss didn't call in on cue."

"There was trouble. Steinheiser's injured. It's a long story."

"Why didn't *you* call?" the other man asked, clearly suspicious.

"Good to see you, too, Callum. Look, the fucking car got shot up. One of the targets is dead. I have the other, Mark Bretton, in the SUV." He nodded toward the vehicle.

"Cellphone?" Callum persisted.

"Yours working?" Trafano snapped back, praying there really was no service out here.

The man checked his screen. "No . . . okay. So the boss is where?"

"By the Trinity monument under a shade I built. I couldn't move him—spinal injury. I ain't a doc."

The two men paced over to the SUV. Trafano steered them away from a view into the back of the car where Abi's body lay. They glanced at Mark through the smashed windshield. He sat motionless in the passenger seat, looking ahead at the dusty track. The air was still, just the purr of the sedan's engine breaking the natural silence. Then came a knocking sound from the rear of the SUV.

"What was that?" Callum said and started to walk toward the back of the car. He caught a glimpse of Steinheiser trying to pull himself up.

Trafano pulled out his gun, fired, and blew a hole in the back of Callum's head. As the man crumpled to the floor, Trafano whirled round. Jaimie was standing close to the SUV, his gun raised, his finger squeezing the trigger.

There was a loud crack and Trafano was drenched in blood and chunks of tissue. The mess splattered across his white shirt, his face, his hair, into his eyes. Steinheiser's man fell forward, half his head missing. Mark stood, looking horrified, the Sig still raised, smoke swirling from the barrel.

They both heard the doors of the sedan slam shut at the same moment and Trafano caught a glimpse of two men pulling out their guns as they crouched behind the front doors of the car. "Get down!" he yelled.

For a second, Mark seemed paralyzed.

"Mark!" Trafano hollered and pulled him down beside him.

Bullets ricocheted off the hood. A window on the passenger side of the four-wheel drive shattered, glass cascading to the dirt.

Trafano stood up, got off two shots, then dropped down again.

Another hail of bullets slammed into the SUV.

Steinheiser's face appeared at the rear window, his eyes bulging. Then he started kicking at the window. More gunfire.

Trafano stood up again, fired three times. A bullet ricocheted inside the SUV and thudded into his arm. He was thrown backwards by the impact, the gun falling from his hand as he yelled in pain.

Mark caught a glimpse of Steinheiser's men on either

side of the black sedan. They fired again, ducking back down as rounds thumped into the SUV.

A new sound broke in over the gunfire.

Mark looked up and saw a helicopter overhead. "Oh fuck!" he exclaimed.

Trafano had pulled himself up into a sitting position and was scrambling to the side of the SUV. Mark could see a gash in the sleeve of his shirt, the fabric soaked with his blood.

The chopper came down low and swept over the cars.

"It's a Chinook. I don't recognize it. Can't see markings, but it's definitely not one of Steinheiser's," Trafano said as they watched the aircraft swing round and head back toward them.

More bullets slammed into the SUV.

An amplified voice boomed out.

"Cease fire! Repeat: cease fire! This is the USAF."

There was an ominous silence. Trafano peered over the SUV's hood. He couldn't see the two gunmen. Steinheiser had stopped thumping on the window.

The men from the sedan started to fire up at the Chinook.

"They're shooting at the chopper!" Mark screamed above the noise.

The helicopter swung round directly over the black car. A machine gun fired. One of the gunmen on the ground cried out in agony. Mark and Trafano saw a black shape fall under the lower edge of the driver's door. The other gunman sprang up and dashed from the car, heading for a ditch at the side of the road. He was running fast across the track, firing his weapon into the air as he went. Mark fired three shots. They each missed the man by a yard.

Another burst of machine-gun fire came from the Chinook and Steinheiser's man was lifted off his feet by the force of the bullets.

The chopper landed, kicking up a great cloud of dust. A figure emerged from the haze, a man in a gray suit, one hand up, shielding his eyes. He was twenty feet away before Mark and Trafano recognized him. It was Hubert Elton Hornsby.

He saw the weapons and raised his hands. "Please," the scientist said. "Lower your guns."

"Why?" Trafano asked, keeping his Beretta aimed at the Englishman.

A man appeared behind Elton-Hornsby. He was wearing a military flying suit and helmet, and he had an M27 automatic rifle clasped in his hands.

"I'm here thanks to your friend Roger Gates," Elton-Hornsby said, staring straight into Mark's eyes. "I've been at the Highfield USAF base about fifty miles northeast of here. It struck me as the safest place to go. Gates flew down late last night. He's very concerned about you . . . and Abigail. Where is she?"

Mark swallowed hard. Elton-Hornsby read his expression in an instant.

"Oh no . . ." He lowered his gaze. When he raised his head he had a steely look in his eye.

"Steinheiser?"

Trafano nodded toward the car. "In the back, bound and gagged. How did you know we would be here?"

"Mark and Abi took shelter in my old shack. I had no

idea where you were headed, Mark, dear fellow. But I knew it wouldn't be back toward the Institute. We followed the tire tracks of the SUV from my place, saw the gunfire bursts. Christopher, you're hurt."

Trafano ignored him. "You could have killed the wrong guys."

Elton-Hornsby produced the glimmer of a smile. "The USAF have some excellent gear. I could almost make out the individual hairs on your chin!"

"So what is it you want?" Trafano asked, giving Elton-Hornsby a cold look.

The Englishman put his hands up. "Same as you, old boy: Orlando Steinheiser."

Chapter 48

The flight to the Highfield USAF base took less than twenty minutes. Steinheiser was kept under guard at the rear of the Chinook. Abigail's body lay covered by a sheet on a military stretcher between the seats in the middle of the aircraft just behind the pilot and co-pilot. Mark, Christopher Trafano and Hubert Elton-Hornsby made a solemn threesome who did not exchange a word the entire journey. A medic cleaned up Christopher's injured arm. It was a flesh wound, but deep, still bleeding. The bullet, the medic told them, had missed an artery by a whisker.

The chopper doors slid open and they saw Roger Gates walking toward the aircraft as the sound of its rotor blades diminished as they powered down. Two airmen lifted the stretcher that Abigail had been laid on and took it down the few steps to the tarmac. Mark and Christopher followed close behind.

Gates raised a hand and the servicemen stopped a couple of feet from him. A few strands of Abigail's wavy blond hair were just visible beyond the edge of the sheet covering her. Gates lowered his fingertips to the stretcher fabric and ran them along the stray wisps.

Mark stood beside him and they looked down at the form under the material. The whine of the chopper blades continued to lessen. Gates turned and the two men hugged, and sobbed their pain.

The sun was big and low on the horizon, the sky and the flimsy clouds beginning to redden. A breeze in off the mountains had picked up, tugging the temperature right down to the mid-sixties.

Ahead of Mark, about a hundred feet away, stood the hulking shape of a Boeing C-40, black against the western sky. He was walking across the tarmac. Christopher Trafano was at his side, his arm in a sling, a jacket over his shoulders. They stopped at the foot of the stairs leading up to the front cabin section.

"So you've decided to stay," Mark said. "Definitely don't want to be part of the inevitable hullabaloo?"

Trafano smiled. "I feel I have some catching-up to do here. There's valuable work to be done at the Institute. You know what it's like: once you accept the truth of your own past, you have to go with it."

Mark extended a hand. "Well, good luck—and thank you."

"Why thanks, Mark?"

"If it hadn't been for you I'd have been dead on the sand beside Abi. And Steinheiser would have gotten away with it all."

"I just regret I didn't act faster. I should have saved both of you."

"Some things are just not meant to be," Mark said and turned to the stairs.

The cabin was an empty shell save for a few seats

lining each side of the space. Mark buckled up and sat silently staring at Abigail's casket strapped to the floor. The engines began to fire up, an intense reverberation as the pilot and co-pilot went through the final checks.

He was alone in the cabin. It was so different to the flight that Mark, as David Ashcombe, had taken with a different casket, a different body, long, long ago in an entirely different age. He studied the wood, a solid ash, let his gaze wander over the brass handles, the lines and curve of the lid. He visualized Abigail's body lying just behind the panels of polished wood, beyond the plush satin and the padding. Her flesh would have already started to decay.

He knew more than anyone that he should be able to deal with his loss. He was privy to a great secret, a secret so few were aware of, a secret that spoke of eternity, togetherness beyond death. But at that moment it offered no help. He was riven by selfish thoughts. He was thirty-five: it might be fifty years before he would be with Abigail again. How was he to live through that? And then the two of them might not meet in the next life or the one after that. It felt like a burden impossible to bear, and so he allowed the self-pity to flood in.

The first tear slid down his cheek, warm at first, then growing chill, sliding off his jaw onto the metal floor. For the first time since . . . since the unimaginable had happened, Mark let his emotions go. The tears followed each other down his face, over his lips to splash in irregular shapes on the floor of the aircraft. The walls shook as the plane accelerated along the runway. Abigail's casket rattled and strained against the straps holding it in place. The lights of the base dwindled and slipped away out of sight as they headed north, toward home.

Mark emerged from the elevator onto the forty-fourth floor of the building on 55th Street, where he had worked for almost a decade, and paused. He could see his colleagues at their workstations, heads down, watching their fingers skim their keyboards, some with chins rested on hands and peering at the screens in front of them. Then he pushed the door open and stepped inside.

Stares followed him as he strode between the desks. His colleague Saul Maddox, from the editorial team, swiveled on his chair and whistled quietly. Otherwise the room was silent. Everyone had stopped typing.

Sam Helmer opened the door of his office as Mark went to knock. He stood frozen to the spot, a completely blank look on his face.

"Your desk is over there, Mark," he said and nodded to a point a row back from the front workstation. "Clear it and get out. You've got three minutes, then I call security."

Mark raised a hand. "Sam . . ."

"You heard."

"I think after you hear what I have to tell you, you'll change your mind."

Helmer's expression didn't change. He looked Mark up and down. "And why should I give you a microsecond of my time?"

"Because," Mark replied, "if you don't, you'll regret it for the rest of your life."

Helmer's eyes narrowed, then he turned toward his desk. "Leave the door open," he commanded.

In the cab headed downtown the radio proclaimed the news. "The Story Of The Century", they were calling it. The conspiracy to kill John Fitzgerald Kennedy had finally been unraveled, the truth exposed. Mark had sat in silence in the back of the car as it stopped and started. He had gazed through the window at the concrete and the stone, the tarmac and the neon and he had tried to find some meaning to it all. But there was no meaning to find. It was as simple as that.

By the time he reached 10th Street dusk was settling over New York and his apartment was filled with shadows. From outside came the blare of a police siren. The air was hot in the main room, the floor burnished with orange haze, the sun dipping behind the water towers, its rays slipping between the buildings.

He walked over to the window and pulled it up. The sounds from the street intensified. The new air came in and cleared out the old, but it was warm air, as warm as the atmosphere of the apartment. To Mark it felt as though he had been away at least a year, perhaps two. He had found love and lost it in an instant. He had made enemies and they had molded his world, shaped his future. But he knew that there was nothing he could have done about it. Events had played out without his influence. Perhaps none of us have any say at all, he thought. Perhaps, after all, everything is random. All of it totally beyond our control—for the moment, at least.

He found his Gibson guitar in its case leaning against

the wall. But he felt no desire to open it, to pull out the instrument and play. At that moment he wondered if he would ever play again, if he would ever *want* to play again. He wandered over to the kitchen and stopped close to the table. He saw the corner of a glossy sheet of paper, the edge of a photographic image that he had forgotten he had ever printed out.

Leaning over, he shuffled the papers aside and saw the photograph of Abigail, the one he had taken after the gig at Johnny J's . . . an eternity ago. He pulled up a chair and sat down heavily, picked up the glossy page and held it in his hands.

"God, I'm missing you already," Mark said. Then he stood up, feeling as weary as the old man he wished he was and paced over to the corkboard in the kitchen. With one hand, he plucked the colored tacks away from the picture of his ex-wife Jill and placed the photo on the worktop. Lifting the image of Abigail, he pushed in the pins at each corner and ran a finger over the glossy paper before stepping back to survey his work.

"Until next time, Abi," he said. "Until next time."

The End

ALSO AVAILABLE IN ARROW

Equinox

Michael White

**A brutal murder. A three-hundred-year conspiracy.
A deadly secret.**

Oxford, 2006: a young woman is found brutally murdered, her throat cut. Her heart has been removed and in its place lies an apparently ancient gold coin. Twenty-four hours later, another woman is found. The MO is identical, except that this time her brain has been removed, and a silver coin lies glittering in the bowl of her skull.

The police are baffled but when police photographer Philip Bainbridge and his estranged lover Laura Niven become involved, they discover that these horrific, ritualistic murders are not confined to the here and now. And a shocking story begins to emerge which intertwines Sir Isaac Newton, one of seventeenth-century England's most powerful figures, with a deadly conspiracy which echoes down the years to the present day, as lethal now as it was then.

Before long those closest to Laura are in danger, and she finds herself the one person who can rewrite history; the only person who can stop the killer from striking again . . .

arrow books

The Borgia Ring

Michael White

A weapon from the past. A secret that has survived the centuries. A deadly obsession.

When a blackened skeleton is unearthed on a building site in the City of London, no one can have the slightest idea of its extraordinary link to a plot to assassinate the Queen of England over 500 years ago.

But there is one very conspicuous clue. On the index finger of the body's right hand is a gold ring topped with a brilliant, round emerald.

DCI Jack Pendragon has just transferred from Oxford to Brick Lane police station – in part to escape his own past. Immediately, he finds himself investigating three particularly gruesome murders. And he will need all the experience he has acquired from two decades on the force to track down a killer for whom an eerie obsession has become total madness. A killer who draws his murderous inspiration from a Renaissance family whose power and cruelty remain a living legend.

arrow books

The Medici Secret

Michael White

**An ancient mystery. A conspiracy of silence.
A secret to kill for.**

In the crypt of the Medici Chapel in Florence, palaeopathologist, Edie Granger, and her uncle, Carlin Mackenzie, are examining the mummified remains of one of the most powerful families in Renaissance Italy.

The embalmers have done their work well in terms of outward appearance. But under the crisp skin, the organs have shrivelled to a fraction of their original size, which means it is difficult to gather a usable DNA sample. Edie and Mackenzie both have serious doubts about the true identity of at least two of the five-hundred-year-old bodies.

And no one can explain the presence of an alien object discovered resting against Cosimo de' Medici's spine.

For Carlin Mackenzie, this is the most fascinating and the most dangerous discovery of his life. For Edie, it is the beginning of an obsessive, life-threatening quest . . .

arrow books